CW00642858

THE ARTIST'S APPRENTICE

CLARE FLYNN

Storm

Ebook ISBN: 978-1-80508-425-9
Paperback ISBN: 978-1-80508-427-3

Previously published as *The Colour of Glass* in 2023 by Cranbrook Press.

Cover design: Debbie Clement
Cover images: Arcangel, Shutterstock

Published by Storm Publishing.
For further information, visit:
www.stormpublishing.co

ALSO BY CLARE FLYNN

Hearts of Glass
The Artist's Apprentice
The Artist's Wife

The Penang Series
The Pearl of Penang
Prisoner from Penang
A Painter in Penang
Jasmine in Paris

The Chalky Sea
The Alien Corn
The Frozen River
A Greater World
Kurinji Flowers
Letters from a Patchwork Quilt
The Green Ribbons
The Gamekeeper's Wife
Storms Gather Between Us
Sisters at War

'When love and skill work together, expect a masterpiece.'
John Ruskin, *The Stones of Venice*

PART ONE

ONE

DALTON HALL, RICHMOND, SURREY

January 1908

Alice was late again. She'd risen early but had been side-tracked by sketching the unusual patterns of frost on her bedroom window. A lecture from her mother was inevitable. Lady Dalton was a stickler for punctuality.

Seeking a diversionary tactic, Alice intercepted the footman who was about to deliver the first post to her parents at the breakfast table.

As she took the silver tray from the man, Alice noticed the handwriting on the envelope that lay on top of the pile – over-large, cursive, but with an almost childlike uniformity of style that made it stand out from the others on the silver tray. Something about it made Alice curious – and oddly nervous.

As she entered the room, her mother opened her mouth to protest at her lateness, but Alice was ready. 'I saw the post coming so I waited for it. I was hoping for a letter from Harriet but there's nothing from her.' She passed the silver tray to her mother and took her place at the table.

Lady Dalton tutted but slit the first envelope open with a paper knife and read the contents.

'That dreadful American woman has invited us all to dinner.'

'What dreadful American woman?' Lord Dalton spoke from behind his copy of *The Times*.

'Mrs Cutler, your stockbroker's wife. You introduced us at the ballet. She has one of those awful rasping voices, like a chair scraping, and wears far too much jewellery. I'll find an excuse to decline.'

'You'll do no such thing.' Lord Dalton folded his newspaper and put it down. Glancing at his son, Victor, he addressed his wife. 'You must accept immediately.'

Alice's nervousness mounted. She had no idea why, but an odd sense of foreboding chilled her. She tried to focus her eyes on the piece of toast she was buttering, her appetite already gone.

'The Cutlers are social climbers. He's in commerce and she's an American *arriviste*.'

Lord Dalton peered at his wife over the top of his spectacles. 'I find her rather charming. And Herbert Cutler is very clubbable. Times are changing, my dear. We need to change with them.' Lord Dalton exchanged another glance with Alice's brother, Victor, who nodded in agreement.

Lady Dalton sniffed derisively. 'Why do we need to change?'

'Because we can't afford not to. Unless we make further economies – possibly even put Dalton Hall on the market – we must accept that we now depend on Mr Cutler. Since he took up the financial reins, he's significantly improved matters. After that nasty business last year with the Knickerbocker Trust, Cutler has steered what's left of my investment portfolio into safer waters. He appears to be making excellent choices, but it will take time before I regain the position I enjoyed before the Knickerbocker collapse.'

'I haven't the faintest notion what you're talking about. Collapsing knickerbockers doesn't strike me as a suitable topic for the breakfast table.'

'I've told you before, my dear. It's an American bank that went under.'

Lady Dalton sighed. 'I still don't understand why that means we should endure dinner with these people. If this Mr Cutler has got your investments back in shape, then he's to be congratulated, but it's not a reason to accept a dinner invitation. I shall most definitely make our excuses.'

'You most definitely will not. There's more than a few shares at stake.' He leant forward. 'Cutler has mooted the possibility of a position for Victor in his firm. A very well-paid position.'

Lady Dalton spun round in her chair to face her son. 'Victor? Is this true?'

Victor's lips stretched into a thin line, and he nodded his head slowly.

Alice stared at him, surprised. Her brother had shown no inclination towards employment, nor had her parents ever expressed any desire that he should seek a job. She had always considered her relationship with him as close. Victor usually confided in her, so her first instinct was to feel hurt that this time he hadn't.

Her mother was clearly unhappy.

'What on earth do you want with a "position"? You're not a bank clerk. You're a gentleman. As the son of a peer, you shouldn't be taking paid employment.'

Victor started to protest, but his mother pressed on, unstoppable in her righteous indignation. 'It's out of the question. What would people think? Working in an office in the city of London. No, no, no. What was the point of an Eton education?'

'It's not in London; it's in New York. I'm to learn the workings of the American stock exchange. All being well, eventually I'll return to a senior position in the London office.' Victor rose from the table. 'Now if you'll excuse me, I'm going for my ride before heading into town.'

Alice watched, dumbstruck as her brother left the room. She'd never felt so isolated. Why hadn't he told her any of this? Ever since they were children, they'd been close confidantes, partners in crime, but lately she'd sensed him drifting away. Had he been ashamed about taking this job? But why? Alice shared none of her mother's ingrained snobbery and Victor knew that.

'Well!' Lady Dalton scowled at her husband. 'You approve of this, Neville? Have you been putting pressure on the boy?'

'He's hardly a boy, Lavinia. Victor has a mind of his own. As it happens it's his idea. He's become friendly with the Cutlers and it seems he has a talent for finances that I'm sorry to say he didn't inherit from me. By the time he succeeds to my title and estate, I expect Victor to be a wealthy man.' Lord Dalton removed his glasses. 'He's already spent a few days in Cutler's London office, working alongside one of Cutler's sons. Turns out he knew the boy already. Met him at the Moncriefs a few months ago—'

'You mean the Moncriefs invited one of the Cutlers? To a house party? Surely not?'

Lord Dalton sighed. 'Many people nowadays don't share your distaste for Americans or their offspring – nor for those in commerce. They have no qualms about "new money" so why should you? The Cutler boys both went to Harrow, so they're not exactly lads from the local grammar school. Times change, Lavinia, and we must change with them.'

'If Victor's agreed to take up this *position*, why must we still accept the dinner invitation? Do these people want to rub our noses in it?'

His lordship's eyes drifted towards Alice before moving back to meet his wife's. A sudden queasiness rose inside Alice. She dropped the piece of toast she had not been eating back onto her plate. She knew only too well what was coming.

'There's something else, isn't there, Neville?' Lady Dalton drummed her fingers on the table. 'Something you're not telling me. I always know when you're harbouring a guilty secret. Out with it!'

'We thought... Cutler and I thought... it would be a good thing if...'

'You're behaving the way you did when you were about to tell me we had to get rid of half the servants. What is it?'

He glanced in Alice's direction, but avoided her gaze 'The Cutler boys are of a marriageable age and—'

'Oh, no! You can't possibly be suggesting... Out of the question. I'll not have you and your stockbroker friend arranging a marriage between our only daughter and one of their horrible sons.'

Alice cringed. She wanted to escape. How could they talk about her as though she were utterly inconsequential? Invisible. Did they even intend to ask what she thought? Did Victor know? Why hadn't he said anything to her? He ought to have warned her.

Lord Dalton banged his palm on the table. 'They're not horrible. You haven't even met the fellows. Face the facts, Lavinia. Alice has little to offer. Nothing more than a courtesy title.'

'She has *breeding*.'

Breeding? Did they think she was a prize-winning piece of livestock being paraded at a county show? Alice looked from one parent to the other, but they seemed oblivious to her presence.

Lord Dalton put his napkin down. 'For the Cutlers, Alice represents a connection to one of the country's oldest families.

If it weren't for the unfortunate mishap with that Yankee bank—'

'And before that with the South American railway that never got built.' Lady Dalton narrowed her eyes.

'All the more reason to stay on the right side of Herbert Cutler.' He shook his head sadly. 'Those deals sounded solid, and I was keen to get in while the price was good. I had no idea the Peruvian scheme involved building the railway across the blasted Andes.'

Lady Dalton had heard it all before and rolled her eyes. 'Are you telling me we have no choice?'

'I'm afraid I am, dear girl. I trust I can rely on you as always?'

Before her mother could reply, Alice pushed back her chair and rushed out of the room.

She ran to the stables, but Victor wasn't there. The stall where his horse was kept stood empty. Apart from a couple of carriage horses and Victor's bay mare, the once fully occupied stable block was untenanted, a victim of the belt-tightening caused by her father's financial difficulties.

She'd have to wait to confront her brother. Alice began pacing up and down, anger mounting. Anger at her parents who treated her like a child – a person without agency, simply there to be used as they saw fit. Anger at Victor for failing to tell her anything. How could he decide to leave the country for America and neglect to even mention it? And was he also a party to this latest plot to marry her off?

Alice kicked the stable door, frustration and fury numbing the pain of a stubbed toe. Her own plans for the morning were ruined. It was a sunny day and she'd intended to take her easel and paints and continue work on painting the view of the Hall from the meadows beyond. Yesterday she'd made a start, but the threat of rain and a cold wind had driven her indoors.

Rage and frustration gradually ebbed out of her, and she

settled onto a bale of straw to await her brother. Eventually the clip of iron on cobbles heralded his return. He trotted back into the stable yard and swung himself off his horse. He didn't look pleased to see his sister waiting for him. Ignoring her, he led his horse past her into the stall.

Alice stared him down, hands on hips. 'You knew all about it. Why didn't you warn me?'

Victor unfastened the girth and lifted the saddle off his horse. 'I was waiting for the right moment. How was I supposed to know that dinner invitation was coming today? I'd have told you eventually.'

'Told me what? That you're about to leave for America or that I'm about to be married off to some man I've never met?'

Victor moved past her and handed the saddle and bridle to the waiting groom who now doubled as a chauffeur, the sole survivor of a once large team of grooms and coachmen. 'Don't worry, Gibson, I'll brush and water Sapphire myself. You get the motor ready.' He waited until the servant had disappeared into the tack room before answering Alice. 'Both.'

She watched in silence as he filled a bucket of water at the yard tap and set it down in the stall for the mare to drink. It was clear he was uncomfortable at Alice cornering him.

'Look, Papa told me not to mention the move to America until the details are finalised. He knew Mama would kick up a stink. As to the other part, I'd have told you but as it's none of my business I thought it better coming from Papa.'

Alice studied his face as he spoke. He didn't look any happier about the arrangement than she was. At least there was that. If he'd tried to pressure her into marrying this man, she'd have found it impossible to forgive Victor. But he looked as glum as she felt.

'Papa said you know the sons.'

'Only one of them. Gilbert. Never met the other one.'

Alice's temper was starting to fray again. He was being so evasive. 'It's a plot to marry me off to Gilbert. To *your friend*.'

'It was mooted. That's all I know.' He had his back to her as he worked the brush over his horse. The strong sweet scent of horse sweat and fresh straw permeated the small space.

'No one's going to force you to marry anyone against your will, Alice. But Gilbert's a decent chap. He's become a good friend. You could do a lot worse. Pass me that rug will you?'

She took the rug from a hook by the door and watched as he draped it over the mare's back and patted her neck again.

When the horse was settled, Victor held open the door for Alice, then followed her out into the stable yard. His voice was impatient. 'I have to get into town for a meeting. Gibson's dropping me off at the station. I'll see you soon. And stop worrying. It will all work out for the best.' He turned back to face her and dropped a quick kiss on her forehead.

'Aren't we even going to talk about America? You've told me nothing. When? How long for?'

'Soon and for a few years at least.'

She gasped, horrified. But Victor was already heading back to the house.

On the day of the Cutlers' dinner party, Alice spent the morning tramping through the woods, then the afternoon sitting sketching, wrapped in a blanket, in the doorway of an old folly that looked like a ruined Roman temple. Whenever she was drawing, she lost track of time, as if the day-to-day world of preordained mealtimes and the weight of social or familial obligations didn't exist.

The son of one of the gardeners came to find her, sent on the errand by the housekeeper.

'Mrs Robinson said to tell you her ladyship has asked for the motorcar to be ready to leave promptly at a quarter to six.'

'Crumbs! I'd forgotten the time.' Alice scrambled about, gathering up her drawing materials. Lost in the pleasure of drawing, she'd allowed herself to forget the looming prospect of the dinner that night.

'I'll deal with that, Miss Alice. You get along,' said the boy. All the servants knew that Lady Dalton was obsessive about punctuality.

Alice gave him a grateful smile and made her way across the meadow towards the honey-coloured, rambling, eighteenth century pile that was Dalton Hall.

She was dreading this evening. Being dragged along in her parents' wake to a formal dinner with people she didn't know. Having to abandon the safe haven of Dalton Hall for the hurly-burly of London was painful. The idea of meeting the man her father pinned his hopes on her marrying was terrifying. What was more, her mother's initial objections had evaporated. Lady Dalton – once she'd got used to the idea – and to the fact that it hadn't been her own – had become increasingly enthusiastic about Alice marrying one of the Cutler sons.

Her coming-out the previous year had been a disappointment. The Honourable Alice Dalton had failed to accomplish the fundamental purpose of the entire debutante palaver – finding a suitable husband. It had been an ordeal. She'd hated making polite conversation with people with whom she shared few common interests, under the critical eyes of everyone present, from the overprotective mothers to the prospective suitors and the other debutantes. The only part she'd enjoyed was the opportunity to compare notes with her best friend Harriet. Their morning-after post-mortems of each evening's events had been the only redeeming feature of the season.

Alice crunched across the gravel towards the house. Under a triangular pediment, the rear elevation was a Palladian structure dissected by tall windows, which looked out over a wide, gravelled terrace and a sweep of lawn to meadows and woods beyond.

Inside, the long case clock in the hall was already showing a quarter past five, so she rushed upstairs to her bedroom, and scrambled into the peach silk gown her mother had insisted she wear tonight. Since Papa had cut back on the servants, Alice was expected to dress herself, because Johnson, the only lady's maid they still employed, was monopolised by Mama, whose own maid had accepted higher-paid employment elsewhere. Not that Alice cared, as she preferred to dress without assistance.

Most of the time.

But now, as she adjusted the satin sash to cover a couple of grease spots, she was all too aware that Johnson would never have allowed stains to pass her eagle-eyed inspection. The frock would have been re-laundered and every trace of the marks vanquished. Alice never paid much attention to her clothes – provided they suited the occasion and the season, she didn't give a fig.

What had caused the offending stains? She tried to recall when she'd last worn the gown. The sash almost covered the small spots, but not quite. She'd need to keep her hands in front of her waist and pray that Mama didn't see. Once they were seated at the dinner table, she'd be safe, and later in the evening if anyone noticed, they'd assume that it had happened during dinner and not that she'd turned up wearing a soiled gown.

Victor and Papa were already in London, so Alice and her mother would be alone for the drive into town.

Taking one last look at herself in the cheval glass, she moved her hands over the offending stain and hurried downstairs, unable to quash the sense that she was about to be offered as a sacrificial lamb to appease her father's creditors.

TWO

HOLBORN, LONDON

The first time Edmund Cutler set eyes on Miss Dora Fisher he was smitten.

She was in a group of young women from the Royal Female School of Art in London, visiting The Central School of Arts and Crafts. The Female School was about to merge with the Central. Edmund, a final year student, was to show one of the groups around the new premises in Holborn. He'd been irritated by the request, wanting to get on with preparing his latest stained-glass samples for the oven. But all irritation vanished when he saw Miss Fisher among the bevy of young women gathered in the lobby.

She had her back to him. With a slight figure and dark hair gathered into a loose bun at the nape of her neck, she drew his eye immediately. When she turned to face him, his throat constricted.

Later, when Edmund tried to decide what it was about Miss Dora Fisher that so instantly and completely captivated him, he couldn't pinpoint one individual feature. She was petite – a pocket Venus. Her complexion was bright and flawless, with a tinge of rose in her cheeks. Under an odd little hat, her hair was the crowning glory – from now on he decided he would recreate it in every Madonna, Lady of Shalott or Saint Joan he portrayed.

He stood in front of the group of women, tongue-tied and unable to take his eyes off the beautiful creature. She gave him a brief glance, before turning away. One of her companions nudged another and said something he couldn't hear. The other girl put her hand over her mouth to stifle a laugh and turned to whisper to her neighbour. The whispering spread like a game of pass-the-parcel throughout the small group. Edmund's skin tingled with a rush of blood to the back of his neck.

Until now, he'd been relatively immune to the charms of the opposite sex. He'd admired a pretty face and responded to an engaging smile, but no woman had threatened his dedication to his artistic studies. But here in the lobby of the Central School he appeared to have lost the power of speech.

It was the vision herself who broke the impasse. 'Aren't you meant to be giving us a guided tour?' She tilted her head on one side as she addressed him.

He swallowed twice before he was able to answer. 'Of course. Sorry. Are you all here? Shall we begin then?' His voice sounded hollow, tremulous, and he told himself to buck up. 'The building is brand new – we only moved here from Regent Street a couple of months ago. We'll start upstairs and work our way down. Follow me.'

He set off towards the main stairway, conscious of the whispered conversations and the intermittent giggling as they followed behind him.

'Just a minute.' The speaker was a stout, red-faced, older woman, who'd introduced herself as Miss Heeley their tutor. 'How many floors?'

'Five.'

'Then shouldn't we work our way upwards so we only need to tackle one set of stairs at a time?'

He shrugged his agreement, although annoyed at the woman for pointing this out, and with himself for not anticipating it. Pushing his embarrassment aside, he asked the group which disciplines they were following. There were two potters, a fashion plate designer, a painter, a stained-glass artist, two needleworkers – one of them the tall tutor – as well as the beautiful young woman who'd caught his attention, who was studying illustration. He felt a ripple of disappointment that she was not the one doing stained glass. This was balanced by satisfaction that the tutor was about to discover that the needlework and weaving rooms were on the top floor and once the new term began she'd have to face those five flights of stairs every day.

They moved through the building, room by room, starting in the basement where the percussion of chisels on stone heralded the stone carving room. Edmund led them through studios and workrooms, some occupied, others empty: pattern designing, life drawing, wood engraving, enamelling and more. The group of women lingered longest in the chasing and *repoussé* room, where more than a dozen young men sat at the long wooden workbenches engraving silverware. Edmund watched, helpless, as the object of his fascination stopped for an inordinate amount of time beside the work-post of a silversmith with a cheeky grin, who made no secret of flirting with her. She leant towards him as he showed her what he was working on and explained the use of the various tools of his trade.

Edmund struggled to summon up the enthusiasm to talk to the other women students about the custom-made workbenches with their semi-circular cut-outs to accommodate each student. He told them that these allowed the men to be close to the object they were working on, as well as to the metal vices and tools nested neatly beside them. As he explained, the young woman continued to flirt with the cheeky-faced silversmith and seemed to show no intention of moving on. Edmund was about to interrupt and usher them all into the bookbinding room, when he caught her looking at him. It was a look that said *I know you don't like this so I'm going to keep on doing it*. He ought to have been annoyed at her, irritated, impatient, but all he could think of was what it would be like to take her in his arms.

Eventually, the needlework tutor prevailed on her to move on. The older woman had an intense gaze that made Edmund feel cornered whenever she asked a question.

'Come along, Miss Fisher,' the woman called. 'Let that gentleman get on with his silver-work. There's still a lot to see. This poor chap here has been waiting patiently to continue our tour.' Edmund was far from thrilled at being described as a poor chap.

As they walked down the corridor, Miss Fisher moved alongside him. 'What kind of illustrations do you do?' he asked her.

The goddess shrugged. 'All sorts.' She waved a hand vaguely in the air.

'But don't you have a specialisation?' he persisted.

Before she could answer, another of the young women interrupted, moving to the other side of Edmund. 'Dora does the most exquisite botanical drawings.'

Edmund turned to Miss Fisher, rejoicing that he now knew her Christian name too. 'Really? I'd love to look at your portfolio some time.'

'Did you hear that, Dora?' the other young woman said, archly. 'The gentleman wants to look at your portfolio. Hope it's ready for inspection.' She uttered the word portfolio as though it was something indelicate.

Edmund was embarrassed and somewhat bewildered. He was unused to the company of young women, having no sisters, and passing straight from Harrow School to the Central, where until now, there had been no females. He hadn't expected girls to have such confidence and to exhibit such *esprit de corps*.

Miss Heeley spoke again. 'What's *your* speciality, Mr Cutler?' Her voice was plummy and patrician.

'Stained glass,' he said, 'two floors up,' pointing at the ceiling.

'Why did you choose that?' Miss Heeley's eyes drilled into him.

Edmund wished the woman would leave him alone with Miss Fisher. He was there to show them around, not to be subjected to a personal interrogation. Eventually, he said, 'It's the perfect combination of both art and craft.'

'What exactly do you mean?' The woman was frowning, her eyes now two narrow slits.

'In stained glass, the creative skills of the painter meet the technical skills of the craftsman. Firstly, creating the image, just like a painting, all the form and colour, but not stopping there. One also needs to understand materials and techniques – the science. The work won't come to life without the artist mastering the technical aspects: choosing from different types of glass, testing the colours, experimenting in the kiln, knowing where to place the leading.'

'I don't see how that's different from any of the disciplines we follow,' the tutor said haughtily.

In his stride now and annoyed by the tutor's determination to be argumentative, he said, 'It's the way the painted glass changes in different light conditions. It never turns out exactly as you imagined. It's never completely predictable.'

Miss Heeley skewered him with her eyes. 'I don't understand what you're trying to say. Please elaborate.'

'Until a piece of stained glass is installed, you never know exactly how it will appear. So much depends on the architecture that surrounds it, the way the light falls on it and through it, the direction it faces. So many factors.'

'Surely that's true of a painting too?' She folded her arms under an ample bosom. 'More so, perhaps, as the artist usually has no control over where and how it is hung.' Her tone was triumphant.

The rest of them were now gathered around, looking at him expectantly. He wouldn't have been surprised if they had chorused *Touché*. Miss Fisher was standing apart from the others, staring out of the window, apparently oblivious to the sparring.

'Yes, that's true,' he said. 'But a painting can be moved. With a stained-glass window, you create it for a specific place. Once it's there, it's there. That's what makes it special. You try to take into account exactly where it will be, how high or low, what direction it faces, the source of light, whether it's shaded by trees or another building. It's like a scientific experiment and despite all the careful calculations and planning, you're never entirely certain how it will look until it's *in situ*.' He glanced at Miss Fisher, trying to establish whether she was listening. It appeared not. 'I suppose that's why it fascinates me so much. The combination of precise planning and serendipity.'

'Excellent answer, young man,' said Miss Heeley, and Edmund felt about twelve years old.

When the tour finished and the women had departed, Edmund headed back upstairs to the glass studio. He had intended to do some more experimentation with different colour mixes and varying times in the kiln. But he had no stomach for it now.

All he could think about was Miss Dora Fisher. He imagined removing her funny little hat, unpinning her hair and running his fingers through it. He closed his eyes, thinking about how it would feel to brush those lips with his own. What did she think of him? Had she even noticed him? No doubt his pontification on the art and craft of stained glass had sounded pompous. It certainly hadn't interested her. But worst of all, Miss Fisher had clearly had eyes only for the silversmith she'd spoken to for so long. Edmund already hated the man, whom he didn't know, with a jealous passion.

Telling himself to put thoughts of Miss Fisher aside, he tidied the workbench and went downstairs to fetch his coat and hat from the basement cloakroom. By the time the ladies of the Royal Female School of Art were due to start classes in two weeks' time, surely he'd have forgotten all about her? There was no reason for them to bump into each other since they'd be in different parts of the building.

He decided to go for a walk by the river before heading home. He would direct his attention to ideas for his entry into the graduating students' competition next term. It would be his final term at the school and he was determined to produce the prize-winning design.

Edmund pushed through the doors and onto Southampton Row just in time to see Miss Dora Fisher slip her arm through that of the young silversmith as the two walked away towards High Holborn.

THREE

GROSVENOR SQUARE, LONDON

In the motorcar, a heavy plaid rug covered Alice's knees and she clutched her coat tightly around her, shivering as the Wolseley rattled through the streets towards central London. Shouting to be heard above the engine noise, her mother lectured her about keeping an open mind that evening and remembering what was best for the family. Alice let the words wash over her and tried not to think about what they meant.

'Of course, we will be guided by your preference, darling, but your papa and I feel the elder son will be more suitable. I gather the other one is rather immature. Your father suspects he's a disappointment to Mr Cutler. Reluctant to join the firm.' Lady Dalton nudged her daughter's arm. 'I imagine the older one will inherit the business. I had no idea until your father explained to me, but they are extremely wealthy.'

Alice gave her mother a smile in acknowledgment but said nothing. It never ceased to amaze her how deep the seam of materialism ran in Lady Dalton – and how little it took for pragmatism to gain the upper hand.

When Alice and her mother arrived at Grosvenor Square, the two Dalton men were already inside the Cutler residence, smoking cigars and sipping whisky. The ladies were ushered into the drawing room where only Gilbert, the elder son was present. Introductions were made but the men showed no desire to break off their conversation, so Alice was left to chat with her mother and Mrs Cutler.

Because the younger brother, Edmund, hadn't arrived yet, dinner was delayed more than half an hour. An increasingly flustered Mrs Cutler repeated her apologies. Alice took advantage of the delay to inspect Gilbert Cutler without appearing to be watching him. He was on the far side of the large drawing room, and she could only see him in profile. But it was a handsome profile. Distinguished. Debonair. She allowed herself to breathe. Perhaps this wouldn't be so terrible.

The clock chimed the half hour and Mr Cutler, visibly exasperated, instructed his wife that the dinner should proceed without the absent Edmund.

Alice was placed between Gilbert Cutler and her father, but as Gilbert helped her into her seat and was about to take his place beside her, her brother, Victor, called across to him, 'You and I have lots to catch up on, Gilbert. Why not leave that seat for Edmund? I want you to tell me about the New York office.' Alice was left marooned beside the empty chair.

Mrs Cutler looked at her husband, but he was deep in conversation with Lord Dalton, so, diplomatically, she turned to Alice and said, 'I hope you don't mind, my dear. Edmund will surely be here any minute.'

Alice knew with absolute certainty that Edmund Cutler wasn't going to turn up at all. She resigned herself to sitting next to an empty chair and to the inevitability of her mother having much to say on the topic on the drive home. But right now, Lady Dalton was happily holding forth to her hostess about her distaste for Mrs Pankhurst and her suffragettes.

'Suffragism is an admission of failure,' she said smugly. 'Any woman who demands the vote might as well admit her own shortcomings as a wife.' She offered a patronising smile to Mrs Cutler. 'The true decisions are made not in the House of Lords but in the home, where we reign supreme. Don't you agree, Mrs Cutler?'

Susan Cutler glanced towards her husband at the end of the table, but he was still engaged in discussion with Lord Dalton. 'I guess so,' she said without much conviction. 'My husband wouldn't stand for such behaviour, that's for sure. Being an American, I don't understand English politics. I leave such matters to him and concentrate on raising my sons and managing the household.'

Lady Dalton's description of their hostess as 'a vulgar American woman' seemed to have no foundation. Alice's own assessment was that Mrs Cutler seemed timid, deferential towards her husband and unsure of herself. The way Mr Cutler had snapped at her over Edmund's lateness indicated he was used to getting his way and the wifely influence Lady Dalton had referred to did not appear evident in the Cutler marriage.

Meanwhile, at the other end of the table the two patriarchs were speaking of such riveting topics as bauxite mining and England's progress in the latest Test match in Australia. Alice couldn't make out what Victor and Gilbert were discussing; their conversation was conducted in low voices, punctuated by the occasional guffaw and they made no attempt to include her, ignoring the usual etiquette.

The prospect of a long dull evening stretched ahead, and Alice wished it was time to leave. She envied the absent Edmund and wondered what excuse he had for missing the dinner. Perhaps his non-appearance was deliberate. Maybe he too suspected a plot afoot to arrange a marriage between her and one of the brothers and had taken evasive action. She took the opportunity to study the other brother more closely. Undeniably handsome, Gilbert had perfectly groomed dark brown hair, a neatly clipped moustache and eyes that hinted at a sense of humour. When he'd been introduced to Alice, he'd seemed diffident, shy even, but was relaxed now talking with Victor – possibly helped by the free-flowing wine.

Alice was all too conscious that this evening was to seal the deal between her father and Mr Cutler. To the Cutlers, Alice offered the cachet of being the daughter of a baronet, albeit one of slender means. In turn, Gilbert, a partner in his father's rapidly growing firm, would offer Alice financial security. And judging by Victor's behaviour tonight, he appeared to be happy that a lucrative position, possibly a seat on the board, had already been lined up for him. Thinking back to that breakfast when she'd first heard of the Cutlers, Alice realised her cooperation was as important to her brother's future as it was to the family's fortune. If she raised an objection to marrying Gilbert Cutler, she risked derailing Victor's plans as well as jeopardising the future of Dalton Hall. The burden of responsibility was hers – even though the choice wasn't.

But now she had an opportunity to study Gilbert she was increasingly open to the idea of marrying him. Contrary to expectation, she found nothing in his looks or manner to object to. With eyes that seemed to draw her in when he looked at her – which so far had been only when they were introduced – Gilbert was the most handsome man Alice had ever seen. When he smiled, revealing straight white teeth, she allowed herself to imagine what it would be like to be kissed by him.

Alice's friend Harriet had recently married a portly middle-aged earl. Harriet's surprise engagement had been a huge relief to Alice as there had been suggestions that the Earl of Wallingford would make a suitable match for Alice herself. Becoming Mrs Gilbert Cutler might be an acceptable fate, after all.

Whether prompted by an unseen signal from his father or his own awareness of her eyes on him, Gilbert Cutler leant forward to address her across the table. 'Do you spend much time in town, Miss Dalton?' The enquiry was banal but his eyes were kind.

'As little as possible, if I'm honest,' she confessed, then immediately wished she hadn't – perhaps Gilbert was about to extend an invitation. 'I mean there are lots of interesting things to do in London, but I'm awfully fond of the country.'

Victor rolled his eyes. 'I'm afraid my sister is never happier than when she's sitting on an old tree stump, painting the scenery.'

'You like to paint?' Gilbert raised his eyebrows. 'What a pity Edmund isn't here. He's an art student. Talented too.'

Mr Cutler Senior broke in. 'Drawing and painting are fine hobbies for a young lady but a disgraceful waste of time for a man. A lot of stuff and nonsense.' He shook his head and drained his wineglass, which was promptly replenished by a hovering servant. 'Edmund's mother convinced me that letting him go to art school would get it out of the boy's system, but there's no sign of that so far.' He glowered down the table at his wife.

'I'm sure Miss Dalton doesn't want—' Mrs Cutler was interrupted by her husband.

'Don't worry, it's the last time I'll listen to her.' Herbert Cutler spoke as though his wife wasn't present. 'As soon as that damn-fool art course is over, Edmund will be joining the firm, like his brother. Isn't that right, Gilbert?'

Gilbert Cutler glanced sideways at Victor. 'If you say so, Father.'

'I can't imagine where Edmund is.' Mrs Cutler gave a nervous laugh. 'I'm really sorry for his behaviour. It isn't with the intent of dishonouring our guests. He's a little absent-minded. I call him Eddie Head-in-Air – after the verse by Mr Heinrich Hoffmann. Do you know it, Lady Dalton? Once my son is absorbed in a piece of artwork, he loses all sense of time and responsibility.'

Alice thought it a pity Edmund wasn't present as she rather liked the sound of him. Remembering she was expected to sustain the conversation, she turned back to Gilbert. 'Are you fond of the countryside, Mr Cutler?'

'Your brother and I met on a shooting weekend, but I fear I made rather a hash of it. I don't know one end of a gun from the other.'

'Are you artistic like your brother?'

'Good Lord, no. I appreciate art, music and the theatre, but entirely as a spectator. I've absolutely no talent for any of them.'

'Exactly as it should be,' Mr Cutler interjected. 'Such frivolities are for entertainment only. One's own endeavours ought to be directed towards the enrichment of one's family and the growth of the British Empire. Now, isn't it time the ladies withdrew? I've a very fine port and a new selection of the finest Havanas waiting for us, Lord Dalton. Unfortunately, my American wife is sometimes forgetful of English conventions.'

'I'm sorry, Lady Dalton. What was I thinking?' Flustered and blushing, Mrs Cutler jumped to her feet and led Lady Dalton and Alice towards the door. Alice trailed behind the two older women who were discussing a petition currently circulating regarding the proposed formation of an Anti-Suffrage League, to counter the women's suffrage movement, following extensive correspondence on the subject to *The Times*. Alice made her excuses and went to the bathroom. If asked her opinion, she'd support Mrs Pankhurst's side, but no one bothered to enquire what she thought.

When she emerged a few minutes later, she heard voices from down the hall. She stepped back inside the bathroom doorway and waited for them to move away.

'I'd lie low if I were you, Edmund,' she heard Gilbert Cutler say. 'Father will hit the roof if he sees you. It's obvious you've been drinking. Stay out of his way and hope he's forgotten by tomorrow evening. What on earth were you thinking?'

A long sigh. 'What's the prospective bride like?'

'That's why you didn't turn up, isn't it? Making sure I'm the one who ends up marrying the wretched girl.'

The blood rushed to Alice's cheeks.

'When I decide to marry it won't be to keep *him* happy,' Edmund said. 'I shall marry for love. Come on, what she's like?'

'Pleasant enough, I suppose. Certainly not a looker.'

'But you'll go along with what Father wants anyway?'

'Path of least resistance, old boy.' There was a short pause. 'Besides I liked her. Reckon she'll make a good wife.'

'Do you think she knows?'

'Imagine so. Before they arrived, Mother said this was likely her last hope, poor thing. And I have to marry someone, so it might as well be her.'

The voices were getting closer, so Alice slipped back inside the bathroom to wait until they were safely past.

Moving to the large mirror that hung over the washbasin, she studied her reflection. Gilbert's words had stung. She had no illusions that she was anything other than plain but presentable, yet it was one thing to acknowledge this herself and quite another to hear someone else say it. It would have been preferable for Gilbert to have rejected marriage to her out of hand as at least it would have meant she'd provoked some reaction. What could be worse than being seen as bland.

Soon after Alice re-joined her mother and Mrs Cutler, the evening drew to a close. As they left the house, Victor announced he was staying in town at his club and would make his way there on foot. 'I need a breath of fresh air,' he said, handing his mother and sister up into the back of the Wolseley. His father was already sitting in front waiting for the driver, who was readying the rugs to drape over the passengers.

'That went rather well, I think,' shouted Lord Dalton, as the motorcar rattled past Hyde Park, heading for the Bath Road.

Neither woman attempted to reply. The noise of the engine

made conversation impossible. Alice shivered under her blanket and longed to be home in bed, but first she'd have to endure a post-mortem of the evening.

When they arrived at Dalton Hall Lord Dalton ushered Alice and her mother into the library where a small fire was burning in the grate. Mrs Robinson, the housekeeper, brought them a tray of tea and a brandy for Lord Dalton.

'All in all, an enjoyable evening, yes?' Lord Dalton rubbed his hands together. 'Herbert Cutler keeps an exceptional cellar. Dashed rude of the younger son not to put in an appearance but, after all, Alice can only marry one of them and I'm rather taken with Gilbert. Seems a fine fellow.'

Lady Dalton glanced at her daughter who was still shivering after the drive home. 'Victor monopolised him. You must talk to him, Neville. All very well he and the Cutler boy being chums, but Gilbert and Alice need to get to know each other.'

'Plenty of time for that once they're married. At least Alice has had a good look at him and can see he's a sound chap. You and I barely exchanged more than a few sentences before we tied the knot. Didn't do us any harm did it, my dear?'

Lady Dalton ignored the remark and focused instead on her daughter. 'I thought he was awfully handsome, didn't you, Alice?'

'Too handsome for me, you mean?'

'Don't be silly, darling. There are far more important qualities needed in a wife than beauty, and I'm sure Gilbert Cutler recognises that.'

'Like being the daughter of a peer of the realm?'

'What's the matter with you this evening? You seem quite out of sorts, Alice.'

Still smarting over the conversation between the Cutler brothers, Alice had an urge to be defiant. 'You say there are more important things than beauty but all you have to say about

Gilbert Cutler is how handsome he is. Am I supposed to be pathetically grateful?'

'Alice! What's got into you?'

'I can't think why you're bothering to ask my opinion at all if the whole thing's already decided. But you're making an awful lot of assumptions, as Gilbert Cutler barely glanced at me, and our conversation lasted about two minutes. He was far more interested in talking to Victor.'

'I told you so, Neville!' Lady Dalton turned to face her husband. 'You must have a word with the boy. Victor needs to know he's upset his sister.'

'You don't like the fellow?' Lord Dalton's eyebrows narrowed.

Alice sighed. 'I didn't say I disliked him. But I can't see him wanting to marry me.'

'Well, he does.' Lord Dalton rubbed his hands together. 'After you ladies retired, Cutler and I thrashed out the details over the port.'

Thrashed out the details? Her father made it sound like selling a horse. Complete with full pedigree. 'Why do I need to marry anyone at all? I'm perfectly happy as I am.'

Lady Dalton crinkled her nose in horror. 'Don't be petulant, Alice. It doesn't suit you. Surely you don't want to turn into one of those bitter old spinsters who hurl bricks through shop windows and write angry letters to the Prime Minister?'

Lord Dalton took a gulp of his brandy. 'The best marriages always offer benefits to both parties. You just need a little time to get to know the fellow. His father has suggested an evening at the theatre, or perhaps a walk in Regent's Park. Once you've spent a little time together, we'll invite the Cutlers for a weekend here. After that we can announce the engagement. No point in wasting time.'

Lady Dalton nodded at Alice. 'We'll have a small dinner here at Dalton Hall just for the two families. In May or June, when the gardens are looking lovely. We could have more guests in for a big dinner on the Saturday and make the formal announcement before we sit down to eat.'

'That's the stuff,' said Lord Dalton, polishing off his brandy. 'Champagne at the ready. Quite a party. What do you say, Alice? Young Cutler's a fine chap and you could do a lot worse.'

Lady Dalton sipped her tea. 'I must admit when your father first mooted the idea I had my doubts, especially with Mrs Cutler being American, but I was reassured tonight. She's not as pushy as one might expect from an American. In fact, she was tolerable company, though I'll never get used to that accent. Americans sound so... lacking refinement. On the other hand, Gilbert's had the benefit of an English education and he's *so...*'

'Handsome? You've already made that clear, Mama.' Alice stared into the fire gloomily. She tried to convince herself her parents only wanted the best for her. She pictured Gilbert Cutler again. Maybe, given time, they'd develop a fondness for each other. Most young women would be delighted to be in her shoes, with such a polite, affluent and, yes, handsome man as a prospective husband.

This match was also the best – possibly the only – chance of her family saving Dalton Hall. She thought of Harriet and her fat old earl. Gilbert Cutler might lack the aristocratic pedigree of the Earl of Wallingford, but she knew with whom she'd rather share her future. Gilbert thought her plain, but her eavesdropping had shown he was ready to marry her anyway. Was her family name and courtesy title really that important?

Forcing a smile, she said, 'Sorry for being so crabby. I'm happy to see Gilbert Cutler again and I'll marry him if he'll have me.'

FOUR

LONDON

Edmund followed Dora Fisher and the young silversmith at a safe distance, uncertain why he was doing it, but unwilling to let her out of his sight. He'd never done anything like this before. It felt shabby and devious, but he wasn't ready to let Dora disappear into the foggy streets without discovering where she lived.

The couple – for it did appear they were a couple as Dora's arm was linked through the crook of the silversmith's – walked at a leisurely pace up Southampton Row to Russell Square, passing the rear of the British Museum and on to Tottenham Court Road. As they strolled, they kept up an animated conversation, Dora laughing and smiling up at the young man. They turned into Goodge Street and stood talking for what seemed an age to Edmund. After receiving a kiss on the cheek, Dora said goodbye to the silversmith. From the opposite side of the street, Edmund watched as she went through a doorway adjacent to a greengrocer. Moments later, an upstairs room glowed with a lighted lamp before Dora appeared at the window and closed the curtains. Meanwhile, the young man loitered in the street, smoking a cigarette. Although it was cold and beginning to driz-zle, Edmund waited, watching his rival.

Taking a last puff of his cigarette, the man ground it under his heel then unlocked the door to an adjacent shop, *F.C. Spindlemann & Son, Engraver & Pawnbroker*. Dora's silver-chaser was her next-door neighbour.

Edmund was relieved. They were neighbours, not lovers.

Relief turned to gloom as his mind played over and over the vision of Dora's arm linked intimately through Spindlemann's. The sound of her tinkling laughter at whatever the man said. The memory of her leaning over the man's work bench, so close that her breast almost brushed his face.

Stop! No point tormenting himself with what might have been between him and the beautiful Miss Fisher. She was spoken for and must be forgotten. He turned and walked away through the streets, his collar turned up against the rain.

Passing a well-lit tavern, he went inside on a whim and sat at a table in a dark corner. His parents were holding a supper party that evening. Both he and his brother had been ordered to attend by his father – the first step in a scheme to form a match with a client's daughter.

The prospect of polite conversation with strangers while his mother desperately tried to meet the expectations of his ungrateful father was unpleasant. He had no intention of being pushed into a marriage himself and couldn't bear to witness his older more compliant brother giving in to paternal pressure. With his hopes about Dora Fisher crushed, it was better to remain here in the warm fug of this public house, numbing his brain with drink. He'd return to Grosvenor Square once it was too late to join the diners.

The following evening, Edmund looked at his father with undisguised disgust. 'Why are you doing this to Gilbert? He doesn't care tuppence for this Dalton girl.'

Herbert Cutler narrowed his eyes. 'Stay out of it, Edmund, unless you're prepared to marry the girl yourself. Fortunately, your brother has a stronger sense of filial duty.'

'You mean he's willing to make himself unhappy rather than upset you?'

'My only aim is to make the Cutler name stand for something. Everything I do is for this family. Everything *you* do appears to be with the sole intent of defying me.'

'Gilbert's lost the will to stand up to your bullying. You've worn him down in every way. You pushed him into becoming a broker. Now you're pressing him to marry this girl just because her father has a seat in the House of Lords and a crumbling old pile somewhere in Surrey. Gilbert doesn't even know her, let alone care for her.'

Herbert Cutler walked over to a side table and poured himself a whisky. 'Gilbert needs to marry. The Honourable Alice Dalton is a good match. The Daltons are one of the most illustrious families in the country. The connection with them will open doors to you too. I'd have thought a little gratitude would be forthcoming for all the effort I make on behalf of my feckless sons.'

Edmund's jaw hardened. 'We're not feckless. Our interests and desires just don't happen to coincide with yours. Both Gilbert and I care about things other than money and status.'

Herbert slugged down his scotch and poured himself another. 'You're a constant disappointment to me. What kind of man chooses to waste his time learning how to paint when he would be better applying himself to the study of markets and building an understanding of how money works?'

Edmund thumped his chest with the side of his fist. 'This kind.'

'You won't get a penny out of me. You're of age so I can't stop you throwing your life away, but I'm damned if I'll help you do it.'

'Throwing my life away? And what exactly are you encouraging Gilbert to do?'

'Gilbert knows what's good for him.'

'He knows life is a lot less painful when he stops trying to stand up to you. You've ground him down, bullied him, threatened him, knocked the stuffing out of him. You're not doing that to me.' Edmund slammed his fist against the arm of his chair.

'Please, Eddie, stop!' Until Susan Cutler cried out, the two men had forgotten she was also in the room. 'It's not good for your father's heart when you argue with him.'

Edmund's lip curled in scorn. 'How can I damage my father's heart when he doesn't appear to have one?'

'Eddie, really!' Susan Cutler's hand covered her mouth.

'Be quiet, Susan, don't interrupt.'

Edmund's mother cringed and retreated into her customary silence. Edmund leapt to his feet and left the room.

The following evening, Edmund was mixing paint pigments in the studio at the Central, trying to create the exact shade of green he wanted. He was the only person in the glass studio as everyone else had left for the day. The house in Grosvenor Square held no allure – especially after the argument with his father. He swirled paint onto his palette, gathered some onto a brush and swept it across a small piece of glass, before holding it up to the light and comparing it with another colour sample.

'Mr Cutler? I can see you're hard at work. Can I interrupt for a few minutes?'

Edmund turned to see Christopher Whall, the celebrated stained-glass artist who had once taught at the Central and was an occasional visiting lecturer. Whall's once-ginger hair was white, although the neatly trimmed beard retained a pale reddish hue.

Edmund was awed by the man. His inspirational guest lecture at the Central had been the highlight of the previous term. How come such an eminent artist knew his name? 'Mr Whall, how can I help you?'

'I've heard good things of you, Mr Cutler, from one of your teachers, Karl Parsons. He and his sister Beatrice work in my studio. He's suggested I get you to show me some of your work.'

Flustered, Edmund hesitated, overcome with nerves. But Whall's eyes twinkled, and he smiled broadly. 'Don't worry. I know I'm springing this on you. Just let me have a look at your sketchbook and any work you happen to have to hand – then we can talk.'

'Of course,' said Edmund, scrabbling about amid the chaos of the workbench to unearth his sketchbook. He handed it to Whall. 'These are rough sketches. While you're looking at them, I'll find the cartoons I've been working on, and some samples of my glasswork.' He darted about the studio, opening cupboards, gathering the pieces, cursing that he'd been taken by surprise and would appear disorganised.

Whall flipped through the sketchbook, then turned to look at the coloured drawings Edmund had laid out on a table.

'This one's for a five-light lancet window intended for a municipal library. The theme we were set was Knowledge and the Arts. I've chosen to portray the nine Muses. Each of the central lights has three of the muses and the two outer ones and the tracery act as framing devices with a rich variety of foliage and flowers as well as elements to convey what each individual muse represents. Stars and planets for Urania, lyres for Euterpe, ballet shoes for Terpsichore and scrolls to convey the various types of poetry and history.'

Whall bent over the artwork and studied it in detail but said nothing.

Edmund laid out several samples of painted glass. 'These are miniatures of the lancets. I finished the leadwork yesterday.' He held his breath.

Whall reached into his pocket, pulled out a pipe and lit it, drawing on it slowly. 'Most impressive. The colour choices are inspired, and your leading is to be commended.' He stepped back and held the panel up to the light from the windows. 'But you'd benefit from recognising when less is more. The colours are beautiful but tend to overwhelm. Have you seen any of my work?'

'I have, sir. St Etheldreda's is very close by.'

Whall snorted. 'Ruined by W.S. Saunders. One of my greatest life lessons. Must be thirty years ago. The poor translation of my cartoons by the manufacturers was what inspired me to learn every single aspect of the craft. It was unheard of then for the manufacturer to consult with the cartoonist.' He sucked on his pipe and shook his head. 'When I saw the finished work in situ I was horrified. The ugliness of the faces of Adam and Eve and the abomination that was a dragon's head. No resemblance to what I'd drawn. I was ready to give up.' He wagged a finger. 'But instead, I decided to beat them at their own game. I mastered the technical aspects, learnt the craft. No point in an artist creating a beautiful design only for it to be ruined by the tradesmen who turn it into finished work. In stained glass, one can't be an artist alone, one must also be a craftsman. Never again would I trust an unknown worker in a glass factory to realise my vision. What do you think?'

Edmund nodded enthusiastically. 'Yes! Exactly! It's why I chose to work in stained glass. Building and creating something that's more than a mere illustration.' He gripped the edge of the table feeling the excitement of talking with a kindred spirit. 'Choosing the right type of glass, doing the cutting, and working out how and where to place the leading is what makes it so absorbing, so all-consuming. Nothing compares!'

'A man after my own heart.' Whall bent over the workbench and examined the lead working. 'This is very good. Very good indeed.'

Edmund was exultant. He could feel his heart pounding at hearing such praise from the country's acknowledged master. 'You were saying about knowing when less is more. What did you mean?'

'Ah yes. I fear you've fallen prey to the temptation of filling your windows with an intensity of colours so that each element competes with another.'

Edmund swallowed and braced himself for the demolition that was about to come.

'I'm a believer in using white spaces and making them interesting. That way you direct the eye to focus on what's most important. And never forget the building itself. Your window isn't meant to compete with it but to show it in its best light. Glass and the architecture in harmony.'

Whall took up a pencil and pulled Edmund's sketchbook towards him. 'May I?'

Edmund watched closely as the older man began to draw a rough sketch. 'Each of your muses will stand out more prominently if you tone down the colours in the two side lancets and the tracery. Try some clear glass, here and here.' He tapped the paper with his pencil. 'In the window at St Mary's in Stamford I used a lot of clear glass to give white light and offset the colours. Let them sparkle!' He picked up his pipe from where he'd set it aside on the workbench. 'The windows in the North transept at York Minster. That's how they did it in the thirteenth century. Have you seen them? *The Five Sisters.*'

'I'm afraid I've never been to York.' As he spoke, Edmund decided that must be remedied.

'*The Five Sisters* window is the largest example of *grisaille* anywhere. So simple, so understated. A glorious, soaring thing of quiet beauty. The *grisaille* is painted so finely and delicately and amongst all that glorious white light there are little bursts of coloured glass. Like an exquisite piece of jewellery. The *grisaille* has varied textures, patterns from the bubbles in the glass and the fine diapering.' Whall shook his head. 'Visit York, Mr Cutler. Stand under that magnificent window and study it. Looking at it will teach you more than you can possibly learn from me. Record your impressions and observations. Keep a notebook in your pocket.'

He cleared his throat and straightened up. 'But I'm forgetting why I'm here. I'd like to offer you a position in my studio at Hammersmith. Karl Parsons is setting up on his own, and I need to take on some new talent. Parsons says you're the best student at the Central. Now I've seen for myself, I think you'd be an asset.' He wagged a finger. 'I flatter myself I'm a good teacher and you'll learn a few things from me. What do you say?'

Edmund stared at the great man, momentarily lost for words. 'You mean it? Yes, yes, yes! Thank you, sir. I'm honoured and gratified.'

'Pay's not a lot but there'll be scope to supplement it as you become more involved in commissions. If you work hard and do great work you'll eventually be ready to abandon me as Parsons has done and set up on your own.' Whall chuckled. 'Alas, it's the penalty I pay for doing a good job as a teacher. But nothing gives me more pride than seeing my assistants prosper.'

'Thank you.' Edmund's grin was wide. 'I won't let you down, Mr Whall.'

As Whall was leaving the studio, he turned back and called over his shoulder. 'And tidy up that workbench, Cutler. I won't tolerate mess in my studio. A place for everything and everything in its place.'

FIVE

PORTMAN SQUARE, LONDON

Alice lost little time before involving her friend Harriet in her parentally orchestrated courtship by Gilbert Cutler. Harriet agreed to chaperone the couple on a walk later that day in Hyde Park.

They were sitting in the sunny drawing room of Harriet's new marital home off Portman Square, an hour before Gilbert was due. Alice counted Harriet as her closest ally and only real friend. A lively redhead whose fondness for desserts had contributed to a figure more ample than deemed fashionable, Harriet didn't care a jot for others' opinions. Whenever Alice was feeling glum a good dose of Harriet's practical attitude always restored her spirits.

'I've never heard of Gilbert Cutler,' said Harriet. 'Should I have?'

'No. His family is frightfully wealthy but it's what Mama calls "new money".'

'How refreshing. Tell me more.' Harriet's eyes widened with the eagerness of a puppy dog.

Alice sighed. 'Nothing more to tell. I barely know him.'

'Come on - you're not blind, Alice. At least tell me what he looks like?'

'Handsome, as Mama keeps reminding me.'

'Details please.'

'Dark hair. Moustache. Fairly tall. Slim build. Quiet. Very polite. Went to Harrow School. Works in his father's firm in the City. Not keen on the countryside. Likes the theatre. That's about the sum of it. Oh, and he's four years older than me.'

'Snap him up! Lucky girl. Anyone under fifty is a big improvement on Lord Wallingford. And so is being taller than he's broad. And you say he's wealthy? And handsome. What more do you want?'

'We've barely spoken. This afternoon is a chance to get to know each other. If it goes well, a visit to the theatre and then another family dinner. Mama and Papa want to get it all tied up in time for a June engagement. Dreadfully embarrassing. Thanks for agreeing to come along. I'd have hated it to be Mama accompanying us.'

'I intend to give your dashing young man the once-over before retreating to a safe distance and letting you love birds get on with it.'

Alice flung herself back in her chair, arms spread wide, eyes raised to the ceiling. 'Honestly, Harriet, don't tease me. The whole business is an ordeal. I just wish it was all done and dusted.'

'Short courtships are better. That's why I agreed to marry old Wallingford right away. No matter how many times I met him I wasn't going to feel any warmer towards the old boy. Frankly, Alice, I'd highly recommend that approach as everyone knows where they stand, and you don't have to pretend you're falling in love. Not that *anyone* would have believed that of me and His Lordship.' She gave a dry laugh. 'But since you're lucky enough to have found a man who's young and handsome, it will probably be different for you. Maybe even the bedroom bit.'

Alice didn't want to think about the bedroom bit.

But Harriet was now in full flow. 'I've learnt to grin and bear it. I deliberately drank nearly a whole bottle of champagne on my wedding night, hoping I'd be so drunk I wouldn't be too aware of what was happening. I needn't have bothered as His Lordship passed out as soon as we got into bed. It was three weeks before he managed to do the dastardly deed. Now I just pray that I'll manage to conceive as soon as possible so he'll leave me alone.' She sighed. 'I can't tell you how grim it is to have that great big gorilla on top of me. Mercifully, it's usually over in a flash.'

Alice screwed her face up. 'Honestly, Harriet, you shouldn't be talking of such things.'

'Why not? I wish someone had talked to me about it. I might have had second thoughts if I'd known what was actually involved. Knowing what I know now I can't help but feel angry that Mummy pushed me into it. All very well her saying it's every woman's burden. But there's a vast difference between being burdened with a man close to one's own age, as was the case for her and Daddy, and being crushed to death by an ugly old bull like the earl.'

Alice squirmed. She sometimes wished Harriet was a little less frank. It would be impossible now to see the Earl of Wallingford without that image appearing in her head. 'If you think any of this is helping, then you couldn't be more wrong. Spinsterhood seems increasingly attractive.'

Harriet came to sit beside her friend on the sofa and took her hand. 'You told me you were facing a dilemma about marrying this Gilbert Cutler. Frankly, I'm trying to make you realise that you don't have a dilemma at all. Grab your young man and his "new money" before he changes his mind. Then get on with the rest of your life. Once we have babies it'll all be different for us anyway.'

·   ·   ·

Gilbert Cutler arrived punctually to collect Alice and her friend. It was a warm spring day and the three strolled the short distance from the Wallingford town house in Portman Square to Hyde Park.

Harriet did most of the talking on the way, interrogating Gilbert on her friend's behalf.

'I hear you went to Harrow, Mr Cutler? My husband, his Lordship, the Earl of Wallingford, is an Old Harrovian. But it must have been several centuries before you were there. He's practically fossilised.'

'Harriet!' Alice suppressed a giggle.

'I haven't had the pleasure of meeting Lord Wallingford but I've heard he's a fine man,' said Gilbert politely. 'The school has some very distinguished alumni.'

'You gentlemen are fortunate going off to school and having adventures and meeting other chaps.' Harriet waved her furled up umbrella in a sweeping gesture before her. 'I would have adored to be packed off to a boarding school, but no such luck. Alice tells me your mother is an American.'

'Born in Boston. She and my father met on board a ship to England on my mother's first visit to Europe. They married in New York soon after her return but settled here in London.'

'How thrilling. You were born in London?'

'Yes. I was, but my brother and I travelled to America most summers with our mother. She has a house on Long Island. Sadly, we rarely visit these days.'

'And your father?'

'Doesn't enjoy vacations. He always stays in London – or in New York City. He's only happy when he's working.'

'Working?' Harriet raised a quizzical eyebrow. 'What does he do that's so all-consuming?'

'Make money. Stocks and shares. That kind of thing.'

'And you?'

'The same. Though I'm still learning the ropes.'

'And do you find making money as all-consuming as your father does?'

Gilbert coughed and looked embarrassed. Alice was beginning to wish she'd never agreed to Harriet joining them and had accepted her mother's offer.

'Not so far,' said Gilbert at last. 'I must admit I find financial matters a bit of a slog. But Father is determined one of his sons should be involved in the firm. And Edmund, my brother, is even less inclined towards finance than I am. He's the artistic one in the family.'

'If it were left entirely to you, Mr Cutler, how would you choose to spend your time?' Harriet looked sideways at Alice to make sure she was listening.

'My dream was always to be an architect. But it was not to be.'

'Why not?'

'Harriet!' Alice threw a sympathetic look at Gilbert. 'We mustn't subject Mr Cutler to a barrage of questions.'

They'd reached the park, so Harriet smiled at Gilbert and patted her friend on the arm. 'I'll leave you to the less inquisitorial approach of my dear friend, Lady Alice. While you stroll together, I'll be on that bench over there reading my book. Come and find me when you're ready.'

Once Harriet was out of earshot, Alice turned to Gilbert. 'I'm sorry about all those questions. Harriet is very forthright.'

'Not at all. Lady Wallingford is charming.'

They walked on in silence, heading towards the Serpentine.

The lake came into view, its surface sparkling under the winter sun. A group of children were gathered near the edge throwing bread to the swans as their mothers or nurses looked on. Alice and Gilbert both started to speak at once.

'Would you like— '

'I find this all— '

'Sorry, you first,' he said.

'I was about to say I find the way our parents have thrown us together rather awkward, Mr Cutler. If you'd prefer not to continue, I'll understand.'

'Not at all. And please call me Gilbert.'

'It's hard to get to know someone when one is conscious of scrutiny from family and friends.'

'I understand. Would you prefer not to see me again?'

'No!' The word was said vehemently. 'I don't mean that at all. I meant it the other way round – that perhaps you would prefer not to see *me*.'

'I would very much like to see you again, Lady Alice. In fact, I was about to ask if you would like to accompany me to a concert. Do you like music?'

'Yes. And it's just Alice. No title. My mother is Lady Dalton. I'm merely The Honourable Alice – and no one bothers with that.'

'Opera?'

'Er... yes.'

'My parents have a box at Covent Garden. This season they're putting on Wagner's Ring Cycle – but I hesitate to suggest it as, somewhat controversially, it's being performed for the first time in English rather than German.' He looked at her anxiously. 'I know Wagner is not to everyone's taste, especially ladies.'

Mildly affronted that her gender could have anything to do with her capacity to appreciate music, Alice said, 'I speak no German and I'm not familiar with the music of Wagner so it would be an excellent opportunity for me to sample it.'

'You're not horrified by the idea of opera in the English vernacular?'

Alice didn't want to admit that her knowledge of opera in any form could be written on the back of a postage stamp. 'Not at all.'

'My mother will be joining us. Possibly Edmund too, and

Father usually puts in an appearance for the beginning and the end. He loathes opera. Only turns up because he thinks it's the place to be seen.'

'What does he do while it's going on?'

Gilbert shrugged. 'Meets other like-minded philistines in the bar and drinks and talks business, I suppose.'

'My family are not connoisseurs of serious opera either. Papa has a fondness for the D'Oyly Carte, but Mama isn't musical at all.' That Alice herself hadn't even attended a performance of one of Gilbert & Sullivan's light operas was more than she was ready to admit. By now, she'd concluded that Gilbert Cutler would make a very acceptable husband and was anxious not to scare him away.

The performance of *The Rhinegold* was a week later, at the beginning of February. Yet again there was no sign of Edmund Cutler. Mr and Mrs Cutler, together with Gilbert and Alice, took their seats in the box and the curtain lifted to reveal mountainous scenery as the haunting sound of the prelude was played by the orchestra. When the Rhine maidens took to the stage, Alice tried to make out what they were singing, but apart from brief snatches, found it almost as hard to follow in English as it would have been in German. But the scenery and costumes drew her into the story, and it was easier to make out the words sung by the baritone, Thomas Meux, portraying Alberich, the dwarf.

Lord Dalton had accumulated a quantity of recordings but rarely played them on the gramophone. Alice enjoyed Puccini and Verdi, but the family collection included no Wagner. There was something hard and masculine about the music, lacking the variety and musicality of the Italians, and the trilling of the Rhine maidens jarred with her – and yet, sitting here in a box while the music enveloped her and the drama unfolded before her eyes, was new and thrilling. If Wagner were an acquired taste, she was determined to acquire it, especially as in the dim light of the box she could see the rapturous expression on Gilbert's usually impassive face.

Gilbert's father's restless fidgeting was distracting. He consulted his pocket watch constantly, clearly unimpressed by the Rhine maidens or the lecherous dwarf. When the orchestra swelled and the cymbals crashed, he took advantage of the cover they afforded to slip behind the curtain and leave the box. Neither his wife nor his son paid his departure any attention.

The music was one continuous piece with no interval in the opera, which lasted over two hours. When it finished, to thunderous applause, Herbert Cutler had somehow re-materialised in his chair.

As they were leaving the box, her hostess asked Alice if she'd enjoyed the performance.

'Very much, Mrs Cutler. It was my first experience of Wagner so I was a little nervous, but it exceeded my expectations.' She hesitated then, *sotto voce,* added, 'I'm sorry Mr Cutler didn't enjoy it.'

'Don't worry about him, my dear.' Susan Cutler smiled. 'I reckon he's tone deaf.'

Alice expressed a need to use the powder room after the long performance and the American woman steered her into it. 'My husband considers cultural events to be good for business but the performance itself unworthy of his attention. I adore the opera and it means I get to come regularly. You must join us again.'

As the two women emerged, Mr Cutler was pacing up and down. 'Hurry up, Susan. I can't abide being stuck in traffic.'

His tone was abrupt. Susan Cutler stiffened, and her smile faded. Alice felt sorry for her, and decided Herbert Cutler was a very disagreeable man.

The carriage and horses were waiting, ready to convey the

party to a supper club in Mayfair. Alice was seated beside Mrs Cutler, immediately opposite Gilbert. There had been no opportunity for conversation until now, but he showed no inclination to break their silence. She studied him, unobserved, while Mrs Cutler maintained a monologue about the opera and her husband stared through the carriage window, ignoring her.

Gilbert's dark hair sat neatly in a lavish sweep above his brow, so perfectly groomed that it might have been carved in marble. Under his opera cloak he was wearing the obligatory evening wear and his shoes shone like well-polished conkers. He wore a white glove on his left hand, slapping the other glove absently against his thigh as he listened to his mother. Glancing up, he caught Alice watching him and looked away quickly. When they'd walked in Hyde Park a few days earlier, he'd been warmer and more approachable. Now there was an invisible barrier between them. Alice wondered if it was because of the proximity of his parents or, more precisely, his father.

To her surprise, when they reached the restaurant, the elusive Edmund was waiting at the table for them. He rose as they approached, kissed his mother lightly on the cheek, nodded almost imperceptibly to his father and, lightly touched his brother's sleeve as he stepped past him, stretching a hand forward to greet Alice.

'Lady Alice, I presume? A pleasure to meet you.'

Herbert Cutler's expression was cold. 'Where were you?' he snapped.

'With friends.'

'Your mother expected you to join us at Covent Garden.'

'It's quite all right—' Susan Cutler started but was interrupted by her husband.

'It's not all right. I won't tolerate your constant defiance and ill manners, Edmund.' Before Edmund had a chance to answer, his father turned away and went over to another table to speak to someone.

Slightly taller than his brother, Edmund Cutler's appearance was altogether more casual. His light brown hair, overdue for a trim, flopped heavily over his brow and curled over his collar. Not in evening wear, he looked dishevelled in contrast with Gilbert's sartorial perfection. No white gloves for Edmund. No gloves at all. Alice noticed his hands immediately. Beautiful hands. Not pale and unused to labour like most men of her acquaintance, Edmund's were large, with long fingers – the hands of a man who used them to make things. When he took his seat again at the table, he steepled them under his chin and studied her with a frankness Alice found unnerving and annoying. She decided at once to dislike him.

'How was the opera?' Edmund's question was directed at her.

'I liked it enormously,' she said. 'It was my first experience of Wagner, so I wasn't sure what to expect. I thought it absolutely splendid.'

'Absolutely splendid? Really?' Edmund looked at her, his head tilted on one side as though doubting her words. 'Rather you than me. The wailing Rhine maidens always give me a headache and I find German such a brutish language.'

'It was in English,' said Gilbert quickly.

'Even worse.'

Mrs Cutler pursed her lips. 'That's not like you, Eddie. You love the opera. And I wasn't aware you had an aversion to Wagner. Is this a new development?'

Alice had a feeling Edmund's aversion was less an aversion to Wagner and more an aversion to The Honourable Alice Dalton.

Edmund ignored his mother's question and instead posed another to Alice. 'And my brother? Is he proving congenial company?'

The blood rushed to her face. Yes, she definitely disliked him. Why would he ask such a question?

'Don't put the poor girl on the spot, dear,' said Mrs Cutler.

Alice was almost relieved when Herbert Cutler returned to the table and set about ordering the food and drink. Clearly another aspect of the Cutler household where he reigned absolute.

Still smarting at Edmund's rudeness, she decided to fend off further embarrassment by turning the questioning on him. 'I understand you're an art student, Mr Cutler?'

'I'm studying the art and craft of stained glass.'

'Stained glass?' she echoed. 'How interesting. Do you learn how to do everything from cutting the glass to putting it together? I've often wondered how it's constructed. Making a picture from all those bits of coloured glass, like a giant jigsaw puzzle.'

He looked at her coldly. 'You make it sound random, like gathering shells on a beach.'

Heat rose in her cheeks. 'As you can tell, I've really no idea.'

Gilbert interjected to tell his brother that Alice was an artist too. She wished he hadn't, as she knew exactly what Edmund Cutler was thinking – that she would be a hobbyist whiling away her afternoons with badly executed water colours. In any case, why should she care what he thought? Yet she felt diminished by his opinion of her.

'You must show me your work some time, Alice,' said Mrs Cutler. 'I'd love to see it.'

'I paint only for my own eyes, Mrs Cutler. I never show it to anyone. My pleasure is in the act of painting and drawing and not in the result.'

Edmund Cutler looked at her curiously, as though trying to weigh up whether what she said was good or bad. At least he dropped the interrogation, to her intense relief.

For the rest of the evening, she barely contributed to the supper conversation but said a silent prayer of thanks that she was being courted by Gilbert and not by Edmund.

SIX

LONDON

Over the following weeks, Edmund viewed the progress of Gilbert and Alice's courtship with disapproval mixed with dismay. His relationship with his brother was close, despite their different interests and Gilbert's willingness to bend to the rule of his father while Edmund resisted. Whenever Alice and her family were to be present, Edmund kept away from Grosvenor Square. Watching his brother's submission was more than he could endure.

One Saturday in late March, the brothers rose early and went for a walk together. Both were keen to avoid their father who used Saturday mornings to rail at them both over breakfast –particularly at Edmund – applying constant pressure for him to abandon his studies and enter the brokerage.

They strolled through the streets of Mayfair to Piccadilly, through Green Park and into St James's Park, where they sat on a bench beside the lake. Edmund pulled his sketchbook out of his pocket and began drawing the pelicans.

'What's the fascination with pelicans?'

'I may want to incorporate one into a window some time,' he said. Pelicans are a common motif in religious iconography.'

Gilbert was amused. 'Where does it come from, Ed?'

'What?'

'Your talent. Your love of art. You certainly didn't inherit it from Father.'

'Don't let's talk about him. I imagine it's from Mother. But who'd know? The poor woman has no outlet for anything that may interest her. It all gets crushed.'

'I thought you said you didn't want to talk about him.'

'I don't. I was talking about *her*. When Grandad was alive and we spent the summers on Long Island, she used to do all kinds of things – watercolour painting, beachcombing, tending the garden. Don't you remember?'

'I suppose I don't.'

'The only outlet she has for anything artistic these days is going to the theatre and the opera when it suits him.' Edmund flipped the page and began another drawing. 'But she spends a lot of time in museums and art galleries when he's not around.'

'I didn't know that.' Gilbert stretched his legs out in front of him.

Edmund saw that, as usual, Gilbert's shoes were polished so you could see your face in them. The contrast with his own was marked. Gilbert's trouser creases were knife sharp.

'Did I tell you I've been offered a job?' Edmund didn't lift his eyes from his sketchbook as he dropped this piece of news.

Gilbert spun round to face him. 'You most certainly didn't.'

'Christopher Whall, the greatest stained-glass artist of his generation, has offered me a position in his studio.'

Gilbert clapped his brother on the back. 'That's wonderful, Ed.' He hesitated then added, 'At least I presume it is? Will you accept?'

'Most definitely. I did so on the spot before he could change his mind.' Edmund grinned. 'It's a tremendous opportunity. Whall receives commissions from all over the world.'

'Where's his studio?'

'Hammersmith. Ravenscourt Park.'

As they were speaking, the pelican that Edmund was drawing decided take off over the lake where it skimmed low before diving for a fish. It emerged, joined the rest of its group and was greeted by the pelicans' strange baritone grunting noises, interspersed with higher pitched shrieks.

The brothers watched the birds until Gilbert spoke again. 'Does Father know?'

'No.'

'Will you tell him?'

'When I start. Which isn't until after the summer. Whall wants me to finish my studies first. Once I start working I'll rent a room nearby and get out of Grosvenor Square altogether. I won't tell him where I'll be living.'

Gilbert looked concerned. 'What about Mother?'

'I won't tell her either. If she knows he'll force it out of her.'

'She'll be devastated.'

'I'll still see her. We can meet somewhere on neutral ground like the National Gallery. But once I'm out of his house I want nothing more to do with Father. Not that it's *his* house anyway. It was bought with Mother's money.' Edmund lifted his pencil and began drawing again, quickly capturing a group of the pelicans at a distance.

'He hasn't given up on you joining the brokerage. He'll kick up a stink when he finds out.'

'Another reason why I don't want to tell him. I don't know how you bear it. Isn't working there dull as ditch water? All those figures. It'd make my head dizzy.'

'It's mindless. Not exactly demanding work. He doesn't trust me with anything that might be remotely interesting.'

'Why do you stick at it?' Edmund paused his sketch and turned to face his brother.

Gilbert looked away. 'I don't have much choice.'

'Of course, you do. I stood up to him. You could too.'

Gilbert shrugged, his expression rueful. 'Maybe I'm weaker than you are, Ed. Or it could be that he hasn't yet found a means of coercing you. As you said yourself, I always take the line of least resistance.'

'I didn't mean that.'

'Yes, you did. And it's true.'

'How's he managed to coerce you?'

That shrug again. Gilbert looked away, took out his fob watch and said, 'I promised to meet a pal at Whites. I'd better get going.'

'That's another thing,' said Edmund. 'I don't see you as someone who enjoys sitting around in clubs.'

'I don't. I told you; I'm meeting someone.' He paused, 'Actually it's the brother of the Dalton girl. Father thinks I should be spending as much time as possible with her family. And Victor's a good chap.'

Edmund chuckled. 'Getting some tips on how to sweet-talk his sister?'

Gilbert pulled a face.

'You really are going ahead with this engagement business, aren't you?'

Gilbert got to his feet. 'I've reconciled myself to the matter. She's a pleasant woman. I could do worse. She's from a good family. Looks aren't everything, Ed.'

Edmund looked at his brother with concern. Gilbert always seemed defeated, worn down. Edmund couldn't understand why he allowed himself to be so easily browbeaten. He wanted to tell him to grow more spine but that would be cruel – and it would never happen. He tried again to dissuade him from this loveless marriage. 'But do you *feel* anything? Do you look forward to seeing her? Do you think about her when she's not there? Do you ever dream of her?'

Gilbert smiled. 'None of those things. But where does love get you? Look at Mother. She believed Father loved her, only to discover that he didn't and he'd married her for money. At least Alice and I are going into this with our eyes open. I have no illusions that she feels any more for me than I for her.'

Edmund sighed and shook his head. 'It seems very cynical.'

'Not at all. We can base our marriage on friendship.' He looked across the park. 'I must be going, or I'll be late for Victor.'

Edmund watched his brother as he walked away in the direction of the Mall. There was something about Gilbert's too-ready acceptance of the arrangement that made Edmund uneasy. But he couldn't pin down exactly why. It was probably his own tendency to oppose anything his father thought to be a good idea. He picked up his pencil and began to draw again.

Immersed in drawing the pelicans, he didn't notice there was someone standing behind him until a voice pierced his concentration. 'Sketching on a Saturday? You're awfully keen, aren't you?'

Edmund slammed his sketchbook shut and spun round. To his astonishment it was Miss Dora Fisher. He bounced to his feet, relieved to see that the young silversmith wasn't in attendance.

'Miss Fisher...' he burbled.

'Mr Cutler, isn't it? I knew it was you from right across the park. Who was that handsome chap with you?'

'My brother.' Edmund's heart was hammering.

Miss Fisher moved around the bench and sat down beside him. 'You don't mind me joining you for a while?'

'Of course not,' he managed, looking around to see if anyone was observing them or if there was any evidence of the silversmith.

'Only I thought I'd come and ask why you were following me home that day, after you'd showed us round the Central.'

His mouth gaped wide – how had she spotted him? He thought he'd been discreet.

She laughed. 'Thought I didn't see you, didn't you?'

Edmund cringed, remembering her and her young man laughing. No doubt laughing at him.

'I stopped to look in a shop window and saw your reflection. You were trying to hide in a shop doorway.' She started to laugh. 'You'd make a hopeless private investigator.'

'Whereas it seems you'd make an excellent one.'

'Come on then, are you going to tell me why?'

Edmund was mortified. Again, he pictured Dora and Spindlemann laughing at his expense. The story was probably all over the Central by now. He gave her a sheepish grin. 'I can't say why. It just happened. I was curious. I'm sorry. I hope your boyfriend wasn't offended.'

'He's not my boyfriend.'

A tidal wave of joy surged over Edmund and his face broke into a grin. 'I'm sorry... I assumed...'

'Because we were arm-in-arm?' She narrowed her eyes, and her face formed a teasing expression. 'It's nothing like that. Stanley and I grew up together. We're next-door neighbours. Our mothers were best friends. He's like a brother.'

Edmund's heart was hammering in his chest. 'So, you don't have a gentleman friend?'

Miss Fisher smiled. Whenever she smiled her cheeks dimpled, and he ached to stretch out a hand and touch her.

'Why? You want to audition for the part?' she asked.

His insides turned to blancmange, and he didn't know how to react. Dora Fisher was so direct. Completely different from the young women he had met until now. Ladies like Alice Dalton. The new female students at the Central. Serious-minded and determined individuals devoted to their art studies. In contrast, Miss Fisher's behaviour was brazen. The way she'd approached him today. She appeared to lack any of the sense of decorum and good manners that most young ladies adhered to. Eventually, he said, 'I suppose I do.'

'Good. We've got that out of the way then. I could tell right away. When you showed us round.'

'It was that obvious?'

'Put it this way, one of the girls said your eyes were on stalks from the moment you saw me, and you barely took them off me.'

He wanted to curl into a tight ball and disappear. 'I apologise for embarrassing you.'

She grinned. 'Don't be daft. I'm teasing you. But I could tell you were jealous when I was talking to Stanley.' She turned to face him. 'Give us some credit though. Stanley's a lovely bloke but he's never going to set a girl's heart aflutter.'

That must mean that perhaps Edmund could. Fuelled by hope, he said, 'You promised to show me your portfolio some time.'

Dora laughed. 'Never mind my portfolio. Aren't you going to ask me to step out with you?'

'Yes...' he said, scarcely able to believe what was happening. Until now he wouldn't have described himself as headstrong. Now he was ready to fling himself at her feet. He'd never met anyone like her. Bold, coquettish – but utterly charming.

'Right then,' she said. 'You can walk me home now. I need to get the dinner cooked for my dear old dad. You can meet him tomorrow afternoon and ask him if he minds if you take me out.' She grinned at him. 'He won't, of course.'

Scarcely able to believe his luck, Edmund said, 'Where? When?'

'I was thinking Regent's Park. You can take me to the zoo. Come by our house after dinner. About two.'

As they walked to Goodge Street, Dora told Edmund she'd seen him and Gilbert leaving the house in Grosvenor Square earlier.

'What were you doing in Grosvenor Square?'

'I always go walking on a Saturday. It's to give Dad time to cool off after the night before. He goes drinking after he's paid on a Friday and he's like an angry bear when he wakes up. Right as rain after a few hours so I make myself scarce. I love to look at the shop windows of the big stores. I walk along Oxford Street. Bourne & Hollingsworth. They do beautiful displays. Marshall & Snelgrove too. Sometimes I cut through to Piccadilly for Swan & Edgars, along to Regent Street and Dickins & Jones, and back home.'

'So, you didn't know I lived in Grosvenor Square?'

'No, but I do now. Very posh. Didn't realise you were a toff.'

Edmund frowned. 'I'm not. My parents just happen to be wealthy. Besides I'll be moving to Hammersmith soon.'

Her face fell. 'Why would you do that?'

'I don't see eye-to-eye with my father.' He weighed up whether to tell her more, then said, 'I'm starting work in Christopher Whall's studio when I graduate.' He glanced sideways to read her reaction. She seemed unimpressed. He added some details about the great man and what an honour it was, but Dora looked uninterested, so he changed the subject. 'Is it just you and your father at home or do you have other family?'

'Just us. He's all right, the old fellow. Bark's worse than his bite. And he only barks on a Saturday anyways. As long as I stay out until it's time to get the dinner ready, he's like a lamb. Can't say as I begrudge him his drinks on Fridays. He's made a lot of sacrifices for me since my mum died.'

'She must have died young?'

'The consumption. She was thirty-four. I was ten at the time.' Her eyes welled and Edmund wanted to put his arm around her so he sat on his hands to stop himself.

'How very sad. What about your father? What does he do?'

'Clerk for the railway. Mother taught art part-time at The Female School. I was good at drawing so she used to bring home bits of paper and crayons and things – only stuff they were chucking out. Dad set his heart on me going to The Female School when she died. Said it would have made her proud to have her daughter a student there.' She looked up at him, eyes wide. 'So, I had no choice really.'

'But you wanted to, anyway?'

'I suppose I did. Dad scrimped and saved to send me there. I couldn't disappoint him, could I?'

'You must be talented. They'd never have taken you otherwise. I remember when I was showing you and your colleagues around the school that girl said you were the best of the class. I can't wait to see your work.'

'Do you really want to see it?' Her smile was beatific. It lit up her face.

'I do. If your work is half as beautiful as you are, it will be exceptional. Was your mother as beautiful as you?'

Dora lowered her eyes. Her shyness contrasted with her earlier boldness. 'People say there's a likeness. Mum married beneath her, according to Dad. She was going to stay with her aunt in Taunton and at the ticket office she realised she'd left her purse behind. Dad took pity on her and issued a return ticket which she promised to pay for when she got back from her trip. He said she had a trustworthy face – but I reckon he was already sweet on her. At first sight. She repaid the debt when she got back a couple of weeks later and he plucked up the courage to ask her to step out with him. He'd no idea she was a doctor's daughter and ought to have been out of his league. He's a good-looking man is Dad, and he's never hesitated to go after what he wants. I suppose I'm a chip off the old block. I like getting my own way.' She gave Edmund a cheeky grin. 'When she agreed to marry him, her family disowned her.'

'It was brave of her to go ahead anyway.'

'Love conquers all,' said Dora, smiling. 'Dad adored her. Worshipped the ground she walked upon.' She sighed, then her

mouth tightened into a hard line. 'That's why I can't blame him
for drowning his sorrows once a week.'

'What was she like?'

'A proper lady. Artistic. Musical too. Accomplished.'

'I meant it you know. About wanting to see your work.'

Dora pulled a face. 'If you must. Before you take me to the
zoo tomorrow. Just a quick peep.' They turned the corner into
Goodge Street. There was a barrel organ playing on the pavement outside the greengrocer's and a number of people standing
in line for *F.C. Spindlemann's*. Edmund imagined they were in
need of a pawnbroker rather than a silversmith.

Dora said, 'This is me. But you know that already, don't
you?' She nudged him in the ribs with her elbow. Indicating the
queue she said, 'It's always busy on a Saturday. One or two
come to claim back their stuff since getting paid on Friday. Most
have already spent their wages on Friday night so need to pawn
things. The rent man does his rounds on Saturdays.' She smiled.
'Don't suppose that happens in Grosvenor Square, does it? See
you tomorrow. Two sharp.'

After she'd disappeared into the side doorway, he waited a
moment, listening to the sound of her heels clattering up the
wooden stairs, before he turned and headed along Mortimer
Street towards Oxford Street. After a few moments he realised
he was whistling.

The following day, Edmund was outside Dora's flat ten minutes
early. He paced up and down impatiently, anxious for the
appointed time. There was a smell of rotting cabbage rising
from the gutter, but the street was quiet after the crowds
yesterday.

When he knocked on the door at two sharp, he was
rewarded by Dora's broad smile and a cheery greeting. He
followed her up the bare wooden stairs to the dwelling above.

The Fishers' spotless flat was modestly furnished. A table and chairs stood by the window and apart from a couple of armchairs, the only other furniture was an upright piano opposite the range fireplace. As Edmund entered, Mr Fisher rose from his seat at the table. He was a short man, of slight build, with a heavy dark moustache that contrasted with the grey of his hair.

'I hear you want to walk out with my daughter?' he said, without preamble.

'Good afternoon, sir.' Edmund, assuming the question was rhetorical, extended a hand in greeting. 'I'm Edmund Cutler. Miss Fisher and I met at the Central School of Art. I'm about to graduate.'

'George Fisher.' He accepted the handshake. 'My Dora says you're a glass painter. What's the point of that?'

Nonplussed, Edmund glanced at Dora, who rolled her eyes. 'Don't give the poor chap the third degree. I already told you, Dad, he makes stained-glass windows for churches.'

'A trade then. I'd hoped for better for my daughter.' He turned to Dora. 'Can't you find a fellow to go courting with who works in a bank or something? A profession that's always in demand. A teacher. A legal clerk.'

Dora stood, hands on hips. 'Cut it out, Dad. I told you Mr Cutler lives in Grosvenor Square. Can't get much fancier than that.' She grinned at Edmund. 'Take no notice of him. He's just trying it on with you. Dad loves to tease, don't you?' She gave her father a mock punch on the arm. 'Now where did I put my drawings?' She looked around the room as though it was a larger space and full of possible places to conceal things.

Edmund pointed to a portfolio on the top of the piano. 'Over there?'

Dora feigned surprise and laid it out on the table where her father was sitting. 'Here, have a look. Make it quick though.'

Edmund bent over the sheets of paper. The drawings were

exquisite. Delicate, detailed, intricate, rich in colours. All forms
of plants, flowers and seeds. He pored over each one, marvelling
at the skill and beauty. 'These are stunning, Miss Fisher. Your
fellow students were right about the quality of your work.' He
turned over the pages, each revealing a drawing more perfect
than the last. 'Mr Fisher, your daughter is extremely talented.'

Dora's father preened, stroking the neat moustache which
adorned his upper lip like a furry caterpillar. 'Takes after her
late mother. Plays the pianoforte too.'

'Stop it, Dad, or you'll scare him off.' Dora gathered the
drawings back between the covers of the portfolio. 'That's
enough. We ought to get going if we're going to visit the zoo.'
She disappeared behind a curtained doorway and reappeared
moments later wearing her coat and pinning on her hat.

When they set off, Edmund raised the subject of her art
again. 'You have an incredible eye for detail and a skill for accurate drawing. Botanical subjects are notoriously difficult. Yours
are stunning. Such detail. Such brilliance in the colours.' He
knew he was gushing but the praise was genuine. He turned to
look at her. 'What do you plan to do when you finish your
course? Book illustration? Some form of design?' He imagined
her working for someone like Mr William Morris, assisting in
the creation of beautiful fabrics and wallpapers.

Dora shrugged. 'Plenty of time to think about that later.'
She fixed her huge brown eyes on him and gave him a look that
liquified his insides.

When they reached the Euston Road, Dora slipped her
hand through his arm. His stomach knotted and his spirits
lifted. It was hard to believe that just the previous morning he
had assumed Dora Fisher to be beyond his reach. Now here
they were, arm-in-arm, walking out like a long-term courting
couple – and he'd already met her father.

As though reading his thoughts, she said, 'What did you
think of my dear old dad then? You mustn't take what he says

seriously, you know. He likes to play the strict father, but he'd never go against anything I wanted.' She bumped her shoulder against his arm as they walked. 'And I reckon right now that includes you, Mr Edmund Cutler.'

Another soaring feeling inside him. 'Call me Edmund, please.'

'I intend to.' She grinned up at him.

'Your work is exceptional. Absolutely beautiful. You're seriously talented, Miss Fisher.'

'Dora to you. And thank you. Nice of you to say so.'

'Believe me, there's nothing nice about it. I'm not prone to complimenting others on their art without justification.' He glanced sideways at her as they walked. 'And you play the piano too.'

Dora pursed her lips. 'Mum taught me, but I hardly touch it these days. Only when Dad pushes me. I was never that interested in practising scales and arpeggios. I just play a few pieces she taught me – Bach, Schubert. That kind of thing. Not really my cup of tea, but it makes Dad happy.'

The afternoon at London Zoo passed too quickly for Edmund. Dora charmed him: delighting in every exotic animal she saw. When she laughed – which she did constantly – Edmund watched her, entranced. She took pleasure in everything around her, visibly excited each time they came upon a new animal. Her tinkling laugh was infectious. Edmund couldn't remember the last time he'd enjoyed himself so much. Her favourite animals were the giraffes, but she laughed joyously at the antics of the monkeys and jumped up and down with glee when Edmund suggested she take a ride on a camel or an elephant. She plumped for the elephant and he helped her into the howdah and stood watching as she and the other passengers were carried on the wooden platform on the beast's enormous back. There was a childlike innocence about Dora that belied her apparent confidence and flirtatious manner. Edmund wanted to wrap her up and protect her.

By the time he escorted her back to Goodge Street, Edmund was completely smitten. He asked whether she enjoyed reading, but she told him she'd little time for anything besides keeping house for her father. 'To be honest, squeezing in the classes at art school and doing the work for my portfolio is hard enough. I'd give it up, but Dad's determined I carry on. Says it's what Mum would have wanted.'

Edmund hated the thought of her being her father's unpaid housekeeper and having so little time for her art. 'I'm glad you were able to come out with me today,' he said. 'It must be hard for you caring for your father while pursuing your studies.'

She laughed. 'It's no hardship looking after Dad. I've always liked cooking and cleaning and doing the laundry. Ever since I was a little girl. If it were up to me, I'm not sure I'd continue at school.'

Edmund was aghast. 'Thank goodness you've stuck with it. A talent like yours shouldn't be denied.'

Her face broke into a smile that warmed the air around her. 'Do you mean that? You're not just trying to get on the right side of me?' She nudged him playfully in the ribs.

'I never say anything I don't mean.' With a rush of affection, he imagined her seated at a table, paints and brushes laid out before her as she focused her attention on her intricate drawings. He pictured himself working in the same room, perhaps at an easel or a workbench. What could be more desirable than being forever in the company of this beautiful woman, this happy, smiling girl, united in artistic endeavours? An Arts and Crafts version of the Brownings, feeding and inspiring each other's creativity, working side-by-side in companionable silence and shared understanding. His skin felt hot and his palms clammy. He glanced sideways at her, wondering if she felt the same.

'I did love that ride on the elephant,' she said, with a wide grin. 'Maybe next time I'll try the camel.'

Next time. There'd be a next time.

He had hoped to linger a while saying goodbye – or to be invited inside again but as they reached the greengrocer's, Dora skipped away from him, opened the door and with a cheery wave was gone, leaving Edmund alone and bereft.

SEVEN

DALTON HALL

June 1908

Alice woke with a sudden impulse to fill the house with flowers. Mama always said it was pointless when the garden was full of them – although Alice suspected it was more a case of her mother not wanting to create more work. Lord Dalton expected his wife to run the house on a shoestring. But today was a special occasion. Today, Alice's engagement to Mr Gilbert Cutler was to be formally announced. A small dinner for the families and one or two close friends. Surely her mother wouldn't be vexed by her making an exception with the flowers today?

Alice sprang out of bed, brushed her hair and dressed hurriedly, before flinging open the window. The scent of lavender rose to greet her from the border below. She leant on the stone ledge, breathing deeply, trying to quell the nervous excitement that bubbled up inside her.

Flower arranging would be the perfect antidote to her anxiety at being the centre of attention that night. It was hardly surprising she was jittery. She barely knew Gilbert. They had only met a few times before this weekend and, apart from the short stroll without Harriet in Hyde Park, had never been alone together. At dinner the previous evening they'd been seated at opposite ends of the table, allowing the perfect vantage point for Alice to view her soon-to-be-fiancé discreetly but he'd done nothing to help her get to know him better. Tonight would be different – as the guests of honour they'd be seated side-by-side.

Gazing out over the lawns toward the ha-ha and the distant woods, Alice thought about yesterday's dinner. She was glad Gilbert's grumpy younger brother hadn't turned up – though it was bad form on his part. Her one encounter with Edmund had done nothing to endear him as a future brother-in-law. He'd been rude to her at the after-opera supper and her eavesdropping on his conversation with Gilbert indicated he thought the match was ill-advised. His absence this weekend was a deliberate snub, but Alice felt only relief.

There was a warm glow inside her as she compared Gilbert to Harriet's husband, a short, stout, red-faced blusterer, who appeared inordinately satisfied with himself.

Alice had always hoped that Victor would marry Harriet. She'd have liked nothing more than to have her best friend as her sister-in-law. But Victor had shown no such inclination and her family's financial position made him a less appealing prospect for Harriet than the chubby middle-aged earl.

Alice nursed the hope that marriage to Mr Gilbert Cutler would eventually prove to be a love match. He'd said little to her at last night's dinner, focusing his attention on the other gentlemen as they discussed movements in the price of sterling against the dollar and fluctuations in the gold standard. Alice brushed that aside – Gilbert was only trying to make a good impression on her family. Once they were married, love would blossom.

She leant further out of the casement window. An early-morning mist smudged the view of the distant woods. It would soon dissipate – there was every reason to expect it would be a perfect summer's day. In the other direction, the once-open fields were being encroached on by the insidious spread of housing. But the herbaceous border was a riot of colour against the pale brick wall that separated it from the kitchen garden. Deep red and pale pink-white peonies, phlox, stocks, the blindingly vivid blue of delphiniums, the pure white of jasmine and a polychromatic display of sweet peas. She'd pick a posy of the latter and tell the maid to put it in a jug in Gilbert's bedroom. And a rose – she'd find the perfect one to offer to him as buttonhole for their engagement dinner that night.

Alice bounded down the stairs, then pulled up short, reminding herself to move with decorum. She didn't want to give her mother cause to reprimand her today of all days. Lady Dalton frequently compared her daughter to an ungainly baby goat and took every opportunity to lament Alice's abject failure to conform to the rules of deportment.

She ambled along the brick-paved path, enjoying the scent from the herbaceous border, gently brushing the early morning dew off a clump of gypsophila as she passed. Approaching the gardeners' wooden shed, she was surprised to hear murmuring from inside, and recognised her brother's voice. He rarely put in an appearance before ten, so Alice was astonished he'd risen so early. He'd never shown the slightest interest in the garden so who could he be talking to in a potting shed at just after seven?

Amused, Alice pushed open the door. She strangled a cry of horror and stood, motionless, like Lot's wife, on the threshold, unable to comprehend the sight in front of her.

Gilbert Cutler, the man she was supposed to be marrying, was perched on the rim of the wooden workbench, tie missing, shirt wide open and his previously immaculately combed hair ruffled so it stood on end with a dusting of cobwebs. He was facing the door but didn't notice Alice at first, so intent was he on kissing the man who stood facing him, pressed up against him and held in place by Gilbert's legs, which were wrapped tightly around the other's back.

Her brother Victor's back.

The sight would have shocked Alice had it been a man and a woman, but two men was beyond her understanding. She stumbled and fell against the side of the doorway as a cry of revulsion escaped from her constricted throat. The men broke apart and Victor spun round, a swearword Alice had never thought to hear bursting from him. Gilbert jumped down from the bench. He looked in anguish at Alice before bending forward to cover his face with his hands.

She turned and half-ran, half-stumbled her way back to the house, where she raced up the stairs to the safe haven of her bedroom. Inside, she turned the key in the door then pressed her back against it as if to keep out what she'd just witnessed.

Nothing could eradicate the image playing over and over in her head. Those legs tightly gripping her brother's frame. The tousled, cobwebbed top of her fiancé's head as he leant into what was unmistakably a passionate kiss. The agonised look before he buried his face in his hands.

Shaking, trembling, unable to control her breathing, Alice staggered to the still-open window and pulled it shut, wanting to close herself off from what lay beyond. Barely ten minutes earlier she'd stood in this same spot, full of hope and excitement about the day ahead. About her life ahead.

She slumped onto the window seat. The same sun was still shining. The same lavender still sent its fragrance drifting up to greet her. The brilliant colours of the flowers in the long border were just as vibrant. She was wearing the same dress. She was the same person.

Yet she wasn't.

If only she were able to cry, to give herself up to the indulgence of tears, but they wouldn't come. She was hollowed out. Numb. An empty seed husk. Catapulted in an instant from joy and innocence to the realisation that her hopes and her future were ruined. Everything had changed irrevocably.

If only she'd gone to the kitchen to borrow Cook's scissors instead of going to the shed for secateurs. She would have tarried to chat to Mrs Wilson and there would have been no need to go anywhere near the potting shed. Alice would have gathered her posy of sweet peas, filled her basket with flowers from the herbaceous border and returned to the house to arrange them. Later, she would have seen Victor and Gilbert at breakfast. Perhaps walked in the garden with Gilbert. The day would have gone as planned. The celebration dinner party that evening. The pop of champagne corks. The beginning of the rest of her life as Mrs Gilbert Cutler.

But now nothing lay ahead. The dinner must be cancelled. The guests dispersed. The engagement called off.

She was haunted by the expression on Gilbert's face before he was aware of her presence. A look directed at Victor. A look of love, of desire, of complicity and trust. Then those eyes had lifted and met hers and for a fleeting moment she had seen shock turn to fear.

Alice climbed back into bed, fully clothed, and pulled the covers over herself, burrowing down in a futile attempt to shut out the world. What would she do? Marrying Gilbert was out of the question. How could she bind herself for the rest of her life to a man who had been making love to her brother?

A sharp knock on the door made her sit bolt upright.

'Open up. Let me in. I have to talk to you, Alice. I have to explain.'

'Go away, Victor.' Her voice was barely audible. Her brother knocked again. Louder.

'Open up, for God's sake, before Mama hears.'

Reluctantly, she rose from the bed, opened the door and went to sit on the window seat, leaving Victor standing awkward and shame-faced.

He brushed a hand through his hair. 'It's not what it seems. We were clowning about. It meant nothing.' The wretchedness in his voice belied his words.

'Clowning about? I saw how he looked at you. I saw what you were doing. That wasn't clowning. It was real.' She squeezed her eyes tightly shut. 'Do you love him? Does he love you?'

Victor made a little choking sound. Alice's eyes sprang open as he began to cry.

'How long? How long has it been going on?'

'Since we met. Seven months ago. At Harry Moncrief's shooting weekend. But I promise it will stop now. He knows he has to marry you and do the right thing. It's his duty. He's an honourable man. I promise you it will never happen again. We both knew this was to be our last weekend. That's why we were there in the garden shed. We were saying goodbye. But—'

'You revolt me. How could you behave that way? It's not natural. It's disgusting.'

'There's nothing disgusting about how Gilbert and I feel about each other. What we feel for each other is beautiful. We love each other. The rest of the world regards our love as wrong. But it's not wrong at all. Loving Gilbert is the best, truest thing that has ever happened to me. He and I know we have to end it today, say goodbye. I promise you, that's what we were doing. Saying goodbye for the last time.' He took a gulp of air. 'I'm going to go to America. Mr Cutler has arranged the job in New York. I promise I won't return to England until long after you're married. Please, Alice. Let's keep this between the three of us. No one else knows. No one else must ever find out. Gilbert's terrified you'll tell Mama and Papa. Or try to call the engagement off. Promise me you won't. Once I've gone away, things will be different. It will all blow over. It's for the best. I'm doing it for you. And for Papa and the family. Your marriage is for the best.' He clutched at her hand. 'I beg you. Please, Alice, don't let anyone else know. There'll be a frightful fuss. Pretend nothing happened and you never saw anything.'

For the briefest moment she entertained the idea. But the image of Gilbert's legs wrapped around her brother's hips wouldn't leave her. Nor would the memory of Gilbert's face and the certainty that he would never look at her the way he had looked at her brother.

'At least the engagement hasn't been announced,' she said. 'Not even a ring to give back.' She was bitter and couldn't help herself. 'Tell Papa I've had a change of heart and you may as well tell Gilbert too. I'm sure he'll be relieved to hear it. Now get out and leave me alone.'

Victor moved to where she was sitting on the window seat. He got down on his knees in front of her, grasped her hands between his and looked up at her with a tear-stained face. 'I beg you, Alice. Don't do this. It will break Gilbert.'

'You should have both thought about that before doing what you did. I don't care if it breaks him. I'm already broken. Crushed. Humiliated. Devastated.' She pulled her hands from his grip and pushed him away. 'Leave me alone. Go and break the news to Papa and your friend. I'm not changing my mind.'

With a cry of pain, Victor got to his feet and staggered out of the room.

Soon after, her bedroom door burst open and her father stormed in, wearing his dressing gown, her mother following in his wake.

'What's going on, Herbert? Why are you so angry?' Lady Dalton's eyes moved back and forth between her husband and her daughter, like a spectator at a tennis match. 'Will someone please tell me what's going on?'

'Your daughter's decided she's not marrying Cutler. According to Victor she's had a change of heart. Tell her that her heart has nothing to do with it.' The baron clenched his hands into fists and shook them at the side of his face. 'Cutler's a perfectly decent man and there's no reason on earth why they shouldn't have a perfectly decent marriage. Talk some sense into the girl, Lavinia.' He turned to leave. 'I expect to see you all within an hour at the breakfast table and I don't want to hear any more nonsense.'

After he'd gone, Lady Dalton sat down beside her daughter on the window seat and took her hand. 'Darling, it's understandable that you're having last minute wobbles. I was absolutely terrified when I became engaged to your father. It's a big step. But it's nothing to worry about. I can honestly say that I've had a very satisfactory marriage. Your father's been a good husband.' She patted Alice's hand. 'Gilbert Cutler may not be from the best of families, but he is a charming and handsome man and a wealthy one at that. And to be truthful, my dear, these days money is becoming more important.'

'Then tell my father to find another means of getting some. I'm not marrying Gilbert Cutler and that's final.'

Lady Dalton looked askance. Alice was usually a biddable and dutiful daughter. 'But why, darling? You were perfectly happy last night. What's brought this about?'

Alice turned her head away and gazed out of the window. The sun had burned off the mist over the woods and the day was warming up. So deep was her sense of betrayal that she decided she owed nothing to Gilbert. 'Gilbert Cutler is more interested in men than in women.' She chose not to mention Victor.

Her mother gave a little chuckle. 'Is that all? Men usually prefer the company of other men. What man wants to spend time with his wife when he could be at a cricket match or a shooting party or conversing over cigars and a decanter of port?' She squeezed Alice's hand. 'Now come on, don't be a silly spoilt girl.'

'I didn't mean like that, Mama. I mean Gilbert Cutler has the kind of feelings for a man that he ought to have for a woman.' She looked down, rubbing at a yellowy-brown streak across her dress where she must have brushed against some lilies as she dashed along the path. 'I mean physically.' Her cheeks burned.

Her mother was still unperturbed. 'Young men have needs that we women don't. And if there isn't a willing servant, sometimes they experiment with each other. When Victor was at school he came home crying after his first term because one of the older boys had tried to kiss him. But he soon got used to it.'

'I bet he did.'

'Boys will be boys. But they grow out of it. And once married they have no need of it any longer. You'll see it will all be fine. We women have other things in life to keep us busy. Having children. Running the home.' Her mother smiled. 'Let's go down and have our breakfast and forget all about this.'

'I'm not marrying Gilbert Cutler. Nothing you or Papa say will change my mind.'

Her mother stared at her open-mouthed. Her eyes narrowed and her brow creased in anger. Before she could reply, a loud explosive bang echoed through the house. For a moment mother and daughter stared at each other, disbelieving that they'd heard a gunshot.

'Stay there. Don't move,' said Lady Dalton, as she rushed from the room.

EIGHT

LINCOLN'S INN FIELDS, LONDON

Gilbert Cutler's engagement to the Honourable Alice Dalton was due to take place on the Saturday and as Edmund was graduating from the Central on the Friday, he had good cause to miss the family dinner that night at Dalton Hall.

His graduation ceremony wouldn't be witnessed by either of his parents: Herbert Cutler disapproved of his younger son's chosen field of study and Susan was unwilling to go against her husband's judgement that the event was unworthy of marking.

Edmund was relieved. His father opposed his chosen path as a student of the art of stained glass, so his absence was neither a disappointment nor a surprise. He'd have liked his mother to be there, but she'd never gainsay her husband. It was good to see Gilbert standing at the back of the hall to show his support.

He waved to Gilbert over the crowd as they poured out of the hall, but seeing Dora he pushed through the throng to her, so he could introduce them. By the time they were outside Gilbert had vanished.

Edmund was grateful to Gilbert for taking the trouble to turn up and felt a twinge of guilt that he wasn't going to reciprocate by being at the dinner at Dalton Hall. It would have meant spending the weekend in close proximity to his father. Edmund wanted nothing to tarnish the joy of his graduation day.

He had much to celebrate – his graduation, the new job at Whall's studio, and, above all, his growing attachment to Dora. To his delight, she agreed to spend the following afternoon and evening with him to mark his graduation.

Their courtship had been rapid so far and Edmund, to his joy and near disbelief, found that she appeared to enjoy his company as much as he did hers.

Having graduated, what could be more perfect than to marry her? Someone who not only shared his artistic talent but was also the prettiest student at the Central. He didn't want to risk losing her now that they were no longer fellow students. Their courtship needed to move to a firmer footing.

He arranged to meet her for a walk in Lincoln's Inn Fields on the Saturday and spent the morning at the school, packing up artwork and tools ready for removal on Monday to Whall's studio.

It being a pleasant June afternoon, they sat on the grass under one of the large plane trees. Dora was wearing a skirt and blouse with a little bolero jacket. In contrast to the simplicity of this costume she'd completed the ensemble with an enormous wide-brimmed hat, topped with ostrich feathers in the style of the day. So huge was the hat that her little heart-shaped face almost disappeared under it. Touched by the sweetness of her face beneath the sophisticated confection, Edmund leant forward to kiss her, clumsily knocking the hat sideways. Dora laughed and unpinned it from her head, casting it onto the grass beside them. 'Only a little kiss,' she said. 'And just the one.'

It was a source of mounting frustration to Edmund that Dora mixed coquetry with a marked reticence when it came to kisses. Part of him respected her modesty and propriety. She claimed that kissing was 'unladylike' - even when there was no one present to observe them. He told himself that a pleasure postponed would make its eventual delivery all the sweeter. Yet, he was disappointed that she didn't seem to experience the same intensity of desire for him that he did for her. Perhaps that was how all women were before they were married, but he hoped fervently that it wouldn't always be that way. It made him all the more determined to marry her so that all the restraint and modesty could be cast aside and they could indulge their love. Meanwhile, her flirting and teasing was sustained torture. Edmund couldn't help wondering whether she took a sadistic pleasure in it. When she laughed her beautiful tinkling laugh, he cast his doubts aside and basked in the warmth of her smile.

Sitting under the tree, their backs against its sturdy trunk and Dora's head resting on his shoulder, neither of them noticed as the breeze lifted the hat from where it lay on the grass and carried it away.

When the hat's disappearance was discovered by Dora, Edmund was secretly relieved. If he'd been more inquisitive about his own feelings and less trusting of them, he might have wondered why. He might have admitted he found the hat vulgar and out of keeping with the simplicity of the rest of Dora's costume. It was a fine hat, but better suited to an older woman. Dora's fresh beauty had no need of such embellishment. But what should have given him cause to ponder the true nature of his feelings was Dora's reaction to the loss: the sudden spark of temper, the creases that cut across her brow, her insistence that Edmund go in search of the missing hat.

While Edmund scoured the shrubberies and gazed in vain into the canopy of the trees, Dora sat in a huff, watching his efforts. Only when he promised to buy her a new one, did she relent. An unplanned expenditure he could ill afford on the tiny allowance his father granted him – an allowance which would doubtless cease altogether when he informed Herbert Cutler he was taking the job with Whall.

Anxious to appease Dora, he offered to take her to The Bechstein Hall where there was to be a Schubert recital. Instead of showing delight, Dora pulled a face.

'I'm not at all keen on that sort of music.' Her bottom lip protruded in a pout. 'It makes me sad and reminds me of my mother. I like the variety acts much better.' The pout dissolved into a smile.

By now, Edmund was prepared to do anything she wanted. 'What about the theatre then?'

'I prefer the music hall. If we hurry, we'll be in time for the next show at that place on The Strand. I saw a billboard this morning and they've got Florrie Forde in the six o'clock show.'

Edmund had no idea who she was talking about but agreed with good humour. He was willing to buy more expensive seats in the stalls, but Dora insisted on the cheap seats. 'It's more fun up in the gallery.' She fanned herself with the programme. Her unalloyed pleasure endeared her all the more to him.

Dora laughed through the performances, from the performing dogs to the ventriloquist and the raconteurs. Her eyes misted over, entranced, during the balletic dance sequence, and she squeezed his hand in delight. Edmund wished he'd realised sooner how easy it was to make her happy – and how happy it made him to do so.

The star of the show that evening was the Australian comic songstress, Florrie Forde, whose rendition of *Oh, oh, Antonio!* was swelled by the audience joining in all the choruses. Dora nudged Edmund, urging him to sing along too, but he had to admit he knew neither the words nor the tune. She rolled her eyes. He was mortified to admit this was the first time he'd ever been to a music hall.

Miss Forde nearly brought the house down with her rendition of a new song, *Kelly from the Isle of Man*. Dora convulsed with laughter while Edmund grinned but remained bemused. Florrie sang about how she had mislaid her sweetheart in

Piccadilly, ending up at the Houses of Parliament where the suffragettes chained her to the grille as she belted out '*Has anybody here seen Kelly? Kelly from the Isle of Man!*' The audience was evidently reading more into the lyrics than he understood himself. But his own puzzlement paled, compared with the knowledge that he had restored Dora's good humour.

Leaving the theatre, she said, 'That song about Kelly was hilarious. Florrie Forde is the best.'

'She doesn't seem to approve of the suffragettes.'

Dora pulled a face. 'Who does? Silly twits!' Dora linked arms with him. 'They're a blooming disgrace. Don't you agree?'

Edmund didn't. But as a man, he felt unqualified to argue with her. Perhaps he was missing something? He'd assumed the extension of the franchise to the fairer sex was both logical and long overdue. But Dora seemed adamant.

'If you ask me, they're all bitter and sad. Bunch of old miseries. Much better to accept that things are the way they are because it makes sense.' She smiled a beatific smile.

As they left the theatre, she clung tightly to his arm and appeared to have forgiven him for her hatless state.

Edmund walked her back to her home above the greengrocer's shop. It was still light, but the air was heavy with smoke. As they walked between the blackened buildings, he wanted to stop and take her in his arms again. That brief kiss under the plane tree had made him hungry for more, but he was a gentleman and would never dream of kissing her in the street. If only they were married, he wouldn't have to tear himself away from her. She'd be all his.

He imagined lying in an enormous bed with her in his arms, knowing they had the whole night ahead of them instead of having to say goodnight on her doorstep and for him to wend his lonely way back to Grosvenor Square. But it would be a long time before he could propose marriage – even though it was what he wanted more than anything. He couldn't support a

wife and family until he'd made his name – and that might take
several years. First, he had to complete his apprenticeship with
Christopher Whall. If only his father weren't so unreasonable
and would pay him a more generous allowance. It wasn't as if it
was all his money. Yes, his brokerage was a thriving enterprise,
but the bedrock of his fortune was Susan Cutler's inheritance.
If his mother's wishes were respected, Edmund would be amply
provided for.

It wasn't that he had a desire to be supported by his parents.
Edmund didn't have a sense of entitlement. But he did have a
burning desire to pursue his art and fulfil his God-given talent.
A little support in these early years was surely not an unreason-
able expectation.

After Dora went inside, Edmund returned to what he
expected to be an empty house, his parents having left the
previous day for the party at Dalton Hall.

As soon as he entered, he knew something was amiss. Their
bags were in the hall, there was no sign of the servants, and he
could hear his mother crying in the drawing room.

He went inside to find her prostrate on the sofa, weeping
into the cushions. His father stood in front of the empty fireplace, hands on the mantelpiece and head lowered. He looked
up as Edmund entered. In the reflection in the overmantel
mirror, Edmund saw his father's usually stony face was
contorted in pain.

'What's happened?' Edmund looked between his parents.
'Why are you home already? I thought you'd be gone for two
days.'

Susan Cutler's sobs grew louder.

'Go to bed, Susan. We'll call the doctor to give you a seda-
tive,' said Herbert. 'I need to talk to Edmund.' His face was
restored to an impassive expression as he rang the service bell.
The housekeeper appeared, ashen-faced, and escorted
Edmund's mother from the room.

'What's going on? Why is Mother so upset?'

'Gilbert's dead.'

'What?'

'Your brother's dead. He shot himself this morning.'

Edmund couldn't process his father's words. He stared at him, trying to force them to make sense. 'What are you talking about? I don't understand.'

'Are you stupid?' Herbert raised his voice. 'Your brother has killed himself with a gun. Do I have to spell it out or draw a picture?'

Edmund's head spun. He slumped onto the couch recently vacated by his mother. 'Why?' was all he could manage.

'That damn fool girl called the engagement off. No idea why, but whatever the reason, it caused Gilbert to take his own life.'

'How could he do that?'

'What do you mean, how? I've told you; the boy blew his brains out with a shotgun.'

Edmund cried out. Why? None of it made any sense. Why would Gilbert do such a thing? He stared unseeing into the middle distance.

His father seemed to gather new resolve from his younger son's presence. He started pacing up and down the room. 'I need to pull the engagement announcement from *The Times* before they go to press on Monday. Thank God, there's still time. If Gilbert had done what he did *after* the engagement was announced, it would have been impossible to avoid a scandal. But we've a decent chance of keeping this quiet. We need to make sure that no whiff of impropriety comes back to tarnish Lord Dalton – or the dratted girl. A tragic shooting accident.' He paused his pacing. 'But it's out of season...' Frowning, he punched a fist into an open palm. 'Deer culling. That's what we'll say. Gilbert unfamiliar with handling guns. Yes, that will do it.'

'Stop!' Edmund stared at his father open-mouthed. 'You're more worried about covering it up to avoid a scandal than understanding why your son took his own life? What kind of father are you?'

'Nothing's going to bring Gilbert back. We need to focus our minds on how we make the best of this dreadful business.' Herbert turned to look his son in the eye. 'I can promise you, Edmund, this is a bitter blow to me. Your brother was the apple of my eye, and your mother is devastated. But we have to make the best of a terrible situation.'

The best? Edmund stared at him in disbelief.

'Shooting accidents are ten a penny. It will soon fade from the collective memory of the readers of *The Times*. We mustn't lose sight of the original reason for joining our fortunes with the Daltons.'

'What are you talking about?'

'I mean that once things have quietened down and the silly girl has been made to see reason, then she must marry you, Edmund.'

NINE

DALTON HALL

The trees met the darkening sky, like smudges of ink on blotting paper. The evening was quiet: a dense silence. Like the end of the world. An owl screeched into the darkness and Alice shivered. The house may be a prison she wanted to escape, but the world beyond was even more alien and frightening.

She wanted to be brave but felt fragile, insubstantial. Dalton Hall, the only home she had ever known, was spoiled, tarnished. The image of her brother in the arms of Gilbert Cutler was seared onto her brain forever. But her own shame and guilt was worse. How could her personal humiliation and disgust be weighed against the loss of a man's life? Perhaps the two men were guilty of unnatural acts, against all principles of decency, but what they'd done was born of love: something private and for their own consciences and the eventual judgement of God. What she'd done had caused a man to take his own life. Nothing could be as bad as that.

The intensity of the look between Gilbert and Victor was not only a terrible shock. It had been a revelation. No one would ever look at her that way. She was destined to remain unloved.

What had driven the two men to behave in this depraved way? Against all the laws of man and God.

Had she been the cause? Was it her coldness? Her inability to show affection or attract it in others? Was there something wrong with her?

Another thought gradually seeped into her consciousness. Did the evident passion between the two men explain Gilbert's readiness to marry her without love or affection? Would marriage to her have been the means of giving Gilbert close access to Victor, and giving them the cover to meet regularly? The more she considered this possibility the more certain she became. She had been duped. She was the innocent pawn in their game. Instead of this knowledge making her feel better, she felt worse.

As she stared into the gathering night, she realised she couldn't stay at Dalton Hall any longer. The prospect was unthinkable. How could she walk through the garden again and pass the potting shed without re-living that terrible sight? Lie here on her bed without being haunted by the memory of the shot echoing through the house? Or ever again enter the room next door to the billiard room where Gilbert Cutler had taken a shotgun out of the gun cabinet and blown his brains out?

If only she'd done what Victor and her mother had begged her to do and put what she'd seen in the garden out of her head. If only she'd put it down to a moment of madness on their part and agreed to go ahead with the engagement anyway. If only she'd swallowed her pride, brushed away her disgust and got on with it. If only. If only. If only.

If she'd done these things Gilbert would still be alive. They could have found a way to accommodate her knowledge – or wipe it from her memory and eventually built a satisfactory life with each other. But her foolish pride and her injured dignity had ruined her future and cost Gilbert his life. It was her fault and she had no right to pretend it wasn't.

Yes, staying here was out of the question. But where could she go? Wretched, she cast about for a way to escape.

Harriet would surely offer her sanctuary. But that would mean Alice letting herself be comforted first, lectured next and finally encouraged to pretend that momentous day had never happened. Harriet's pragmatism and determination to make the best of things was not an appealing prospect. And Harriet, like everybody else, would believe Gilbert's death was a terrible unhappy accident and Alice would have to endure her pity, not her understanding. She could never share the terrible truth of why he'd killed himself and what had prompted it. Not even with Harriet.

But staying at Dalton Hall would be worse. The look of disappointment in her father's eyes, the pity in her mother's and hatred in Victor's would be more than she could bear.

Alice didn't attend Gilbert's funeral. Because her engagement had not been announced, Lord Dalton and Herbert Cutler judged it better that neither she nor Lady Dalton were present. Still in shock from what had happened, Alice had been prescribed a bromide by the family doctor.

The day after the funeral she was asked to join her parents in the drawing room. Still groggy from the medication, she made her way downstairs for the first time in days. Victor was not in evidence. Alice hadn't seen him since that fateful Saturday morning, and she assumed he was staying in town after the funeral. Avoiding her. It was a relief. She dreaded the thought of the hurt and accusation that would be in her brother's eyes. Even though logic told her she was the innocent party in everything that had taken place, Victor wouldn't see it that way. Gilbert had taken his own life not because he'd been involved in an illegal liaison but because of fear that Alice's refusal to go ahead with marrying him would expose it.

The drawing room was chilly, in spite of the season. Dalton Hall was draughty and her parents rarely indulged in the luxury of a lit fire after May was out. When she entered the room her parents were sitting but Lord Dalton got to his feet and began pacing up and down. Lady Dalton patted the seat beside her on the Chesterfield and Alice went to join her mother.

She looked from one to the other, wondering what was coming next. Eventually her mother spoke. 'Your father and I would like to put something to you. He will explain.' She folded her hands in her lap and sat upright.

Lord Dalton looked uncomfortable and coughed. Alice wished she were back in her bedroom. Whatever was about to transpire was not going to be pleasant.

'I've spoken at length with Herbert Cutler,' he said at last. 'He and I believe that the reasons for uniting our families are as strong now as before. Possibly more so as we share grief over the loss of Gilbert's life and the fact that it happened here at Dalton Hall.' He coughed again nervously.

A shiver spread through Alice's body.

'Herbert Cutler is by nature a pragmatist and has made a suggestion that your mother and I believe will bring about a satisfactory conclusion to this sad and sorry affair.' He moved across the room and sat in a stiff-backed wing chair opposite Alice and her mother.

Impatient, Lady Dalton stated, 'We all agree you must marry the younger son.'

'What?' Alice gasped. 'You're not serious.'

'Indeed, we are. Don't rush to judgement, Alice,' said her father.

His wife nodded. 'Since your engagement to Gilbert was never announced, it will appear quite natural for you and the other one... what is his name? Edward...? Edgar...? *Edmund.* That's it. Yes, for you and Edmund to become engaged.' Lady

Dalton twisted sideways in her seat to face her daughter. 'Obviously we'll need to wait a little time before it's announced, out of respect to the wretched Gilbert. But what could be more natural than you and Edmund being drawn together in mutual grief and affection?'

Alice's jaw dropped. She could scarcely believe what she was hearing. 'I don't like Edmund. And he doesn't like me either.'

Lady Dalton patted her shoulder. 'You don't have to like him, darling. That will come in time. I wasn't frightfully keen on your father when we were first married, but one learns to rub along.'

Lord Dalton appeared oblivious to his wife's words. 'Alice, my dear, you know we have your best interests at heart. This marriage has much to commend it. You'll be financially secure. The nasty experience of Gilbert's accident will be forgotten. The relationship between our two families will be cemented further.'

'What does Edmund Cutler think of your plan?'

'I'm sure he'll be happy to go along with this, provided you're willing, Alice.'

'You're *sure*? Does that mean he doesn't know yet?'

'His father is talking to him now.' Lord Dalton got up and began pacing again. 'I do hope you'll agree, Alice.'

Lady Dalton pursed her lips. 'Of course she'll agree. Alice is a sensible girl and has always taken our counsel.'

Their counsel? When had she ever sought counsel? And for what? Alice's palms were sweaty and she rubbed them against the sides of her skirt. 'It was my fault,' she said at last. 'That Gilbert killed himself. It was because I refused to go through with marrying him. How can I possibly marry his brother knowing I was the cause of his death?'

Lady Dalton leant forward. 'Don't be silly, dear. Of course, it wasn't your fault. That young man must have had other reasons to take his own life. It was nothing to do with you.'

'Quite so,' said Lord Dalton. 'And from now on, no more talk of him killing himself. It was a terrible accident. Even the coroner said so. The young man wasn't used to handling guns.'

'Papa, you know that's not true. There was no reason for him to be near a gun.'

'Stop it at once, Alice.' Her mother stood up. 'I won't hear any more of this. You're still in shock from the dreadful accident, but I want you to put all these silly notions out of your head. Neville, tell her to stop, please.'

Lord Dalton gave Alice a rueful smile. 'Your mother's right, Alice. Nothing will bring the boy back. The best way to honour Gilbert Cutler's memory is for you to marry his brother.'

Lady Dalton looked gratefully at her husband. 'Exactly so.'

Alice lowered her head, defeated. The unsaid undercurrent to this entire conversation was that this marriage was a financial necessity for her parents. Having been the cause of the tragic loss to the Cutler family, how could she now refuse to do what was clearly of paramount importance to both families?

All fight had gone from her the day Gilbert shot himself. There was no point in resisting.

TEN

GROSVENOR SQUARE, LONDON

At the same time Alice Dalton was facing her parents in the drawing room of Dalton Hall, Edmund Cutler was under attack in Grosvenor Square. His mother, although a witness to the discussion, played no part in it, sitting quietly, hands clenched, on the far side of the room. Herbert Cutler stood with his back to the fireplace, hands clutched behind him, chest puffed out, as he waited for Edmund's response. When his father first raised the idea of Edmund marrying his late brother's intended on the day of Gilbert's death, Edmund had brushed the suggestion off with an angry and incredulous refusal. Since then, he had ensured he was nowhere near his father.

But today being in each other's presence was unavoidable because of the funeral. The only guests at the short ceremony had been Lord Dalton and his son Victor, as well as half a dozen colleagues from the brokerage firm. Now, with everyone gone, there was no one between father and son.

Edmund knew better than to suppose his father would let the matter drop. When he set his mind to something, Herbert Cutler was a terrier with a rabbit in his mouth.

'I've talked this over with Lord Dalton, and we intend to

wait a couple of months and then announce your engagement to Lady Alice. As far as the world is concerned, there was no engagement between the girl and Gilbert, even if there was an understanding between them. What could be more natural than you becoming close to each other in shared loss and sympathy?'

'You disgust me.' Edmund turned away from his father and glanced at his mother who dropped her eyes. He would get no overt support from her.

Herbert Cutler turned to his wife. 'Leave us please, Susan. I want to speak to Edmund alone.'

Susan Cutler threw her son an apologetic look and slipped from the room.

When she was gone, Herbert walked over to a side table, opened a silver box and took out a cigar which he proceeded to trim with a cutter before lighting. Blowing a ring of smoke into the air, he moved back and took up his place again in front of the fireplace.

'If you don't marry the Dalton girl you will reap the consequences. You will no longer be welcome under this roof and your allowance will cease forthwith.'

'You think I care about money?'

His father raised a hand imperiously to silence him. 'As the academic year has ended, you'll cut all ties with that art school and begin work at the brokerage. The marriage to Alice Dalton will take place before the end of the year. You and your bride can live here at Grosvenor Square, although of course you may choose to reside at Dalton Hall on high days and holidays.'

Edmund started to speak but was cut off by another outstretched palm from his father.

'I have not finished. Any attempt on your part to countermand my wishes will have repercussions for your mother. You may not care for money, but I believe you care for her.'

'What the hell do you mean? What are you threatening?'

'You'll find out if you test me.'

A lump formed in Edmund's throat. This was his worst fear. His father was a bully and not beyond resorting to physical violence to get his way. When Edmund was a child, his mother sometimes winced when he tried to hug her and he suspected she had bruises concealed under her sleeves. It hadn't happened recently, but it didn't mean it wouldn't. He turned to face his father. 'You're utterly despicable. Completely without a moral compass. What's Mother done to deserve your abuse? All she ever did was foolishly believe you cared for her and then gave up everything to marry you and live here, far from everything she's ever known. You've stolen her money—'

'Stolen her money? What drivel. I'm her husband and what was once her money is now mine. You sound like one of those damned idiot suffragettes. When a woman marries, she is subject to her husband. Your mother wants for nothing.'

'My mother wants for everything she deserves. A husband who actually cares for her. A husband who is a father to her sons instead of a tyrant who thinks everything boils down to money.'

'Everything does.' Herbert Cutler blew a smoke ring. The pungent smell of the cigar filled the room and Edmund felt nauseated. 'You'll learn soon enough, just as your brother did, that life becomes much easier when you stop trying to defy me. Gilbert understood that his nasty little perversions could only remain secret if he took a wife. But he was careless. The business with Dalton's son was beyond the pale.'

'What are you talking about?'

A sneer disfigured Cutler's face. 'You didn't know?'

'Know what?' Edmund was uneasy. He could see the glint in his father's eye. 'What didn't I know?'

'That Gilbert was a pervert. A criminal, no less.'

Edmund's mouth fell open. What was his father implying?

'You didn't know he was of the Oscar Wilde persuasion? A

ho-mo-sex-u-al.' Herbert Cutler was clearly enjoying himself as
he made this revelation. 'You thought you were close to Gilbert,
didn't you? Thought you knew him well? You didn't know him
at all. I told him I'd beat it out of him if he didn't mend his ways
and the best way to do that was to marry. I must admit I hadn't
realised Victor Dalton was of a similar persuasion. That slipped
past me entirely.'

Edmund slumped forward in his chair. It all made sense.
Gilbert's willingness to marry Alice, in spite of feeling nothing
for her; his fear of their father and refusal to gainsay him. And
this morning, at the graveside, the little sob that came from
Victor Dalton before he covered it up by blowing his nose.
Edmund looked up. 'Does Mother know this?'

'If she does, it's not from me. And I hope not at all. Your
mother is a respectable woman and wouldn't conceive of such
an unspeakable topic – or for her own son to be implicated.' He
looked down his nose in an extended sneer. 'Gilbert's name is
not to be mentioned in this house again. The Dalton boy starts
in the New York office next week, then he'll be safely out of the
way too. He may be a pansy, but he has a way with numbers.' A
smile of smug satisfaction creased his face, and he drew again
on his cigar.

Edmund was dumbstruck. If only Gilbert had confided in
him. He'd probably viewed it as too risky. Edmund had let his
brother down. He thought of their last walk together, to St
James's Park the morning he'd met Dora. Since he'd begun
courting Dora, he'd barely had time for his brother. That day
Gilbert had been about to meet Victor Dalton. Gilbert had
seemed on the point of telling him something but had stopped
short.

'Why did Gilbert kill himself?'

'An accident with a shotgun. You heard the coroner's
verdict.'

'I heard the verdict but not why the coroner gave it. How much did you pay the man to secure it?'

Herbert Cutler chuckled. 'I didn't need to waste my money. Why on earth would a young man on the eve of his engagement – on the very threshold of happiness – want to end his own life? Ergo, it must be a tragic accident. And with the testimony of the brother and Lord Dalton, as well as Gilbert's lack of experience with guns, it's hardly a case for Sherlock Holmes.'

Cutler pulled his Hunter from his pocket and looked at the time. 'I have papers to review in my study. I await your answer, Edmund. I've told your mother we will host the Daltons, including Lady Alice, a week on Saturday for dinner. That will give you both an opportunity to renew your acquaintance and then we'll agree the finer details.' Tucking his watch away, he strolled out of the room.

Edmund was cornered, an animal caught in a trap. He weighed up his options and found them all undesirable. He was all too aware of the lengths his father would take to ensure his compliance. What was behind the veiled threat about his mother? How could he risk putting her in jeopardy? Unthinkable. Herbert Cutler would be as ruthless in executing this threat as he'd evidently been with his older son.

The only way out of marrying the wretched Dalton woman was to make it legally impossible. The only way to achieve that was to be already married. Even his father would stop short of encouraging bigamy. And he wanted to marry Dora, didn't he? More than anything else in the world.

And yet something held him back. It seemed too rash, too hurried, too impetuous, particularly when he was about to start a new job at the Whall studio. His future wasn't yet secure. How could he support a wife on an apprentice's wage? What if she were to fall pregnant? How could he provide for a family? His father would cut him off without a penny once he found out about the job, let alone about Dora. He'd need to pay for somewhere to live – hard enough for himself alone but nigh on impossible for the two of them. His mother would want to help but she had no control over her own money.

Walking always helped him think more clearly so Edmund headed towards the Embankment, striding but without any real purpose or destination, other than to work off his excess energy. His thoughts raged as he struggled to find a solution.

Marrying the Honourable Alice Dalton would be intolerable. He suspected she may even have been involved somehow in his brother's decision to take his own life. In any case, he felt nothing for her. The thought of being chained to the woman for the rest of his life was worse than a death penalty. A sentence of life imprisonment. And it would mean giving up Dora.

Dora, Dora, Dora. He loved her. Longed for her. She haunted his thoughts. But that didn't mean he was ready to be catapulted into a marriage that would guarantee their poverty and a loss of his self-respect. It was too soon. While he'd never doubted he would eventually ask her to marry him, he had envisaged it happening once he'd made his way in his chosen career, built his artistic reputation, and secured his place as a trusted member of Whall's team, earning a share of commissions. That wouldn't happen overnight. He had to prove his mettle first. It would take months, possibly years. His teacher at the Central, Karl Parsons, had worked for Whall for years alongside teaching at the school and was only now breaking independently. The situation was hopeless. In time Edmund might get a teaching position to supplement what he'd earn with Whall, but it was still likely to be a hand-to-mouth existence.

Most of all, he was concerned for his mother. His father was a vindictive man and Edmund didn't doubt for a moment that his threat was serious. Herbert Cutler had always appeared to despise his wife, resenting her, even though she was the source of his fortune. Gilbert's death had broken Susan Cutler. Edmund had never doubted his mother's affection for him but her feelings for his older brother were special. There had always been a close bond between them, a co-dependency. He, on the other hand, had been a free and independent spirit since an early age. How could he possibly cast her adrift with no one to defend her? At least while the brothers had lived at Grosvenor Square, there had been a stay on their father's behaviour – but there would be no protection for her were he to abandon her to take up the job with Whall and marry Dora.

Over too many drinks in the Princess Louise, Edmund reached the decision he'd been dreading. He must put his responsibility as a son first, marry Alice Dalton and take up the position in his father's brokerage firm. But, before that, he needed to acknowledge what he was sacrificing.

After a sleepless night he set off at dawn to catch the first train to York.

It was a pilgrimage. He'd promised Christopher Whall to view the Five Sisters window in the Minster, to learn from it and apply that learning. He would no longer be able to fulfil the last part of that promise. Marriage to the Dalton woman would be the end of his artistic education. This trip was to formally say farewell to his hopes and dreams.

Edmund crossed the bridge towards the Minster, its magnificent pair of towers rising imperiously above the surrounding buildings. He stood, gazing up at the Gothic magnificence, drinking in the details in the stonework, the soaring elegance of the structure, the thrust of the flying buttresses and the tangible sense of history as he stepped inside the huge Medieval building. The nave was awe-inspiring: apparently the largest of its kind in the country. This building also housed the largest collection of Medieval stained-glass windows.

Edmund walked around, breathing in the heavy scent of candles. Someone began to play the organ and a chill ran up Edmund's spine as music flooded the space. Everywhere he looked, another example of glass made his heart race. He took

out his sketchpad from his pocket and began to draw and make
notes, already forgetting that his intention in coming here had
been to bid farewell to his craft. He stood under the Great East
window, marvelling at its size – as big as a tennis court. The
guidebook told him it was the work in 1405 of John Thornton, a
celebrated glazier from Coventry. Edmund gazed up at the vast
window, drinking in every panel, every colour, every scene from
the *Book of Genesis* to *Revelations*.

After a while, he tore himself away and went in search of
the object of his journey. The Five Sisters window comprised
five tall, slender lancets, soaring upwards, pointing towards
heaven like a line of shining spears. Edmund was rooted to the
spot, unable to take his eyes off it. The audacity of the work.
What bravery in using a monochrome *grisaille*. When close,
pinpricks of brilliant colour danced, indiscernible at a distance.
Whall was right – it was like a piece of filigree jewellery.

Until this moment, Edmund had taken little pleasure in
grisaille, preferring to indulge his love of colour with vivid
splashes of contrasting hues, and leaving the soft greys, pale
greens and white of *grisaille* to small areas of background. This
window defied that, reversing the norm and creating a subtle,
breath-taking monochromatic work. He slipped his sketchbook
back into his pocket and stood, lost in a trance, as he drank in
the beauty in front of him.

Eventually he moved towards some votive candles and lit
one, then knelt in a pew and prayed for the soul of his
brother. Edmund was not a religious man, but he had a strong
sense of the spiritual. It was inevitable if you devote so much
time to the study and creation of stained glass, most of whose
subjects were of a religious nature. His brother's death had
caused him to dwell more than usual on whether there was an
afterlife. If there were, would God be merciful and look
kindly upon Gilbert? Kinder than society ever would have
done. Gilbert may have had inclinations that went counter to

the teachings of the Church and the law of the land, but surely such inclinations came from deep within him? No man would willingly follow such a dangerous path as homosexuality, unless he had no choice. Gilbert's proclivities must have been innate to his nature. Surely that must mean they were God-given? No matter what anyone else said, Gilbert had been a good man and deserved his place in heaven – if it existed.

Edmund stayed inside the Minster until the light was fading. As he walked back to the railway station, he accepted it would be as impossible for him to give up his art as to stop breathing. He'd felt a connection to the Medieval artists and craftsmen who had laboured to produce those magnificent windows. It was as though these long-dead men had called out to him. Stained glass was his vocation. It could not be denied. Today his very soul had been touched and he'd experienced a calling. From God? It didn't matter. It was enough that it had happened, viscerally, completely, undeniably.

He was going to take up the position with Christopher Whall but he had to find a way to do so while protecting his mother. There had to be a way.

The train roared through the English countryside, past towns and villages, but Edmund was blind to them all. His eyes were closed but inside them the images of the magnificent windows were burnt onto his retinas. His nerve endings jangled in excitement and anticipation. He still had a problem to resolve – but it no longer seemed insurmountable. He was suffused with blind faith that a way ahead would appear to him.

It struck him that he hadn't thought of Dora at all that day. But now her beautiful face dissolved the images of the Five Sisters.

The way forward came to him in a flash. If she loved him as much as he loved her, she'd help him resolve the problem. Crazy to take all this upon himself. The decision wasn't his alone to make. He had no right to decide things that involved her, without her playing a part in the process.

Dora might be unwilling to accept a proposal when it came with so little security. It was unfair to expect her to share the sacrifices that must be made if they were to marry. If she was unwilling to do that, he would be forced to strike a bargain with his father. He'd have to agree to marry Alice Dalton – but it would be strictly on condition he could continue with his chosen career.

Edmund wasted no time before speaking to Dora. If she were to refuse him the pain would be preferable to the agony of uncertainty.

Marriage would mean her abandoning her studies – at least temporarily – as Edmund would be unable to afford the fees at the Central and could hardly expect George Fisher to continue supporting his daughter after her marriage. Edmund didn't know what a railway clerk's salary was, but he imagined it wasn't large. Supporting Dora on Edmund's apprentice wages would be a challenge. They'd be forced to live in a rooming house. He hated the thought of being unable to give her a proper home of her own. Dora had a right to expect one. He'd work harder than any man alive to win Whall's respect and move as rapidly as possible up the ladder – but it wasn't going to happen overnight.

The rain had stopped when he reached Goodge Street and knocked loudly on the door. It was Saturday morning and he remembered that she tended to leave the flat to her father on Saturday mornings. He was about to walk away when Dora appeared in the window above him. She waved and he heard the clatter of her shoes as she hurried downstairs.

'You never said you were calling today,' she said, smiling as she opened the door. 'Come in. Dad's out. I was about to start getting the dinner ready.'

Edmund reached out and grabbed her hand. 'I must talk to you, Dora. It's important. Can we go for a walk?'

Her brow furrowed. 'Give us a sec. I'll fetch my coat.'

When she returned, Edmund steered her towards Russell Square, wanting to avoid anywhere near Grosvenor Square.

'Dora, I don't know how to tell you this,' he began.

'Just say it, Edmund.' Her face was stern, and he realised she was anxious.

'I haven't told you much about my family.'

Dora touched his sleeve. 'Is this about your poor brother? The funeral must have been terribly sad for you.'

'It was.'

'Of course. It's never a good idea to mess about with firearms. Easy for accidents to happen. Your poor mother. It must have been ghastly for her burying her own son.'

He winced. 'It was painful for us all.' He didn't want to think about it or about Gilbert.

But Dora didn't read his mood. 'Your brother was so young and so handsome. I can't believe I saw him with you in the park that day and now he's gone. It doesn't seem right.'

Edmund gritted his teeth, impatient. He wanted to get this over and for his agony to end. 'I need to talk to you about my father.'

'Oh, yes?' She raised her eyebrows. 'What about him?'

'He's a man who always expects to get his own way.'

Dora gave a nervous chuckle. 'Don't all men?'

'I'm afraid he isn't a very pleasant man. Ruthless is the word I'd use to describe him. He's made my mother's life a misery and his constant bullying may have been the cause for Gilbert...' He reminded himself the suicide was meant to be a closely guarded family secret. 'Gilbert's nervous state and lack of attention may have contributed to his carelessness in handling the gun.'

Dora tightened her lips and gave him a sympathetic look. 'How awful. Having a father you don't get along with. I'd be lost without my dear old dad. He may grate on my nerves at times, especially when he's had a few drinks, but he's always been good as gold to me.'

Edmund sighed. This was proving harder than he'd anticipated. 'Gilbert was about to be engaged to be married. The announcement was due the day he died. It was a marriage that suited both families.' He sucked in a deep breath. 'And, as is usually the case with my father, there was a financial aspect to the arrangement.'

They'd reached Russell Square and Edmund guided Dora towards a bench under a tree.

'Not there,' she said. 'It was raining earlier. We'll get dripped on.' She indicated another bench. 'Over there.'

Edmund took out a handkerchief and dried the wooden slats before she sat. She was wearing a short, black velvet jacket over a plain skirt. Her hat – the one he'd bought for her – was of a more modest size than the one it had replaced, but Dora had trimmed it with an extravagant clutch of pheasant feathers which trailed down over one side and made up for what the hat brim lacked in width. He brushed aside the thought that sometimes dogged him whenever he was with her – a wish that she'd show a little more restraint in her millinery tastes.

'My father wants me to marry Gilbert's intended.' It was out. He'd said it. He held his breath, waiting for her reaction.

Dora started to laugh. A hollow nervous laugh.

Uncertain, Edmund shuffled his feet. 'He also wants me to join his firm. He's threatened to cut me off without a penny if I refuse.'

She stopped laughing and gazed up at him. 'So, go on, marry her then.' Her tone was frosty. 'See if I care.' Then she made a little choking sound. 'I thought... I thought you...'

Edmund reached for her hand, but she jerked it away.

'I can't possibly marry The Honourable Alice Dalton.'

'Why ever not? Do tell.' Her tone was now sarcastic. '*The Honourable* no less. So, what was I? A passing fancy? A bit on the side?'

'No! I can't marry her because I'm in love with you, Dora.'

A hint of a smile quivered at the edge of her lips. 'Well, you'd better hurry up and ask *me* to marry you then.' Her lip trembled. She lowered her eyes.

Edmund grasped her hands and wrapped them in his. 'Oh, Dora, I imagine it every waking moment. I can't think of anything I want more than for us to belong to each other. I dream about it every night. Us being together.'

Her eyes shone. 'So why are you looking so worried? You look as though you've lost a pound and found sixpence.'

'Because it's not so simple. I told you – my father will cut me off without a penny. I'll be on a very modest salary with Mr Whall at first. Probably for a couple of years. I'll barely be able to support myself, let alone you. I can't expect you to put up with that.'

'Then get another job. Work for your father.'

Edmund's head jerked back in surprise. 'I can't do that. Working for Whall is what I've been striving for ever since I started at the Central. Surely you know that?'

A cloud passed over her face and her eyes filled with tears. 'You want that more than you want me?'

He squirmed. 'Of course, I don't.'

'Then I don't understand. You tell me you want to marry me and then you say that you don't.'

He clasped her hands more tightly. 'No! I do want to marry you, Dora. But I'm trying to tell you that I'm not in a good position. I'd hoped to make my reputation first and to have reached a point in my career when I could propose to you, knowing I'd be able to support you financially.'

'What about that big house you live in, in Grosvenor Square?'

'I'll have to move out when I take up the job with Whall.' He stroked the back of her hands. 'And to tell you the truth, Dora, I can't wait to leave. It's like being in prison living there. You've no idea what my father's like.'

'I'm confused, Edmund. Completely confused. You tell me you love me and want to marry me and then you say you can't. Are you trying to tell me you want to marry this Honourable Alice Whatsername? Do—'

He interrupted her. 'No! I can't think of anything worse. I love *you*. I want to marry *you*. But it's not fair to expect you to accept a life of poverty as a consequence. At least in the beginning.'

'So we can wait, can't we? Though not too long I hope.'

'That's just it. We can't.' He turned his head away. 'Unless there's a legal reason why it can't happen, Father will force my hand and push me into marrying Alice Dalton.'

'How can he do that?' She pulled her hands from his grasp. 'You're a grown man. He can't drag you kicking and screaming to the altar.'

'He's made it abundantly clear that if I fail to marry her, the person who will be made to suffer is my mother.'

Dora looked sceptical. 'What are you saying?'

'He's a violent man. He's struck her in the past. Not recently. But when Gilbert and I were younger. It's why she's so cowed and frightened. He knocked all the spirit out of her.'

Edmund leant forward, elbows on knees, head in hands. 'She married him for love. Went against her father to do so. As soon as the ink was dry on the marriage licence, my father began to torment her. Believing herself in love with him, she complied with everything he wanted, but it was never enough.' Edmund felt a twinge of guilt speaking of his mother in this way –she'd hate him telling someone outside the family – but he had to make the circumstances clear to Dora. 'He forced her to live here in England. At first, he let her spend the summers with us at her house on Long Island. But once my grandfather grew ill and was incapable of standing up for his daughter, Father refused to let her see him. When Grandfather died that was it. The only time she gets to return to America now is if it suits Father for business purposes. Mother has no other family there. Now that Gilbert's gone, she's utterly broken. I can't let her suffer anymore.'

'So, you're breaking up with me?'

'No!' He reached again for her hand, but she jerked it away. 'I'm trying to say that the only thing that will prevent Father forcing me to marry the wretched Dalton girl is if it's a legal impossibility. If I'm already married. But I can't expect you to agree to marry me unless you understand the implications. It would be a struggle at first. A terrible struggle. That's not something I can expect you to enter into willingly.' He took her hand and this time she let him.

Edmund swallowed, barely able to breathe, watching as she mulled it over.

'Of course, I'll marry you, dearest Edmund,' she said at last.

He pulled her into his arms and held her pressed against his chest, waves of relief mingling with anxiety over what he was asking of her. He didn't care a jot for himself – he'd always known his father would cut off his allowance, but was he right to drag Dora down with him? Except he wouldn't be pulling her down. It would be a short-term sacrifice. He would work harder than anyone to rise in his chosen profession. One day soon he'd make it up to her.

'I'll have to ensure that my father has no reason to believe my mother is involved in any way.'

'She isn't. It's between you and me.'

Edmund heaved a sigh of relief. 'You won't mind then if I don't introduce you to her until after we're married?'

She kissed him lightly on the cheek. 'I'm marrying you. Not your family.'

'And you don't mind it being a struggle financially – at least at first?'

Dora looked up at him and held his gaze. 'You could always move into Goodge Street.'

'I'll be working in Hammersmith.'

'There's the train. Or the tram.' She smiled at him. 'And it would mean I could carry on looking after Dad. He relies on me.'

Starting married life as the lodger in his father-in-law's home was not what Edmund had in mind. But he could worry about that later. Dora had said yes and that was all that mattered.

He held her in his arms and kissed her tenderly. When the kiss ended, he told her about his revelation at York Minster. As he described the arresting simplicity of the monochrome window, she stiffened beside him. Perhaps she was disappointed that he hadn't asked her to accompany him on his day trip to the north.

'It's not fair of me to go on about it when you haven't had a chance to see it too. When we're married and I manage to save up a bit, we'll go together. You could paint it. Capture the delicate intricacies. It's like fine embroidery, only sparkling. Oh, Dora, I can't wait to show you.'

She smiled then changed the subject. 'You'll have to ask Dad about marrying me. He won't object. He should be back from Euston by now. He was doing a shift this morning to cover for a colleague.' She smoothed her hand over the fabric of her skirt. 'It's time I got home and got the dinner on. You can join us.' She stood up and slipped her arm through his in a proprietorial fashion. 'I know you'll be short for cash, but you will be buying me a nice ring, won't you, Edmund?'

ELEVEN

Lady Dalton and Mrs Cutler had reached an understanding that the nuptials between Edmund and Alice would take place in the following spring with an engagement formally announced at Christmas.

'The courtship can begin in the Fall,' Mrs Cutler suggested. Lady Dalton agreed.

Later, she informed her daughter 'Over the next couple of months it's only right and proper that we respect the tragic death of Gilbert and not throw you and Edmund together too quickly. Susan Cutler and I think it's best that the two of you don't rush things. Obviously, we all want the matter settled as soon as possible, but we must allow time for the Cutlers to mourn their son'.

It wasn't said, but Alice concluded that there was also a belief by the two mothers that proceeding cautiously would allow time for Edmund to look more favourably on marrying her. At least she wasn't expected to socialise with him at all in the meantime. As the days and weeks passed, maybe she'd become more reconciled to her fate. Perhaps he would too.

. . .

Alice was staying for a couple of days with Harriet at the latter's home in Portman Square. Morose and saddened by recent events, she'd taken up her mother's suggestion that a short break might raise her spirits. She enjoyed spending time with Harriet – their friendship was solid despite their very different personalities and approach to life.

Alice was sticking to the fiction that Gilbert's death was an unfortunate accident and hadn't told her friend about what she'd seen in the garden shed. A slip of the tongue could lead to a scandal and Alice was terrified by the prospect of the truth coming out. But she had revealed her parents' wish that she now marry the younger brother, Edmund – as well as her own misgivings on the subject.

'Why not give this Edmund chap a chance, Alice?' Harriet said. 'He might not turn out to be as bad as you fear.'

'I've said I'll agree to marry him – assuming he asks me, but I don't have to like him. I'm doing it for Mama and Papa. If it weren't for them, I'd be more than happy to remain a spinster.'

Harriet tutted. 'Of course, you wouldn't. You're not old maid material. I'm not for a moment suggesting you have to fall in love with the man, only that you keep an open mind. You may have got off on the wrong foot, but I can't believe he's as dreadful as you're making out.'

'He's worse. He tried to persuade Gilbert not to marry me. He's rude. He's abrupt. He clearly holds me in contempt.'

'You've only met the man once.'

'That was enough.'

Harriet tilted her head on one side and studied her friend's face with an intensity that made Alice uncomfortable. She felt like a specimen on a dish for her more worldly-wise friend to inspect. They were close, yet Alice was more reticent about her feelings than Harriet was. Being offered up in marriage to a man she disliked was a humiliation. Why couldn't Harriet see that?

'Come on, he must have some good points. After all, he's an artist. You have that much in common.'

Alice curled her lip. 'Not according to him. He more or less accused me of being a dabbler. Anyway, he'll have to give up his artistic career as his father insists he takes Gilbert's place in the family firm. He's bound to blame me for that too.' Alice thought for a moment. 'He's only a stained-glass artist. That's hardly more than someone doing jigsaw puzzles.'

'Oooh! Cutting!' Harriet laughed. 'Cheer up, old girl. There's no point in double-guessing the poor man. If you've come round to agreeing to marry him then surely, he will too. Give the fellow the benefit of the doubt. He may surprise you. Successful marriages are based on other considerations than love. Once you get to know one another, respect may grow. But if you go into this determined to dislike him, you'll be guaranteed to make each other miserable.'

Alice considered her friend's words. Edmund Cutler was an insufferable, arrogant man but at least he had some artistic leanings – even if stained glass was in her opinion a lesser calling than painting. He wasn't as handsome as Gilbert, but he was still a good looking man – especially in comparison with Harriet's earl. Maybe she was being too picky.

Harriet stretched her arms wide. 'Look at me. I close my eyes and grit my teeth whenever his Lordship comes near me, but we're perfectly civil with each other and in consequence I reap the benefits.'

Alice stretched her lips into a grim rictus smile. 'Benefits?'

'Living here in Portman Square. He's mostly in Norfolk. I need to be available for Royal Ascot and the odd charity dinner. All he expects is that I deliver an heir and a spare as soon as possible.'

'But that's the worst part, isn't it?' Alice couldn't comprehend how Harriet was prepared to share a bed with the earl – even if only occasionally.

Harriet grinned. 'I just close my eyes and grit my teeth. The first time was vile, but after that I barely noticed. Mummy told me it's a useful time to plan the seating for dinner parties or think about what to ask cook to prepare for the coming week's menus. And I do enjoy being the Countess of Wallingford and having accounts at all the best dressmakers. The old boy is fabulously rich.'

'You make it sound rather mercenary.'

'It is! But practical too – who'd want a life of poverty? No, thank you. Lack of money can turn even the most loving marriage sour. Anyway, it looks like I've done my duty on the childbearing front. His Lordship will almost certainly leave me alone from now on.' Harriet smiled. 'I wasn't going to tell you yet, but it seems I'm to make Lord Wallingford a very happy man early in the new year.'

'You're...?'

'Yes. I am going to have a child.' Harriet leant forward and touched Alice on the elbow. 'I'm praying it will be a boy. It's already proving to be a wonderful excuse for him to shower me with gifts.' She grinned. 'And the best thing is, it will almost certainly mean the fat old fellow will leave me alone in my bed.'

Harriet pregnant? A gulf opened up between them. The balance of their friendship had shifted when Harriet married but now motherhood? 'How do you feel about becoming a mother?'

'Thrilled to bits. I can't wait.'

The gulf widened. Alice was happy for Harriet but inside she knew their relationship would change forever. 'I'm delighted for you.' Alice put her arms around her friend.

'One day soon, you could be feeling the same way. You may not relish being a wife, but I'm sure you'll be as happy as I am at the prospect of being a mother. Now, my dear sweet friend, I'll send for some tea, then once we've had it, we're going to stroll over to Hyde Park and join the rally.'

'The rally?'

'Women's suffrage. I went to a meeting of the Women's Social and Political Union last week and they think the numbers will be enormous today. Women are travelling to London from all over the country. It's why I asked you to wear white.'

'I didn't know you were a suffragette?'

Harriet grinned. 'I joined as soon as the meeting ended. And now I'm determined to recruit you.' She looked more animated than Alice had ever seen her. What had got into her?

Alice pulled a face. 'I've no interest in politics. If I had the vote, I wouldn't know what to do with it.'

'Then we need to remedy that. Besides, it will give you something to think about. Take your mind off your own troubles.'

'You know my mother is thinking of joining the other side?'

'The other side?'

'There's talk of establishing an opposition group against the suffrage. Mama is trying to recruit Mrs Cutler. Lady Jersey is chairing a meeting next month to set it up, and Mama wants me to go with her.'

'After you listen to the speeches this afternoon that will be utterly unthinkable.'

Alice very much doubted that. 'Does Lord Wallingford know you're mixed up in this?' she asked.

'Of course he doesn't. Nor does he need to. I've no intention of doing anything too radical but I can offer some financial support and I've been helping out, distributing leaflets and doing some administration in the office. It's terrific fun.'

'But what's the point of a gathering in the park? What good will that do? It won't change anything.'

Harriet gave a weary sigh. 'You live in an ivory tower, Alice. Don't you ever read the papers? Mr Asquith claims the vast majority of women don't give a fig about having a vote. He's laid down a challenge, so we need to prove to him and his government that there is a huge strength of feeling in support of the cause.'

Alice had some sympathy for Mr Asquith but wasn't going to say that to Harriet. 'What's the point of going to the park?'

'It'll be a massive demonstration of how widespread our support is. You've no idea how many women will be coming. They'll be pouring into London from all points of the compass. Dickins & Jones has completely sold out of white dresses.' Harriet jumped up. 'I almost forgot.' She went over to a cupboard at the corner of the room and took out some fabric. 'Sashes. To show our support. These are the colours. Purple and green.' She slipped a sash over her bodice and handed the other to Alice. The sash bore the words 'Votes for Women'.

'I'm not sure it's a good idea for you to be joining a rally when you're expecting a baby, Harriet. I'll come to the park with you. To make sure you're safe. But I'm not going to be part of it or wear a sash.' Alice folded her arms.

'At least take it. Put it in your handbag. Just in case.'

Alice rolled her eyes heavenwards but did as instructed, curious to find out more. It would be a relief to have something else to think about other than her own problems.

As soon as they left the house, Alice sensed something in the air. A buzz of excitement radiated through the streets, growing, along with the crowds, as they drew nearer to the park. Once inside the gates, Alice was staggered by the number of people. In her entire life she'd witnessed nothing like it. A teeming mass of humanity, some of them curious onlookers, but an impressive turnout of white clad women, many wearing the purple and green sashes and carrying posters and banners. Votes for Women! Women Unite! Universal Franchise! as well as banners bearing the names of the towns and cities from where the women delegates had come. One of the largest was the Manchester contingent, carrying placards heralding that they – led by Mrs Pankhurst – were the First in the Fight.

The sun blazed down upon the throng as they poured into Hyde Park from all directions having marched on foot from Paddington, Euston and King's Cross stations as well as Trafalgar Square and the Embankment. Brass bands lent a carnival atmosphere to the proceedings. There was a collection of raised platforms on which eminent speakers, from Keir Hardie of the Labour Party to George Bernard Shaw, were to lend their support to the cause.

Alice looked around her. It was as though the entire country had turned out that afternoon. Awe-inspiring. A sea of straw boaters signalled there were almost as many men here as women. Whether doubters, supporters, or mere onlookers, there was no indication that anyone was out to cause trouble and the atmosphere was festive and celebratory.

Somebody thrust a leaflet into Alice's hands. As she took in the words, she wondered why the injustice of the status quo had never struck her before. How could it possibly be right that women, half the population, should be denied any say in electing the government that would make the laws that bound them? How could it be right that a woman, on marriage, had virtually no rights at all – not even over her own children? And how could a single woman pay her taxes and own property and yet have no influence whatsoever over the laws that governed her? Where was the justice in that? Alice opened her reticule, took out the purple and green sash and slipped it over her head.

That evening, exhilarated but exhausted, Alice climbed into her father's Wolseley to be driven back to Richmond. Harriet stood on the pavement to say goodbye. She leant into the motorcar and tweaked the suffragette sash across Alice's chest. 'Better take that off before you see your parents. We don't want them deeming me a bad influence.'

'Which of course you most certainly are.' Alice grinned. 'Thank you for persuading me to come to the rally. It's been an eye-opener. If you think I may be able to help, I'd love to get involved.'

'Don't worry. You will be.'

As the car drove off, Alice drew the purple and green sash over her head, folded it carefully and slipped it inside her handbag. If she was to pursue her interest in the cause of women's suffrage, she must do so in secret, at least until she was married.

TWELVE

It was all happening so quickly.

None of it was of Edmund's choosing. He'd certainly wanted to marry Dora, but not in this hurried manner. It was tawdry, furtive, as though it were something to be ashamed of. But in the end, he'd had no choice. Either marry Dora with undue haste or risk being roped into a loveless marriage with Lord Dalton's daughter.

His mother paid a rare visit to his room the day after his proposal to Dora. She knocked on the door and asked if she could talk with him.

'It's about marrying Miss Dalton. I'm sorry it's come to this, Edmund,' she said. 'I know you're not happy about it. You're being punished for Gilbert's terrible accident. It's so unfair since you weren't even there. If anyone's to blame, it's the Daltons for letting him handle a gun when he's not used to it.' She perched on the edge of a chair, twisting her hands round and round in the endless twitching fashion she'd adopted since her elder son's death. 'Marriage wasn't something Gilbert sought, and I know he accepted it for the sake of appearances.' She stared at the back of her hands then folded them in her lap, only for the twisting motion to begin again after a few moments. 'It mattered little to him about the woman concerned. For you, I know it's different.'

Her face was lowered but Edmund could see that she was blushing.

'I know you've no feelings for the Dalton girl, but—' Looking up at him, she gave him an apologetic smile. 'I rather like her and I'm sure, given time...' Her voice trailed away.

Edmund sat on the end of his bed. 'I'm not marrying The Honourable Alice Dalton.'

His mother's face crumpled. 'But Eddie, if you persist in going against your father's wishes, I'm afraid...' Her expression was anguished.

Edmund reached across the gap between them and took her hand. Closing his eyes he took a deep breath. He'd have preferred to keep his mother in the dark but it felt wrong to lie to her. He also wanted to avoid getting more embroiled with the Daltons when the marriage to Alice wasn't going to happen. 'I'm not marrying her because I *can't*. I'm engaged to someone else, Mother.'

Susan Cutler snatched back her hand from his as though she'd been burnt and it flew up to cover her mouth. 'Engaged? To whom? How? When?' Her eyes were wide, and he could see the fear in them. 'When your father finds out he'll force you to break off the engagement. Who is she?'

'Her name is Dora Fisher. I met her at the Central.'

'Her background?'

'Her father's a railway clerk. Her mother's dead.'

Susan's lip trembled. 'Your father will pay her off. You know what he's like. He'll write a cheque large enough that Miss Fisher and her father will be compelled to accept.'

'That's cynical of you, Mother, to assume Dora's feelings are so shallow.'

'Not cynical. Realistic.'

He knew there was justification in his mother's words. The kind of money Herbert Cutler could offer would be life-changing. Dora's circumstances would make it impossible for her to refuse, no matter how much she cared for him. Edmund got up from his perch at the end of the bed and moved across to the window. 'Then I'd better hurry up and marry her before he finds out.' He gazed out over the gardens of the Square, as if a solution to his problems would manifest within the green canopy of plane trees.

'It takes weeks for the banns to be called.'

'Then we'll marry in a register office.'

'That makes no difference. You still have to give notification in advance.'

Edmund's face fell. He hadn't envisaged that. 'We'll elope.'

'It's the same even at Gretna Green these days. I read a magazine article about wedding customs just a month or so ago.' Her mouth turned downwards. 'It's different in New York. Herbert and I were married at short notice there. It only takes twenty-four hours. My father would never have approved of our marrying.' Her eyes welled up and she turned her head away.

The bitter irony of that. Herbert Cutler's philosophy was *Do as I say not as I do.* 'There has to be a way around it. Surely?'

Susan Cutler's face was pale and Edmund could see she was shivering. He felt a rush of affection for her. He hadn't wanted to involve her at all, but he'd seen no means of avoiding telling her something of his plans. She twisted her hands together, knuckles white. 'I can't advise you, Edmund. It's better that I know as little as possible. I'm a terrible liar. Your father would soon force it out of me.'

That was true. She would become the butt of Herbert Cutler's anger. Frail and fragile since the loss of her son, she'd be an even more vulnerable target for her husband's anger. Edmund's insides clenched at the memory of finding her, face bloodied, on the drawing room floor when he was eleven. It would haunt him to his grave. It must never happen again.

'My worry is for you, Mother. Him taking it out on you. I shouldn't have told you.'

'I'm glad you did. Just don't tell me any details until it's done. It'll all be dandy as long as he believes it's a shock to me too.'

Edmund hoped she was right but he was afraid. 'I'm scared he'll be so angry he'll take it out on you.'

'Don't worry. If you love this girl you must marry her. I told you. I'll be fine and dandy.' Susan rose from the chair and wrapped her arms around her son, laying her head against his shoulder. He could feel her body shaking as she held him. She tilted her head back and looked up at him, her hand caressing his cheek. 'Whatever you decide, Edmund, you have my blessing. I'm sorry you won't be marrying the Dalton girl. Despite your father's reasons for promoting the match, I felt it was a good one. But if you truly love this Miss Fisher and have made her promises, then you must honour them. I wish I could offer you financial support but you know I have no access to funds.'

'I do love her, Mother,' he said, and gave her a tight smile. 'And the money is immaterial.' Though that wasn't strictly true. Lack of cash was going to be a serious challenge.

'The best way to deflect your father's attention from this is for me to spend as much time as possible with Lady Lavinia and her daughter. The poor girl will be horribly let down.'

'I doubt it. I have every reason to believe The Honourable Alice Dalton has as little desire to be married to me as I do to her.'

She kissed him and left the room, her eyes welling with tears. Edmund felt wretched.

. . .

Edmund settled on a register office wedding. He judged it less likely that notice of the event would reach his father. It was no easy feat to persuade Dora. She had entertained hopes of a fine wedding in the church where her parents had married, and, despite his constant reminders that the marriage must take place without his father discovering, Dora was difficult to appease.

One sunny morning as they discussed their plans while walking in Regent's Park, Dora leaned her head on his shoulder and entwined her fingers with his. 'I don't understand why you won't introduce me to your parents. I'm sure once we meet, your father will feel differently about us marrying.'

'You don't know my father.'

'Exactly. That's what I want to put right.'

Her bottom lip pushed out in a pout that made him want to kiss it away. Just a look from Dora, and Edmund was soft clay in her hands. But he was uneasy at her refusal to accept that the rift with his father would be permanent once Herbert Cutler found out about their clandestine marriage. Edmund continued to stress that, once married, he'd never again cross the threshold of the house in Grosvenor Square. But Dora gave him a knowing smile that made him feel she saw him as a naughty child to be indulged and she herself knew better. Nothing he said appeared to change this.

Guilt nagged at him. How could he go through with the marriage when Dora was wilfully seeing an altogether different future for them? Yet, whenever he stressed that their life, once married, would be far from the trappings of luxury, Dora would smile and repeat that she understood perfectly and all that mattered was that they would be together.

Susan Cutler was true to her word and extended frequent invitations to the two Dalton women, for tea, gallery visits and the occasional afternoon concert. Gilbert's recent death ruled out more active entertaining, but the regular presence of the

Daltons in Grosvenor Square satisfied Herbert Cutler that matters were progressing as planned between his remaining son and Alice Dalton.

Edmund was agonising over the outlay for a wedding ring for Dora. He understood why it was important to her but every penny counted. As soon as they were married he would be taking on the support of his wife on an apprentice's modest earnings.

He was sitting reading in the drawing room one Sunday morning, a week before the wedding was scheduled. Herbert Cutler had left for his habitual weekend golf game. It was one of the rare times when Edmund and his mother were free to talk and relax without the edginess that Herbert Cutler's presence caused. Susan came in and sat on the sofa, patting the cushion beside her for him to join her.

She opened her hand to reveal a small velvet box. Taking Edmund's hand she placed the box on his palm.

Nestled inside among folds of deep blue velvet was a ring.

'Your grandmother gave it to me before she died,' Susan said. 'I wanted to wear it when I married your father, but he wouldn't let me. He saw my wanting to wear a ring that had belonged to my mother as casting an aspersion on him, so he took me to Tiffany's and chose this.' She held her hand out, her upright fingers at a distance and a shimmer of distaste on her face. 'Of course, my own money paid for it.' She gave a little sigh and stared into the middle distance. 'I'd intended the ring for Gilbert's wife, so it's right that you give it to your bride.'

It was a simple but exquisite gold band inset with diamonds.

'Oh Mother! I can't thank you enough. This means so much to me. I've been worried about finding the money for a ring.' He flung his arms around her, drawing her small thin body close.

'I ask only one thing. Don't let your father know I've given it to you.'

Edmund frowned. 'Will he notice it's gone?'

Susan gave a bitter laugh. 'Of course, he won't. He's never even seen it. Just don't tell him. Please.'

Edmund went to the register office in Camden Town – far from Herbert Cutler's milieu. The notices for forthcoming marriages were posted in a cluttered display box fixed to the wall of the building and the likelihood of his father or any of their acquaintances being in the area, let alone spotting it, was virtually nil.

The wedding ceremony was booked for the earliest possible date after the banns were posted. Not a moment longer than necessary. Guilt about leading the Daltons to believe that marriage to their daughter was likely to happen mingled with a determination to avoid having to meet Alice Dalton in the meantime. His mother had proved an invaluable ally, continually stressing to both her husband and Lady Dalton that it would be disrespectful to Gilbert's memory to effect a meeting sooner.

Edmund prayed that his mother's advocacy for the Dalton marriage would convince Herbert Cutler that she knew nothing of his planned nuptials when he eventually found out.

When the wedding day arrived, Edmund was excited but nervous. He'd known Dora less than a year but in that short time his whole life had changed. His only sadness was that his brother and mother were not there to witness his marriage. But it was no time to feel melancholic. He and his beloved Dora would be joined forever. Never again would he feel the wrench he experienced whenever he left her on the doorstep of the flat in Goodge Street. Never again would he spend a night alone in his bed.

He got to the register office early and had to pace up and down in the street until the weddings ahead of his were completed. When Dora arrived on her father's arm, Edmund's heart somersaulted. Wearing her little black bolero jacket over a white muslin dress trimmed with a broderie anglaise border, she looked more beautiful than ever. Her face was lit by a smile that warmed him and set his pulse racing. Under a cartwheel-style hat her hair fell in soft curls and she carried a posy of pink carnations and baby's breath. But it was the radiance of her smile as she saw Edmund that stopped his breath. It lit up her face and made him more certain than ever that he had been right to marry her.

All the witnesses to the ceremony were on Dora's side: her father, Mrs Spindlemann and a sour-faced Stanley. Mr Spindlemann was absent as he was required to attend to the shop. After the knot was tied in what Edmund thought was the briefest, most clinical of procedures, the wedding party returned to Goodge Street where Dora had prepared sandwiches and a platter of boiled ham and tongue, supplemented with slices of fruit, an iced fruitcake, bottles of beer for the men and sherry for the two women. Edmund was torn between shame that it was such a miserable repast and satisfaction that it was different from the feast that would have been offered had the marriage to Alice taken place. At the thought of that, he shuddered and turned to gaze at Dora. Her pale skin was like fine bone china. Her hair was dressed with more care and attention than usual so that the rogue tendrils that habitually graced her neck were carefully anchored by wide tortoiseshell combs. She could have been a model in a Pear's soap advertisement.

The diamond wedding ring on Dora's finger caught the sunlight streaming through the window. She held up her hand and examined the simple gold band inlaid with diamonds. 'It's so beautiful. Thank you, my darling Edmund.' She tipped her head to one side. 'Are the stones real?'

He took her hand in his and ran his finger over the ring which fitted perfectly. 'The diamonds are real. The ring's an heirloom. It belonged to my grandmother.'

Dora recoiled. 'You've given me a second-hand ring? You want me to wear a ring some other woman wore? Why would I want your dead grandmother's hand-me-down?' She tugged at it, trying to pull it off her finger, her face twisted with anger. 'I want my own ring.'

Mortified, Edmund froze.

Mrs Spindlemann reached for the bride's hand. 'Let me have a look at your ring, ducks.' She grasped Dora's fingers and bent them to allow her to examine the wedding band. Reaching into a pocket in her skirt she pulled out a jeweller's magnifying eyeglass. 'Very nice indeed,' she declared. She gently elbowed Dora. 'No wonder my Stanley wasn't good enough for you. You've married a man of means, ducky.' She gave a little conspiratorial laugh. 'Best diamonds I've seen in many a year. Worth a pretty fortune, if you ask me. And I know.' She turned to signal to her son. 'Come and get a peep at this, Stanley.' She handed him the eyepiece.

Stanley took Dora's hand in his and bent his head to study the ring on her finger. Edmund bridled at the way the silversmith lingered over his examination, holding her fingertips while muttering and sighing. Eventually, Stanley said, 'You're right as always, Mother. That's a beaut! Those diamonds'd fetch a small fortune down Hatton Garden.'

Dora's mood transformed. 'It's an heirloom, it is. Handed down from my Edmund's grandmother in New York. From one of the finest jewellers in the world.'

The declaration was met with approving sighs and nods from the Spindlemanns and relief from Edmund.

But something inside him had shifted, like the first vibration in a tectonic plate. He looked at Dora. Her beauty was incontestable, but today had revealed something else in her. Something venal. Base. Shallow. Unworthy of the elevated position he had afforded her until now. He pushed the traitorous thoughts to the back of his head. He was being over-critical. Dora's behaviour was no doubt down to wedding day nerves.

George Fisher clapped his hands and raised his glass of beer. 'A toast to the happy couple. Welcome into the Fisher family, Edmund.' He made an expansive gesture, sweeping his arm around the room. 'My new son-in-law is a proper gent. But my girl shouldn't be intimidated by that. Dora's mother, my dearest departed wife, Felicity, was a lady, and my girl has her blood flowing through her veins.'

He turned to face Edmund. 'I want to make something clear, lad. Don't ever think this girl isn't good enough for you and your fancy diamonds. She's pure gold, just like her ma was.' He puffed out his chest then his stern expression shifted into a smile. 'Now there's plenty more to drink here.' He put an arm around Stanley's shoulder. 'Stan, why don't you run next door and tell that father of yours to shut up shop and come join us in toasting the good health of my darling Dora and her new husband. Dora, girl, let's show that fella you've married what a great performance you can give on the old joanna.' He raised the lid of the piano. 'Go on, play my favourite, *Oh Mr Porter*.'

Dora settled herself on the piano stool, positioned her fingers over the keys and started to play, singing in a voice that captivated Edmund. He'd never heard her sing or play before and watching and listening to her now, he was overwhelmed by a mixture of desire and admiration. Her voice was sweet as a nightingale's, her dexterity on the keyboard fluid. As the Spindlemanns and George Fisher joined in the choruses, the doubts about Dora vanished.

After the wedding guests left, Edmund tried to help Dora clear the plates away, only to be met with a scornful laugh by George and affronted pride by Dora.

'What are you thinking? It's not your place to do that. It's my job to look after both of you.' She gave him a big smile, as she moved between the parlour and the scullery.

Knowing he couldn't put it off any longer, he said, 'In that case I'll go over to Grosvenor Square and tell my parents we're married. I won't be long. If my father's true to form I'll be kicked out of the house.'

Dora looked up at him sharply and untied her apron. 'The dishes can wait. I'm coming with you. It's time I met my new in-laws.'

George picked up a newspaper and began to read, disassociating himself from the conversation.

'Not a good idea, my love,' said Edmund. 'Father will be rude and angry. Better not to put yourself in the firing line.'

Dora folded her arms. 'I'm your wife and I'm coming with you. That's that.'

Edmund turned to George, who shook out the newspaper and refused to be drawn in. 'Nothing to do with me, son. When my Dora makes up her mind you'd do well to take heed.'

Heart sinking, Edmund stood in the doorway as Dora shrugged on her coat and pinned on her hat – the one with the extravagant pheasant feathers.

Half-an-hour later they were on the doorstep of the house in Grosvenor Square. Deciding it was inappropriate to use his keys, he rang the doorbell. Moments later, it was opened by the housekeeper, who looked at him in surprise. Her eyes widened further when she saw Dora standing beside him in her elaborate hat.

'Mr Edmund, have you forgotten your keys?'

'Are my parents at home?' he asked, ignoring the question.

'Mr Cutler is in the drawing room and your mother is dressing for dinner which is to be served in an hour. They're being joined by Lord and Lady Dalton. Will you be dining with them?' The housekeeper, clearly bursting with curiosity, cast another sly glance at Dora. 'Shall I announce your guest?'

'That won't be necessary.' Edmund steered Dora towards the drawing room.

Her eyes darted around. No doubt she was overawed by the grandeur and scale of the town house. Glancing up at him, she grasped his hand. He gave her a smile and squeezed her hand in reassurance.

Herbert Cutler, in a wing-backed armchair, was sipping a whisky. He looked up and frowned when he saw his son. 'Edmund? So, you've condescended to join us for dinner?'

Dora stepped out from behind her husband.

Cutler's eyes narrowed and he threw a quizzical look at his son.

'Father, allow me to present my wife, Dora. We were married this morning.'

Herbert Cutler spluttered his whisky, then slammed the glass down on a side-table. 'What are you talking about, Edmund? Have you lost your mind?'

As he spoke, the door opened and Susan Cutler came in. She stopped on the threshold, her brow creased and her eyes fearful. 'Edmund?'

Edmund repeated the introductions, careful to avoid any indication that he had already alerted his mother to his marriage.

Dora gave Susan Cutler a wide smile then moved to greet Herbert. Edmund pulled her back and drew her towards him, wrapping an arm protectively around her shoulders.

'I wanted Edmund to invite you to the wedding. I'm really sorry, only...' Dora's voice trailed away.

'My son knew all too well that I would have moved heaven and earth to prevent such an appalling marriage.' Herbert Cutler's steely eyes bored into Dora. 'A woman like you is clearly beneath him.'

Stung, Dora's shoulders went back. 'I've nothing to be ashamed of. I may not live in a fancy house in Grosvenor Square but no one's going to make me feel small or inferior. Your son asked me to marry him, and I accepted. It may come as

a shock to you and I'm sorry. I wanted him to tell you before-
hand, but he wouldn't have it.' She pushed her bottom lip out.
'He reckoned you'd try to press him into marrying that woman
with a fancy title but he's a grown man and has made up his
own mind. I'll have you know we're living in the twentieth
century.' Dora put her hands on her hips.

'Shut up.' Herbert Cutler got to his feet, slugged back the
rest of his drink and walked across the room to pour himself
another one. 'In half-an-hour our guests are arriving, and I want
you both gone.' He turned to Edmund. 'The marriage needs to
be annulled. As quickly as possible.'

Enraged, Edmund took Dora's hand and faced down his
father. 'There'll be no annulment. We took our vows seriously.'

Cutler ignored his son. He appraised Dora with a sneer of
disgust.

'Where in God's name did you find this creature? Look at
the hat. Is she a costermonger? Pretty face I'll grant you, but you
could have had what you wanted from her without marrying
her. Marriage is about reputation, property, one's position in
society. This girl will drag you into the gutter.'

'Don't talk about me as though I'm not here!' Dora was red
in the face. 'I've never been so insulted in my life. I'll have you
know my grandfather was a doctor and my dad's got a good job
with the railways. I've nothing to apologise for. Just because you
live in a fancy house doesn't make you a gentleman.' She folded
her arms and stared her father-in-law down.

Edmund wanted to hit his father, but it would only make
matters worse. This was exactly what he'd wanted to protect
Dora from. He turned to his mother. 'Please apologise to the
Daltons for me. I had no desire to hurt Miss Dalton's feelings,
but I never colluded in the charade of this attempt at an
arranged marriage.' He took Dora's arm and steered her towards
the door. 'Let's go. I can't bear to spend another minute under
his roof. Goodbye, Mother.'

As they passed Susan Cutler, Dora stretched out her arm to reveal the ring on her finger. 'By the way, Mrs Cutler, my neighbour is a jeweller and says these are the finest quality diamonds. Worth a pretty penny I gather. Thanks for that.'

Susan Cutler went pale. Edmund made a little choking noise as he bundled Dora out of the room.

Once they were out in the street, Edmund, trying to rein back his anger, said, 'Why in God's name did you mention the ring?'

'I was only being polite. But it seems no one in Grosvenor Square knows what good manners are. Didn't even invite me to sit down. I've never been so insulted in my life. Comparing me to a costermonger and a common prostitute.' She stopped walking and scowled at Edmund. 'You should have punched his nose.'

'I *told* you what he was like but you wouldn't listen. I also told you he was likely to take out his anger on my mother. And now you've let the cat out of the bag and made it clear that Mother knew about us by mentioning the ring.'

Dora rolled her eyes. 'Who cares about the blooming ring? What does it matter compared to what he said about me?'

'Only that he's now likely to use her as a punch bag.'

'Don't be daft.'

'You've no idea, have you? Why else do you think I didn't do more? I don't want him to take it out on her.' Edmund thrust his hands deep into the pockets of his coat and avoided looking at her. He started walking at a fast pace, so Dora almost had to run to keep up with him.

'Never mind her. What about me?'

'He wasn't going to hit you.' Edmund kicked the base of a lamppost.

They were silent the rest of the way back to Goodge Street.

He waited as she opened the front door but didn't follow her in.

'What're you waiting about for?' Dora stood in the doorway.

'I'm not coming in.'

She stared at him as though he were insane.

'I'm going to the studio.'

'Suit yourself.' Dora stepped inside and slammed the front door behind her.

THIRTEEN

Since the July rally in Hyde Park, Alice continued to visit
Harriet as often as possible and always to coincide with a
meeting of the WSPU. Not only were the meetings inspiring
but since they'd opened her eyes to the cause of women's
suffrage, her life had felt more purposeful. How on earth had
she been indifferent to the subject before?

Alice took care to keep her involvement in the movement
concealed from her mother, who continued to maintain that
women were far too clever and influential to need anything so
inconsequential as a vote. Meeting women from all classes of
society was novel and refreshing and brought home to Alice
what a sheltered life she'd led. The only women she'd met
outside her social class until now had been servants. Fraternisa-
tion with them was frowned upon and would have felt awkward
to both sides. But amongst the members of the Marylebone
branch of the Union, Alice experienced camaraderie, unity and
a sense of belonging she'd never known before.

One day, she was in the WSPU office, stuffing envelopes
with newsletters for members when she became aware of
someone standing close to her. A woman in her forties was

gazing at her with intense interest. Alice hadn't seen her at the meetings before.

'It's Alice, isn't it?'

'I'm sorry. Have we met? I do apologise but I can't recall. I've met so many women at the meetings.'

The woman smiled. 'Yes, we've met. Many years ago.' She had hair the colour of ripe wheat, a clear bright complexion and hazel eyes. 'You were a small child. But you so resemble your mother that I knew at once it had to be you.' The woman extended her hand. 'Forgive me, I'm Eleanor Hargreaves.'

Alice accepted the proffered hand. 'Are you a friend of my mother, Mrs Hargreaves?'

'I'm afraid I haven't seen Lavinia in more than twenty years. Twenty-three to be precise.' The woman looked around the room, which was a hive of activity, before turning to Alice again. 'Could you be spared from your duties here for half an hour? I think we ought to talk and I'd much rather do it over a nice cup of tea.'

Mystified, Alice mumbled her agreement, then went to make her excuses to Harriet. 'Do you mind awfully if I slip out for half an hour or so? There's a lady over there who is an old friend of Mama and she insists on me joining her for a cup of tea.'

'Go ahead. See you later. But don't forget we have to drop off this lot at the post office on the way home.' Harriet indicated the growing stacks of envelopes.

They went to a nearby tearoom. Mrs Hargreaves led Alice to a table at the rear of the near-empty café. While they waited for the waitress to bring the tea and scones, they chatted, mostly about the suffrage movement, with Mrs Hargreaves explaining that she was in London for a few days to visit The British Library.

'I'm assisting my husband in research for a book he's writing on the Reverend Gilbert White. You know, the celebrated naturalist.'

Alice didn't know but decided not to admit that.

'We live in Hampshire. Not all that far from Selbourne, where White lived. My husband's a clergyman but, like his hero, he has a passion for all things of the natural world.'

Mrs Hargreaves poured the tea then fixed her gaze on Alice. 'You have no idea who I am, have you?'

Alice shook her head.

'I'd rather hoped there might still be a photograph of me at Dalton Hall.' Seeing Alice's blank expression, she pressed on. 'I'm your aunt, Alice. Your father's sister.'

Alice gasped. 'Papa has no sister.' Then conscious she was accusing the woman of lying, added quietly, 'At least none I'm aware of.'

'You weren't even five years old when I left Dalton Hall.'

'You lived with us?' If Alice's eyes were any wider, they'd have popped out. 'Why hasn't anyone mentioned you?'

'I'm afraid I left under a cloud as far as your mother was concerned. I'd hoped Neville would have been a little more understanding, but it seems not. I wrote many times to him, but my letters were all returned unopened. I suspect that was down to your mama.'

'Why? What happened?'

'I fell in love with someone inappropriate.'

'The Reverend Hargreaves?'

The woman looked amused. 'No. Not my husband – although I suspect Lavinia would have regarded him as equally unsuitable. I was only sixteen when I formed an attachment for a young man. As it turns out, your parents were quite right about his unsuitability. Albert Darley was a travelling salesman. Utterly charming, dashingly handsome and completely untrustworthy. I met him when I was out for a walk. I tripped over and twisted my ankle and he helped me up and escorted me home.

By the time we got there he had extracted a promise that I'd meet him the following week and over the course of that summer he charmed me into believing myself in love with him. He made a lot of empty promises that we would be married, closely followed by reasons why we must always wait just a little longer. I think one of the servants saw us together. There was a huge row and your parents insisted I give Albert up. I refused, determined to marry him. There were threats and things said that would have been best left unsaid and, to cut a long story short, I ran off with Albert. By the time I discovered he was already married, with a wife and two small children in Stoke-on-Trent, I was expecting a baby.'

Alice realised she was staring open-mouthed at the woman. Yet Mrs Hargreaves seemed sincere and credible and who would willingly make up such terrible things about themselves?

'What did you do?'

'After I told him about my condition, Albert Darley abandoned me. We were living in lodgings in Winchester at the time. Being a commercial traveller, he was away as often as he was home. It was several days before I found out he wasn't coming back. He wrote a letter to say he was sorry but his duty as a husband and father came first, and he was going home to his family. He appeared to have conveniently forgotten that he had started another one.'

Eleanor Hargreaves looked down at her untouched scone, then took a sip of tea. 'I'm much younger than your father. I always suspected I was a late surprise to my parents. When Albert Darley abandoned me, I was still only seventeen. Albert was twenty-nine.'

Alice gasped. 'Seventeen! What a dreadful thing to have happened to you.'

'Then the landlady told me Albert owed arrears of rent and she wanted me out. I didn't know where to turn. I swallowed my pride and wrote to your father, begging to be allowed to return to Dalton Hall. My letter was returned. I walked the streets of Winchester looking for work, but I had no references and no experience doing the kind of jobs available. I didn't even have the money to get me home to Dalton Hall.'

Alice bit her lip, her eyes welling as she tried to imagine her aunt's plight. It was hard to believe this of the elegant, self-contained woman sitting opposite her now.

'I was in despair and deeply ashamed, Alice. Unfit for tough reality because I'd led a privileged life, cosseted at Dalton Hall. I even contemplated ending my own life. Your parents had always assumed I'd marry someone suitable – probably of their choosing – or at worst would have remained at home as the spinster sister. I hadn't even come out in society when all this happened. I was terribly young and naïve.'

Instinctively, Alice stretched her hand out and touched that of Eleanor Hargreaves to offer comfort. 'But you managed. What happened?'

'I lost the baby. It was raining. I was exhausted, starving hungry, cold and at rock bottom. I walked and walked for hours. I'd no idea where I was or where I was heading. As I walked, I begged God to give me the courage to end my life and to forgive me for doing so. Then I experienced a sharp pain and knew at once I was losing my unborn child.' Eleanor looked around, suddenly conscious of the need to avoid anyone overhearing. 'I knew next to nothing of such matters. I thought I must be dying and believe me, Alice, I hoped I was.'

She told Alice how she had been found barely conscious by a woman who had been delivering a basket of eggs to a nearby village.

'Mrs Shepherd understood what had happened to me. She was a widow who'd carried nine children and miscarried five of them. Somehow, she got me to her cottage, put me to bed and cared for me. She fed me broth and bread and gradually my strength returned. If she hadn't happened upon me that day, I'd surely have died.'

'Thank goodness for Mrs Shepherd.'

'And that's how I met my husband.'

Fascinated by her aunt's story, Alice realised her tea was going cold. She gulped it down.

'Walter Hargreaves was the local vicar. Mrs Shepherd asked him to call at the cottage and pray for my recovery and for the soul of the dead child. He came again the following day and every day after that, and we talked. Gradually I became aware I was falling in love.' She gave a shy smile. 'After the shallow roots of my attraction for Albert Darley, my feelings for Walter grew slowly but bedded in deeply. But that's enough of me. I want to know all about you, Alice. I'm proud and delighted to know you're involved with the suffrage movement.'

The frankness of her newly discovered aunt made Alice feel the need to be more open than she would normally be. 'Mama doesn't know I'm involved. She believes women have no place in politics. I hate being deceitful, but I have no choice. The cause matters to me but I can't risk my parents finding out.' She looked up at Eleanor Hargreaves. 'Is that cowardly of me?'

'Not at all. There's no active group where I live. I come to meetings when I happen to be in London. The important thing is to do what one can.'

'Does the Reverend Hargreaves know?'

Eleanor grinned. 'Walter and I have no secrets. And yes, he heartily approves.'

'Imagine! Papa would have a fit if he knew what I did when I visit Harriet. As for Mama... But I'm to be married next year. Things may be different then.'

Eleanor beamed. 'That's marvellous. Tell me about him. Your fiancé.'

Alice blinked and lowered her eyes, embarrassed. 'We're not officially engaged yet. I barely know him. We've only met once. I was engaged to his older brother, but he died in an accident.'

Her aunt's face filled with concern. 'Oh, Alice, I'm so sorry.'

'Don't worry. I barely knew him either.'

'I see.' Eleanor frowned.

'I've come to accept it. To be frank, I care little whether I marry or not and I suspect my husband-to-be has as little interest in me as I in him. I'm sure we can come to an accommodation. And I'm all too aware that my choices are limited, Mrs Hargreaves.'

'Please call me Eleanor. It's probably a bit late for Aunt, but we don't need to be so formal.' She looked at Alice intently. 'Love can come at any time, you know.'

'Or not at all.' Alice gave her a tight-lipped smile. 'But the cause of women's suffrage goes on.'

'I suppose Victor is married now?'

'No.' A disturbing vision of her brother held between the thighs of Gilbert Cutler struck her. She took a gulp of air. 'Victor will be leaving soon. He's going to America to be employed in the firm of my future father-in-law. He's a stockbroker.'

'That sounds exciting. It seems the fortunes of your two families are already closely linked.'

Too closely, Alice thought, but merely nodded.

Eleanor Hargreaves wrote down her address and extracted a promise that Alice would write. 'Remember, Alice, if ever you need anything please contact me. I'd hate you ever to feel as alone and friendless as I once was.'

When Alice returned with Harriet to Portman Square she was surprised to find her family's chauffeur parked in the Wolseley outside the town house. He hadn't been expected until the following day. Gibson told her he'd been sent to bring her straight home to Dalton Hall where her parents needed to speak with her urgently.

Mystified, Alice said goodbye to Harriet and climbed into the back of the motorcar.

'Write to me at once and let me know everything is all right – as I hope it will be,' said Harriet, blowing a kiss up to her.

This summons home by her parents was a reminder that everything Alice had learnt at suffragette meetings impacted little on the reality of her day-to-day life. She was expected to comply with the wishes of her mother without question.

During the drive out of London, Alice replayed the conversation with Eleanor Hargreaves in her mind. It had been both enlightening and shocking. Alice was disgusted that her mother had kept the existence of her sister-in-law secret. While Eleanor was Papa's sister, Alice had no illusions that the choice to write her out of the family history was entirely of her mother's making. It pained her to acknowledge it, but her father was governed by the wishes of her mother. Alice tried to imagine pretending that Victor didn't exist but, despite what had happened in the gardener's shed, she couldn't do it. She may have fallen out with him, but were Victor ever to need her, she'd come to his aid. The pain in her aunt's eyes when Eleanor spoke of Alice's parents meant it was hard not to think badly of them.

Perhaps there was a way of healing these old wounds. All this happened over twenty years ago. Surely enough time had passed for her parents to forgive and forget? Eleanor was no longer a young girl under the age of consent, but a respectable married woman. A clergyman's wife no less.

An idea formed in Alice's head. She'd invite Eleanor to her wedding. When the invitations were sent out, she could tell her mother Eleanor Hargreaves was a friend she'd met through Harriet. That was close to the truth anyway. Times were changing and so were attitudes. What better occasion than a wedding to bring families together and heal old wounds?

The thought of her looming marriage to Edmund Cutler made her heart sink again. Whenever she was at a WPSU meeting she pushed the thought of her future nuptials to the back of her mind, but now her talk with Eleanor had moved it to the forefront and the familiar sinking feeling made her uneasy.

But there were upsides to marrying Edmund Cutler. It could provide the chance to reunite and reconcile her father with his sister. And the opportunity, once married, for Alice to become more closely involved with the votes for women cause. She didn't imagine Edmund would care one way or another how she spent her time. The best she could hope for in a marriage with him was indifference. She'd be free to pursue her own interests. There was also the possibility of eventually having children. Harriet was joyous at her pregnancy. Motherhood had never held much appeal for Alice, but perhaps she'd feel differently if she were expecting her own child. If Harriet and Lord Wallingford could rub along together, why couldn't she and Edmund Cutler? The marriage may even help assuage the burden of guilt she carried over the death of his brother.

As the Wolseley scrunched onto the long gravel driveway of Dalton Hall, she spotted her mother standing under the portico at the front of the house, awaiting her arrival.

'What took you so long?' Lady Dalton snapped. 'We sent for you hours ago.'

Alice glanced at Gibson, who was holding open the car door for her. 'Harriet and I were out taking tea with friends when Gibson arrived. Then the traffic was heavy.'

'Your father is waiting in the library for us.'

Alice handed her hat and gloves to the housemaid and followed her mother into the hallway.

The moment she entered the library, Alice sensed something was very wrong. Her mother glanced at her father then looked away quickly.

'It seems there is urgent business in Mr Cutler's office in

New York,' Lady Dalton said. 'Victor has travelled to America to sort it out. His ship sailed from Southampton this morning.'

'What?' Alice spluttered. 'He's gone? Without saying goodbye?' It stung.

'There was no time to let you know.' Lady Dalton plucked at the fabric of her sleeve. 'Mr Cutler insisted Victor leave immediately. He'll no doubt return to England on leave some time in the next few years. It's a big responsibility for Victor and a chance for him to prove himself.'

Lord Dalton looked away, staring into the empty fireplace. 'Your mother's right, Alice. We mustn't begrudge Victor the chance to make his way in the world.'

Alice knew all too well that her parents' enthusiasm for Victor taking this position was financially based. Somehow her snobbish mother had swallowed her misgivings about 'new money.' Maybe the fact that her son was earning it on the other side of the world made that easier.

'I can't believe he's gone without saying goodbye.' Victor must still blame her for walking into the garden shed that morning and breaking off her engagement. With him out of reach in New York, there was no hope of healing the wounds. She lowered her head and stared at the back of her hands. Perhaps a long absence was best. It would give Victor time to forgive and forget. Yet it was hard not to reach the conclusion that the real reason for the Cutlers packing him off across The Atlantic was to remove him from any whiff of scandal. She wished she hadn't allowed Victor to give her the cold shoulder since Gilbert's death. She should have found a way to talk to him, to clear the air between them.

Then it struck Alice. Victor would not be at her wedding. She gave a little cry.

Lady Dalton glanced sideways at her husband and gave him a meaningful look.

He coughed, clearly nervous. 'I'm afraid we have some bad news, Alice.'

She froze. What more was there? All she ever heard lately was bad news. Just as she had adjusted to each downturn, another appeared. She held her breath, braced for whatever it was.

'Your marriage to Edmund Cutler is off.'

Bad news? How was that possibly bad news? She felt profound relief.

Her father was grave faced. 'I'm afraid Mr Cutler informed his parents this morning that he was married yesterday.'

'Married?' Alice was dumbstruck. 'Yesterday?'

'It appears he and the woman concerned undertook a register office wedding. All very clandestine. Mr Cutler is trying to get the marriage annulled but there's little hope of that as his son is defiant.'

'It's so humiliating,' said Lady Dalton. She closed her eyes, her lips in a hard line.

Lord Dalton shook his head. 'Of course, Cutler's disowned him. The young man has refused to join the brokerage too. Intends to carry on with his stained-glass window making. As you can imagine, Cutler's hopping mad.'

Alice realised she'd been unconsciously holding her breath. She took in a gulp of air.

Lady Dalton shook her head. 'It's scandalous. The Cutler family have treated you abominably, Alice. The woman he's supposedly married is some little trollop he met at his art school. The daughter of a railway clerk at Euston Station, for Heaven's sake. A marriage in a shabby register office somewhere in North London. Utterly dreadful. Can you imagine? The shame of it. Poor Susan Cutler. She may be an American, but even Americans would draw the line at such vulgarity.'

'He must have been desperate to avoid marrying me.' Alice spoke quietly. It appeared neither parent heard.

'So, you see, Alice, it's an absolute blessing that Victor has gone to America. We must rely on him now to safeguard the future of the family.' Lord Dalton had a hang-dog expression.

In that moment Alice despised her father. How had they come to this? How had he been so profligate that he was forced to use his children as the means of preserving the family seat and assuring its future?

Lady Dalton was clearly of a different mind. 'Of course, if you hadn't been so headstrong in rejecting Gilbert Cutler, none of this would have happened.'

'That's enough, Lavinia. What's done is done. It's not fair to blame Alice. The blame clearly lies with the Cutler boy. Damn fool he must be.'

'May I go to my room now?' Alice stood up.

Her mother was about to protest, but Lord Dalton waved his hand in dismissal.

She fled upstairs, slamming the bedroom door behind her and moving over to sit in the window seat. The window was open, and she could smell the sweet scent of tobacco flowers drifting up from the garden. She leant out and saw them glowing, an ethereal fluorescent white in the gathering dusk beyond the dark bulk of the lavender plants.

Alice wanted to curl into a small tight ball. The suddenness of Edmund marrying was a slap in her face. Utter humiliation. He must hate her deeply to go to the extreme of organising such a furtive wedding. None of the Daltons' acquaintances would dream of marrying in a register office. It was not the kind of thing respectable people did. Edmund Cutler lived in Grosvenor Square and came from a wealthy family. His motivation was clearly expediency. A desperate measure to avoid having to marry Alice. She choked back her tears. Self-pity wouldn't serve her now. She cared nothing for Edmund Cutler. It was just wounded pride on her part.

Remembering her conversation with her new-found aunt

that afternoon, Alice resolved never to marry. Eleanor may have found happiness with her vicar, but it had been at a cost. And her terrible treatment by the man she ran away with was even worse than Edmund Cutler's behaviour. Men were cruel and heartless, lacking all consideration and kindness. Her own parents were hardly a model for marital contentment. The Earl of Wallingford saw Harriet solely as a means of securing his lineage. Alice herself had been offered like a traded commodity to both Cutler brothers, neither of whom had wanted her. If this was marriage then she wanted no part of it. She was weary of being like an unclaimed parcel, a piece of uncollected luggage. She'd be a spinster and be proud of it until the day she died.

And this would be the last night she'd ever spend under her parents' roof. Alice no longer cared where she went, as long as it was away from Dalton Hall.

FOURTEEN

RAVENSCOURT PARK, HAMMERSMITH

Edmund let himself into Whall's studio. He'd intended to continue working on cutting the glass pieces for a small hallway window he'd been asked to assist with, but he slumped at the workbench, head in hands and eventually went to sleep.

After an indeterminate time, during which night fell, he woke to hear the door opening. The electric light above his head flickered and lit up, making him blink, momentarily confused by his whereabouts.

'Good Lord! What are you doing here, Cutler? I thought you'd taken the day off.'

Edmund had told nobody about his nuptials, wanting to avoid any possibility, no matter how unlikely, of word getting back to his father in time to stop the marriage. He looked up guiltily at Christopher Whall. 'I got married today.'

'Married? Then why on earth are you here?'

'It's a long story, sir.'

'Then you'd better come into the house and I'll get Florence to make a pot of tea.'

Fortified by the tea and a ham sandwich provided by Florence Whall, Edmund unburdened himself of his story.

Whall listened in silence apart from the odd request for clarification.

When Edmund had finished, his boss shook his head. 'You poor devil. What a mess. That father of yours has much to answer for. But might his actions and words stem from grief over the tragic death of your brother?'

Edmund snorted. 'Grief? The only thing that motivates my father is greed. It guides everything he does. That and an insatiable desire for power.'

'Then I'm sorry. As a father myself I can't comprehend his behaviour. Let's turn then to the question of your bride.'

Edmund lowered his eyes and shuffled his feet.

Whall looked at his wife, who was sitting at the other end of the deal kitchen table, their short-haired terrier on her lap. 'My dear, do you have a perspective to offer from the feminine point of view?'

Florence Whall pursed her lips. 'Poor girl. Abandoned by her groom on her wedding night. What were you thinking, Mr Cutler?'

Shame shuddered through his body. 'I was angry. And afraid. For my mother.'

'Bad enough that one woman is mistreated without you starting on another. The last thing you ought to do is behave like your father.' She fixed her eyes on Edmund while absently stroking the little dog.

'I'd never harm Dora!' The thought was appalling. 'Never!'

'There are more ways to cause harm than physical blows. Put yourself in her shoes. How would you feel?' Her expression was sad rather than accusatory. 'Newly married. Meeting the in-laws for the first time only to be insulted by her new husband's father. Is it any wonder she put her foot in it about the ring? And then, to cap it all, the groom runs off and leaves her on her own.'

Remorse overcame him and he gave a strangled sob, then

coughed, took out his handkerchief and blew his nose. 'You're right, Mrs Whall. My behaviour was unforgivable.'

Christopher Whall touched him on the shoulder. 'You love this young woman?'

'Yes, yes!'

'Then go home to her at once.'

Edmund needed no further encouragement. He scraped back his chair and got to his feet. 'Thank you both.'

'One more thing, Edmund,' said Whall, using his given name for the first time. 'As you've a wife to support, there'll be an additional two shillings a week in your wage packet from now on.'

Edmund shook his boss's hand, full of gratitude. 'Thank you, Mr Whall. That will make a big difference.'

'Look after her, son.' Whall put an affectionate arm around his wife's shoulders. 'As the Bible says, a good wife has a price more than rubies. You've given up a lot for her – and for stained glass. The road to artistic success and recognition is an arduous one with many challenges. Mrs Cutler will be an essential support to you. You must love and treasure her, no matter what.'

Edmund caught the last tram back to the West End. Approaching the greengrocer's in Goodge Street he realised he'd forgotten to ask for a key and would have to knock.

A red-eyed Dora opened the door, candle in hand, misery etched onto her face.

Edmund's heart melted and all traces of his earlier anger left him. He took her in his arms. 'I'm sorry, Dora. So dreadfully sorry, my dearest darling.'

'Dad's let us have his bedroom and moved his things into my little one.' Her lip trembled. 'I thought you'd never come home, and I'd have to move them all back again.'

Edmund was about to point out that his plan was to find them digs in Hammersmith or Turnham Green, but if George Fisher was prepared to make sacrifices to accommodate him in his home, then Edmund must have the good grace to accept. Their outgoings would be lower – and more importantly, it was what Dora wanted. Whall's words about loving and treasuring her resounded in his ears.

The Goodge Street flat was small but much more spacious than the alternative, which would be a cramped room in a shabby building with shared facilities. Dora had made a big effort to make it comfortable and cosy. She'd made it clear she would cook and bake and keep house for him and her father – something she clearly wanted to do. She'd still have the pianoforte to play when she chose, and being near the heart of the West End, the flat was walking distance from the Central, should she eventually return to her studies. He could see the merit in the plan. And if Dora was happy, that was all that mattered. Wasn't it?

FIFTEEN
DALTON HALL

During a sleepless night, Alice weighed up her options. There seemed to be only two: staying at Dalton Hall and living with her parents' disappointment in her or seeking refuge with Harriet at Portman Square. The first was intolerable and the second would signify dependence, not to mention humiliation.

When it first formed in her head, the idea of seeking help from her newly discovered aunt seemed crazy. Yet, despite the brevity of their acquaintance, there had been something about Eleanor Hargreaves that made Alice trust her. Having gone through far worse privations at an even younger age, her aunt was well-placed to sympathise with her plight. Alice had an instinctive sense that Eleanor would do anything she could to help her. Their chance meeting and their shared belief in the importance of women's suffrage seemed portentous signs.

She decided against writing to her. The delay while she waited for a reply would give Alice the chance to change her mind. She didn't want to accord herself the time to withdraw from a plan that just a while ago she'd have considered foolhardy.

She got out of bed, pattered barefoot across to the window

and parted the curtains. The dawn hadn't yet broken and the fading moonlight was sufficient for her to see that it was just after a quarter to five by the clock in the archway leading to the stable yard. Better to leave now under cover of darkness, before the servants were up and about. Hurriedly cramming as many essentials as she could fit into a holdall, she dressed quickly and left the house.

Her parents would soon find out that she'd taken the train to London but there was little risk of them tracking her down beyond that initial journey, once she'd been swallowed up into the maw of the metropolis. Besides, there was little reason for them to try to find her. Her parents saw her as a saleable commodity more than a daughter. Her relationship with her family had never been close. Apart from Victor until... but she didn't want to think about all that.

At the end of the long gravel drive, she paused at the gates and looked back past the oak and cedar trees towards the grey slate roof of the house, silvered in the moonlight. The eighteenth-century Palladian wing of the house was out of sight, concealed by foliage, but the old Jacobean east wing was a dark bulk against the lightening sky. She swallowed, a wave of sadness striking her at leaving her home. But no matter how happy she'd been there in childhood, everything had changed now. And unless her father's circumstances underwent a dramatic transformation, it was likely the house would eventually be lost to the family anyway. Better to leave now on her own terms than to have it taken from her. Anyway, this wasn't the first time Dalton Hall had almost been lost. The English Civil War had cast the family into near ruin and crippling debt. Her ancestors had reversed their fortunes then by an astute combination of advantageous marriages and ventures into foreign trade. Perhaps Victor would achieve a similar rescue. It was clear her father was never going to accomplish it himself.

By the time she'd walked the mile and a half to the railway

station, the dawn had broken but it was still too early for her parents to have registered her absence. After consulting the ticket clerk she bought a single ticket to Waterloo.

Remembering her promise to write to Harriet, she penned a few lines while on the train. She kept to the brief facts – that her marriage had been called off and she was going away. Guiltily, she added that she was keeping her destination secret so her parents couldn't come after her. Sealing the envelope, she reflected on how unlikely that would be. She ended by wishing Harriet the best for the birth of her baby.

At Waterloo, she melted into the crowds of bowler-hatted businessmen and office clerks hurrying to work. She posted the letter then bought another single ticket for the nearest station to where her aunt lived. The train was almost empty, most railway passengers heading into the capital rather than out of it at that time of day.

It was a walk of just over two miles from the station to the village of Little Badgerton. Alice saw the church steeple and heaved a grateful sigh – the handles of her travelling bag were cutting into her palms and her shoulder ached from the burden of carrying it. She switched hands again and trudged on along the country lane.

The stone-built church appeared to be very old but the squat tower topped with a small spire was likely a more recent addition. Her stomach contracted as she drew nearer. What she had believed several hours ago to be a sensible plan, now seemed foolish and presumptuous. Her family had rejected her aunt, so why would Eleanor Hargreaves extend Alice the kindness that had been denied to herself?

Postponing announcing herself at the vicarage, Alice went into the church. It was empty, the air weighted with the scent of flowers, old timber and candle wax. She slipped into a pew close to the rear of the nave. The silence and the ecclesiastical smell calmed her racing heart.

Alice had no idea how long she'd been sitting in the church, but she was suddenly aware that she was cold and her joints had stiffened. It had been a strange day since her departure from the home she had known all her life, fleeing like a thief under cover of darkness. And now she could delay the inevitable no longer. It was time to face her aunt.

She got to her feet, stretching her aching limbs, when the silence was broken by the creak of a door at one side of the transept.

The vicar – for it could only be he as he was wearing a dog collar and cassock – noticed her at once and approached, smiling. He removed his round spectacles and tucked them into the pocket of his cassock before extending a hand in greeting. 'Good morning. I don't think I've had the pleasure of meeting you before.'

She told him her name, omitting the honorific.

'I'm here to see my aunt... Mrs Hargreaves.'

His face broke into a broad smile, and he reached for her hand again, wrapping it in both of his. 'Of course. I can't begin to say how happy Eleanor will be to see you. She told me about your recent meeting in London.'

Alice felt some of the tension ease from her body. But it was one thing to renew an acquaintance, quite another to seek a place to stay.

He was already ushering her out of the church. 'You're in luck. Usually, my wife makes parish visits in the morning, but today is her day for preparing her Sunday school class so she's at the vicarage.'

'Oh, but I don't want to interrupt her.'

'You won't be interrupting.' He smiled conspiratorially. 'Actually, she improvises the classes. Wings it, as they say in the theatre. But her weekly "preparation" is an excuse for Eleanor to enjoy one morning without the constant demands a parish makes on the incumbent's poor wife. She'll be delighted to see you. She's barely stopped talking about meeting you.'

They found Eleanor Hargreaves in a sunlit room at the back of the vicarage, where she was engrossed in a book. She dropped the book and jumped to her feet to greet her niece. 'Alice! What a wonderful surprise!'

The vicar said, 'I'll leave you two together – today's the parish council and the other members have high expectations regarding punctuality.' He chuckled, eyes twinkling. 'Alas, I frequently disappoint them.'

Eleanor Hargreaves embraced Alice then called the parlour maid to bring a tray of coffee and biscuits. 'Or would you prefer tea, Alice? You must have set off very early – you'll be hungry. Luncheon isn't for another two hours but I can ask Cook to prepare you a late breakfast.'

'No thank you. Coffee and biscuits will be perfect.'

Alice glanced at the jacket of the book her aunt had been reading. She read out the title. '*No Surrender*. Who's refusing to surrender to whom?'

'Women – to those who would silence us.' Eleanor tucked the book beside her. 'I'm nearly finished, then you shall have it to read. It's about our struggle for the vote. But it's a novel. You'll love it. Now, tell me what brings you here?' She frowned. 'Not trouble at Dalton Hall, I hope?'

Nothing but the whole truth was needed if Alice hoped to fall on the mercy of her aunt. She began with the morning of her planned engagement to Gilbert and offered a stumbling and embarrassed account of what she'd witnessed in the garden shed. Describing out loud what happened that morning was mortifying, and she avoided her aunt's eyes. Eleanor reached her hand out and took Alice's. 'My poor darling. That must have been a terrible shock. Did you tell your parents what you'd seen?'

'I tried to explain to Mama, but she brushed it off and acted as though I was exaggerating and making something out of nothing.'

'And Victor?'

'He couldn't deny what happened between them but promised their relationship was over and begged me not to break off the engagement.' She told Eleanor how she'd insisted on calling it off, and Gilbert's subsequent suicide. 'So, I have a man's death on my conscience. And Victor will never forgive me. He didn't speak to me after it happened, stayed at his club in town and avoided me. Then he went to America without saying goodbye.'

Eleanor Hargreaves shuddered, her face betraying her sadness. 'How could you have possibly known what that young man would do? And Victor was probably in shock – and feeling guilty too. You mustn't blame yourself.' Eleanor shook her head slowly, her eyes welling up. 'It's not a popular opinion, but if anyone is to blame it's a world that judges a man so harshly if he doesn't conform to the expectations of society.'

She paused, waiting while the maid brought the tray into the room.

When the maid had left, Eleanor poured the coffee. 'For a young man to take his own life he must have been truly distressed and utterly without hope. I imagine he was unable to face the consequences of his nature.'

'His nature?' Alice put down her cup. 'Don't you mean his behaviour? His perversions? For a man to kiss another man in that way goes against the laws of the land and *against* nature.'

Eleanor tilted her head slightly. 'I'm not so sure. For men to take the kind of risks Gilbert and your brother took, I struggle to believe it would be a deliberate choice. You were a little girl when Oscar Wilde was tried for immoral acts and sentenced to two years of hard labour. There was so much publicity around that trial and then more recently when he died in poverty in Paris. I find it hard to believe anyone would risk being found out unless they were genuinely and hopelessly in love. It must require a lot of bravery to admit to those kinds of feelings.' She touched Alice on the arm. 'I know it's no consolation to you, but it sounds as though your poor fiancé truly loved your brother. It also explains why Victor has left the country.'

Alice stared at her, dumbfounded.

Eleanor took a sip of coffee. 'But one thing is clear to me.' She fixed her gaze on Alice. 'You, Alice, did nothing wrong. Once you knew Gilbert had feelings for your brother, it was unthinkable that you'd want to proceed with the marriage. Victor will eventually understand that too – but assuming he loved Gilbert – he's doubtless too full of grief and guilt to think straight at the moment. He was angry with you, even though you were an innocent victim, but I have a feeling he is a tortured soul himself.' She stared at the back of her hands. 'Poor Victor. I will remember him in my prayers and hope that his transfer to America will bring him peace, allow him to forgive himself and build a new life.'

Alice put down her coffee cup. Her aunt's words had cast a new light on matters.

'Let me refill your cup.' Her aunt took the cup and saucer from her. 'All that happened some time ago. Back in June? What's brought you here today? I thought you mentioned you were about to marry the younger brother.'

Alice bit her lip. 'Last night I was told he married someone else.'

Eleanor gasped. 'I'm dreadfully sorry, Alice. Was there no warning?'

'No. But then we hadn't actually begun courting. Mama and his mother decided we needed to observe a couple of months of mourning then have a short engagement. The parents cooked the whole thing up between them. I had no say and evidently he didn't either. I suppose I can't really blame him if he already had a sweetheart. I didn't want to marry him anyway, but that doesn't stop me feeling humiliated. And it's all Papa's fault for trying to use me to improve his finances.' She filled Eleanor in on the details of the abortive wedding plans. 'I don't know why I even care. He was a horrible man and I feel sorry for the poor fool who married him.'

'Do you know her?'

'Gracious, no. According to Mama she's "a little trollop".'

Eleanor Hargreaves said nothing, but Alice noticed an almost indiscernible smile playing around her lips.

'I mean, I'm only quoting what Mama said. Anyone who'd choose to run off and marry that obnoxious man has to be an idiot.'

Eleanor smiled. 'You've certainly had a rotten time, Alice. I'm delighted you turned to me. You're welcome to stay here indefinitely and I speak for my dear Walter too.'

'But he doesn't know I came to stay yet.'

Eleanor nodded at the cloth holdall at Alice's feet. 'I imagine he has a pretty good idea.'

'I'll only stay as long as it takes for me to find employment somewhere. Perhaps I could become a governess or a lady's companion. Something that comes with live-in accommodation.'

'You're determined not to return to Dalton Hall?'

'Completely. I'll never go back there.'

A little tightening of her aunt's lips. 'Will you at least write and tell your parents you're safe? Don't close the door against any possibility of reconciling. You may change your mind about them when you've had some time to reflect.'

'I won't. Anyway, they wouldn't even bother to reply. Look what happened to you.'

'That was different. For a start, Lavinia is only my sister-in-law. She's your mother. And I did something wrong in running away with Albert Darley. You've done nothing wrong.'

Alice folded her arms. 'My reasons aren't about me, but about them. I've seen them both in a new light. Mama is snobbish and intolerant. She doesn't see me as a person – only as a pawn. She projects her own views of the world onto me, regardless of mine. And father's let his vanity cloud his judgement. They've pushed Victor out of the country and they don't care a fig what happens to me. Now all their attempts to marry me off have been scuppered, I'm just a burden to them.'

After a few moments, Eleanor said, 'Very well. But forget about finding a job with a place to live. Now that I've found you I have no intention of letting you go. I'm going to put you a delightful bedroom overlooking the garden. Rose will draw you a bath and you can relax until lunch is served. Later we can talk. I have so much to ask you – we've almost a lifetime to catch up on.' She jumped up and pulled her niece into a hug. 'Thank you for turning to me, Alice. You've no idea how much it means.'

SIXTEEN

It was a miserable wedding night. When Edmund took Dora in his arms she pulled away.

Thinking she was understandably nervous on their first night as a married couple, he doused the lamp as they undressed in the dark. Until now, Dora had been resistant to his kisses – something he'd put down to modesty. But he'd hoped things would be different now that they were man and wife. Yet now they were free to make love at last, Dora made it clear she was reluctant to do so. They lay side-by-side in the same bed, separated by an invisible line that Edmund felt unable to cross.

Days spent working in the studio reinforced Edmund's conviction that he'd found his vocation. His joy at following his passion was tempered by wretchedness every time he climbed the stairs to the flat.

Dora was cheerful as she served up the supper, happily chattering about her daily routine – trips to a nearby market, walks in the park and her favourite pastime of window-shopping.

Finally, she allowed him to consummate the marriage. The circumstances were unromantic. Instead of turning away from him when he got into bed beside her, she told him to do what he wanted to do. Astonished by the coldness of the invitation, he was paralysed.

'Go on then. Hurry up. Before I change my mind.' Her eyes were closed, and he could see that she was shaking.

Anxious to reassure and relax her, he leant over and began to kiss her gently. As soon as his lips met hers he forgot all the awkwardness of the past week. Her coldness must have been Dora's way of punishing him for what had happened after the wedding party. Although even now, he sensed she was submitting rather than actively participating. When he tried to remove her nightgown she tugged at it, pulling it back down over her body.

'Stop it. That's not decent.'

She made no sound, other than a small cry of pain when he entered her, and his own breathing was overwhelmed by the creaking of the bed springs.

When he ran his fingers through her hair, she grasped his wrist, jerking his hand away. 'Don't muss up my hair. I've just brushed it out.'

He was hurt, but nervous and anxious not to annoy her further, he said nothing. All his longings had led to this arid act that she clearly wanted to be over as quickly as possible.

When it was done, he lay motionless on his back staring at a narrow beam of light across the ceiling. He was hollowed, dismayed that his dreams for this moment had culminated in a cold and mechanical act. They had never been so physically intimate and yet so utterly far apart.

'I hope I didn't hurt you,' he said.

Silence.

'What's the matter, Dora? Tell me what's upset you. If I don't know, how can I make things better? Didn't you know what would happen?'

Nothing.

He waited, but when she remained mute, he tried again. 'I love you, Dora. I only want to make you happy.'

In the darkness came the sound of a snort.

Pain stabbed deep inside him. 'I thought you loved me too?'

'I'm fond of you. But *love*? I love looking at clothes I can't afford to buy. I love singing along at the music hall. I love chocolate. It's nothing personal, Edmund, but I can't imagine loving you or *anyone*. I just don't feel that way about other people.' She paused. 'Apart from my dad, but that's different.'

'You didn't like what we just did, did you? But it will get better. Once we're more used to each other.'

'Do be quiet and go to sleep, Edmund.'

He turned on his side, his back to her, but sleep eluded him. How had it all gone so wrong?

The following Sunday Edmund went to see his mother while his father was at the golf course. His worst fears were realised. When he walked into the drawing room, she turned away from him. Her face bore the marks of fading bruises and beside her chair a stick was propped which he gathered she was using to help her walk. She brushed away his concerns and begged him not to do what he wanted – which was to await Herbert Cutler's return and dish out the same treatment to him.

'No, Eddie, please! It'd make things worse for me. Your father was angry but it's passed now. And it's not as bad as it looks.'

'What do you mean? Your face must have been black and blue and you're using a stick. Have you seen a doctor?'

'Yes. I told him I fell downstairs. Nothing's broken. Just a sprain. Honestly, I'm perfectly all right now. It won't happen again.'

Edmund punched one hand into his open palm. 'I'd like to give him a taste of his own medicine.'

She placed a hand on his sleeve. 'It would make things worse. You know that, Edmund. Enough about me. How about you? I'm sorry Dora was treated so rudely. She's such a pretty girl. No wonder you fell for her.' She smiled but her face was sad.

'I warned her. I begged her not to come with me. She wouldn't believe me. I'm sorry. After your kindness in giving us the ring.'

'At least now she understands.'

'Yes,' he said. 'Of course.' But he knew Dora didn't.

When he returned home, Edmund suggested a walk in Regent's Park. As soon as Dora had washed the dishes from the Sunday dinner, she went into the bedroom, returning wearing a dress Edmund had never seen before. It was in a pink grosgrain fabric with leg of mutton sleeves and a tight waistline that dropped in a V-shape at the front while two rows of decorative fabric buttons descended, military style, from waist to hem. Edmund caught his breath. She looked stunning, the pale pink contrasting with the burnished brown of her hair. Giving a twirl, she smiled, then rushed over and dropped a kiss on Edmund's cheek.

'You look beautiful, Dora. I haven't seen you wearing that before.'

'That's because it's new.' She went back into the bedroom from where he could hear her opening the small cupboard where she kept her clothes. 'So's this,' she said. On her head was another extravagant hat– this one adorned in a profusion of pink ostrich feathers. 'Do you like it?' Her face was like a child's at Christmas.

Edmund blinked. If only she had stuck to the perky little hat she'd worn the day he met her at the Central. It had been perched on top of her glorious hair, and its size and shape had perfectly complemented her delicate features. The oversized confections she had taken to wearing overwhelmed her so that one saw the hat rather than the person. But he suppressed his reservations and delivered the expected compliment. It was a relief to see her so happy.

They walked towards the park in silence as he wondered where she had obtained the money to buy these new clothes. The housekeeping he handed over to her – the entirety of his wages – wasn't enough to pay for fashions like these. But something made him proceed with caution rather than confronting her. Perhaps her father had gifted her some money.

It was a fine day, and the park was busy with couples taking a Sunday afternoon constitutional, many listening to a brass band and others hurrying towards the zoo. They found themselves by the boating lake and Edmund suggested they take a ride in a boat.

'No thank you very much.' Dora shuddered. 'I'm not going out on the water. I've no wish to drown.'

Edmund looked across at the families with children happily paddling the wooden boats around the lake, fearless of the prospect of drowning. 'It's only four feet deep,' he said. 'You wouldn't drown, Dora. The boats are sound and the weather's perfect.' He smiled at her, amused by her evident misgivings. 'Besides I'm a strong swimmer and I promise I'd rescue you.'

'I told you, no,' she snapped. 'I'm going nowhere near that lake. It's bad luck.'

Puzzled, he asked why.

'Dad nearly drowned there when he was fifteen. It was in winter, and the lake was frozen. He was sliding about on the ice and there were lots of people skating. The ice cracked and they all fell into the freezing water. Hundreds of people including him. He was lucky someone pulled him out from under the ice and dragged him onto the bank. Forty people died in the lake that day.'

'I didn't know.'

'Well now you do. I think they should have filled it in completely, but they just drained it and made it shallower.' Dora's lip jutted out. 'It's horrible. Like a graveyard.'

Shocked, Edmund said, 'They didn't leave the bodies there, surely?'

'Course not. But it's still horrible and it gives me the willies. My dad could have died.'

'Well, let's be thankful he didn't.' Edmund gave her a reassuring smile.

They walked on until the boating lake was out of sight, then went to sit on a bench. There was an ice cream cart and Edmund went to buy her a cornet. Dora took off her white gloves to eat it and he felt a rush of affection for her, despite the absurdity of her hat. As she held the cone up to lick the ice cream he noticed her wedding finger. Instead of the pretty gold band with the delicate inset diamonds, she was wearing another ring, larger, unsubtle, with a cluster of diamonds surrounding a pair of oversized garnets.

He reached for her hand and drew it towards him. 'What's this? Where's the ring I gave you?'

'Gone.'

'What do you mean? What have you done with it?'

'When the Spindlemanns told me how much it was worth, I asked them to flog it up Hatton Garden and I got this one, plus the money to treat myself to some new clothes. The stones are only paste but no one would know and at least it's not some old hand-me-down. I got to choose it myself.'

He let her hand fall and stared at her, open-mouthed.

She tutted. 'Don't get all funny with me. After the way your parents insulted me, you can't seriously expect me to want to wear a ring that belonged to your family.'

'It was a precious heirloom.'

She rolled her eyes, exasperated.

'My father beat my mother black and blue because of her giving you the ring. Do you have any idea what she went through as a result?'

'She didn't give it to me. She gave it to you because you were too stingy to buy me a new one.'

Indignation gave way to remorse. It was wrong of him to place the blame for his mother's beating entirely on Dora. It was his fault. He had defied his father to marry Dora, knowing full well that there might be consequences for his mother. And yet his father could hardly have blamed her if the ring hadn't been mentioned.

Dora pursed her lips. 'Anyway, you said how nice my new gown is. Surely you want your wife to look pretty. Don't you care?'

'Of course, I do. But it doesn't take fancy clothes to make you pretty, Dora. That ring was special. I wanted you to wear it. I wanted one day for you to hand it down to our first child. My mother suffered so you could have it.'

She huffed. 'You're exaggerating about him hitting her. I don't believe it. Rich people in fancy houses don't beat up their wives.'

Edmund stared at her, trying to follow her crazed logic.

'It's done now. And it was *my* ring to do with as I chose. You should have told me if it came with conditions. I happen to think I got a splendid bargain. A special dress, a wonderful hat and a replacement ring that I got to pick myself.' She held her hand out, fingers splayed to show off the ring. 'It was the loveliest in the Spindlemann's shop.'

These last words stung most deeply. The thought of Stanley and his parents helping Dora choose a replacement wedding ring and no doubt cajoling her into selling his grandmother's one was a bitter pill to swallow.

Edmund's mouth felt dry. He watched her licking the rest of her ice cream, telling himself he'd better accept he had made a terrible mistake in marrying her, and try to find a way to carry on. Constantly churning over his decision to marry her, wishing he'd acted differently, would change nothing. He must try to make the best of things, no matter how difficult that would be. He was tied to Dora for the rest of their lives.

The sale of the ring was a watershed. His marriage was increasingly fraught and miserable. Edmund sought consolation from working in Christopher Whall's studio. His love for his craft grew daily. There was a strong fellowship among the assistants and Whall was a patient and good-humoured teacher. Every day, when he got a chance for a short break, if the weather was fine, Edmund walked in the adjacent Ravenscourt Park and if it was raining, visited the public library in Ravenscourt House. While the work was a welcome distraction, his walks were troubled by a growing acknowledgment that his feelings for Dora had evaporated.

They'd now been married for two months and their relations were increasingly strained. Conversation was forced, shallow and inconsequential. Dora rarely demonstrated any affection towards him, let alone love. He had never felt lonelier.

She was only willing to have marital relations once a week on a Friday night. That was the night that George Fisher went to the pub and returned after closing time to collapse almost comatose onto his bed. Dora was concerned that sounds travelled through the thin partition walls of the flat. Edmund softened his harsh judgement of her – although remaining disappointed by her lack of affection and failure to respond with any enthusiasm to his lovemaking. She still refused to let him see her naked and turned away whenever he so much as removed his shirt. Edmund resolved to raise again the idea that they find a place of their own to live. Even though George Fisher was affable and welcoming, Edmund felt like an inter-

loper. The bond between father and daughter was strong. He
was always going to play second fiddle.

He set aside his dislike of the music halls and went with
Dora to a variety show. The performance was crude and
raucous – as were the people around them in the gods. But he
nursed the hope that doing this for Dora would make her happy
and perhaps more willing to show him some affection. Sitting
next to her in the darkened hall he reached for her hand and
watched as she sang along with gusto to the choruses, roaring
with laughter until tears ran down her cheeks. How little they
had in common. How incapable he was of ever making her
happy. These glimpses of the joyful Dora he'd fallen in love
with made him bitter and angry – not at her – but with himself.
This laughing happy-go-lucky Dora had mostly given way to an
unsmiling woman who looked at him from under her impossibly
long eyelashes with resentment that he sometimes thought
bordered on disgust.

Edmund believed the only reason she had agreed to marry
him was that she had laboured under the misapprehension that
once they were married, his father would have a change of heart
and offer them financial support. Her ambition of moving up in
the social hierarchy had been dashed by her humiliation in
Grosvenor Square. It was clear she laid the blame for this on
Edmund rather than his father.

He knew now he had never loved his wife and never would
– nor could. His dream of an artistic fellowship – a communion
of souls – had vanished. Dora's portfolio gathered dust on top of
the wardrobe. The more he knew her, the less he understood
her. Only her undeniable beauty remained to mock him for his
shallow infatuation and lust.

One Friday evening, they were sitting alone in front of the
fire in the parlour, George having left as usual for his weekly
pilgrimage to The One Tun. Edmund was immersed in reading

The Stones of Venice by Ruskin. Looking up, he caught Dora watching him.

She smiled at him. 'What are you reading?'

He told her.

'Huh,' she snorted. 'Only you would read a book about stones.'

'It's not about stones. It's about architecture.' But she'd already lost interest,

slumped in a chair, idly thumbing through the pages of the *Penny Illustrated Paper*.

'What are *you* reading then?'

'I'm just looking at the pictures. The articles are boring. Unless it's a murder. I do like them. But they're thin on the ground at the moment. This magazine is full of dreary stuff about how people celebrate Christmas. Look.' She thrust the newspaper towards him. 'Christmas decorations in a fire station!' She made a scornful sound. 'Why would anyone be interested in that? As bad as you and your dreary old books.' She cast the paper aside. 'We never seem to get a decent murder these days.'

A decent murder?

She leant back in her chair and studied him as though he were an unusual specimen in a museum. 'By the way, I'm expecting a baby. Due next June according to the doctor. Dad's promised to buy us a cradle. I've seen a darling one in the window of Maples.' Dora's eyes narrowed as she took in his shocked reaction. 'I'd better get the dinner on.' She got up and went into the kitchen, leaving Edmund trying to comprehend her words. She'd told her father before she'd told him!

Shaken, he followed her into the kitchen. 'Are you serious, Dora? We're really going to have a baby?'

'So it seems.' She shrugged. 'Although I think it would be more accurate to say *I'm* going to have one.'

'You don't seem very pleased about it.'

'Why would I be? I've never been keen on children. And Mrs Spindlemann warned me it hurts like billy-o when the baby comes.'

So, Mrs Spindlemann had also been told before him.

'It's going to be crowded here,' she added.

'Then we'll move. I'll start looking tomorrow.'

'Not Hammersmith. I'm not going out to the suburbs. If you can't find somewhere better that's central, we'll stay put here.' She took some potatoes from the vegetable basket and started to peel them, while Edmund stared at her, trying to process the news.

She continued scraping as she spoke. 'You'll have to ask your father to give us some money so we can afford a bigger place. We haven't had a penny out of him and he's rolling in it. It's his grandchild. Having a baby's expensive. We'll need more than Dad's cradle. You have to ask for some of what's rightfully yours.' She put down the potato and her knife, then wiped her hands on her apron and turned to face him. 'Once your father knows he has a grandchild on the way he'll change his tune. Maybe he wants nothing to do with *you*, but he'll have a different attitude to a baby who's done nothing wrong.'

'What are you talking about? Are you saying *I've* done something wrong?'

'You must have done, for him to cast you aside like that.' She narrowed her eyes. 'And don't you dare say your mistake was marrying me.'

'My father's getting nowhere near our baby.'

Dora snorted. 'What about your precious mother then? Don't think I don't know you sneak off to meet her every now and then. I've seen you.'

'What?'

'I followed you last Sunday. You went to the British Museum and she was waiting on the steps for you.' Dora gave a little chuckle. 'I was checking you didn't have a fancy woman.'

Edmund stared, staggered by what she was saying. 'Why are you so angry with me, Dora?'

She put the potatoes into a saucepan, added salt and filled the pan with water. 'I shouldn't have married you. You and your fancy airs and graces and your great big house in a posh square. So much for that, eh? I should have settled for Stanley. He asked me often enough. I thought I was bettering myself in choosing you, but I've ended up worse off than if I'd married him. At least he makes a good living and has a share in a business that one day will be all his.'

Edmund's head jerked back in shock. 'What are you saying? Are you in love with Stanley Spindlemann?'

Dora lit the gas under the pan. 'Don't be daft! In love with Stanley? Where does love get you? I've told you, Edmund, I don't believe in all that guff. But Stan's a decent man and he makes more than a bob or two, what with the shop and his silversmith work. He doesn't have daft pie-in-the-sky ideas like you. Solid, he is.'

'You wish you'd married him instead of me?'

Dora cocked her head to one side and looked thoughtful. 'Maybe I do.' Her mouth formed a rueful smile. 'Marrying you was meant to be a step up the ladder. Dad always reckoned I should aim high because of who my mother was.' She gave a long slow sigh then turned to look at him, hands on hips.

'Stan would have married me like a shot. And he wouldn't have kept pestering me to move to blooming Hammersmith or to go back to that stupid art school.'

She pulled her apron off, flung it on the table and went into the bedroom, slamming the door behind her.

Edmund sank into a chair, head in hands.

Susan Cutler was waiting outside the National Gallery when Edmund hurried up the steps. She looked pale and had lost weight. Her eyes were sad. A light had gone out in her since Gilbert died. And she was still walking with a stick. Edmund swallowed, guilt and remorse flooding through him, as it did whenever he saw her.

Once they were inside, she said, 'I can't stay long. Your father's golf game was cancelled and instead of going to Sunningdale, he's staying in town and meeting someone at his club. I've no idea how long he'll be. I can't stay out long and risk him discovering we've been meeting.'

'You think he suspects? I don't want to put you at risk.'

'I wouldn't be here if he suspected anything.'

Anger welled up in Edmund. 'Has he been hitting you again?'

'No. He hasn't laid a hand on me since that day ... but we've been through all this before, Edmund.'

'I know, but I wish—' He squeezed his hands into tight fists.

'Don't. It was a fit of anger and if I give him no cause, I'll be perfectly safe. Now tell me about you.'

'Dora's having a baby.'

Her eyes widened. 'Edmund! That's wonderful. I'm very pleased for ...' Her voice trailed away. 'You don't look happy about it.'

For a moment he was going to tell her the whole miserable story, but he didn't want her pity. He didn't want to say out loud that he'd made a terrible mistake. Especially since his mother had suffered for it.

'Dora wants me to ask Father for money. She seems to believe that the knowledge he is about to become a grandfather will encourage him to reconcile.'

'Ah.' Her lips tightened.

'Exactly.'

'If anything, it will make him angrier. He's been spending a fortune on lawyers, trying to find a way to extricate you from the marriage. But a baby... that makes it impossible, short of divorce, and he won't want the scandal.'

Ironically, the idea of being extricated from his marriage was appealing, but he couldn't possibly abandon Dora now there was a child on the way. Nor could he give his father the satisfaction. 'It'll be hard financially and will likely set me back a few years but I'm happy about becoming a father.'

Susan smiled and took his hand, stroking the back of it. 'I think it's marvellous. What does Dora think?'

Edmund shrugged, unable to confess that his marriage was a spectacular failure. 'Still adjusting to the idea. She's not used to children, being an only child. She'll feel differently once the baby arrives.'

'You know I don't have access to money, or I'd help out.' She unhooked her earrings and placed them in his palm, closing his fingers over them. 'Take these and sell them. They're not worth much but it should help a little. But don't let Dora know where the money came from. If your father finds out—'

That made his mind up. 'I won't put you at risk again.' He pressed the earrings back into her hand. 'Keep them. I have to support my family myself. I had a pay rise from Mr Whall when I married and if I carry on making progress I'll soon be involved in bigger commissions. I chose my career and I chose to marry Dora so I take full responsibility.' He wished he could say he regretted neither decision but that would be true only of one of them.

As the months of Dora's pregnancy passed, Edmund spent less time at home. The atmosphere in the flat was increasingly claustrophobic as if Dora's swelling belly diminished the cramped space further. As her time drew nearer, sharing the marital bed became harder, as she was restless during the night, so Edmund took to sleeping on the couch in the parlour.

The baby was born early – and rapidly. Edmund returned home from work one evening to find George at the table eating fish and chips out of the newspaper.

Edmund looked at his father-in-law in surprise. 'A fish supper? Where's Dora?'

'Resting.' George beamed at him. 'Our girl's had a busy day today. The baby arrived in a hurry. Mrs Spindlemann helped deliver her as there was no time to fetch the midwife. That woman's a treasure.'

Edmund didn't wait to hear more. He dashed into the bedroom. Dora was sitting up in bed, propped against the pillows, suckling the new baby. She jerked the bedsheet up to cover her exposed breast. 'It's polite to knock first. Come back when I've finished feeding her.'

He remained rooted to the spot. 'A girl.' He felt a surge of joy. 'May I see her?'

'Not while she's feeding. It's not decent. I'll call you when she's done. Greedy little thing she is.' Despite her dismissive words, Dora was grinning.

Edmund returned to the parlour and sank into a chair.

'A real bonny baby isn't she?' said George.

'I couldn't see her properly as Dora was feeding her. She threw me out.'

'Oh, right. She's a good girl, my Dora. Modest, like her dear mother.'

Edmund said nothing.

When Dora called to him, the baby was asleep. Edmund gazed at her little face and his chest contracted. His own child. His daughter. At that moment he knew he would do anything to protect her. Anything at all. 'May I hold her?'

Dora looked dubious but then nodded. 'Try not to wake her and don't let her head flop back. Put your hand underneath to support it.' She smiled as he took the child gently and cradled her in his arms.

The baby was perfect. A miniature miracle. Tiny eyelids tightly shut, a button nose, a little rosebud mouth, and a covering of dark silky hair on her head. 'She has your hair,' he said. 'She's beautiful.'

'A bit scrunched up,' was Dora's response. 'But she's sweet, isn't she?' She grinned at him. 'I'm glad we've had her. She's got your eyes.'

He felt an unexpected rush of affection for Dora. 'Well done – and thank you.'

'We did all right, didn't we? It all happened very quickly. At least Mrs Spindlemann saved us the one and sixpence we'd have had to pay the midwife. Now leave me to sleep as I'm very tired.'

'We need to choose a name.'

'Already decided. She's going to be Charlotte, after my mother.'

Argument would be futile – and having no objection to the name anyway, he nodded and handed Charlotte back to Dora.

SEVENTEEN

Alice settled quickly into life with her aunt and uncle in Little Badgerton. Determined not to be a drain on the household expenses, she was keen to find a paying job.

'No need for that, Alice,' said her aunt. 'I can't imagine how I managed before you came. You were a stalwart at the Mothers' Union tea yesterday. You lightened the load considerably.' She paused. 'But I'm being selfish, aren't I? Perhaps a part-time job would be good for you. Did you have anything in mind?'

'That's just it. I'm qualified for nothing. I have no experience. No skills. I'm hoping getting a job may be the means of acquiring some.'

Alice was arranging garden flowers in a vase. 'All I need is someone prepared to take a chance on me. Just a few mornings a week. I don't want to give up the parish work I'm doing with you.' She hesitated. 'I was also wondering about starting a local branch of the WSPU.'

Eleanor clapped her hands. 'What a splendid idea.' Then something caused her to frown. 'Definitely a women's suffrage group, but perhaps not the WSPU. I'm not sure about some of their tactics. All the window-smashing that's been happening lately. I don't think you win people around by vandalising their property.'

'None of us in our local London branch did anything like that.'

'Maybe not. But it's on the increase. Mrs Pankhurst and her "Deeds not Words" is fuelling it. Believe me, Alice, I'd like nothing more than to hurl a toffee hammer through the window of some of those politician's houses but if a cause is just, it can always be argued with words.'

'Only if people are prepared to listen to the arguments. So far the politicians are proving extremely obdurate – in particular Mr Asquith.'

'True. But violence achieves nothing other than to alienate people.'

'So what should we do?'

'The National Union of Women's Suffrage Societies is committed to campaigning peaceably. There's a branch in Farnham. Why don't we pay them a visit tomorrow and get some information about establishing an offshoot in Little Badgerton?'

Alice grinned. 'Splendid idea.' She hesitated a moment. 'But what will Walter say? His parishioners may not approve of his wife and her niece being involved in the campaign for the vote.'

'Walter's a staunch supporter. He thinks it's a disgrace that we're denied the right to vote. Some of the most vocal supporters of the cause are clergymen, and Walter's no exception.'

The next day, Alice and Eleanor took the pony and trap and drove into Farnham. They were met by a Miss Dodds, a rather officious woman who clearly resented them interrupting her morning.

'As you're in Hampshire you need to affiliate with a branch

in the same county. The nearest is Petersfield. Since Little
Badgerton is only a village it hardly seems worth setting up a
full branch but I'm sure the Petersfield lot will suggest how to
establish an offshoot.' The woman turned away to get on with
what she was doing.

Alice persisted. 'What kind of things would we need to do?'

The woman waved a hand dismissively. 'Not up to me.
Speak to the parent branch and find out what they need. It'll be
the usual stuff. Fund raising. Recruitment. Missionary work.
Publicising events and speakers at the parent branch as I
imagine your village is too small to attract speakers in your own
right.' She peered at them over a pair of spectacles that needed
polishing. 'Have you had any involvement in the cause at all?'
She folded her arms. 'The NUWSS aren't interested in
breaking windows, so if you're a militant you can forget about
joining us.'

Alice was indignant. 'I've never smashed a window in my
life and I've no intention of starting now.'

The woman went to a desk at the back of the cramped
office, opened a drawer and took out a piece of paper and
thrust it at Eleanor. 'Here's a checklist of the kind of activities
and tasks that need to be done. But speak to Petersfield first.'
She thumbed through a booklet filled with names and
addresses. 'The only name I have is Mrs Badley. She's the wife
of the Headmaster at Bedales. Now, unless there's anything
else, I have to get to the printers to pick up some fliers. Votes
for Women!' She spoke the last three words with a perky
energy.

Thanking her, they left the office.

'What an odd woman.' Alice rolled her eyes.

'She was rather lacking in the social graces. But suffragists
are a diverse lot. After all, the only thing that we have in
common is a desire for the vote.' Eleanor unhitched the pony
and climbed into the trap. 'You're right though. I'm jolly glad

Miss Dodds wants nothing to do with us. Let's hope we get more of a welcome in Petersfield.'

By chance there was a public meeting scheduled at the Corn Exchange in Petersfield the following week. When the two women arrived, the hall was packed to hear a series of local speakers, including Mrs Amy Badley from Bedales School. She spoke of the importance of equal opportunities in education, citing the example of her husband's pioneering school which had been co-educational for the past ten years.

Before the arrival on stage of the main guest speaker, there was a musical interlude provided by a string quartet and the serving of tea and cakes. Alice and Eleanor squeezed through the throng to reach Mrs Badley, who welcomed their offer to help the cause.

'We were fortunate enough last year to have Mrs Pankhurst herself address us at the school and that helped drum up a lot of local interest. There's unequivocal support among the teachers as well as many of the villagers in Steep, and we have a growing interest here in the town too.' Mrs Badley, gave a little shrug and looked about her. 'Of course there's a big difference between sympathy for the cause and active participation. And I myself can't do as much as I'd like, given my duties at the school.'

The bell rang to herald the imminent arrival on stage of the speaker. 'Catch me after this finishes and I'll have some suggestions for how you could help.'

And so the Little Badgerton Women's Suffrage Society was born. At first, the only members were Alice and her aunt, so their priority was to drum up support. Most of the responsibility for this fell on Alice, as calls on Eleanor's time as the wife of the vicar were extensive.

Armed with propaganda leaflets supplied by Mrs Badley, Alice began a systematic canvass of the village, knocking on doors and attempting to engage the woman of each house in a discussion of the importance of extending the franchise to women. All too often her reception was cool.

'My husband wouldn't like it.'

'I'm far too busy to bother with that.'

'I'm not interested in politics. Better to leave it up to the men. They understand that kind of thing.'

'Huh! That's just for posh women with plenty of money. Not for the likes of me.'

'It's all very well for girls like you with plenty of time on your hands. I've a husband and five children to care for.'

Her attempts to counter these objections usually resulted in a rapid closing of the door.

Disheartened and weary after several fruitless days of trying to gather support, Alice was on the point of giving up.

'No one cares two hoots about the suffrage,' she declared over lunch one day. 'The working people are all too busy, and the wealthy think it's beneath their dignity. I had a humiliating experience at a big house outside the village today. I knocked on the door and explained I was there to speak to the lady of the house.' She gave Walter a sheepish look. 'The maid showed me into the drawing room, which was full of people. All men actually. It turns out it was a gathering of the committee of the local Conservative party. They took one look at me and my Votes for Women sash and threw me out. The maid must have thought it would be a jolly jape.'

To her relief, Walter didn't laugh at her, but put a hand on her shoulder. 'I can imagine how that must have felt, Alice, but don't worry about those old duffers. If they'd any sense they'd have offered you a drink and asked you to explain why you believe women should have the vote.' He shook his head. 'Short-sighted. It'll have to happen eventually. They could have seized the opportunity to win your goodwill as a potential future voter. They're like King Canute commanding the tide to recede. Don't give up. I haven't known you long, but you strike me as a plucky young woman. Remember, you have right on your side.' He sighed. 'Even if days of pounding the lanes doesn't yield a single volunteer, you will at least have increased those women's awareness of the Cause. We'll put a notice in the parish newsletter about the group. You never know, there may be someone who wasn't ready to sign up on her doorstep but may yet seek you out.'

Grateful, Alice thanked him and set forth again after lunch with renewed energy.

By the end of the month, the Little Badgerton Women's Suffrage Society had grown to include Miss Trimble, a young schoolteacher, Mrs Collins, the wife of the local doctor and – rather reluctantly – Miss Pendleton, who played the church organ and had been 'encouraged' by the vicar to enrol. In spite of her initial hesitance, Miss Pendleton soon proved to be an enthusiast for the cause and went about her tasks with gusto.

Alice's door-knocking also gained her a friend. Viola Fuller lived in a cottage just off the road between Little Badgerton and Petersfield. Viola's husband was a travel writer and away from home for extended periods, leaving his pregnant wife to cope with two small children. Alice never met Robert Fuller. During the periods when he was home in Hampshire, he spent his days closeted in his study writing and guarded his time with Viola jealously. Viola was clearly as in love with her husband now as the day she'd met him when she was sixteen and he was working as a gardener to support his attempts to build his writing career. But his long absences took their toll and Viola's loneliness was palpable.

Walter Hargreaves referred to Viola as 'The Wanderer's Wife,' but knew little of her since the couple didn't attend church. Despite protests from both Alice and Eleanor that it was unfair to reference a woman as a mere adjunct to her husband, the name stuck between the three of them.

Before long, Alice came to depend on her impromptu visits to her friend, as Viola was the only source of interesting conversation outside the vicarage. Sometimes Viola held the door open only a crack and told her Robert was at home and she was unable to invite her in. Though hurt at first, Alice soon accepted this and made sure to avoid calling when she knew The Wanderer was in residence.

It was only after she'd known Alice for several months that Viola told her she and Robert weren't actually married. 'Robert says the only thing that matters is what's between the two of us. The vows we make to each other. There's no need for the law or the church to be involved. We both believe marriage is an outdated institution and a form of servitude. A couple should be together because they choose to be, not because a piece of paper declares it to be so.'

Alice was shocked although she could see some merit in the sentiment. 'Don't you feel insecure?' she asked her friend.

'Why should I? We're together because we love each other. That's not going to change.'

Viola had been baking and the small kitchen was filled with the aroma. She cut a slice of lardy cake and handed the plate to Alice, cutting another slice for herself. 'But I do worry sometimes for the children. It doesn't matter while they're small but once they go to school … should someone find out… other children can be so cruel. I'd hate for them to suffer for something they have no say in. It's why I took Robert's name.'

'Have you told him about your concern?'

Viola smiled. 'Yes. But he brushes it off. Says we're bringing up our children to be resilient and independent.' She sighed. 'But that doesn't stop me worrying. When he's away on one of his journeys, or shut up here in his study, it's I who will have to deal with the tears and anguish if they're bullied.'

Alice stretched out a hand and placed it over her friend's. Viola eased hers away with an apologetic smile. 'Sorry. I'm feeling a bit low today. Missing Robert. That's all.'

Viola didn't mention her marital status again, but increasingly Alice sensed that there was a deep vein of unexpressed unhappiness in her. Her friend confided that Robert suffered from periodic bouts of depression – black moods and anger when he would storm out of the cottage and spend hours walking alone through the countryside.

'Robert experiences everything with an intensity that's hard to match. He's a passionate man – in so many ways – and I'm grateful that he chose to love me. At times I wonder why... what he sees in me. When he disappears on one of his walks, I worry he won't come home. Then he'll appear with armfuls of wildflowers and make everything magical again.' She twisted her hands together. 'I'd hate to be with an ordinary man. One who sets off every morning for the office and behaves like every other man. Robert's unpredictable, quixotic, clever – the cleverest man I've ever known, endlessly fascinating, and talented. And he makes me feel beautiful. Quite a feat!' She laughed. 'I hope one day you too will find a love like ours. Not the black moods – I wouldn't wish those on anyone – but the passion, the closeness, the all-encompassing love.'

Alice said nothing. Sometimes she wished that too. But she had long since stopped believing it would happen.

Over breakfast one morning, Eleanor turned to Alice. 'Are you still interested in a part-time job? Or have votes for women taken you over completely?'

'Most definitely I'm interested. Miss Pendleton and Mrs Collins have picked up a lot of the administrative burden, so I have some free time.'

'Colonel Fitzwarren over at Padgett Hall – the big house on

the Liphook road – is writing his memoirs. He needs someone
to decipher his handwriting and type them up. I immediately
thought of you. I told him you had no training in stenography,
but he seems to think that isn't a problem. He also wants help to
catalogue his library but says that can wait until the manuscript
is completed. It could be a job of quite long duration. He'd want
you every weekday from nine until one.'

'The Mothers Union meetings are on Tuesday mornings.'

'We can move the timing to the afternoon if you're
desperate to come along.' She gave Alice a cheeky smile. 'But
you did say all the talk of children and babies was tedious.

'Sorry. I did, didn't I? How rude of me.'

'Not at all. You're quite right. Other people's children are
not a source of fascination. I only go because I have to show my
face.'

'What's the colonel like?'

Eleanor chuckled. 'I'll leave you to find out. But put it this
way, I wouldn't be at all surprised if you were soon begging to
return to the Mothers' Union meetings.'

'My goodness. I've just realised Padgett Hall may be the
place where the Conservatives were having their meeting and
threw me out.'

'Very probably. Colonel Fitzwarren is the local party
chairman.'

'Then he won't want to give me the job.'

'If you turn up wearing a Votes for Women sash I'm sure he
won't, but I don't imagine you were planning on doing that,
were you?'

'Of course not. A time and a place.'

Colonel Fitzwarren was a tall man with a stoop. His grey hair
was thinning on top but he had a heavy moustache with abun-
dant side whiskers, matched by a pair of spectacular eyebrows

that resembled an overgrown hedgerow. His face was hung with deep wrinkles like a rucked-up carpet.

To Alice's relief he didn't appear to connect her with the unwelcome sash-wearing intruder who had encroached on his committee meeting.

He spoke with a bark and was clearly more comfortable addressing men on a battlefield than dealing with a young woman seeking employment. 'Wanted a man for this job, y'know. Doubt a young filly will be up to the task but there's no one suitable in the district. Told the vicar's wife I'd give you a try-out but if you're not up to it you're out.' The bushy eyebrows bristled as though alive, as he frowned his disapproval.

She waited.

'I suppose I'll be saving on wages.' The brows took flight upwards as he almost smiled, adding, 'A chap would obviously have to be paid more, so there is that.'

Alice wanted to get up and leave, but she swallowed her annoyance. Doing a good job and proving him wrong was all part of advancing the suffragist cause.

'One week's trial. That's all you'll get.'

'Can you tell me something about the nature of the work?'

'Transcribing my memoirs.' He peered at her. 'You squeamish? Can't have you fainting at the mention of blood or death. No smelling salts in this house. No call for them. Never married. Never will.'

She gritted her teeth. 'No. I'm not squeamish. When would you like me to start?'

A grunt. 'No time like the present. Come.' He strode across the room and opened the door to a large study, overlooking a paved terrace and lawns that ran down to a stream with a copse on the other side. Two walls of the room were lined with bookshelves. The heavy oak desk was piled with papers and the wall behind it covered with framed maps of Africa and India. A collection of military regalia, including a trio of highly polished infantry swords, was displayed over the fireplace. A side table bearing a typewriter faced the window. At least she would have a view of the garden. The only other furniture in the room were a winged leather armchair, a tiger skin rug – complete with fierce gaping fangs, and a gramophone.

Alice went across to the smaller desk and picked up the first sheet of paper. The colonel's handwriting was spidery and required some concentration to decipher. She read the first paragraph and sighed inwardly. Any hope that the memoirs would prove an interesting read vanished.

'I expect you to check the spellings of all the place names using the wall maps. There's a supply of paper and typewriter ribbons in the cupboard. Now what are you waiting for? Chop chop!'

Alice slipped off her coat and, lacking anywhere else to put it, draped it over the back of the chair. She sat down and set to work.

Three hours later, Alice left Padgett Hall and walked back towards the village. Any elements of the colonel's life story that might have had the potential to spark interest were reduced to yawn-inducing tedium by the turgidity of his prose. She'd been tempted to rephrase some of the more monotonous stretches but realised it would amount to a complete rewrite of the manuscript and was bound to elicit the old man's disapproval. But treating the transcription as a mechanical exercise was likely to send her to sleep. Untrained in stenography, she decided to set herself targets for speed and accuracy so at least she could emerge from the experience with a useful skill – even if she used only two fingers.

The day was unseasonably warm for early October so Alice carried her coat over her arm. Postponing her return to the vicarage, she turned off the road and followed a track up a hill towards a ridge. The climb was steep but the ground was firm underfoot and she wanted to attain a vantage point that would offer a view over the surrounding countryside. Her blouse was damp against her back as she pushed upwards, her summer coat slung over one shoulder. Eventually, she entered a copse where the ground levelled out. The leaves of the trees were turning yellow, the colour of ripe lemons, contrasting with the dark greens lower down.

When she emerged from the copse, the land fell away in front of her in a steep escarpment. Moving out of the shade, she settled on a tree trunk, gazed out over the panorama and drew a deep breath, filling her lungs.

The sun blazed in a last defiant act of summer, warming her skin. But everywhere there were signs of approaching autumn. The changing colours, the abundance of fruits and berries, a V-shaped flight of geese swathing across the cloudless sky. Portents of colder, bleaker days to come. She shivered despite the warm temperature.

A long winter lay ahead. A winter of trudging along muddy lanes five mornings a week to transcribe the colonel's tepid words. If only there were more blood and guts – so far the military man had no grounds for fearing she'd need smelling salts – unless it was to revive her from sleep. She told herself she was fortunate to have work, to have a home at the vicarage and the companionship of the Hargreaveses, having broken free from her previous life. Free from her cold and calculating parents. From her perfidious brother. From men who didn't want to marry her. From an existence lacking all purpose and direction.

She picked at the tree trunk she was sitting on, letting the rotting bark crumble under the pressure of her fingers. Now, she had many calls on her time. Many interests to pursue. She didn't want suffragism to take her over completely, so the job at Padgett Hall and helping Eleanor with her parish duties did at least add some more variety to her days. And there was no reason why she shouldn't start sketching and watercolour painting again. After the business with Gilbert, she'd lost the

urge to create, but her new circumstances and more positive
outlook could be the spur she needed. Looking about her, she
committed the scene to memory. Tonight, she'd try to recreate it
on paper.

Gilbert Cutler was always there, a ghostly presence in the
background, waiting to trip her up and deal her a blow – even if
the blows were softer since Eleanor had helped to put them into
perspective. Along with the sadness and guilt, there was a
nagging feeling that, despite accepting a future of spinsterhood,
she may be missing out on something or someone. The Hargreaveses' happiness had tempered her acidic view of matrimony.
It would be overstating things to say she was disappointed, or
even lonely, but it was hard not to occasionally succumb to
wondering what might have been.

She rubbed her fingers against the fabric of her skirt,
brushing away the residue of bark dust, then got to her feet and
made her way back to the road.

PART TWO

1913–14

EIGHTEEN

Five years later, 1913

The November sun emerged from a bank of cloud and Edmund could smell woodsmoke drifting like incense from a series of soaring red brick chimneys which rose above the treetops. He thrust his hands deep into his pockets, glad that he'd worn his heavy overcoat and not the gaberdine he'd almost put on when leaving London. An anxious shiver rippled across his stomach. Had he left his fountain pen and notebook on the train? No, they were safely tucked in the breast pocket of his jacket. It was hard not to suffer from nerves when today marked the chance for his first personal commission. He mustn't botch it.

Since joining Christopher Whall's studio he'd risen from apprentice to the most trusted and valued of the studio staff. Edmund had absorbed all the knowledge and experience he could from Whall, assisting him in the execution of numerous projects from cathedrals to municipal libraries, private houses and small churches. He was more than ready to take on an entire project in his own right. All he needed was a client willing to commission him.

In the years since his marriage, as well as becoming a father, he'd lost his mother – tragic news he'd discovered from an announcement in *The Times,* read in the library during his lunch break. Her death was sudden, apparently a heart attack. It sent him into a state of guilt and misery that his marriage had contributed to her decline. But more than anything, her death cemented his hatred of his father for the years of abuse.

Edmund and Dora had achieved a kind of *entente cordiale,* although their marriage remained an arid desert. He couldn't fault her love for Charlotte. Dora was a good and caring mother. George Fisher's declining health had forced the role of carer on Dora too – but it was one she embraced without a word of complaint.

Edmund supposed his marriage was no worse than many and better than some. But it fell far short of the hopes and dreams he'd nursed when he'd married Dora. Perhaps now, if he won this commission today, things might improve. There'd be more money – a longstanding source of Dora's discontent. He wasn't optimistic but all he could do was live the best life he could. And his daughter was a constant joy – as was his art.

The lane took a sharp twist and there in front of him was Bankstone, the house with the towering chimneys. Another flutter of nerves. It was larger than he'd expected. A honey-coloured render covered the walls, contrasting with the red brick of the chimneys and window surrounds and the clay tiles of the steep sloping roofs. The mullioned windows sparkled as the low-lying sun struck them. A fine building, exemplifying the best of the Arts and Crafts style. His stomach fluttered again: this time with excitement.

Edmund stepped between the yew hedges, through the woven willow gate into a well-tended garden and approached the front door. He pulled the bell and it echoed inside the house. As he waited on the doorstep, which appeared to have been fashioned from a millstone, he glanced down. The half-hour walk from the railway station had coated the shoes he had so carefully polished that morning with a fine patina of dust. He flicked each leg back and rubbed his shoes in turn against his trousers, before realising he'd spread the grime to them too. Mind you, the woman who had summoned him here was unlikely to be concerned by a bit of dust on either shoes or trousers. He wasn't interviewing to be a butler or valet.

It seemed an eternity until the door creaked open and a stern-faced housekeeper appeared. A woman of about fifty, she looked Edmund up and down and didn't appear to be impressed by what she saw.

'Mrs Bowyer was expecting you ten minutes ago.'

Edmund felt his neck redden. 'I'm sorry. The train was late. Apparently a problem with the signals at Clapham Junction.'

The housekeeper sniffed as she ushered him inside 'No point giving me your excuses. It's no concern to me what time you turn up or whether you turn up at all.' She looked at him with disdain, his grubby trouser legs unlikely to have skipped her notice. 'But *she's* a stickler for punctuality.' Softening a little, she added in a more conciliatory tone, 'The late Commodore Bowyer was a naval officer. He expected the house to be run like a ship and she shows no sign of changing things now he's gone.' The woman gave a long-suffering sigh.

By now they were deep into the interior of the house, having passed through a series of interconnected rooms and hallways. Edmund barely had a chance to take in his surroundings during the woman's monologue. She showed little respect for either her employer, or for Mrs Bowyer's guests. Not that he'd had much personal experience recently with the conduct and deportment of servants.

'In here,' the housekeeper said. 'She's waiting for you. And don't blame me if the tea's cold. It was there on time even if you weren't.' With that she clicked open a latched wooden door and left him.

Edmund walked into a large double aspect drawing room, occupying the end of one wing of the house. The brick-framed windows gave onto a formal country garden on one side, which Edmund recognised as the handiwork of Mrs Jekyll, the acclaimed plantswoman, and to lawns sloping away to woodland on the other. He would have liked to gaze out on the garden, his eyes drawn to the ornamental stone well at the centre and the subtle silvery green and white of the planting. But he turned his attention to his prospective patroness.

Mrs Bowyer was drinking tea at the fireside – a huge stone and brick inglenook which dwarfed the meagre excuse for a fire. A small woman, dressed in mourning, she was wearing an old-fashioned costume of black bombazine, her grey hair coiled on top of her head. Widow's weeds. She glanced up as Edmund approached and gestured towards a matching chair. Her face gave away nothing she was thinking.

'I hope you don't mind pouring for yourself, Mr Cutler, but I suffer from rheumatism in my hands and it's as much as I can manage to raise a cup. I hope it hasn't stewed in the pot. You'd better sup it quickly as Mrs Harrison will be back to clear the tea tray at five bells.'

Edmund hesitated, unsure whether to offer her his hand before deciding that it was evidently not expected. As a craftsman, his only reason for being here was to render a paid service, so perhaps it was understandable that the lady of the house chose to dispense with the social niceties. Unsure what his hostess meant by 'five bells', he suspected it was a form of maritime time-keeping.

The woman waved a hand in the air dismissively when he apologised for the train delay. The tea was still reasonably hot – but stewed. Edmund drank it down in a few gulps and waited for Mrs Bowyer to speak again.

'How old are you, young man?'

'I turn twenty-seven in two weeks.'

'Married?'

'Yes, with one child.'

'A son?'

'A daughter.'

Her expression indicated that she viewed a daughter as a blight not a blessing.

'My friends Mr and Mrs Hinkley suggested I approach Mr Whall, but he was already committed to a commission overseas. It was he who recommended you. But you seem exceedingly young. Hard to believe you are a father.' She gazed at him over the top of her teacup as though challenging his word.

Edmund didn't respond, fearing it could cause her to doubt him more.

'The Hinkleys have a most wonderful stained-glass window done by Mr Whall. Fleurs-de-lys and flying geese. Quite delicate and understated. But I prefer a denser pattern myself.' She leant forward in her chair and put down her cup. 'I am awfully fond of the wallpapers of the late Mr William Morris. My husband and I chose Morris & Co papers for our small parlour and three of the bedrooms.'

'Is that what you have in mind, Mrs Bowyer? A close repeating pattern? Because––'

'Certainly not.'

She gave him an exasperated look and Edmund's heart sank. He shouldn't have interrupted her.

'I want two stained-glass windows. The first, for this house, will be a portrait of my dear departed husband. The second is to commemorate him in the parish church here in Little Badgerton.'

At that moment, a bell rang five times and, on cue, the door opened and the housekeeper reappeared to collect the tea tray. Once she'd gone, Mrs Bowyer rose to her feet and moved briskly towards the door.

'Come, Mr Cutler. I can't abide dawdling. This way.'

He followed her out of the sunny drawing room into the darker depths beyond. They went down a ceramic-tiled corridor and into a formal dining room where Mrs Bowyer halted and pointed upwards at a portrait in oils above the fireplace. It was of a bearded man in late middle age, holding a pipe and wearing a tweed suit, as though dressed for the country.

'This is my dear late husband, Commodore Algernon Bowyer. What do you think?'

Edmund hesitated. Was he expected to comment on the quality of the artwork – which he felt was third rate – or the appearance of the man – which was unremarkable? He decided to refrain from offering an opinion on either. 'The commodore must have been an impressive man. My sincere condolences, Mrs Bowyer.'

'He was indeed.' She looked gratified. 'A truly remarkable man. But will you be able to do him justice in stained glass, Mr Cutler?' She narrowed her eyes and fixed her gaze on him.

Edmund gulped. He hadn't envisaged the commission would involve a likeness. He'd expected to be asked to render a classical montage, a biblical story or possibly a rendition of an idealised bucolic scene. But an elderly man in a Harris tweed suit? He turned to his hostess and said, 'I can certainly attempt to reproduce this in glass, but I'm puzzled why, when you have such a magnificent portrait already, you wish to replicate it in stained glass?'

Mrs Bowyer shook her head rapidly as though it were on a spring. 'No, no, no, no, no.' The denial was staccato, like a hungry woodpecker. 'You can use this painting as a reference to create a likeness but I want you to portray my husband in full dress uniform.' She gazed up at the portrait with a wistful expression.

Edmund was dismayed. It was dispiriting for his first commission, his chance to demonstrate his skill and creativity, to be curtailed by such prosaic subject matter. What a waste of his hard-earned skills. Such an uninspiring portrait may as well be constructed in cheap factory glass. Why employ a skilled artist when subtlety and artifice would be subordinated to near photographic accuracy?

He struggled to conceal his disappointment. Collecting himself, he said, 'You mentioned a second window for the local church. Do you have a subject in mind for that?'

She gave a sigh of resignation. 'My husband's name was Algernon so I would have liked it to be Saint Algernon but I've been informed by the vicar that there's no such saint. The name apparently is of Norman origin and means "with moustache" and as my dear Algernon had a full beard that's clearly not a fruitful avenue to pursue.' Mrs Bowyer tutted. 'I suggested a portrait on the same lines as I intend for the house but the local vicar is not minded to agree. He fears a non-religious portrait would set a precedent and has asked instead that we create a window to feature the saint the church is named for.' Her mouth turned downwards.

'And that is?' Edmund leant forward.

'Not a suitable person to commemorate my husband.' She sighed again. 'For a start it's a woman: Saint Margaret.' She made her odd jerky little head shake again as though shivering in horror. 'What's worse, Saint Margaret is apparently the patron saint of expectant mothers and servant maids.' She raised her eyebrows in horror. 'Most inappropriate. My dear Algernon would not have been happy at all.'

'I understand,' he said. 'Does the vicar have any alternative suggestions?'

'I'm rather hoping you'll be able to suggest something agree-able to him. I find the fellow tiresome and would prefer not to engage in further debate. He really has been most unreason-able.' She leant her weight on the back of a dining chair and fixed her eyes on Edmund. 'The wretched man ought to be grateful for the generosity of my late husband in bestowing such a gift on the church. To quibble over the execution seems to me to be the height of ill manners.'

Deeming it wise not to be drawn further, Edmund asked to see the site of the planned window and to understand more about the career and achievements of the late commodore.

Mrs Bowyer said, 'Mrs Harrison will show you the window. I'm feeling drained.' She sighed volubly. 'After that, I suggest you go to look at the church. I've told the vicar to expect you. Mrs Harrison has prepared a bedroom for you. Tomorrow morning, I will meet you in the library and tell you more about dear Algernon and we can discuss your ideas for the church.'

Edmund hadn't anticipated an overnight stay. As Mrs Bowyer finished speaking, Mrs Harrison materialised. It was as though she sensed the moment she was needed – or more likely she hovered, listening outside doors. She led Edmund down a long corridor and upstairs into another wing of the house where she showed him a small spartan bedroom overlooking the garden. Daylight was beginning to fade.

'You're in here. There's electric light throughout the house. We don't light fires in the bedrooms until December, so you'll have to manage without if it's cold. Since you haven't any baggage to unpack, I'll show you the window she wants to replace, then you'd best hurry to St Margaret's before it gets dark.'

The chosen window was on the upstairs landing of the main wing of the house. It was a wide, brick, mullioned window which, as well as illuminating the landing, sent light down via an open galleried balustrade into the double height hallway below. Immediately, Edmund saw the possibilities of a mixture of clear pale slab glass to maximise the light, and some delicate, subtle staining to cast a shimmering cascade of colour into the hall below. Shame it would be used to render the image of the uniformed naval officer. There were two mullions and Edmund would be forced either to divide the image between three panels or shoehorn it into the central one, necessitating a full-length portrait or a smaller head and shoulders with something in the background to fill the rest of the space. Had Mrs Bowyer anticipated this?

He turned to the waiting Mrs Harrison. 'I'll make some sketches and take measurements when I return from the church.'

The housekeeper gave a shrug. 'Suit yourself. So, you're going to do it, are you? Hope you realise what you're letting yourself in for.'

St Margaret's was half a mile from Bankstone. The dusk was drawing in and the temperature dropping, so Edmund walked briskly.

The brief meeting with Mrs Bowyer had unsettled him. He'd been hoping that creating the memorial window would establish his reputation and allow him to move out of the shadow of Christopher Whall. The work might even win him a coveted place in the Arts and Crafts Exhibition; perhaps even a mention in *Country Life*. The publicity would have generated further commissions and helped secure his future as an independent artist. But no one was likely to show interest in a window portraying a uniformed naval commodore. Such a dull, uninspiring subject. His only hope was the church and, from what Mrs Bowyer had told him, the vicar was unlikely to be amenable to the kind of unusual and arresting work Edmund had dreamt of creating.

But he had a wife and child to support and still nursed the dream of opening his own studio, perhaps renting a space next to one of the leading glass manufacturers such as Britten & Gibson. For that, he'd need to earn significantly more money than he could as Whall's assistant.

At the thought of Dora, his spirits became bleaker. The old

adage, *Marry in haste, repent at leisure*, had proved all too true –
even though he couldn't fault her as a devoted mother to their
daughter.

Since Charlotte's birth, his marriage had become one in
name only. Night after night he was rebuffed by his wife in bed.
If it were up to Dora, marital relations would be non-existent
but sometimes Edmund was unable to stop himself – usually
after a couple of drinks. Dora was a beautiful woman and lying
beside her in bed without physical contact was more than a
saint could bear – and Edmund was a full-blooded man with
natural urges and desires. She never resisted him – he would
never force himself on her – but her distaste was evident. Afterwards, he'd feel ashamed and riddled with guilt at his loss of
self-control. He saw himself as a failure and was convinced that
by failing in his marriage he was also failing in life.

So Mrs Bowyer's assumption that he would stay at Bankstone that night was not unwelcome. It would be a relief to
escape Dora's accusatory gaze and her litany of trivial
complaints.

In the modest flat above the greengrocer's shop Edmund got
along well enough with George Fisher, but once Charlotte
arrived, the already cramped accommodation had become
oppressive, particularly on the weekly washday. George had
developed a hacking cough which Edmund feared was tubercu-
lar. But the doctor informed them that it was a non-infectious
lung disease. Although it was likely to prove fatal, at least the
family members were not at risk. George's declining health
necessitated early retirement and Dora was adamant they
remain in Goodge Street so she could care for her father.
Whenever Edmund brought up the subject of moving elsewhere she flew into a rage, followed by the demand that he seek
a reconciliation with his own father and take a well-paying job
in his brokerage firm so they could afford to live somewhere
more spacious in central London.

Edmund tried to push these gloomy thoughts from his mind as he trudged along the lane. A few cottages indicated the beginning of the village and beyond them was the church of St Margaret's. A solid stone-built structure with a sturdy tower topped by a short spire, it was surrounded by an overgrown graveyard. Edmund pushed open the heavy oak door, its creak echoing loudly through the gloomy interior. The only light was from a pair of guttering candles in a side chapel and the last weak light of the dying day entering through the west-facing windows.

He should have called first at the vicarage as he had no idea which window had been selected. Apart from what looked like an early Victorian factory-glass rose-window behind the altar, all the windows were lancets in clear leaded glass. Edmund walked around, absorbing the atmosphere, which was sepulchral and sombre. He'd have to return in full daylight to take measurements and undertake a full inspection of the designated space.

A door creaked on the left of the chancel, followed by a click. Light illuminated that corner of the church.

'Mr Cutler, I presume?' The voice was confident and carried across the empty pews. 'I'm Reverend Hargreaves.' The clergyman moved towards him, hand outstretched. He had a welcoming smile that immediately relaxed Edmund. 'Sorry the church was dark. I was writing my sermon and didn't notice the time. Delighted to meet you, sir.'

Relieved at the vicar's affability, Edmund shook hands.

'So, you're the gentleman Mrs Bowyer has chosen to realise her generous gift to the parish?' Was there a faint note of sarcasm in the way Hargreaves said 'generous'? All doubt was removed when he added, 'A gift with strings,' and gave Edmund a smile of resignation.

'Strings?'

'Mrs Bowyer's generosity is less about the glorification of

God than the sanctification of her late husband.' He tightened his lips. 'I had to put my foot down over her request for a portrait of the old sea dog himself. The man never set foot in the church. St Margaret's is a place of worship and that doesn't extend to the worship of individual wealthy parishioners, even those who have served their king and country. I'm afraid Mrs Bowyer and I have reached an impasse and I'm hoping you can resolve it. I suggested a portrayal of our namesake, St Margaret, but that upset her. She seems to think it would enrage her late husband to be associated with a female saint.' He shook his head.

Edmund was puzzled. 'Why is Mrs Bowyer so keen to dedicate a window here in the church when she's already planning one at Bankstone? And particularly if her late husband didn't worship here?'

'Social acceptance.' The vicar spread his hands out, palms up. 'Bankstone was completed only eighteen months ago. The commander fell ill and died soon after they moved here from Portsmouth on his retirement from the navy. Bankstone was to be the fulfilment of a dream. The poor chap barely had a chance to enjoy it. Now Mrs Bowyer is alone and keen to make connections in the area. Most of the leading families in the county have been here for generations and, between you and me, they consider anyone under the rank of admiral or a peer of the realm to be of the lower orders.' He chuckled. 'Mrs Bowyer has plenty of money. From her side of the family. Her father made a fortune in trade. Some form of wholesale grocery business and she was his only heir. Round here it's "old" money that counts – or even *no* money but with the right family pedigree – certainly not money from trade. I believe Mrs Bowyer intends her munificence to open doors that would otherwise be closed to her. She also wants public recognition of the old boy's life.' Reverend Hargreaves shrugged. 'I told her as tactfully as possible that a donation towards the roof repairs would be more welcome but she wrote me a cheque for that and then declared that she still wanted her memorial window. She considers my stance that this is the house of God as an irritant to be brushed off.'

'Are you obliged to accept her offer?' As soon as Edmund uttered the words he regretted them. He needed this commission badly.

'I was left in no doubt that the cheque for the roof was conditional.' Reverend Hargreaves smiled. 'I'm afraid my principles fly away like dandelion clocks in the face of a promise of filthy lucre. I make no apology, Mr Cutler. Anything to eliminate the line of buckets we need to place in front of the altar when it's raining.'

'And the chosen window?' Edmund looked around him.

The vicar nodded. 'Another bone of contention. Mrs Bowyer wants a window in the middle of the nave but I've put my foot down as it would look odd, being the only decorative window among the plain glass. And to be honest, I like as much natural light as possible.' He smiled. 'Not what you want to hear, I'm sure. But she and I have reached a satisfactory compromise. Over here.' He led the way to a side chapel occupying the opposite side of the chancel to the vestry.

'Later than the main body of the church. Added in the late fifteenth century.'

Edmund looked at the window opening. It consisted of five lancets with elaborate tracery above. There was plenty of scope to exercise his creativity in these apertures. Already, as he stared up at the window, he envisaged a *grisaille* to maximise the flow of light into the chapel in the tracery above, and more vibrant colours in the lancets below.

He turned to the clergyman. 'I understand you want the subject matter to be of a religious theme. I wonder whether we could achieve that along with the support of Mrs Bowyer were

we to select biblical stories of a nautical nature. I'm thinking of
Jonah and the whale, Noah and his ark—'

Hargreaves interrupted. 'The parting of the Red Sea, Jesus
walking on the water. Yes! I like that idea.' He rubbed his hands
together.

'And didn't Jesus also calm a storm?'

'Yes. On the Sea of Galilee. Perfect!' The vicar was enthusiastic.

'Do you think Mrs Bowyer will agree?'

'Why don't you put it to her? It will be better coming from
the artist rather than me. And it would help if you gave her the
impression I took some persuading. Believing I'm less than
happy is bound to make her more favourably disposed.' Hargreaves chuckled again. 'Why don't you come to the vicarage and
join Mrs Hargreaves and me for a sherry? Mrs Bowyer doesn't
drink and the only thing the late commodore kept in the house
was rum.' He pulled a face.

Mrs Hargreaves was a handsome woman who appeared to be in
her forties, perhaps ten years younger than her husband. She
greeted Edmund with a warm smile. 'Come into the parlour,
Mr Cutler. It's nice and warm.'

A fire was blazing in the inglenook fireplace that dominated
one wall of the modestly but comfortably furnished room. The
tension he hadn't realised he'd been carrying in his body all day
ebbed away and Edmund relaxed. He took a seat close to the
fire and looked around him, luxuriating in the simple surroundings. This was the kind of home he'd dreamt of living in eventually, when he had been courting Dora.

The Hargreaveses sat on a sofa opposite him. Mrs Hargreaves leant forward eagerly. 'Have you decided what you're
going to create for us, Mr Cutler? I can't wait to hear.'

'Mr Cutler has a plan that may even win over Mrs Bowyer,'

said her husband. 'Biblical scenes of a maritime nature. Jonah and the Whale, Jesus walking on the water and the parting of the Red Sea.'

'You clever chap.' Mrs Hargreaves clapped her hands. 'What a brilliant solution. Mrs Bowyer can't possibly object to that.' She turned to her husband. 'It will also be useful for explaining the Bible stories to the parish children. More relevant than a depiction of poor old Saint Margaret.'

The Reverend Hargreaves took his wife's hand – a gesture of love and affinity which was reflected in his eyes when he glanced at her. Edmund experienced a pang of envy. In just a few minutes with hardly a word spoken, it was apparent that the Hargreaveses had the kind of marriage he'd aspired to but failed to achieve. A marriage where volumes could be communicated in a rapid glance, where a hand had only to reach out and it would find the other's waiting to receive it. He took a sip of sherry and suppressed a desire to escape. The casual, unremarkable happiness of the Hargreaveses underlined how miserable his own marriage was.

As though divining his thoughts, Mrs Hargreaves asked, 'Are you a married man, Mr Cutler?'

Edmund told her he was and had a four-year-old daughter.

'Then you're a lucky man.' Mrs Hargreaves' eyes were wistful. 'Sadly, we've not been blessed with children.'

The vicar touched his wife's hand. 'But we've been delighted to share our home for the past few years with our niece.' He glanced at his wife. 'We must invite Mr Cutler to supper. It will be an opportunity for him to meet Alice.'

'Splendid idea.' Mrs Hargreaves clasped her hands. 'My niece works for Colonel Fitzwarren up at Padgett Hall and I'm afraid he can be rather crotchety. The poor girl has her patience tried on a regular basis. But there's so little gainful employment to be had in the area and sadly nothing that could fulfil her artistic bent.'

'Your niece is an artist?'

'Not a trained one, but certainly a talented one.'

The Reverend Hargreaves replenished their glasses. 'Do your commissions often take you far from London, Mr Cutler?'

'As far afield as Germany. Assisting my employer, Mr Christopher Whall, but as a rule I work out of his studio in west London. I'm hoping to establish my own studio. Little Badgerton is within easy travelling distance of London so I can be here when required—'

The clergyman and his wife exchanged glances. 'Hasn't Mrs Bowyer told you she expects you to base yourself at Bankstone?'

Edmund was taken aback. 'She kindly offered to put me up tonight, but—'

'Mrs Bowyer intends you to remain at Bankstone for the duration of the project. She's set aside a large outbuilding in the grounds for you to use as a studio.'

Edmund gasped. 'But I'll need my tools and equipment. A kiln. And most of all I need assistance. I can't bring one of the apprentices with me as they can't be spared from other work – all the studio assistants are involved in multiple projects. If I undertake everything myself it will considerably lengthen the duration of the project, not to mention add to the cost.' He was crestfallen.

'Where Mrs Bowyer is concerned money appears to be no object. She'll pay to install a kiln and any necessary equipment, as well as cover the cost of any necessary staff.'

Mrs Hargreaves interrupted her husband, 'More to the point though, Walter, there's the question of Mr Cutler's wife and daughter. I'm not sure how Mrs Bowyer will feel about accommodating them at Bankstone too.'

Edmund shook his head emphatically. 'It's out of the question. Mrs Cutler and our daughter can't leave London. My wife's father is a semi-invalid who requires care.'

The couple exchanged another anxious glance. 'That could be a problem then, unless you're willing to be apart from your family for the duration of the project.'

Edmund paused, drawing a deep breath. Being away from little Lottie would be painful but an enforced absence from Dora would be a blessing. 'The life of an artist who is dependent on commissions means we're accustomed to long periods of separation.' The fire crackled and a small shower of sparks flew upwards into the chimney. 'What's troubling me more is the question of sourcing a trained assistant here.' He couldn't afford to lose this commission. How long had he waited for a significant project like this one? There had to be a way round the problem. 'Perhaps I can find a young man in the area willing to learn the craft.'

Mrs Hargreaves leant forward, her eyes fixed on Edmund. 'What kind of things would such a person be required to do? What qualities must they possess?'

'A steady hand, a propensity for hard work...' He frowned as he listed the requirements. 'Ideally an ability to draw, but most of all a willingness to learn. The work would involve preparation and conservation of my materials, keeping the workshop in order, mixing paints to my exact specifications, taking accurate measurements.' He sighed, hands gripping his knees. 'It's painstaking work and often tedious. Do you think such a person could be found here in Little Badgerton? And even assuming they can, would such a person accept a position that has no long-term future once this commission is completed and I return to London?'

The Hargreaveses exchanged one of their knowing glances before Mrs Hargreaves replied. 'We may have a solution.' Another glance at her husband. 'How would you feel about employing a young woman?'

Edmund shrugged. 'Mr Whall has always employed women. Some of the best apprentices are women. Indeed there are many impressive stained-glass artists who are female. You have someone in mind?'

'Our niece. Her duties at Padgett Hall are concluding and as I mentioned she's a keen artist.' Mrs Hargreaves gave him a broad smile.

Edmund felt cornered. 'Perhaps I've been unclear. While drawing ability is desirable, it's not as necessary as more menial skills. To put it bluntly I need a dogsbody. Someone unafraid of hard work, much of which involves organisation skills. I admit I'm likely to be the worst of employers – a man who wants his mark to be on every aspect of the work – the art and the craft – and given the time constraints of this project I'll have little chance to offer the kind of teaching a student could expect at an art school or in a large studio.' His voice trailed away. Was he protesting too much? 'Of course, if your niece is prepared to do such work and can accept that it's unlikely to lead to long-term employment...'

'You can ask her when you come for supper. How about next week? Thursday's the best day for us as there are no parish activities that evening.'

Edmund thanked them.

'That's settled then.' Mrs Hargreaves' eyes shone. 'I've a feeling your arrival here in Little Badgerton will offer Alice a welcome release from her toils with Colonel Fitzwarren. You'll find her a quick study: meticulous, enthusiastic and eager to learn. Indeed, I'm sure you'll get along famously.' She rose from her chair. 'Don't you agree, Walter? Now, unless you want to face the wrath of that waspish Mrs Harrison over at Bankstone, you'd better get yourself back there before she rings those dreadful bells.'

Edmund put down his glass and jumped to his feet. 'Thank you so much for your hospitality, Mrs Hargreaves. It's been a pleasure meeting you. I look forward to renewing our acquaintance next week.'

As the Hargreaveses showed him out, he realised it had indeed been delightful meeting them. Apart from a residual doubt about the suitability of their niece to fulfil the duties of an assistant and concern about finding a theme for the window to satisfy both Mrs Bowyer and the vicar, he headed back to Bankstone with a renewed sense of purpose.

NINETEEN

Alice wished Eleanor was here with her. It was the weekly meeting of the Little Badgerton Women's Suffrage Society. The atmosphere had become volatile. The young schoolteacher, Miss Trimble, had proposed the group increase their commitment to the cause and undertake more aggressive and subversive acts. 'We're getting nowhere. We simply must step up. How can we possibly justify sitting around talking and writing letters to our member of Parliament when Emily Davison gave up her life.' She was referring to the death of Davison under the hooves of the King's horse at the Epsom Derby. 'We're just a group of well-meaning women who have achieved absolutely nothing.'

Her proposition was met first with a stunned silence followed by horrified disagreement from the majority of members, but sympathy from some, including the wife of the publican of The Red Dragon and Mrs Collins, the doctor's wife.

'What exactly are you suggesting? asked Miss Pendleton, who played the organ at St Margaret's. 'Bomb the parish hall?

Smash Colonel Fitzwarren's windows? Chain ourselves to the vicarage railings?'

Miss Trimble was aghast. 'Of course not. But surely, we can do something more radical that we're doing now.

A murmur went round the parish hall as the women discussed what that something might be.

'What on earth for?' said Miss Pendleton eventually, raising her voice above the crowd. 'We all know violence does no good and makes no difference. I for one have no desire to be arrested, holed up in a cell in Holloway Prison and have a tube shoved down my throat.'

A collective shudder greeted her remark.

'But we do need to do more, don't we?' The speaker was the postmistress – someone who rarely spoke up at meetings.

Alice intervened. 'We're doing all we can. Short of violence. We've always agreed we wouldn't want to go as far as that. Violence is a tool used by men. Aren't we better than that? If we use those tactics we play right into the hands of the men who oppose us. Every one of us went on the Pilgrimage last summer. That earned a huge amount of publicity. Not to mention growing sympathy.'

Miss Pendleton backed her up. 'It was vital to show that we don't all use extreme tactics. To be honest Mrs Pankhurst's escalation has set the cause back no end. More harm than good.'

Alice knew Miss Trimble was posturing. The schoolmistress would never summon the courage to hurl a brick through the colonel's window. Her proposal was simply voicing their collective frustration at the lack of progress in securing the vote.

Back in July they'd all enthusiastically participated in the Pilgrimage, the coordinated national walk to London from various points of the compass. The optimism that event had engendered had resulted in nothing more than publicity and a general sense that while the tide of public opinion was moving in their favour it fell far short of the revolution that was required to sway Parliament.

The discussion eventually fizzled out and they moved back to covering plans for a fund-raising event before Christmas.

Disheartened, Alice returned to the vicarage and found her aunt and uncle deep in conversation.

Eleanor looked up when Alice came in. 'We had a guest for sherry. The gentleman Mrs Bowyer has hired to create the stained-glass window in the side chapel.'

Alice was itching to tell her aunt about the meeting, but Eleanor was in full flow.

'A Mr Cutler. From London. Impressive qualifications. Studied under Mr Christopher Whall, no less.'

Alice, who was about to share her frustrations with Eleanor, paused. Did you say Mr *Cutler*?'

'Yes, Cutler. Nice chap. We've invited him for dinner.'

Alice's throat constricted. She'd never told her aunt the name of the man she'd been led to believe she would be marrying. Stained glass? It had to be him. But Cutler was a common enough name, wasn't it? No, there couldn't possibly be two men called Cutler practising in the creation of stained glass, could there? An impossible coincidence.

She tried to swallow but could barely breathe. That loathsome man. And Eleanor and Walter had invited him to dinner. Her head was spinning. Even if she found an excuse to miss the dinner it would be impossible to avoid him within the confines of Little Badgerton – especially as his work would necessitate frequent contact with Walter as well as visits to the church.

She wanted to scream. To howl. To rush upstairs and pound her fists into her pillow.

Then Alice realised her aunt was speaking to her. 'So we thought, Walter and I, that you'd be a perfect candidate for the job. You're so artistic, so talented. Mr Cutler says the job is a rather low-skilled one – more of a dogsbody he said – but I'm sure he was exaggerating.'

Eleanor looked at Walter who took up the thread. 'Since the colonel has made it clear that he no longer requires your services now that he has his nephew... well we thought it might be interesting for you.'

Alice froze. Surely not? Had she heard properly? A job? Working for Mr Cutler? This couldn't be happening.

Eleanor was oblivious to her niece's panic. 'Mr Cutler intended to do the commission from his studio in London. Walter had to tell him Mrs Bowyer won't stand for that. The poor chap was worried sick he wouldn't be able to find an assistant willing to learn the craft, so naturally we thought of you. Of course, if you don't want to, Alice, you can say so. It might be rather menial for you but we did think it could be an interesting new string to your bow. And Mr Cutler is a most charming man. We both liked him immediately, didn't we, Walter?'

Walter concurred with enthusiasm.

Charming? Likeable? It couldn't possibly be the same Mr Cutler.

Eleanor looked concerned. 'Have we put our feet in it, Alice? Would you rather have taken a break from working? After all that time with the colonel you deserve to.'

Alice straightened her back and steadied her voice. 'Not at all. I'll be glad of a change. As you say, it's a chance to learn a new skill.' She spoke the words but didn't mean them. But if she was horrified by the prospect of working in close proximity with Edmund Cutler – assuming it was him then *he* would be even more so. *He* was the one who had jilted *her*.

Conscious that she was uncovering a devious and vengeful streak in herself, she took satisfaction from it. Becoming an assistant to a stained-glass artist would be a new challenge. A skill to acquire. What could be so hard about making a stained-glass window?

When she'd met the insufferable Edmund Cutler, he'd had the airs and graces of a master Renaissance painter. She smiled. In working with him she'd be like a mosquito, a constant irritant. And she'd show how his self-importance was no more justified than that of a bricklayer or a roof thatcher.

If, as she hoped, it was a mere coincidence and this was another Mr Cutler, there was still the chance to learn a new skill. It had to be better than the Mothers' Union.

TWENTY

The following morning, Mrs Bowyer reacted with disdain when Edmund mooted the idea of using nautical-themed scenes from the Bible. Her head drew back, her brow narrowed, and he saw her suck in a breath ready to demolish his proposal. Then he remembered what the Reverend Hargreaves had said, and quickly added, 'I was rather hoping you'd suggest a way to make the vicar more amenable to the idea. He's agreed to give it some thought but I got the impression he has a strong preference for a window dedicated to St Margaret.'

'He has?' Mrs Bowyer raised an eyebrow. 'The man's an idiot. Bible stories relating to the sea, eh? Like what?'

'The parting of the Red Sea, Jesus walking on the water, Noah's Ark. That kind of thing. Perhaps you have some suggestions yourself, Mrs Bowyer?'

'Not sure about Noah's Ark. Can't abide animals. Nor could my dear Algernon.'

'I had in mind to keep the animals in the background and focus more on the ark and the dove.'

Mrs Bowyer gave it some thought. 'Nautical scenes, you say?'

'Yes. To underline your late husband's distinguished maritime career whilst staying true to ecclesiastical norms.'

She stared at him. Her steely grey eyes narrowed. Edmund held his breath.

'And the vicar is not enamoured with this idea?'

'His instinct is that Saint Margaret herself would be a better subject. I'm reluctant to adopt that route though as before he died Sir Edward Burne-Jones made a beautiful window to Saint Margaret and I doubt anyone could better that.'

Mrs Bowyer was aghast. 'I want this window to be exceptional. Not second best to some other fellow's. No, it won't do. I've told you already I won't have my husband commemorated by the patron saint of women in childbirth.' She fanned her face with a handkerchief. 'I shall call on the Reverend Hargreaves this morning and remind him of a thing or two.' She lowered her voice to a conspiratorial tone. 'It's thanks to me he no longer needs to fill the church with buckets to catch the rainwater. The man is obstinate. But when I make up my mind, I usually get my way. Now I come to think of it, using Biblical scenes is an inspired choice and will enhance our church while doing justice to the stature and reputation of my husband.'

Edmund smiled. 'If anyone can win over the vicar, I am sure it's you, Mrs Bowyer.'

The woman threw him a sceptical glance, before wagging her finger. 'He needs reminding that she who pays the piper calls the tune.'

Edmund's expression was non-committal.

'That's settled then, Mr Cutler. Mrs Harrison will show you the building where you can work. There's also a cottage where you and your wife and child can stay. Rather cramped but you'll be more comfortable there than here in the house.'

Edmund was about to explain that his wife and child couldn't join him because of Dora's care of her ailing father but Mrs Bowyer was still talking.

'I require you to report to me once a week to inform me of your progress.' She tapped her knuckles on the table in emphasis. 'I understand from my friends, the Hinkleys, that it's usual to produce drawings first.'

'Yes, of course. I'll be taking exact measurements then will execute some rough sketches for you to approve before I proceed to the preparation of cartoons.'

'Just show me the drawings and then report to me on progress. I don't want to hear anything technical.' She waved her hand in a dismissive gesture. 'I've no idea what equipment you'll need, so talk to Mrs Harrison about that. She can order anything you require.' She picked up a handbell and rang it. The housekeeper appeared almost immediately.

To Edmund's relief, the outbuilding set aside for his use was a good fifty yards from the house and concealed from it by a small copse. Little risk of his patron dropping in unannounced. Stone-built, it pre-dated the house and had presumably been a barn or stables for whatever building stood on the site before the construction of Bankstone.

Inside, it was empty apart from a big deal table with a couple of wooden chairs, and a line of metal hooks along one wall, possibly once used to hang up bridles or tools of some kind.

He stood in the centre of the room with hands on hips, tilted his head back and gazed up past the rise of the rafters. The red-tiled roof looked intact and watertight. There was no sign of starling nests and no water stains on the floor. The building was sound.

Mrs Harrison looked around her. 'I had one of the gardeners' boys clear the place out and get rid of the junk. Old plough shares and rusty tools. One of the gardener's lads can lay a fire for you each morning. It's cold but a fire should take the chill off. You'll need to sweep the place out yourself. I can't spare anyone to do it.'

He murmured his assent, looking round at the dangling cobwebs and the scattering of dead leaves.

Mrs Harrison sniffed. 'Mrs Bowyer said you'll be wanting to set it up in a particular way.' She folded her arms. 'What does a stained-glass window maker need then?'

'I'll be returning to London tonight and will come back the day after tomorrow with my tools. There are some items I'll have to send by a carrier – easels, sheets of glass, and such like.' He gestured towards the longest wall. 'I'd like to have lots of shelving over there, if possible. And a workbench fitted against this wall here.'

'You don't want the table?' She ran her fingers along its edge, frowning.

'The table is perfect, but I need a workbench as well.'

'I'll send the local carpenter up for your instructions then. What else?'

Edmund hesitated. 'I understand Mrs Bowyer requires me to work entirely from here, but I need to get the glass fired in London.'

'She wants you here. Doesn't want you working on other things at the same time. That's why you can't keep going back and forth to London. What's this firing?'

'The cut glass for the panels needs to be fired in a specialist kiln to fuse the paint. I'll do all the work here but I'd like to oversee the firing, even though I'll use a professional glassworks to do it. It won't involve a lot of time away. Just a trip for each panel.'

'Can't we order one of these kilns and put it in here? She won't like it if you're up and down to London all the time. If you aren't skilled at doing that part of the job and need a professional, maybe Mrs Bowyer would prefer to find someone who can do the whole thing.'

Edmund swallowed. 'No, no, I can do it. In fact I prefer to do my own firing. It's just the expense of buying the kiln.'

'Presumably there's a cost to using a glassworks? And travel expenses?'

'Yes.'

'Then better to install a kiln here.' She folded her arms. 'Anything else?'

'Is there a supply of water?'

The housekeeper pushed open a side door. 'In here. But the water's not heated.'

There was a large butler's sink and a series of store cupboards. Perfect. 'Cold water's more than adequate, Mrs Harrison.'

'The late commodore had the building kitted out so the architect and builder could use it while the house was being built. There's a privy too.'

The woman moved to the wall and flicked a switch. 'He had the electricity put in, but there are oil lamps in the cupboard if you need them too. If that's all, I'll send one of the housemaids to get the carpenter.'

'I'm happy to go and call on him myself.'

'No. The housemaid'll fetch him. He's her father and he does lots of work for Mrs Bowyer. First, I'd better show you the cottage. I warn you, it's not large. Only the one bedroom so your little girl will have to sleep in the main room. There's a divan there that will probably suit.'

'My wife and daughter won't be staying here. My father-in-law is chronically ill and my wife cares for him. Moving here is out of the question for her.'

'I see.' The woman frowned and he sensed disapproval – or disbelief. 'Well take a look at the cottage anyway. You'll be more comfortable there than in the big house. You can come up and take your meals in the kitchen.'

After seeing the cottage, which he liked enormously despite it being smaller than the London flat, he spent the afternoon drawing up a list of supplies and discussing his requirements for fittings with the carpenter. Edmund was excited by the prospect of having his own custom workshop – even if it was only temporary. The building was spacious and light, with a pair of large windows that overlooked open meadows. He felt lightheaded, almost dizzy with a mix of pride and achievement as he headed on foot to the station to return to London. He'd worked so hard for this.

But doubts preyed at the back of his mind. Acknowledging them caused his head to drop as though their weight pulled on his spine. First, Dora's likely reaction to learning that his stay at Little Badgerton would be a protracted one. Being away from her would be a release. But a source of guilt. She had no choice but to remain with her father. And there was Lottie to think of too.

Edmund's dread mounted as he neared Goodge Street. What kind of mood would she be in? Dora's behaviour was unpredictable. Sometimes - increasingly rarely – she was civil, even cheerful, humming as she went about the household chores, laughing as she played with Lottie, crawling around the floor with the child as they pretended to be cats. More often, she was sullen and unresponsive, ignoring Edmund's questions, tossing her head and raising her chin before turning her back on him, but refusing to be drawn as to the reason. Worse were the fits of rage that occasionally consumed her when, at the slightest perceived setback – spilt milk, a cracked egg, bad weather derailing her plan to take Lottie for a walk – she would fly into a blind rage, directed at him.

Being stuck all day in the small flat in Goodge Street was part of the problem. That and the declining health of her beloved father – the coughing had got worse and he was now completely bed-ridden.

She no longer played the piano, claiming she had no time. The only time the instrument was played was when little Charlotte hammered at the keys in random self-expression. Edmund dared to suggest that perhaps Dora could teach the child to play properly but was greeted with a withering stare. She passed most evenings slumped in her chair staring into space, a silent brooding succubus, immune to any attempt he made to draw her into conversation. He had given up encouraging her to take up botanical illustrations again. As a mother to a small child, returning to art school was out of the question, but Edmund pleaded with her not to abjure her talent. When he'd given her a gift of a new paintbox and brushes, she'd shown no pleasure but had given a heavy sigh. 'I hate art. I hate painting. That art school ruined my life.' It was all too clear that she meant she hated him and it was meeting him that had ruined her life. He found the paints later unopened at the back of the kitchen drawer.

So, that evening, as he walked towards the greengrocer's shop, the pit of his stomach was hollow. It was almost eight o'clock. Lottie would be fast asleep. He cursed that he'd have to wait until morning to see his little girl and must content himself with looking down on her sleeping face. She was the one source of joy in his family life, the only reason he didn't walk out of that miserable top floor flat never to return.

Dora would be bound to use his stay at Bankstone as an excuse to play the badly treated, long-suffering wife. Edmund foresaw how she would react. She'd fix her gaze on him from under her improbably long eyelashes, her perfectly formed eyebrows would furrow, and her beautiful Cupid's bow mouth would spit forth resentment. She'd accuse him of neglecting her, failing to provide properly for her, while her eyes would blame him for destroying her dreams and making her utterly miserable.

As he climbed the last flight of stairs, he sensed something was amiss. Opening the door he heard sobbing, a despairing mewling sound, a keening. Instead of Dora sitting by the fireside or washing dishes in the scullery, little Charlotte was standing in the open doorway to the bedroom she shared with her mother, her face streaked with tears. When she saw her father, she hurled herself across the room into his arms. Edmund scooped her up, holding her body against his chest as she buried her face in his shoulder. Tiny, vulnerable, inconsolable.

He looked about as he murmured to her in an effort to bring comfort. No sign of Dora. The door to the small back bedroom where George Fisher slept was ajar. Edmund moved closer. His father-in-law lay on his back in the bed, eyes wide open but lifeless and his face white against the blood-spattered pillow beneath his head. Edmund backed away. Where the hell was Dora?

He carried Charlotte into the main bedroom and laid her gently on the bed, sitting beside her. Her small dimpled hand reached for his and his heart melted as he wrapped his own around it. Her sobs were fading as with his other hand he stroked her forehead. 'Where's Mummy?' he asked.

'Don't know.'

She began to cry again, so he took out his handkerchief and wiped her eyes and runny nose.

'I had a bad dream so I called for Mummy,' she said. 'She didn't answer so I got out of bed and went in to see Grandpa.' The tears flowed again. 'I couldn't wake him up. Why won't he wake up, Daddy? What's wrong with him?'

'Don't worry, my sweet, Daddy's here now.' He gulped in a breath and steeled himself. 'Grandpa's gone to Heaven. He's being looked after by the angels.' He stroked her soft dark hair. After a while, her breathing became more even and she drifted back to sleep.

He was feeling drowsy himself, until the door to the flat opened. He heard feet rushing across the floor followed by a terrible wailing from Dora. Edmund dropped a kiss on Charlotte's head and went to comfort his wife.

She was kneeling beside her father's bed, her arms stretched out in front of her in futile supplication, like a Pièta of a weeping Mary in front of the body of Jesus. Behind her Mrs Spindlemann and Stanley hovered.

Mrs Spindlemann saw Edmund, nodded in acknowledgement, then turned to her son. 'Go home, Stan. Nothing you can do here now.' Wordlessly, Stanley left the flat, throwing a scowl in Edmund's direction as he departed.

'I'll make a pot of tea then I'll leave you in peace,' Mrs Spindlemann said, backing out of the room.

Edmund placed a hand on Dora's shoulder, but she shrugged it off.

He joined the next-door neighbour in the scullery.

Mrs Spindlemann bustled about the room, filling the kettle and readying cups. 'When did you get here, Mr Cutler? I wasn't gone long and the child was fast asleep.' She set the kettle on the hotplate.

'What do you mean? I came home to find Charlotte in tears at finding her dead grandfather. Where was Dora?'

Mrs Spindlemann paled. She reached up to the shelf and brought down the teacups. 'That's unfortunate. Sorry that had to happen to the little ducky. I was sitting in for Dora. Poor old George had a bad coughing fit. Blood'n'all. He were in a bad way. I came in 'ere to fetch him some linctus but it was too late. When I went back into his room he was gone. It was that quick.' She warmed the teapot with water from the kettle and measured out the tea leaves. 'Naturally, I needed to let Dora know he'd passed away. Since the little one was asleep I ran down to The Oxford to fetch Dora home. It's only five minutes away. I never thought the poor lamb would wake up while I was gone. It took me a while to find them in the theatre. What else could I do, sir?'

'Them? The Oxford?'

'Oh didn't you know?' Mrs Spindlemann looked sly. 'I

thought Dora had told you. She's always loved the music halls. She goes with our Stan. He loves it too. She said you were happy about it as you aren't keen on the variety shows yourself.'

Edmund stared at her, stupefied. Eventually, he said, 'Thank you for making the tea, but I'd like you to leave now, Mrs Spindlemann.'

The woman nodded. As she was leaving, she paused in the doorway and looked back at him. 'He'd do anything for Dora would my Stanley. If you don't mind me saying, it isn't right that a young woman should be alone so much. That girl needs a bit of jollity in her life.'

Before Edmund could respond she was gone.

He took a deep breath. How had it come to this? Why hadn't Dora told him? He'd have gritted his teeth and accompanied her to the music hall. He remembered their few trips there and how she had cried with laughter at the corny jokes and sung along to the song choruses - while he'd endured it. Why hadn't he made more effort? But the truth was plain. They were completely unsuited to each other. They wanted different things, had different pleasures. Why had he failed to understand this before he asked her to marry him? A slave to her beauty, he'd looked no deeper.

Leaving her child and terminally ill father with a neighbour while she gallivanted with a man who was not her husband was not the behaviour expected of a wife and mother. But blaming her would be wrong, when the root cause lay with him. Then his anger rose again as he thought of Lottie's distress at finding herself alone with the dead body of her beloved grandfather.

If he was in pain about this, so would be Dora. He couldn't deny that she was a good and caring mother who doted on her child and lavished affection on her. Who was he to begrudge his wife some pleasure in an otherwise empty life? He felt no jealousy about Stanley, only sadness. If Edmund had never set eyes on her in the Central that day, she'd doubtless be married to

Stanley by now and happier. Edmund's haste to wed her was a curse he'd brought upon himself. And where had it got him? Silent evenings. Lonely nights. Passionless arid intercourse on the few occasions she submitted to his advances. But it had also produced Charlotte, the love of his life, who brought joy to him whenever he was with her.

He poured two cups of tea and took them on a tray into the parlour. It was time to persuade his wife to leave her father's bedside. He put his arms around her tentatively and helped her to her feet. Dora offered no resistance and leant against him as he led her into the parlour, closing the door to George's bedroom behind them.

She shed no tears but her face was wracked with pain as she sat, rigid, her eyes devoid of expression, staring at the empty fireside chair where George had sat before being confined to his bed. His pipe was propped on its rack on the mantelpiece where it always rested, a tin of tobacco beside it.

Edmund tried to get her to sip the sweet tea. 'Come on, it'll do you good. You've had a shock.'

'I should have been here with him. Holding his hand when he went. I'd no idea it was that close to the end. I'll never forgive myself.'

'Mrs Spindlemann says it happened quickly. He didn't suffer. He's with your mother now.'

Dora took a sip of tea. 'Easy for you to say that.'

Edmund said nothing. Words were inadequate.

'His lungs were that bad he should have been in that sanatorium out at Pinewood that the doctor mentioned. If we'd had the money...' She raised her eyes to his, reproachful.

Here it was. The *entente* was over. Edmund braced himself for the recriminations to begin. 'When the doctor suggested it, Dora, you said you wanted to care for your dad yourself. And he was adamant he wanted to die in his own bed.'

She didn't reply.

'Your father was very sick. Take comfort that he died in familiar surroundings and that you cared for him as best as you possibly could. Until just a few months ago he was still managing to make his weekly trip to The One Tun. And enjoying his pipe.'

'Shut up. I don't want to hear anything you have to say. If you'd swallowed your pride and asked your stinking rich father for money we'd not have been stuck here like this, with Dad trapped in the flat, unable to manage the stairs anymore. You make me sick, Edmund. I wish I'd never clapped eyes on you.'

He wished it too.

Dora got up, setting her unfinished tea on the table. At the door to the bedroom she said, 'You'll have to go to the undertaker tomorrow. There's the death to register too. I can't face any of that.'

'Yes, of course.'

When she was gone, he quenched the oil lamp and sat in a darkened room, head in hands. He had ruined both their lives. There was no denying it.

The death of his father-in-law meant Edmund remained in London for longer than he would have liked. A telegram to Mrs Bowyer, explaining the circumstances, elicited a curt response that she expected him to return at the earliest possible date.

In between making the arrangements for George's funeral he gathered the materials he needed to send to Little Badgerton and arranged their despatch. Dora was like a wraith, barely eating and drinking, neglecting her appearance and lying on her bed for hours. Edmund took on the task of arranging the funeral, taking his daughter with him, grateful to have such an unprecedented opportunity to spend time with his little girl. Most of the funeral plans had been arranged in anticipation of his death by George himself, using the proceeds of an insurance policy he'd taken out as a young railway clerk, so there was relatively little left to do.

The service took place at All Saints church, in nearby Margaret Street. George had not been a regular church goer, but it was where he and Dora's mother had been married. Edmund knew the place by reputation. A Gothic Revival church, it was tucked away between densely packed buildings.

The interior was an assault on the senses, an explosion of colour, an extravagance of shapes and textures. Edmund was bedazzled whichever way he directed his gaze. Stained glass played a more minor role than usual. In place of windows, the lower wall areas were adorned with vibrantly coloured tiled friezes, portraying Biblical stories and the lives of the saints.

Beside him in the pew, Dora appeared oblivious to the kaleidoscopic surroundings, keeping her eyes lowered, avoiding looking at the coffin, placed in front of the elaborate chancel screen.

Edmund felt a rush of pity for his wife. She'd lost both parents and was trapped in a loveless marriage, with only Charlotte to bring her consolation. He thought of the death of his own mother three years earlier. He hadn't wanted to provoke a confrontation with his father by appearing at the funeral but had made his way to Highgate Cemetery and watched from a distance as his mother was laid to rest. Only when the cortege had departed had he ventured up to the grave to lay a posy of anemones on the ground and say a silent goodbye. What a miserable life Susan Cutler had lived since her ill-fated marriage to Herbert. Last time he'd stood in this spot was Gilbert's funeral. His brother was interred in the same grave. At least his mother was reunited with her elder son.

The death of his mother had roused sympathy from Dora but it had soon become the basis for a renewed attempt on her part to get Edmund to approach his father for money. Since he blamed his father for Susan's premature death, he was adamant there'd be no thawing of relations.

Here now in this church, marking the death of his father-in-law, Edmund reflected that neither his nor Dora's families had been blessed with good fortune. It was hard not to conclude that their union had made matters worse.

When the service ended, Dora caught her husband gazing up at the ceiling of the church. 'Nice, isn't it?' she said, to his surprise. 'Mum and Dad were married here. It's where I always wanted to be married. Not in some seedy council office.' She turned away from him to follow the coffin as it was carried out of the church. Stung by her words, Edmund followed behind her.

George Fisher's interment took place at Brookwood Cemetery in Surrey, accessed via the Necropolis Railway from its new dedicated station on Westminster Bridge Road. The rail trip was a miserable business, with only Edmund and Dora, Mr & Mrs Spindlemann and Stanley, and three of George's retired former colleagues. They travelled in silence apart from the occasional whispered exchange between the elderly rail retirees. Dora was mute, gazing through rain spattered windows with unseeing eyes.

Later, back in Goodge Street, because of Mrs Bowyer's expectation of his speedy return, Edmund could no longer postpone talking to Dora about their future. Once Charlotte was asleep in bed, he broached the subject.

'This commission is more extensive than I envisaged. My client, Mrs Bowyer, insists I remain on site for the duration.'

Dora looked up and threw him a withering look. 'How convenient for you.' She went to stand by the window. Outside, a dense smog obscured the buildings on the opposite side of the street.

He ignored her caustic tone, knowing it must have been a stressful day for her. 'All three of us can go to Little Badgerton.'

The words were out before he thought what that meant. While nothing would make him happier than his daughter being here with him, the thought of Dora moving into the tiny cottage he'd inspected that morning was not appealing. Edmund realised he'd been looking forward to living as if he were once more a bachelor. Away from the mood swings of Dora and his own abiding guilt at having married her. But it was too late to retract the offer. And getting Lottie away from the London smog – experiencing nature first hand – was alluring.

'There's a cottage in the grounds of Bankstone which Mrs Bowyer has offered us rent-free. We'd save on paying rent here. The village is pretty and there's a school where Lottie could go, and plenty of fresh country air. The countryside there is beautiful. I'm sure it would inspire you to start illustrating flowers again. And the scenery's glorious. The walking—'

'I like walking along streets. Looking in shop windows. Choosing the kinds of houses I'd like to live in if you weren't so blooming hopeless. What do I want with the countryside?'

He stared at her, struggling to comprehend. 'You love the parks. It's like living in the midst of one glorious park. Honestly, Dora, you won't know until you've tried. It would be a new beginning for us. We may be even able to stay on permanently and I could run the business from there.'

Dora's expression was sour, her eyes full of contempt as they swept over him. 'The business? What business? You act like you're a huge success but you're nobody.' She turned again to stare out into the sulphurous fog. 'Charlotte and I aren't budging. London's our home.'

He swallowed, hope draining from him, before rallying for another attempt to win her round. 'Come for a few days at least. Have a look. If you don't like it, you can come back here and we'll never mention it again. But think of Charlotte. Country air will be better for her than being in the city. At least come and see for yourself.' He hated pleading with her. It was demeaning, but he had to do it. He was the architect of their unhappiness and he had to take every chance to try to make some kind of future, for his daughter's sake. A change in their circumstances and surroundings may even enable them to build something from the rubble of their marriage.

'Stop!' Dora folded her arms like a barrier. 'I'm sick and tired of telling you. I'm not moving. I'm a city girl and I always will be. I love London and Charlotte does too. Do what you jolly well like, as long as you keep paying the rent on this place, send me my housekeeping and settle the bills. Go and live in the country. Stay with your fancy woman.'

Edmund's hands balled into tight fists and he buried them in his pockets. 'For God's sake, Dora, Mrs Bowyer is an elderly widow. She's not my fancy woman. You're being preposterous.' His mouth set hard. 'We need to talk about this properly, I have to leave early tomorrow morning and I'd like you to come with me. Just for a few days to have a look. Then, if you like the place, we can give the landlord notice here and arrange the removal.'

She spun round and rushed at him, landing a stinging blow with her hand across his face. 'I told you. I'm not leaving here. Now shut it.'

Edmund slumped back into a chair, face smarting and pride at rock bottom. Dora went into her bedroom and slammed the door behind her.

TWENTY-ONE

It was Alice's last day at Padgett Hall; the last time she'd do this daily walk after almost five years in the colonel's employ.

When Colonel Fitzwarren had told her he'd no longer require her services due to the return of his nephew from India, she'd been surprised and more than a little offended. While there'd been no love lost between them, she believed she'd done an excellent conscientious job for the man. To be dismissed in such a peremptory manner was discourteous and unfair.

When she'd asked if he was unhappy with her work, he'd blustered at her, reminding her that his preference had always been to have a man to do the job. He'd claimed that his nephew's knowledge of the army and of India made him far more suited to the job.

While her gender was undeniable, Alice had never felt the lack of specialist knowledge of India, since the colonel would never have permitted her to change a word – other than to ensure the correct spelling of place names.

He'd given her less than a week's notice. After almost five years toiling over his hieroglyphics and transcribing his mind-numbingly boring tales of empire. Five years of heaving books off shelves, dusting them, sorting them into alphabetical order, listing the titles and authors in a ledger book before returning the volumes to the shelves – where she was certain they'd never be touched again. Even though the colonel never appeared to read any of them he continued to add to his collection, with brown paper parcels arriving from a London book dealer on a weekly basis. Alice had been like Sisyphus pushing the boulder up the hill in a never-ending cycle. But now that cycle was ending – at least for her.

As Padgett Hall came into sight, Alice felt a surge of discontent. It hadn't been the most interesting job and the colonel was far from congenial company, but the wage he paid her kept her in clothes and art materials and allowed her to make a modest contribution to the Hargreaveses for her keep. To be jobless would rob her of independence.

Working for Edmund Cutler – for she was increasingly sure it would prove to be him – would at least keep her in funds. But she had to acknowledge that her antipathy for him was doubtless reciprocated, so he might refuse her the job, once he knew who she was.

Skirting the Georgian house, Alice crossed the rear stable yard and entered via the back kitchen door as the colonel had always stipulated, thus underlining that he considered her one of the servants. She took off her coat, hung it up in the boot room and headed for Fitzwarren's study.

A military march was already blaring from the gramophone. The colonel, smoking his pipe and reading *The Daily Telegraph* barely glanced up when she came in. Her cheery greeting was met by a grunt. She was about to ask him when he expected his nephew, but decided not to bother.

The morning dragged and she heaved a sigh of relief when at last the carriage clock chimed and she was able to leave. He said goodbye – but there was no word of thanks.

Alice trudged back towards the vicarage. She swung open

the gate and was heading up the path when the door to the adjacent church swung open and Edmund Cutler emerged. She pressed herself up against the trunk of a chestnut tree and hoped he wasn't coming to the vicarage. To her intense relief he turned left after he went through the lych gate and walked away in the direction of Bankstone.

She watched him recede into the distance and realised she was shaking. A tide of dislike for him washed over her. All the wretchedness she'd experienced when he rejected her to marry someone else. The terrible memory of what she'd witnessed in the garden shed. The falling out with her parents. The separation from her brother. Nothing but unhappy memories she'd thought were behind her forever.

Life was unfair. Fate was playing a cruel trick on her by Cutler turning up here in this little Hampshire backwater. Tears of anger threatened but she brushed them away before they fell. Pushing back her shoulders she took a deep breath. She wouldn't give him the satisfaction of being miserable. She wouldn't let him ruin the happiness she'd found in Little Badgerton. She was stronger than that. A proud suffragette. That arrogant insufferable man wasn't going to get the better of her.

TWENTY-TWO

When Edmund returned to Little Badgerton, to his surprise he was greeted warmly by Mrs Bowyer when he called on her after inspecting the embrasures in the parish church again. He gave her his assurance that there would be no more protracted absences and he would do his utmost to make up the lost time. She offered some unexpected words of sympathy about the death of his father-in-law.

That night was the appointed date for dining at the vicarage. Mrs Hargreaves sent a maid to the studio to check that Edmund had returned and establish whether he was able to fulfil the invitation. He assured the young woman that he would be there as planned.

Now he needed to deal with his expectation that the Hargreaves' niece was likely to prove an unsuitable assistant, putting unnecessary strain on his relationship with the vicar. He liked the Hargreaveses. Liked them a lot. Saw them as allies and possibly friends while he tackled this work, away from the camaraderie of the studio and the support and good counsel of Mr Whall.

So, it was with a degree of foreboding that Edmund

approached the vicarage that evening. If the niece was willing to take on the job, he'd feel obliged to offer it to her. But how would a young woman, whose only working experience was the cataloguing of old books, adapt to the world of creating stained glass? A well-bred woman wouldn't welcome being asked to sweep the floor, keep the benches clean and tidy, and undertake every menial task he threw at her. What if she besieged him with questions and pestered him to teach her the more artistic elements of the job? A potential source of conflict and a recipe for difficulties with the vicar, whose goodwill was vital to the successful completion of the commission.

He'd have to stress that the work would be uncongenial. If he painted a grim enough picture, the young lady might excuse herself and save him the embarrassment of turning her down. Then he could seek out a strong lad from the village to do the job instead.

A housemaid opened the front door and showed him into the room where he'd been received in the previous week. The vicar and his wife were again side-by-side on the sofa, but there was a third person in the room as he entered, sitting in front of the fire with her back to him.

'Mr Cutler,' Mrs Hargreaves said. 'May we offer our sincere condolences on the death of your father-in-law. I understand the gentleman lived with you and your wife?'

Edmund acknowledged that he had.

The vicar shook his head. 'That must have been hard for your poor wife. A blessing that you happened to be there at the time of his passing.'

He indicated the other person in the room. 'Allow us to introduce our niece, Alice.'

The young woman rose and turned to greet him.

Something about her was familiar, but Edmund struggled to place when or where they could have met. Tall, with a fresh complexion and hair pulled back into an untidy bun, there was nothing particularly memorable about her features.

Nodding in acknowledgement of his greeting, she settled back into her chair.

Perhaps she reminded him of somebody else. His brain raced through the possibilities. Not a student at the Central. No one at the studio. Not a past client. Certainly not a friend of Dora's. Since his marriage, his world had constricted, narrowed into these few threads.

Eleanor Hargreaves returned the conversation to his recent bereavement.

'Your father-in-law had been ill for some time?'

'Lung disease.'

'Poor man. How awful for Mrs Cutler.'

'Yes it was a terrible blow. She nursed him and is distraught. They were very close. She lost her mother when she was young.'

'You and your daughter must be a great comfort to her.' Mrs Hargreaves smiled sadly.

Edmund nodded, mutely.

'Will they be coming here to join you?'

'Sadly not. My wife isn't fond of the countryside and prefers to stay in London.'

'How are you finding Bankstone?' Mrs Hargreaves asked, changing the subject as she handed him a sherry. 'I trust you've been made welcome there?'

'Mrs Bowyer has been most accommodating. The building that is to be my studio is perfect. The local carpenter took advantage of my absence and has effected all the work needed to make it a fully operational studio space.'

'Excellent news!' The vicar clapped his hands together. 'Mrs Bowyer called on me in your absence to inform me of her new idea for the church window.'

'What did she say?' Edmund asked.

The vicar raised his glass in a gesture of tribute. 'Clearly, you are an accomplished diplomat as well as a fine artist, Mr Cutler, as she appears to believe that the idea of biblical tales of a maritime nature is entirely her own.'

Edmund grinned. 'Did you give in gracefully?'

'Of course I didn't.' Hargreaves chuckled. 'Mrs Bowyer is satisfied by nothing short of the complete annihilation of her opponent and who am I to disappoint her? So I suggested instead that we dedicate the window to St Erasmus, the patron saint of sailors. Told her his martyrdom would be an inspiring subject and entirely fitting as a tribute to the late commodore.'

Edmund was aghast. 'But—'

'Fear not! Once I told her the poor chap had his entrails pulled out by a windlass she was outraged.'

Eleanor Hargreaves groaned. 'Really, Walter, one day your sense of humour is going to land you in big trouble.' She pulled a face. 'Is that really how he died?'

'Yes, they tried all kinds of other ways to kill him, but he was indestructible. Nothing worked.'

Alice spoke for the first time. 'Don't you mean *God* saved him? You *are* meant to be a vicar.'

Her voice was also vaguely familiar, and Edmund was all the more certain he knew the young woman from somewhere. But where?

'I don't have a lot of time for the gruesome stories of martyrs,' said the vicar. Eleanor shuddered. 'I'm jolly relieved poor Mrs Bowyer didn't embrace the idea. Can you imagine explaining that image to the Sunday school children?'

Alice smiled. 'They'd have loved it, the little horrors.'

Edmund sipped his sherry. 'Anyway, it's a relief to know that we have accord among all parties and I can get on with designing my window.' He glanced sideways at Alice, wondering how to broach the question of her becoming his assistant but her next question relieved him of the need to speak first.

Alice swivelled in her chair to face him. 'My aunt has told me you need an apprentice, and you are open to it being a woman.' Without waiting for a response, she went on, 'I'd like the job.'

Edmund swallowed. He hadn't expected such directness. 'It would be wise for you to understand first what is involved. You may have expectations that I won't be able to meet.'

'I don't care about money.'

'I didn't mean that. Not that I can offer much on that score either. But rather that the work of a junior assistant is of a lowly nature.'

'Did you once do it yourself?'

'Yes. I did.'

'Then it must be an essential step and I'm ready to undertake it.' She tilted her head up and looked him in the eye. 'I'm not afraid of hard work, Mr Cutler. Not when it leads to learning something new.'

Edmund stared at his shoes. He glanced up at the Hargreaves, hoping they'd rescue him, but they were waiting for his answer as expectantly as their niece. He was on his own. 'I'm afraid I'll have no time to teach you. Mrs Bowyer wants the project completed as soon as possible. May I suggest—'

'—I said I want to *learn*. Not that I want to be taught. I have eyes in my head. I can learn by watching you.'

His stomach sank as he imagined trying to concentrate on his work while she hovered at his elbow and peppered him with questions.

He had to be blunt. 'I work in silence. Concentration is essential to me. I can't keep stopping to explain or answer questions.'

She gave a long sigh. 'I'm evidently not making myself clear. I'm not a talkative person. But I am an observant one. I also love to study. I'll take full responsibility for my own learning. I want only the opportunity to watch and learn from you. And as for the menial tasks, anything will be a pleasant change after years of lugging piles of dusty tomes on obscure military campaigns down from shelves, entering their titles and the authors' names in a ledger and putting them back on the shelves. All accompanied by military marches on the gramophone.'

She smiled but it didn't reach her eyes and he couldn't help thinking the smile was more for her relatives' benefit than for his. 'The colonel's music collection consists of about thirty scratchy recordings and I was expected to work my way through the pile, keeping the machine wound up, starting at the beginning again when the pile was exhausted. All while he paced up and down, complaining about the state of the world and the shortcomings of our government as well as the abominations that are Irish Home Rule and Woman's Suffrage.'

Edmund had no way to counter that. The woman certainly had spirit. 'I can't promise the work won't be tedious and repetitive but at least you won't be subjected to marching music or politics. As it happens, I've always had a weakness for the underdog, so my sympathies are with the Irish and I can see no possible justification for denying the franchise to women.'

Eleanor Hargreaves grinned at her niece and nodded.

Alice kept her gaze fixed on Edmund. 'Thank you. You won't regret it.'

So that was it then. The decision had been made and he could only hope she was right. 'How long are you contracted to the colonel?'

'I'm not. I worked for him for the past five years but his nephew has returned from India and has agreed to finish cataloguing the library. I've been dropped like a hot cake. Today was my last day.'

'I'm sorry,' said Edmund.

Alice gave a little derisive snort. 'Don't be. It's a blessed release. The nephew is ex-army himself. Fell off his polo pony and has been invalided out. He's more than happy to work for his uncle.'

Yet again Edmund had a sense of *déjà vu*. Where had he seen her before? Contrary to his expectations, he liked her. She had spirit.

The maid announced dinner and they moved across the hallway into the dining room.

As soon as he entered, Edmund's eyes were drawn to a series of paintings. Watercolours, each in a simple gilded frame, they were breathtakingly beautiful in their subject matters and the detail of their execution. The brushwork was delicate but confident, the colours subtle, with flashes of boldness. Above all they had a simplicity that his trained eye knew belied the artistry that had gone into them. He walked over to study them more closely.

'These are exquisite.' He paused in front of one. 'The detail on the trees in this one is remarkable. And the light, the way it plays on the foliage.'

'Alice's work,' said Mrs Hargreaves proudly. 'We had to browbeat her into letting us put these few pictures up. She insists her painting is for her eyes alone. Claims her pleasure is entirely in the act of painting and drawing and not in the result.'

Edmund paused. Someone else had once said the same thing to him. He recalled a conversation with another young woman about painting. *My pleasure is in the doing and not in the result.*

Dear Lord, the niece was The Honourable Alice Dalton!

Disconcerted, he turned away from the paintings and moved over to the dining table. He glanced at her again. He'd only met Alice once. At that awful supper after she'd gone to the opera with Gilbert. But it was her. It had to be her.

She lowered her gaze, avoiding eye contact.

Edmund spoke quietly. 'Your work is exceptional. With

such a talent you ought to devote yourself to your art. I have nothing to teach you.'

No one spoke for a few moments until Eleanor Hargreaves broke the silence. 'But surely you can understand, Mr Cutler. With such skills at her disposal, my niece is keen to apply them in a new direction. She is genuinely eager to learn about stained glass.'

Alice lifted her eyes and met Edmund's. 'Someone once accused me of assuming that the creation of stained glass was a random act, like gathering pebbles on a beach. I'm keen to make amends for that lack of judgment on my part.'

Edmund drew his mouth into a narrow line and nodded, defeated. Alice Dalton was about to become his assistant and there was nothing he could do about it.

TWENTY-THREE

Alice went into the workshop behind Bankstone, palms clammy, even though it was a crisp late November day. Edmund Cutler was bent over a sketch pad, which he put aside when she entered the room.

Swallowing her nerves, she opted to get the awkwardness out of the way quickly. 'I want to thank you,' she said.

He glanced sideways at her. 'Don't thank me until you've seen what's involved. I doubt you'll want to thank me then.'

He was so snappy. She gritted her teeth and pressed on. 'That's not what I meant. I'm thanking you for not revealing that we'd met before. My aunt and uncle don't know that you're the man to whom I once believed myself about to become engaged.'

His back stiffened, then he turned away.

She was determined to see it through. 'I had no idea you'd already made promises to someone else. It would have been a kindness to let me know.'

'Look, Miss Dalton, Miss Hargreaves, whatever you want to be called, we met only once. I owed you nothing.'

She bristled. 'I didn't say you owed me anything. We were

both pawns being manoeuvred by our parents. I didn't want to be married to you any more than you did to me. And I'm glad you did what you did as it was the trigger for me to break away from all that I loathed about my old life.' She added the *coup de grâce*: 'And I'd have hated to be married to you.'

'Good. That's settled then.' He rubbed his hand against his neck. 'No need to thank me for not revealing that we'd met. I didn't actually remember you anyway.' He turned back to his sketch pad.

If Alice had disliked him on their first meeting, she loathed him now. Edmund Cutler was hateful. But she needed to work and she had to admit she was fascinated by the chance to discover more about the medium of stained glass.

'Where do I start?' she asked, hanging up her coat on a hook by the door. 'Tell me what you'd like me to do.'

'You can start by sweeping this place out, while I sort through my tools. I can't work in chaos, so I'll expect you to keep the studio in order.'

Testing her. Assuming the Honourable Alice Dalton considered herself too grand for menial work. She'd prove him wrong. The arrogant man.

She set about sweeping the floor, first sprinkling water to settle the dust as she'd seen the housemaid at the rectory do. When the job was finished, she looked around, satisfied, and pushed her hair back from her face, securing it with a pin. Her hands and the cuffs of her blouse were filthy, so she undoubtedly now had a dirty face. Scrabbling in her satchel, she pulled out an old Liberty print scarf and tied it round her head to keep her hair out of the way then went to wash her hands and splash water on her face.

Edmund was wearing a heavy cloth apron like a butcher's. Why hadn't she thought to bring an apron for herself? Tomorrow she would – the housekeeper must have a spare one she could borrow until she had time to make herself a couple.

He was arranging tools on the deal table but glanced up at Alice. Noticing her head gear, his lips twitched in a smile. 'Come over here and I'll show you the tools. Your job will be to keep them in order. I can't abide it if I can't immediately lay my hands on the right instrument.'

The tools and brushes were all lined up and spaced equidistantly. She hadn't expected him to be so organised. Edmund Cutler, despite his casual bohemian appearance, his overlong hair and unpolished shoes, seemed to be a man of precision and order.

'You need to keep everything in perfect condition: paintbrushes clean, cutters sharp and ready to use.'

She listened intently.

'If you're to assist me, you'll need to learn the craft first. I want you to forget about painting, regardless of your undoubted flair. Until you know how to cut glass to my satisfaction, you won't be holding a paintbrush in here.' He fixed his eyes on her. 'And if that doesn't happen, I won't require your services at all.'

'It will happen. I'll make sure it does. I want to learn.' It was true. She'd prove the odious Edmund Cutler wrong.

He signalled her to move closer while he detailed each of the tools and explained their purpose. 'Most people prefer wheel cutters but I like the old-fashioned fixed head diamonds. The thicker handle sits better in my hand.' He picked up a cutter and demonstrated how to hold it. 'Here, you try with the wheel cutter. Keep a light touch, using your forefinger to guide the diamond head as you apply the merest pressure. Try it.'

She took the cutter in her hand.

'Not like that. It's not a pen or a paintbrush. It needs to be placed between the first and middle fingers not the thumb and first. Otherwise you'll press too hard and crack the glass.'

Alice bit her lip and adjusted her hold. How was she supposed to know? Insufferable man.

He took the cutter from her and demonstrated how to use it

on a piece of glass. 'Press enough to feel it bite. Don't let it skid over the glass. Imagine a ploughshare in a furrow. The line should be so light it's barely visible. Not throwing up glass dust. Look closely. Like this. Now you try.'

Choking back her fury, she took the cutter from him. The wooden handle was warm from his hands. She positioned it over the glass. His fingers moved to rest on top of hers as he guided her hand forward. They were standing close together and she could feel the warmth of his breath as they watched their joined hands slide over the surface of the glass. 'Lightly. Let it glide. No sound, no grating noise. Like that. Now try on your own.'

She did as he told her and felt the gentle motion of the diamond blade under her fingers, leaving the faintest of lines, barely visible. Drawing back, she looked up at Edmund for his verdict, doubting the line was deep enough.

His bottom lip jutted forward and he frowned.

Alice waited for the inevitable criticism.

'Good,' he said. 'Now do it again.'

She repeated the process in a new straight line through the centre of another glass off-cut. Edmund leant forward and examined it. 'Most students apply too much pressure when they start. It appears you're a natural.'

His tone was grudging. Alice felt a shiver of pride.

He picked up the piece of glass and placed his fingers on either side of the near-invisible cut she had made, so that the glass sprang apart. 'Use your knuckles as a hinge. Don't push too hard.'

Alice did as directed with the second piece of glass and felt a surge of relief as the glass separated cleanly into two pieces.

Edmund remained begrudging in his praise. 'Probably beginner's luck.'

Alice bristled. 'Why should it be? You explained and I did it. Why would I not keep on doing it?'

He frowned again, then went on to show her how to cut a curved line.

The morning passed rapidly as they worked in silent concentration. Alice cut a series of increasingly complicated shapes as directed. Edmund explained the pressure points and the correct order of making each cut so as not to fracture the glass. It was like a lesson in physics or geometry and she listened carefully, determined not to let herself down. She completed every task he set her, without error, experiencing a growing sense of satisfaction as each piece met his exacting require-ments. She hadn't expected to like the cutting part – indeed she hadn't even expected to do it, imagining that Edmund would have used her skills to help him with drawing. Until now she'd imagined that using sharp instruments and cutting up glass was a masculine pursuit and would prove difficult and tedious, yet there was something deeply relaxing and satisfying in the exercise.

They halted just before midday and Edmund went outside and sat on a wooden bench to eat. The spot was sheltered by an overhang in the roof. He unwrapped sandwiches prepared by the cook at Bankstone and called Alice over. 'There's cheese and cucumber and these are ham and piccalilli.'

'I'm sorry, Mr Cutler, I'll remember to bring my own sand-wiches tomorrow. I didn't think.' She sat down next to him on the bench, trying to keep as far from him as possible.

Edmund waved a hand dismissively. 'I asked the cook to make enough for us both. And you may as well call me Edmund.'

'Then you'd better call me Alice.'

Edmund gave a half-smile. 'Actually, I ought to call you Dalton. We use surnames only in Whall's studio.'

Alice nibbled at the cheese sandwich. 'I suppose that's why you didn't want to take me on. Because I'm a woman.'

'What's that got to do with it?'

'You were reluctant to give me a chance. I suppose it's unusual for a woman to want to work in stained glass.'

'What nonsense,' he said, abruptly. 'There are three women working for Mr Whall, including his daughter, Veronica. She's highly talented. All the women are.'

Alice tightened her lips. 'I didn't know that. I suppose I'm used to doors being shut against women.'

'Not in the Arts and Crafts movement. And certainly not in stained glass. Haven't you heard of Lowndes and Drury?'

Alice shook her head.

'Lowndes is Mary Lowndes. She and Alfred Drury, who was one of my teachers at the Central, set up their firm to provide services to people like me who prefer an alternative to commercial glass manufacturers. They rent out studio space and equipment. Mary is an accomplished stained-glass artist. They're based in Fulham in London. I'd be working out of there now if Mrs Bowyer hadn't insisted on me basing myself on site.'

'I've heard of Mary Lowndes,' Alice said. 'She chairs The Artists' Suffrage League. She's done lots of artworks for the NUWSS. Posters and banners and so on. I had no idea she was a stained-glass artist too.'

He glanced sideways at her but said nothing. They ate in silence until eventually Edmund spoke. 'I can assure you, my reluctance to take you on was based on your lack of training and not on your gender, Alice.'

At least he had used the past tense when referring to his reluctance.

'I thought you were going to call me Dalton.'

'I've had second thoughts.' He grinned. 'Alice is rather a nice name and has the merit of being yours and not your family's.' He reached into his knapsack and pulled out an apple which he cut in half with a penknife, handing a piece to her.

She decided not to pursue that line as it was probably related to Gilbert. 'Thank you.'

'So, you're involved in women's suffrage?'

'Yes. Is that a problem?'

'Of course it isn't.'

'I set up a little branch in the village. We're really just an offshoot from Petersfield but we're doing our bit to build support.'

'Good for you,' he said. Was he being sarcastic? Certainly rather patronising.

They lapsed into silence, enjoying the winter sun on their faces as they finished their simple meal. When the sun moved behind clouds, Alice shivered and got to her feet.

Edmund stood up too. 'Now we shall see how you paint on glass.'

'But I thought—'

'You're able to cut glass well enough, so you now need to learn to paint on it. The two things work in harmony.' He avoided her gaze and moved towards the work bench. 'I didn't expect you to take to cutting so quickly, but since you have, there's no point in delaying.'

Alice's fingers were itching; she longed to take a brush in her hands and experience for the first time how it would feel to apply paint to the medium of glass. Her gratification was to be delayed as Edmund embarked first on a lengthy discourse on pigments and how to mix them. She watched as he demonstrated, wondering if she would be able to remember the vocabulary he was using as he described the ingredients. Words that had previously meant nothing to her, like oxidation, gumarabica and iron oxide, now took on an unexpected exoticism as he described them. He told her that most artists bought their pigments readymade but, encouraged by Christopher Whall, he'd become used to mixing his own.

At last, when he'd finished with palette knife, gum and powders, he took up a rigger brush, dipped it in the colour and diluted it to make a small coloured pool on his palette. As he had done in cutting the glass, he now got Alice to repeat each step after he demonstrated, reminding her to stir up the paint solution each time she dipped or mixed, so the pigment didn't separate into sludge.

When she was ready, he told her to make some marks with the paint on a piece of glass. At first he asked for simple curving lines of different thicknesses, all the time demonstrating first. Alice was astonished to discover that not only were the effects variable based on the style, thickness, and pressure of the brush, but also by mixing the pigments with sugar or treacle rather than gum-arabic. Hours passed unnoticed as they tried flat washes and hard outlines. He got her to trace from cartoon drawings and showed her how to get them as close as possible to the originals. Constantly, he held the glass she was working on up to the light to show how it changed the luminosity, transparency and the very colour itself.

'I had no idea,' she said.

'Of what?'

'That glass painting was so subtle and infinitely flexible. I never imagined the effects could be so dramatically different and that there are so many factors to consider.'

'Indeed,' he said, and she sensed he was suppressing a smile. 'I remember you telling me when we first met that making a stained-glass window must be like putting together a jigsaw puzzle with bits of coloured glass.'

Alice felt her face burning. 'Oh my goodness. I did, didn't I? I'm sorry. That was rude and presumptuous of me. Spoken entirely from ignorance. I'm mortified that you remember.' She pulled herself up. Why was she apologising?

'Your words made quite an impression. Since you were the guest of my brother, I had to remind myself it was not the time and place to put you right.'

This out-of-the-blue reference to the past, to a time when Gilbert was alive, broke the spell between them. It was an intrusion – as though Gilbert's presence had manifested in the room and chilled the atmosphere. From that moment on, other than Edmund's instructions and explanations, they worked in silence for the rest of the afternoon.

When the daylight faded, Edmund showed her how to replace the tools in the correct order, cover the pigments, tidy the workbench and set aside the samples they'd worked on. 'Keeping the studio in good order and the tools always ready to use will save time tomorrow.' He looked thoughtful. 'That was one of the first things I learnt from Mr Whall. A glass-painter's tools and workshop – or indeed that of any artist – should be handled with as much care and kept in as good order as you would expect of a surgeon in the operating theatre. Mr Whall was a stickler for it and I can honestly say it was a lesson that took me time to fully absorb, but one that I came to appreciate more than any other.'

His tone had softened and Alice was relieved. The realisation dawned on her that it mattered greatly what Edmund Cutler thought of her. She may not like him as a person, but she wanted to gain his respect as an artist and, more than anything, she wanted him to share all he knew about his craft with her. What he had said about Mary Lowndes had fired her imagination and made her determined not to disappoint as his apprentice. Alice had a powerful desire to learn to become a true artist-craftswoman. That meant turning herself into a sponge to absorb everything Edmund Cutler could teach her. And, above all, ensuring she didn't give him cause to regret taking her on as his assistant. She made an unspoken vow to become the best apprentice he could hope for so that one day she, like Mary Lowndes and Veronica Whall, would become a stained-glass artist in her own right. What did it matter that the man was arrogant and distant? It was the artist she wanted to impress.

She pulled the scarf off her head, folded it and put it inside her bag. The front of her white blouse was spattered with paint.

It appeared Edmund had noticed too. 'I should have warned you to bring an apron. I'm sorry.'

She waved a hand lightly. 'No matter. I'll bring one tomorrow.'

Alice glanced down at the workbench and the neatly restored ranks of tools and equipment. As soon as she got back to the rectory, she was going to put to rights the corner of her bedroom where she kept her paints and easel. How many times had she burrowed about through the chaos trying to find a particular brush, only to find it hiding amongst a heap of pencils, or lying under the bed, caked with dried paint? Tonight, she intended to go through her palettes and paint-boxes, clean and tidy them, make sure all her pencils were sharpened to perfection and neatly placed in a jam-jar.

'You've done well, today.' He looked at her with serious eyes. '*Really* well.'

'I loved it. Much more than I expected. Every minute.'

Edmund gave a wry smile. 'Even sweeping the floor?'

'Even that.'

'It's fortunate Lord and Lady Dalton weren't able to see you. I doubt they'd approve.'

'Well, they'll never know. We are estranged. Didn't my aunt tell you?'

'No. She didn't. But presumably she was unaware of any connection between us.'

There it was again. The past breaking into the present.

'Mr Cutler, Edmund, I'd prefer it if we could avoid any reference to our previous acquaintance. As far as my aunt is aware, you and I have never met before. She knows little about my past circumstances. We met by chance, around the time we... I... the time I left home. My father had never mentioned having a sister. When I fell out with my parents, I turned to Eleanor. I had nowhere else to go and she and Walter were kind enough to take me in.'

Alice took a deep breath. Raking all this up was horrid. 'I hadn't expected to meet anyone from that unfortunate time in the past. You can imagine how surprised I was to hear that a Mr Cutler had been awarded the commission to do the memorial window. I think it would be better for both of us if we behave as though we were complete strangers until the Hargreaveses introduced us.'

'Very well.' He narrowed his eyes, adopting the same expression he had worn that morning – detached, cool, business-like. 'Tomorrow morning bring a notebook and pencil and meet me in the church. I need to take the exact measurements of the embrasures. Your job will be to record them.'

Without another glance at her, Edmund put on his coat and left the studio.

TWENTY-FOUR

As the days passed, Edmund witnessed Alice's growing enthusiasm, no matter how dull the task or how menial. Patiently, she transcribed measurements in a notebook, annotating rough sketches of the embrasures in St Margaret's and Bankstone. He'd expected her to complain when required to do routine technical work rather than painting, but Alice was prepared to do whatever he asked of her. She kept the workshop clean and tidy to the point where he began to feel guilty.

Mrs Bowyer showed little curiosity about the details of what they were doing and never visited the studio. Once a week Edmund was summoned to the morning room to provide a briefing on progress. Alice was not invited to attend.

One morning, Alice was beside Edmund in the draughty church as he roughed out his ideas for the composition of the window. Caught up in his work, Edmund was oblivious to the temperature. He saw her shiver, but she said nothing. Later, back in the studio, he worked up the design and drew more detailed versions in full colour. His trust in her was growing and he decided to get her to translate his rough sketches into detailed templates in the actual size. Alice couldn't conceal her

delight. Edmund made no comment but took unexpected pleasure in her evident joy.

From time to time, he sought her opinion on the colour
choices and the composition of the windows, treating her as an
equal. Aside from essential communication, Alice maintained
her distance and rarely spoke. That suited Edmund. While
valuing her contribution and growing skill, he had no desire to
get to know her better. There was a part of him that felt guilty
about his treatment of her five years ago. At the same time,
while he hated to dwell on it, deep down he held her partly
responsible for Gilbert's death. Yet there was a sense of
companionable collaboration as they concentrated on the task in
hand and hours passed in just a few moments. He sensed that
after the tedium of working for Colonel Fitzwarren, Alice found
being Edmund's assistant a fulfilling and rewarding occupation.

The church window was to be executed with a dominant
colour palette of vivid vibrant blues, consistent with the
maritime theme. Mindful of Mrs Bowyer's strictures against
animals, Noah's ark was shown afloat, with the dove circling
overhead bearing its olive branch.

The dove was not to be the only bird. Edmund pulled a
sketchbook from his coat pocket and flipped through the pages
until he found what he was looking for.

'Some old sketches I made long ago. I want to remind
myself of how a pelican looks. I'm going to put one in the
central lancet beneath the tracery. What do you think?'

'Why a pelican?' She put down her paintbrush and looked
at him, curious.

'It's a Christian motif. The pelican in the wilderness was a
symbol for Christ's sacrifice. She pecked at her own breast,
drawing blood to feed her starving fledglings.'

Alice screwed her face up. 'Ugh. What a horrible image.
Why would you want that in the window?'

'It's part of Christian iconography and present in a lot of

Medieval windows.' He drew in a sharp breath. 'In truth, it's because it reminds me of my brother and the last morning we spent together.'

Her face paled at the mention of Gilbert.

Edmund looked away and studied the drawing closely. 'We were in St James's Park. Watching the pelicans being fed.'

'I didn't know they had pelicans there.'

'They arrived in the seventeenth century, a gift from the Russian ambassador.'

He kept his eyes down but sensed she was watching him. After a lengthy pause, he continued.

'Gilbert asked me why I was drawing them, and I told him that one day I might put them in a window. I've never had an opportunity until now.' He turned to look at her. 'We chatted a while then he left me to finish the drawing. Went off to meet someone at Whites.' He looked at her, eyes steady. 'Your brother.'

Alice said nothing.

He kept his eyes on her as he spoke. 'You found out about what was going on between them, didn't you? That's why you broke off the engagement.'

It was her turn to look away. 'We hadn't actually become engaged. Not officially.'

He stared at her, trying to read her expression.

'But yes. I found them together. I walked in on them in the gardener's shed.' Her voice broke. 'I'd no idea. It was a terrible shock. I didn't even know men could feel that way about each other.'

Edmund felt sorry for her. He had an urge to wrap his arms round her. He resisted. Had he pushed her too far, dragging all this up? After all he'd agreed not to refer to their past connection. 'If it's any consolation, I didn't know about their relationship either. Not until my father told me.'

'He knew?'

'Guessed probably. Once I knew, it all made sense and explained a lot about Gilbert.' Edmund put down his pencil. 'I'm sorry you had a shock, Alice. It must have been hard. Not only finding out about Gilbert, but your brother too.'

She looked down. Edmund sensed she wanted to talk about it. But then his resentment of her rose up. He'd lost his brother. Hers was merely in another country.

Although reading his mind she said, 'It was my fault Gilbert died.' Her voice shook. 'If I'd done what Victor asked me and tried to forget what I'd seen... if I'd gone ahead with the engagement, your brother wouldn't have taken his own life.'

'You don't know that,' he said. He could tell her pain was real.

'Why else would he have killed himself if not for fear that it would all come out?'

Edmund flinched, his lips tightening. 'Gilbert wasn't a happy man. After his death, I started to understand why. It must have been hard to live a lie. Day after day, pretending he was somebody he wasn't. He'd always been a dutiful son, probably out of fear of the consequences if my father had found out about his inclinations.' Edmund sighed. 'He hated the brokerage firm, hated having to kowtow to our father. He was never able to stand up to him.' Edmund looked her straight in the eye. 'Not out of a lack of courage. Gilbert couldn't bear conflict. I hope he and your brother had some moments of happiness.'

He turned away, conscious that his eyes had welled up and not wanting her to see. 'Do you think they did?' His voice was barely a whisper.

Alice reached for his hand. 'I'm certain they loved each other. I refused to accept it at the time and thought it unnatural. Victor was distraught when Gilbert died. It's part of the reason why he went so quickly to America. Wanted to get away from us all. From the memories.' She paused, squeezing her eyes shut. 'I saw how they looked at each other. It was undeniable. They loved each other.'

Realising she was still holding his hand, she dropped it abruptly. 'Sorry. I didn't mean... You're the only person I can talk to honestly about this.'

He looked down at the open sketchbook again, remembering that morning in St James's Park. 'I won't use the pelican after all.'

'Why not? It's important to remember your brother.'

'There's another reason why I remember that morning and it's not a good memory.'

She looked at him, curious.

'A bad decision I made.' He snapped the sketchbook shut, aware he'd let his guard down. 'I'm going to go for a walk. You can get on with that cartoon.' He walked away without another word, desperate to escape the confines of the studio, the ghost of his brother and the knowledge of his own terrible mistake.

TWENTY-FIVE

Nothing more was said about Gilbert's death over the next days as Alice and Edmund continued to work together. The past had retreated into the shadows.

'Mrs Bowyer doesn't approve of you,' Edmund said one morning after his weekly meeting with his client. 'She was complaining today that you're one of those window-smashing suffragettes.' He gave her an amused lop-sided grin. 'The old girl told Mrs Harrison to make sure none of the servants fall under your spell. Said if there was any such nonsense among her staff it would lead to instant dismissal.'

Alice stared at him, her mouth open.

'She suggested I find another assistant.'

Alice was speechless, terrified at the prospect of losing her place working with Edmund.

'I told her there was absolutely no chance of me doing that as you're the best apprentice I've ever had the good fortune to work with and apart from anything else I'm wholly in support of women having the vote.'

'I am? You are?'

'Of course.'

'Thank you. That means so much to me.'

'What does?'

'That you consider me your best apprentice.'

He shrugged. 'It's true.'

Alice swallowed and resisted a sudden urge to fling her arms around him and thank him for his faith in her.

'You support women's suffrage even though your mother was against it?'

He frowned. 'What gave you the idea she was against it?'

'The first time I met her, she and my mother discussed it. Mama was encouraging her to join the Anti-Suffrage League.'

'I imagine she was being polite to your mother while avoiding incurring my father's wrath. Besides, your mother being against it didn't stop you.'

'No. Actually it was a spur to me.'

Edmund smiled then turned away and bent his head over the cartoon he was working on. After a while, he looked up. 'What made you leave home? Why come to live with your aunt? Surely you had a much grander life at that big old pile in Surrey?' He turned to face her, leaning his weight against the workbench.

Alice decided to tell the truth. 'After my parents said you'd secretly married, I was humiliated. They blamed me. Saw me as a disappointment.' She stared down at the back of her hands. 'Victor was always the favourite and he was gone. All I was good for was an advantageous marriage. When that fell through for the third time—'

'The third time?'

'Before you and Gilbert, they were manoeuvring to marry me off to Lord Wallingford.'

Edmund's eyebrows shot up. 'He must be thirty years older than you.'

'Thirty-three.'

'How could you have married him? No wonder you refused.'

'I didn't actually get the chance to refuse. My best friend, Harriet, didn't share my scruples. She was only too willing to trade herself for title and money. I was immensely grateful. My parents were enraged.'

'Surely they couldn't countenance you marrying a fat gouty old fool like Wallingford?'

'My mother lectured me at length about putting the family first and saving Dalton Hall. My father was too ashamed to do so. It was his bad financial judgement that caused our problems. But he was clearly disappointed. When Harriet scooped the earl up, Mama was livid. Harriet's willingness to marry him made my own reluctance so much worse in her eyes.' Alice sighed. 'When it was suggested I marry Gilbert I could hardly refuse. And I must say, the prospect of marrying Gilbert was infinitely more appealing than the Earl of Wallingford.' She twirled a pencil through her fingers and glanced at him, trying to gauge his reaction, but Edmund's face was inscrutable. 'I was just something to be bartered by my parents.'

'And your brother?'

'He told me to stand up to them about the earl. Said it was unthinkable. But he said nothing when your brother was put forward as a suitor.'

Edmund's eyes narrowed.

She rubbed her forehead. 'Since my parents' plans for me came to naught it remains for Victor to turn the family fortunes around. Good luck to him. Have you heard any news of him? He left without saying goodbye to me.'

'No.' Edmund shook his head. 'I have no contact with my father. When I married, he disinherited me and forbade my mother from having anything to do with me. She died two years ago. I found out when I read the announcement in *The Times*.' He sighed. 'He used her money to start the firm. He's a man of no principles and no honour. Worse. He treated my mother abominably. I blame him for her premature death.'

'I'm sorry. I didn't know she'd died. I liked your mother. She was a kind woman.' She thought for a moment. 'Eleanor told me you have a little girl. Does she see her grandfather?'

'No. I'd never allow him near her. Besides, he's disowned me. My mother had a heart attack and died without ever seeing her granddaughter. I couldn't even give her a photograph to keep for fear my father would find it.' His voice broke and he turned away. 'Excuse me.' He grabbed his coat from the hook on the back of the door and left the studio.

Alice moved to the window and watched as he strode towards the woods.

It was only three o'clock, but he didn't return that afternoon. Alice finished the task he had set her then cleaned and tidied away the tools.

The next day when Alice arrived at the studio, she found Edmund threading pieces of coloured glass together.

'What are you doing?'

'Making a wind chime for my little girl. A birthday present.'

'You must miss her?'

He avoided her eyes, bending his head over his task. 'Desperately.'

She heard a tremor in his voice and felt for him. 'Do you have a photograph?'

He pulled a wallet out of his jacket pocket and took out a well-thumbed image. The child was pretty, with delicate features and her hair a mass of dark waves. She was smiling sweetly at the camera.

'What a beautiful child. What's her name?'

'Charlotte. I call her Lottie, to my wife's annoyance.'

'You must be proud of her.'

'She's the best thing in my life.' He said it with a fierceness that surprised Alice. 'It breaks my heart to be away from her.'

Alice wanted to ask why his wife was so reluctant to move to join him in the cottage Mrs Bowyer had provided him. As far as Alice could gather, the cottage was a comfortable place, if small, and since the death of Edmund's father-in-law there was surely no barrier to his wife leaving London. Likely their London home was far grander. But Alice sensed he would be resistant to talking about his private affairs.

Edmund set aside the glass wind chime and returned to the main task. They were cutting pieces for the church window, building up the biblical scenes. Alice doing pieces to form the ark, while Edmund concentrated on the figure of Christ walking on the water.

Alice no longer felt hostile towards Edmund. Her preconceptions about his arrogance were proving to be wrong. Yes, he was moody and unpredictable, but she had a respect for him that was veering close to admiration.

She paused and watched him as he worked, his hands moving over the surface of the glass. Nice hands. Large. Capable. Long fingers. Not idle elegant ones but fingers used to making things. Fingernails clean with well-defined half-moons above the cuticles. Callouses where the glass cutter sat. He held up a piece of glass to the window, turning it to catch the natural light then placed it on the bench again, fixed on the task. Focused. Lost in concentration. He picked up another piece and compared it to the first. Then he turned and caught her looking at him and frowned. Alice dropped her head and got on with her own work.

TWENTY-SIX

Just before Christmas, they were working as usual in the studio when they heard a motorcar pull into the driveway of Bankstone. They paid no heed, assuming it was the weekly grocery van or a guest for Mrs Bowyer.

About ten minutes later, the door burst open, bringing a blast of cold air into the studio. Dora stood on the threshold, a huge smile on her face. 'The housekeeper said I'd find you here.' She looked around and shivered. 'This place is in the middle of nowhere. Took forever to find it. I thought I had the wrong address. How do you stand it?' Then she noticed Alice. 'Who's that?'

She spoke as though Alice were a piece of furniture. Swallowing his irritation he introduced them. 'This is Miss Dalton, my assistant.' He turned to Alice, 'Miss Dalton, this is my wife.'

Dora looked Alice up and down then presumably decided she merited no further attention. 'We need to speak in private, Edmund.'

Alice required no prompting. She put her coat on.

Dora, showing no interest, stepped aside and Alice left.

Dora was wearing a new hat – a more elegant confection

than usual, trimmed with a single pheasant feather. But what left Edmund open-mouthed was the fur coat. She did a little twirl. 'What do you think?'

'Where did you get that coat? And the hat?' He went over to the window. The motor on the drive was a sleek model with well-polished brass lamps. A uniformed chauffeur was leaning against the bonnet smoking a cigarette.

Edmund was appalled. Had George left her an unexpected fortune? How was that possible for a lowly railway clerk? But how else had she found the money?'

'What do you think? It's Persian lamb. Nothing but the best, eh?' She laughed, a high tinkling laugh – a sound he hadn't heard Dora make for a long time.

'How did...?' he started to ask, then shook his head, disbelieving what he was seeing. 'Where did you get the money?'

Dora moved across the room and sat at the table. Ignoring his question, she said cheerily, 'Charlotte's with me. That housekeeper over in the big house is giving her a cup of Ovaltine and a chocolate biscuit. I thought it best you and I talked first, then you can see her.'

'Lottie's here?' His face broke into a grin.

'Don't call her that. I've told you a thousand times. It sounds so common.'

Edmund leant forward, his hands on the table, bewildered. 'What's going on, Dora?'

'I have some wonderful news, so I wanted to deliver it in person. An early Christmas present for you.' She peeled off her gloves and laid them on the table in front of her. 'I went to see your father. Thought it was time he met his granddaughter.'

'You did what?' He felt the blood drain from his face and his fists clenched involuntarily.

'Calm down! I told you it's good news. He was charmed by our little Charlotte and insisted we move into the house in Grosvenor Square. To be honest, I think the old boy's rather lonely. I reckon he misses your mother more than he expected. Anyway, whatever – he adores Charlotte. She's very taken with him too. She misses her grandad and now she has a grandpa who spoils her rotten. He's been spoiling me too.' She leant back in the chair. 'Though no more than I deserve after what I've been through. Reckon he feels bad about how he behaved towards me before. But we're getting on famously now. He's got a gramophone and we've been listening to the music hall songs together.'

Edmund stared at her, speechless.

'He says he's ready to forgive you. So you can move back to Grosvenor Square too.' She fumbled in her reticule and pulled out a key which she pushed across the table to him. 'The rent on Goodge Street is paid to the end of the month. Here's the key so you can get anything you've left there. The landlord's happy for us to leave the furniture but he won't pay much for it.' She folded her arms and fixed her gaze on him. 'Come on. Tell me you're pleased. You didn't have to do any crawling and begging yourself and you have me to thank for that. There's only one condition. Your father wants you to join the firm. Just think, Edmund. We'll have so much money. Charlotte will have nothing but the best.'

Edmund moved away to the other side of the room. He couldn't bear to look at her. Everything about her filled him with self-loathing – what kind of fool was he that he had once believed himself in love with her?

All he wanted now was to get Dora out of the workshop. He was desperate to see Lottie - even though it could only be a brief meeting. He took a deep breath, forcing himself to remain calm. 'I made my feelings absolutely clear. Nothing's changed. I told you I'll never cross my father's threshold as long as he's living there. I can't believe you'd do this, Dora. That you'd use our daughter as a bargaining chip to squeeze money out of him. He's a violent man who beat up my mother.'

'Rubbish! He's a kind and charming man. He treats Charlotte and me like princesses. Charlotte deserves to know her relatives. She deserves to have money spent on her. As do I. My dear old dad may not have had much money but he made me feel like a princess too.' Her eyes filled with tears. 'I thought you would too, Edmund. But all you wanted was to change me.'

'I don't want that man near my daughter.'

'*Our* daughter. And he has every right to see her. Spending time with her is doing him a power of good. He's not a well man, you know, and having me and Charlotte there lifts his spirits. Don't be so selfish, Edmund. Make it up with him before it's too late. Why are you so blooming obstinate?' She picked up her gloves and made a little sneering sound. 'It's her, isn't it? That woman you're working with. What's that all about? What kind of man has a girl as an assistant?'

'She's a talented artist.'

Dora's lip curled. 'She's your fancy woman, isn't she? I should have guessed. Men only care about one thing. She's plain as a pikestaff – but they say women like that are grateful if a man pays them attention. Her sort tends to make free with their favours. That's what's going on, isn't it?'

'You're being ridiculous. She's the local vicar's niece and not like that at all.' He clenched his fists. 'You dishonour her. She's a hard-working apprentice who is making a significant contribution to my work.'

Dora snorted. 'I bet she is. I saw how she looked at you.' Dora gave him a scornful look and got to her feet. 'Let's get one thing clear. You'll not get a divorce from me. I'm not bringing shame on Charlotte. And your father won't stand for it. When I married you, I became a member of the Cutler family and it's staying that way. It's up to you whether you do the decent thing and come to live with your father, your lawful wife and your daughter. But suit yourself. Live in a dump like this but don't come crying to me. You'll have to come to Grosvenor Square if you want to see Charlotte.' She glanced at what he saw was a wristwatch. Another gift from his father. 'It's time I left. I hadn't realised this place was so far from London. You'd better go and say hello to her. No more than ten minutes so make the most of it. I'll wait in the car.'

Edmund raced towards the house and found his daughter holding court in the kitchen to an audience of Mrs Harrison, Cook and two of the maids. The little girl was reciting nursery rhymes. Dora had evidently omitted to tell her they were visiting him as the moment he appeared she screamed with delight and flung herself into his arms. 'Daddy, Daddy, Daddy! What are *you* doing here?'

It was not only Dora who had a new wardrobe. Charlotte was wearing a smart new cherry red coat with a shiny pair of boots. In her hair was a matching red ribbon. Edmund looked at her little face with its peach-soft skin, rosebud lips and big blue eyes. His heart swelled with love for the child. How could he bear to be parted from her?

He crouched down to greet her. 'This is where I work, sweetheart.'

Her arms were around his neck and her legs wrapped around his middle as she clung to him like a monkey and pressed kisses against his face. He breathed in the sweet choco-latey smell of her and cradled her head with its mop of dark silky curls.

'We came in a big motorcar, Daddy. Mummy says it belongs to your daddy. He's my new grandpa. We live in his big house. Are you coming back with us? Please, Daddy! There's lots of room in the motorcar for you.'

It was breaking his heart to see her for only a few minutes before her mother spirited her away.

The Bankstone servants were exchanging quizzical looks, but he ignored them. 'Would you like to see where Daddy works?'

'Yes please.'

He strode with her in his arms across the meadow to the workshop and sent up a silent prayer that Dora would have the grace to afford him a little more time.

He gave her a tour of the studio, lifting her up to sit on the workbench while he held up pieces of coloured glass for her to look through in the wintry sunlight streaming through the window.

'They're so pretty, Daddy. Just like my klidy.'

'You have a kaleidoscope?'

'Yes. Grandpa bought it for me. He's always giving me presents.'

Edmund felt nauseous. He was losing his precious child. His father would turn her into a spoilt brat – ably aided by Dora who could give a masterclass in entitlement. He thought of the unfinished wind chime. How could it possibly compete with the fancy kaleidoscope and all the expensive toys Herbert Cutler showered upon her?

The horn of the motorcar tooted and reluctantly he swung his daughter down from the bench and, taking her tiny hand in his, led her back to her mother.

Edmund's shoulders slumped as he watched the burgundy-coloured Vauxhall glide away down the lane. As the car vanished, he kicked a stone with force down the pathway, then went back into the studio.

TWENTY-SEVEN

Alice half ran back to the vicarage, her head spinning with thoughts and questions. Edmund had led her to believe that he was married to a rail clerk's daughter but the elegant woman who had burst into the studio was expensively dressed, and the shining motorcar on the driveway with its uniformed chauffeur spoke of money – and plenty of it.

Edmund had told her he'd been cut off by his father when he married, yet there must have been some form of reconciliation, as his wife wouldn't be able to afford those clothes on a craftsman's earnings. What urgent business had brought Dora Cutler to Little Badgerton? What did it mean for Edmund's future here?

Alice's overriding thought was how beautiful Dora was. No wonder Edmund had married her. How could he bear to be apart from a beauty like her? Did her unannounced visit mean he would be returning to London?

Fear of losing the job she had loved from the first day chilled Alice. Working with Edmund had given her a sense of purpose, filled her days with meaning, with satisfaction and pride in her craft. Was all that to be snatched away? Edmund was sometimes irascible, moody, silent. Did being separated from that beautiful creature he'd married account for those mood swings? They were months away from completing the commissioned windows. Surely he wouldn't abandon the project at this stage?

Another possibility struck her. Dora Cutler intended to move here to Little Badgerton. The death of her father would have removed the only obstacle to her relocating.

Alice couldn't imagine Dora agreeing to live in what Alice understood to be a tiny cottage. She seemed far too grand. And Edmund had never mentioned this possibility. But why else had she turned up? It had clearly been a surprise to Edmund.

Whatever happened it meant a likely end to the growing collaboration between herself and Edmund. Their companion-ship in the studio, their mutual endeavours, and their shared past would mean nothing in comparison to his marriage and family.

But everything to her.

She started to run faster, her heart thumping and her thoughts jumbled.

At the vicarage, neither Eleanor nor Walter was at home. Alice rushed upstairs and shut herself in her bedroom where she paced up and down, trying to reassure herself that nothing would change - yet certain that everything would.

She went to stand at the window and looked out over the garden. It was a sad spectacle: the trees bare, the ground hard and with little sign of life. She shivered, overwhelmed by a longing for spring. Glum and helpless, she watched a pair of blue tits pecking at the branches of a tree outside her window, searching for insects. Instinctively she reached for her sketchpad and began to draw them. Her breathing calmed and she let her mind focus on capturing the birds on the paper.

This was what she loved most about drawing and painting – it was a form of meditation. The concentration needed released her brain from her paralysing worrying and the endless imagining of future scenarios. Whatever happened, she would always have this. And she would also have her life here – the Hargreaveses, the suffrage society, the friends she had made in Little Badgerton, especially Viola. And maybe, just maybe, her fears about Edmund Cutler ending the project would prove to be unfounded.

Alice had been back for a couple of hours when he came to find her. The housemaid knocked on her bedroom door to tell her Mr Cutler was waiting in the drawing room.

When she went in, he looked annoyed.

'Are you coming back to the studio?' He sounded impatient and there was a flash of anger in his voice.

'Mrs Cutler?'

'Has gone back to London.'

'You're going too?'

'Of course I'm not,' he snapped. 'We've two windows to finish. We've wasted enough time this morning. We need to get on.'

A tide of relief akin to joy surged through Alice. She hastily put on her coat and hat and followed him out of the door. Walking back to Bankstone, Edmund said nothing and Alice was too overwhelmed to say anything herself.

The fragility of her involvement in the stained-glass enterprise had been exposed to her. She had surprised herself by the strength of her feelings about what they were undertaking and how utterly bereft she would have been if their work had come to a halt.

When the house was in sight, he turned to her. 'Mrs Bowyer wants the Bankstone window installed by April. She says the church one can wait.'

'Really? What happened to impressing the landed gentry?'

He looked at her sharply. 'Maybe she sees that as less

important than commemorating her husband in a place she will see every day. Maybe she's less concerned with impressing others than remembering him.' He kicked a stray pebble to the side of the lane, sending it skittering across the frost-hardened ground. 'Mrs Bowyer is genuinely heartbroken that she lost her husband just as their dream of a life together, on dry land, in the house of their dreams had come to fruition. She truly cared for the commodore. No matter how cynical your uncle is about it.'

Alice felt rebuked. Did he think her cynical too? He was always so prickly. 'No doubt you're right. There's never been any love lost between Walter and Mrs Bowyer, and he barely knew the late commodore.'

'She's an irascible lady but the more I've come to know her, the more I respect her. Yes, she's vain and impatient and demanding but she's been kind to me and anyway she's the client.'

They'd reached the studio and he pushed open the door. Alice could smell the lingering scent of Dora's perfume – lily of the valley.

She hesitated, then decided to plunge in and ask Edmund what she was dying to know. 'I thought perhaps your wife might be moving here? Now that she no longer has to care for her father.'

Edmund's brow furrowed and Alice wished she hadn't asked. It was none of her business.

'No,' he said. 'She dislikes the countryside.' He moved across to the table. 'Let's wax up the central panel. I want to get it fired tomorrow. We may need to do multiple firings to get the commodore's features right.'

They set to work, piecing together the glass and attaching the pieces with bits of wax onto a sheet of plate glass. The work took the rest of the day and then they stood back and looked at it.

The naval officer was standing at the prow of a ship looking out through a telescope over a blue ocean, topped with white crests. Where the sea met the sky there was a blazing sun, sending shimmering reds and oranges onto the water at the horizon.

'Let's lay the cartoons for the two panels on either side.'

Alice carefully placed the coloured drawings for the left and right panels on the table. The rich blues of the sea extended into each. They bore maritime motifs – a sextant, a capstan, a pair of dividers, and a compass, as well as more decorative images including a pod of dolphins, flying fish and a flock of seagulls. There was an outcrop of rock in the right panel supporting a lighthouse.

'I still think we should have put in a mermaid.' Alice tilted her head on one side.

Edmund shrugged. 'So do I, but she was adamant it would be trivialising her husband's metier.'

'It would be such a beautiful addition. Just here.' She pointed to an area of the cartoon. 'Are you sure you don't want to try asking her again? If we were to do another cartoon incorporating the mermaid, she might just change her mind. Surely, she wants the window to be as beautiful as possible. Don't we owe it to her to give her the best?'

Edmund smiled and ran a hand through his hair, pushing it away from his forehead. For a moment he reminded her of Gilbert. Almost as handsome but in a less polished way.

'You're right, Alice. You're absolutely right. Thank you. We need this window to be the best we can do, and we must try as hard as possible to convince Mrs Bowyer.'

'Maybe you could tell her Walter hates mermaids.'

To her surprise Edmund roared with laughter. It was the first time she'd ever seen him laughing. She felt a little rush of happiness that she had been the cause.

. . .

They were sitting by the fireside eating bread and cheese for their lunch.

Edmund glanced sideways at Alice and asked how she'd come to be involved in the suffrage movement.

She told him about her best friend and the afternoon when Harriet had persuaded Alice to come to the rally in Hyde Park. 'After that, there was no going back. These days I don't have as much time to work for the Cause, but I still feel as strongly and there's now a good group of local women who have taken up a lot of the administrative burden.'

'Have you done anything active? I mean breaking windows or setting fire to postboxes?'

'Nothing like that. If we're going to win the struggle, it will be achieved by reasoned argument, not irresponsible violence. Some of the recent actions amount to terrorism. I can't understand how burning churches and planting a bomb in Westminster Abbey will achieve anything other than set us back.' She sighed. 'Picking on the church is ill-judged. Clergy like Walter are among the biggest supporters of the movement.'

'Why do they do it then?'

Alice was surprised he was interested. Glancing at him, she saw his curiosity was genuine. 'Desperation. Frustration. A long history of broken promises. I understand what's driving them. I just don't agree with their methods. I prefer large scale peaceful protests. Tangible, visible demonstrations of the massive support we have.'

'I'm inclined to agree. The women in Whall's studio all went to the rally at the end of that big national march to London last summer. Several of us went along to cheer them all on. Some of those women had walked all the way from Scotland.'

'The Great Pilgrimage! I was there! I walked from here to London. It was marvellous. One of the most memorable things I've ever done or am likely to do.' She clasped her hands. 'Thousands of us, marching side by side, through towns and villages. We were on the route that started in Portsmouth. It was jolly hard, so I can't imagine how those who came from the West Country or the North managed it.'

He frowned. 'I read in the papers that some places gave the marchers a hostile reception.'

'Most people cheered us on. But yes, there were spots of trouble. Men who should have known better. Our little group joined the main march in Petersfield. The crowd there was pretty hostile and someone pelted us with tomatoes. Not nice, since we were all wearing white blouses.' She grinned. 'Better than bad eggs though. I imagine they thought we were militants. I suppose it's easy to lump us together and make assumptions.'

Alice put another log on the fire and they watched the sparks fly upwards. She was delighted that they were talking about the cause that was so precious to her and that Edmund's questions were sincere. These days it was hard to remember how fractious their relationship had been. 'The worst thing was the rain. But we were all in it together. A huge sense of camaraderie. Knowing that women had already got the vote in Australia, New Zealand and other countries spurred us on. Why should we lag behind the rest of the Empire? That and seeing all those stupid men wearing sandwich boards that said women don't want the vote when we quite evidently do!'

'Well you have my admiration and respect. I'm afraid my wife is one of those who don't want the vote.'

'Really?' Alice was open-mouthed.

'Not out of any strong conviction against it.' He stared into the fire. 'Dora has a lack of curiosity about the world in general and politics is something that doesn't exercise her at all.' He gave a dry laugh. 'About the only thing that does interest her is crime.'

'Crime? Is there a lot where you live?'

'No. Reading about it. She said to me once there was nothing she liked more than a good murder.'

Before Alice could respond, he got to his feet and went back to the workbench where he was in the process of selecting samples of glass to create the sky.

Curiosity aroused, she wanted to ask him more but knew him enough now to understand when he deemed a conversation closed.

A couple of days later Alice was sorting through pieces of glass when she found the glass wind chime Edmund had been making for his daughter. It was broken into pieces.

'What happened to the wind chime? Did you drop it?'

He shrugged.

'I thought it was to be Lottie's birthday present! Aren't you going to fix it?'

'No point.'

She turned to look at him. 'How so?'

Edmund sighed. 'She wouldn't be interested in a home-made gift. My father showers her with toys. She told me she has a kaleidoscope. Why would she want a wind chime?'

'Because unlike a kaleidoscope, it makes a beautiful sound. And most importantly because it was made with love by her skilful daddy.'

He smiled. 'I wish that were true.'

'Why wouldn't it be?'

'Because my wife and my father will be busy instilling in Lottie the belief that only expensive shop-bought toys are worth having.'

Alice stared at him.

'What?' he said, defensively.

'You don't seriously believe your daughter would think that way?'

He looked away and pretended to examine a piece of glass against the light.

'Do you?' she persisted. 'I thought better of you than that, Edmund.'

'What do you mean?'

'You're sounding like a victim. You told me how much you love your little girl, so I absolutely refuse to believe she doesn't love you just as much.' She gathered the pieces of glass together. 'You must fix this. Lottie will adore it.'

He moved across to the workbench and gathered together the pieces. 'I'll mend it tonight.'

Alice nodded – but she sensed he wasn't telling the truth. There was something seriously wrong between him and his beautiful wife. Something so bad that it meant he was separated from the daughter he adored.

TWENTY-EIGHT

Early on Christmas morning, before she was expected to join her aunt at church, Alice slipped out of the vicarage and went to the studio. Edmund would be spending Christmas in London with his family and Alice wanted to finish work on the alternative cartoon incorporating the mermaid. It would save time and avoid any delays on the preparation of the window panels if she could get it done while he was away.

When she opened the door she sensed there was someone there before she saw him. Edmund was in the corner laying a fire in the hearth.

She called his name in surprise and made him jump. 'What are you doing here?'

He dropped the log he was holding. 'I could ask you the same question.'

'I came to work on the mermaid. I have a couple of hours before church. Why aren't you in London?'

His mouth stretched into a hard line. 'I'm not going.'

She was about to ask why but stopped herself. Better to let him tell her if he chose.

'My wife and daughter are spending Christmas with my father. I've sworn never to enter his house again.'

'You can't spend it alone!'

'I don't much care for it. I'll treat it as just another day.' He laid another log on top of the kindling in the grate. 'Christmas is painful since I can't spend it with my little girl.'

'Then you must come and spend it with us.'

He protested, but she took hold of his arm. 'Don't build the fire any bigger. We'll only be here for an hour then you're coming with me to the service at St Margaret's and back to the vicarage for Christmas dinner. We have an enormous turkey. Please, Edmund. Eleanor and Walter will be delighted to have some company other than me to share the day. And they'd be horrified to think you were spending Christmas alone.'

Edmund hesitated.

Alice was hearing no dissent. 'Let's get on with what we need to do here and then head off to the service.'

'Thank you. I'll come for Christmas dinner but not the service.'

As they were packing their work away, Alice noticed the pieces of glass from the wind chime he'd been making were still in a heap on the workbench. 'You haven't sent your little girl her present.'

'She'll have her pick of Hamleys. Maybe I'll send it for her birthday.'

He turned away. Alice realised he was overcome with emotion, his eyes bright with unshed tears. To save his embarrassment she said, 'I'd better get going. The service starts in twenty minutes. See you at the vicarage in an hour.'

'Wait a moment, Alice. I don't want to tell Walter and Eleanor about my family circumstances.'

'I understand. We'll think of another reason for you being on your own.'

'What though?'

'Could you say your wife or daughter has an infectious illness and you need to stay away?'

He shuddered. 'I'm not tempting fate.'

'Then what about them visiting relatives in the north of England and it being too far for you travel for just two days?'

'That's a possibility.'

She smiled at him. 'Or you could decide to say nothing. I'll merely tell them I found you planning to spend the day on your own to catch up with work so I put my foot down and dragged you kicking and screaming to join us.'

'Would they believe that?'

'You know Walter's convinced Mrs Bowyer is an absolute tyrant. It will allow him the opportunity to think even worse of the poor dear and imagine she's driving you to work harder and faster.'

'That hardly seems fair.'

'Nothing's going to change his opinion of her. We don't have to say that's what's happened. We'll just let him jump to that conclusion.'

He grinned at her. 'You're quite the schemer, Alice.'

'I have many talents when I put my mind to it.'

'I'm all too aware of that.' When he smiled his face lit up and she couldn't help noticing how handsome he was.

She looked away. It was getting all too easy to like Edmund Cutler the more she got to know him. In fact, she was beginning to like him rather too much.

No one noticed Edmund was alone in the cottage. Mrs Bowyer was spending the festivities at her sister's in Lancashire and had given the household time off to join their own families so there was no one at the big house. Edmund had to acknowledge that Alice's invitation was a welcome one. The alternative of eating the cold pork pie he'd bought yesterday at the butcher's was too depressing when compared to a festive Christmas dinner. He didn't want to wallow in his own misery – although he was uncomfortable about the Hargreaveses discovering the sorry state of his marriage.

But as Alice had suggested, her aunt and uncle welcomed him with open arms and were far too discreet to question his reasons for staying in Little Badgerton. After the meal, they all retired to the drawing room where Eleanor played the piano, before they settled down to a game of cards. Edmund was relaxed and genuinely enjoyed being in the company of the Hargreaveses and their niece.

It was with a deep sense of contentment that he took his leave and walked back to his cottage at Bankstone. Today had been delightful. The love the Hargreaveses so evidently had for each other and for their niece was palpable. There was laughter and a constant flow of conversation that they hadn't hesitated to include him in. It reminded him of the camaraderie of Whall's studio – a communion of likeminded people enjoying each other's company.

As he pushed open the door to the cottage, loneliness enveloped him again. When he'd married Dora, he'd envisioned a happy family life like the one he had witnessed today. But his abiding thought as he settled in his bed was how things might have been had he not believed himself in love with Dora. He'd be married to Alice Dalton. And would that have been such a terrible thing?

TWENTY-NINE

'Is the Hargreaveses' niece still working for you?' Mrs Harrison watched as the cook doled Edmund out a bowl of stew in the Bankstone kitchen one evening some weeks later. 'Only I didn't see her about today. I always see her going up the path. Regular as clockwork she is.'

Edmund told her Alice was still in his employ, resisting the temptation to add that it was none of the housekeeper's business. Alice had been in Winchester attending a regional suffrage meeting but he wasn't about to tell Mrs Harrison that.

'She doesn't like it, you know. Mrs Bowyer. Mentioned it again when I took in her tea at four bells. Said it isn't decent: a young unmarried woman working unchaperoned with a married man.'

Edmund looked up and shook his head in disbelief. 'That's a matter for Miss Dalton herself or for the Hargreaveses as her relatives. She's not a child. It's no concern of Mrs Bowyer.' Imagining Mrs Harrison was more likely expressing her own views than Mrs Bowyer's, he forked a piece of mutton and chewed it slowly. If only she would leave him in peace to eat his supper.

'Oh, I think you'll find it is her concern. This being her property and you being her employee.'

Edmund continued to eat, stifling his irritation. He resisted the temptation to correct her that he was not an employee but was working on a commission. 'If Mrs Bowyer has a concern, I'm sure she'll raise it with me herself.'

'What with Miss Dalton being one of those 'votes for women' types... It's not right you know. Against the natural order. Women aren't suited to voting on political matters. Mrs Bowyer says they're too easily swayed by men's personal qualities. They'd just vote for the best-looking candidate.' She laughed. 'And we can't be having that, can we?'

Edmund rolled his eyes.

'They lack judgement, do women. At least that's what Mrs Bowyer reckons. What do you think, Mr Cutler?'

'Would you say *you* lack judgement, Mrs Harrison?'

'Me? Certainly not. But I'm merely a housekeeper, so even if women of property got the vote it wouldn't apply to me, would it? I don't worry myself over things that are never going to affect me. Can't understand why that young woman should be going round Little Badgerton stuffing leaflets through people's letterboxes and using the parish hall for meetings. The hall's for respectable things like the Sunday School and the Mother's Union. The vicar should know better.'

Edmund cut a thick slice off the loaf of bread, tore off a chunk and mopped up some of the stew's rich broth.

Mrs Harrison pulled out a chair and sat down opposite him, watching as he finished his meal. She ate her meals with the other servants at some indeterminate hour and Edmund was relieved that he was neither expected to join them nor Mrs Bowyer herself. Mrs Harrison rarely bothered to give Edmund the time of day so it was unusual to have her company now. It was not something he sought.

The housekeeper was evidently in an inquisitive mood.

'Seems strange that a woman like Miss Dalton would want to do such work. She used to be employed up at Padgett Hall. Worked for the Colonel for a few years but he dumped her as soon as his nephew turned up. After a respectable job like that it's a bit of a come-down to be clearing up after you, Mr Cutler. All due respect, but it's hardly the thing for a young lady, and her being the niece of the vicar's wife.'

Edmund put down his cutlery, took a swig of water and leant back in his chair. 'Miss Dalton is doing highly skilled and intricate work.'

Mrs Harrison tutted. 'Out of sight all day long inside that building with you. It's not right, if you ask my opinion.'

'I didn't ask your opinion.'

'It's a crying shame your lovely wife decided not to stay here. Mind you I can understand why. A lady like her wouldn't want to be cooped up in that tiny cottage. Pity though as we were all quite taken with little Charlotte.'

He said nothing.

'Cook and I did wonder why you don't rent a bigger place in the village. Something more suitable for Mrs Cutler.' She coughed and then leant towards him, elbows on the table. 'But maybe she wasn't too happy about Miss Dalton either.'

Irritated, he decided it was fruitless to argue with the woman.

But Mrs Harrison wasn't finished yet. 'There's many of us reckons Miss Dalton has "A Past", if you know what I mean. She turned up all of a sudden out of nowhere and moved in with the Hargreaveses. Where did she come from and what's she doing here instead of being at home with her family? I smell a whiff of something not right. Has she told you anything, Mr Cutler? Dropped a hint at all?'

Edmund scraped back his chair and got up from the table. He wanted to tell her to go to hell but decided to give the woman an answer to quash her suspicions. He borrowed from Colonel Padgett's nephew. 'I believe Mrs Hargreaves is her only living relative and that Miss Dalton moved here after her parents died in India.'

'Died? Funny no one's mentioned that.'

'Cholera, I believe. Sad business.'

Mrs Harrison's lower lip jutted out as she pondered this information. 'Mmm. So she must have a lot in common with the Colonel's nephew? Them both coming from India and having no parents.' She gave a low chuckle. 'That could be interesting. The Colonel's going to hold a reception for the nephew up at Padgett Hall. Mrs Bowyer's been invited and I'm helping with service. I'll have my eye on Miss Dalton then. See how the two of them get along.' She narrowed her eyes and stared straight at him. 'Maybe there'll be a romance afoot. How would you feel about that, Mr Cutler?'

Her tone was taunting and seemed also to contain a veiled threat. Edmund put down his napkin, nodded at his tormentor and left the house to head for the refuge of his cottage.

Mrs Harrison was correct. Colonel Fitzwarren announced he was giving a party to mark the return to England of his nephew, Leonard, and introduce him to the neighbourhood. The guests consisted of anyone the old man considered of sufficient stature to warrant an invitation – mostly Conservative Association friends, fellow golf club members – largely the same people – and their wives. Other guests included Mrs Bowyer, the vicar and his wife, Miss Pendleton and Doctor and Mrs Collins. Alice was included, presumably as an adjunct of the Harg-reaves household rather than as Colonel Fitzwarren's former secretary.

The room was crowded and rather airless, the canapés dried

up and over reliant on the use of fish paste and gentleman's relish, and the wine insufficiently chilled. Colonel Fitzwarren's cook was evidently more accustomed to preparing plain fare of the kind her employer had eaten in the officers' mess and at boarding school. Nonetheless, there were plenty of takers for the food on offer.

Alice arrived with her aunt and uncle and the discomfort she'd experienced as a debutante returned as soon as she entered the room. Polite party conversation was not her forte and she loathed small talk with people with whom she had little in common. Miss Pendleton spotted her and hurried over to convey an over-detailed description of the planned activities of the Petersfield women's suffrage group. Alice sipped her wine and nodded absently, relieved not to have to mingle. She'd already read the local area newsletter that Miss Pendleton was drawing heavily upon. When her interlocutor was engaged by another guest, Alice drifted towards the far side of the room away from the mêlée and pretended to be studying a couple of oversized paintings in ornate gilded frames. The first was a sweeping panorama of the African veldt with a herd of wildebeest running across the plain, pursued by native warriors bearing spears. It was paired with a second painting – of a similar scene – only this time the pursuers were the pursued – the tribesmen were being mowed down by a troop of musket-firing British soldiers. She shuddered with distaste, glad that at last she was freed from transcribing the endless accounts of her former employer's butchery of both Zulus and Boers.

'Damned fine paintings, don't you think?'

She turned to face a man of about her own age and height. He stood beside her in front of the second artwork, leaning his weight on a silver-topped cane. He had a military bearing in spite of what was a pronounced limp. She formed a snap judgement – she didn't like him.

'The subject matter's not to my taste, I'm afraid,' she said rather more brusquely than intended.

He gave a laugh that managed to combine patronisation with mild contempt. 'I suppose we can't expect you, a mere gal, to appreciate such a magnificent work and such a glorious military victory. S'pose you prefer pictures of frolicking lambs in the fields.' He guffawed and Alice looked about her trying to identify an escape route. But he wasn't letting her go so easily. He stretched out a hand in greeting. 'I'm Leonard Fitzwarren, nephew and heir of our esteemed host. And you are?'

She shook his hand, which was clammy and cold. 'Alice Dalton. I'm the niece of the vicar's wife.'

'Ah! I understand you and I have much in common.' He grinned at her while still managing to convey an air of superiority.

'How so?'

'Firstly, I understand you were helping the old boy with cataloguing his library. Afraid I did you out of a job.' His expression was supercilious. 'Not really suitable work for a young woman though. Takes another ex-military man to understand these things.'

'Secondly? It sounds like there's a secondly.'

He waved an index finger. 'Not just a pretty face, eh? No flies on you! Yes, the second thing is that we have India in common.'

'I beg your pardon?'

'Didn't you know? I'm an old India hand too. Indian Army. Until I took a tumble in a polo game. Stationed near Calcutta. Gather we both lost our parents over there. Cholera's a nasty business.'

Alice stared at him blankly. 'I think you—'

Leonard Fitzwarren pressed on. 'Where were you billeted?' He didn't wait for an answer. 'India gets in the blood, doesn't it? They invalided me out. Wanted to stay out there but it's hard when you can't do all the things you used to do, so I thought a complete change of scene would do me the power of good. Intended living up in town but the spondulix go much further in the country. And just between us ...' He bent forward, tapping the side of his nose and lowering his voice. 'Once it dawned on me that the old boy has no other living relatives I thought I may as well stick close and keep in his good books.' He guffawed again. 'Any tips from you on doing that? He doesn't have much time for the ladies so you must have done something right to have lasted so long.'

Alice was flummoxed. She didn't know how to start answering the barrage of disconnected questions and comments, but Leonard Fitzwarren already appeared to have moved onto new conversational pastures. 'You ride, Miss, Miss, er ...?'

'Dalton. And no, not since I was a child.'

'Understand the hunting's rather good here. It'll take a while getting used to foxes after tigers though.'

'Surely you don't hunt tigers on horseback?'

'No. We stalk them.' He licked his lips with relish and Alice, feeling sorry for the poor tiger, looked around again for a means of extricating herself. She was bemused by his references to her having dead parents and an Indian background, but imagined he'd mistaken her for someone else. Since he showed no further interest in her history, she let the subject slide.

He moved closer, giving her no choice but to study his countenance. His skin was pallid, considering he'd only recently arrived from the tropics. Under a prominent forehead his widely spaced eyes had a slightly vacant expression. Sleek with pomade, his hair was swept back from his face and he sported a neatly trimmed moustache. The scent of either his hair treatment or his aftershave lotion caught the back of Alice's throat as he leant towards her. The smell of alcohol on his breath joined the already unpleasant mix. The party had clearly begun for Leonard Fitzwarren several hours ago.

Fitzwarren stepped back slightly, still surveying her as though she were a piece of meat. He brushed her hand with his fingers and she shuddered. 'I think you and I should get to know each other better. Shall we take a stroll round the conservatory? It's rather noisy in here. I can barely hear myself think.'

Alice didn't imagine thinking was something Leonard Fitzwarren invested much time in – particularly as he was unaware that thinking was usually conducted inaudibly.

He nodded his head in the direction of the open French windows.

Trapped, Alice looked about her. The Hargreaveses were deep in conversation with a couple on the far side of the room and there was no sign of Miss Pendleton. She opened her mouth to make an excuse, but Leonard Fitzwarren placed a hand firmly in the small of her back and steered her towards the open doors. Definitely a few glasses too many.

No other guests were in the conservatory. The room was a jungle of green plants which appeared to have been given free rein to run wild. She'd never been on this side of the house when working for the colonel. Leonard Fitzwarren guided her to a far corner, away from the entrance. Her discomfort mounted. Heavy foliage blocked the view of the drawing room, and they were in a narrow space between the overlarge plants. She told herself that at least forty guests, including her aunt and uncle, were only a matter of feet away so nothing untoward could happen.

'I've heard you're one of those suffragettes,' he said, eyes narrowing.

'Yes, I am.' There was no reason to apologise.

His face broke into a smile that was more of a snarl. 'Only two reasons for women to want to get involved with that nonsense.'

Alice stiffened. 'It isn't nonsense. But what might those reasons be?'

'Either they're women who can't get a man to look at them.' He tilted his head back appraising her. 'And I think we can probably rule that out in your case.'

Alice took a step back.

He reached his hand out and with a sudden jerk pulled her towards him so close that she could feel his breath on her face. He let his walking cane fall. 'And the other reason is that they're fast and easy. The kind of gals men don't marry, but like to have fun with.'

Alice tried to pull away but her back was against the glass frame and his body was blocking her from getting past him.

'You're drunk, Mr Fitzwarren. Why don't we go back inside and we'll find you some water.'

'Not drunk at all.' His body was crushing her against the glass.

Encumbered by the wineglass in one hand, she put the other up to his shoulder to push him away but he was too strong. She let her glass fall and renewed her efforts with both hands.

The shattered glass scrunched under his feet. 'I'll bet we could have some fun together. Don't tell me you're not like that,' he said, breathily. 'I know your type. Convinced you don't need a husband, but more than happy for a bit of the old how's your father.' He placed a hand on her waist, restraining her. He was surprisingly strong. 'I've had my eye on you since you walked in this evening. You've that look about you. The woman serving the buffet tipped me off that you were a colonial too so I thought I'd explore what else we have in common.' He bent his head and pressed his mouth against hers, his tongue trying to force her lips open. His hand moved from her waist to squeeze her breast.

Reflexively, she jerked her knee up and rammed it into his crotch, remembering Victor once screaming in agony when she'd accidentally hit him there with a cricket ball when they were young.

The effect was instant. Fitzwarren doubled over, clutching himself. 'You bitch. You ugly man-hating bitch.'

Alice squeezed past him and made her way back to the crowded drawing room, relieved that no one appeared to have noticed their absence. She tapped Eleanor on the shoulder and whispered, 'I'm going to walk home. I have a headache.'

Her aunt wanted to accompany her, but Alice insisted that she knew the route like the back of her hand even after dark, from her years working for the colonel. 'The walk will do me good.'

A familiar voice from over Alice's shoulder said, 'I'll see Miss Dalton home, Mrs Hargreaves.'

She turned round to find Edmund Cutler standing behind her. 'I didn't know you were here, Mr Cutler.'

'Mrs Bowyer asked me to accompany her tonight but she's decided she's had enough. We can take you as far as Bankstone in the carriage and then I'll walk you home to the vicarage.'

Before Alice could answer, Eleanor said, 'That would be most kind, Edmund. Thank you.'

Alice mutely followed him into the hallway where he helped her on with her coat. Mrs Bowyer was already installed in the carriage.

Alice settled into the seat opposite Edmund and beside Mrs Bowyer. It reminded her of another night and another carriage – with Gilbert opposite her as she sat beside his mother after the opera. The night she'd first met Edmund.

Mrs Bowyer twisted round to scrutinise Alice. 'You're the vicar's niece? I hear you're assisting Mr Cutler with my windows.' She made a tutting sound. 'Do you consider it a suitable occupation for a young woman? It would not have been considered so in my day.'

Alice decided not to debate the point.

'I suppose you think I'm an old dinosaur. But it doesn't seem right for a young lady to do manual work and particularly to be shut up alone with a man all day.' She tutted again. 'Does the vicar approve?'

'He does.'

The woman gave a snort. 'Why doesn't that surprise me?'

Defiant, Alice said, 'I used to be shut up alone all day with Colonel Fitzwarren.' Then as soon as the words were out she wished she'd kept quiet.

'The colonel is a man who has served his country. A pillar of the community. Mr Cutler is from London. Things are different there.'

Edmund rolled his eyes. He'd clearly had this conversation before. 'I've told you, Mrs Bowyer, Miss Dalton is an excellent artist and craftswoman and has proved an exemplary pupil. I'm fortunate to have secured her assistance.'

In the dark of the carriage, Alice blushed.

'I suppose, Mr Cutler, you are a respectable married man, after all. Otherwise I'd have had to put my foot down.' She sighed a heavy sigh. 'I'm so glad to have got away from that tedious party. I'd expected to find more interesting people there. I rather thought the Favershams and the Bolingbrokes would have been there but apparently they are up in town. Truth told, I can't abide Colonel Fitzwarren. I can't imagine what possessed me in accepting his invitation tonight. All those awful braying golfers and India hands. Utter snobs.'

The carriage swung into the driveway of Bankside and the coachman helped Mrs Bowyer out and into the house.

Edmund held his hand out for Alice as she got down. 'I hope you don't mind walking the last part,' he said, apologetically.

'Not at all. I'd intended to walk all the way back from Padgett Hall anyway. But you don't have to accompany me, Edmund.'

'I want to.'

They set off along the lane which was illuminated by a full moon.

After a few moments, he spoke. 'I saw you disappear into the conservatory with the guest of honour.' Did she imagine it or did Edmund's voice have a slight edge.

'Not by choice. I didn't really have any say about it,' she said. 'He practically bundled me through the door. He was extremely drunk.'

'Really? You're saying you didn't choose to go with him? It didn't look that way to me.'

She stopped walking. 'What are you implying?'

He buried his hands in the pockets of his greatcoat and walked on then halted after a few steps. 'I don't know. I just didn't like you talking to him.'

'Why?'

'Because I didn't like him.'

'You spoke to him?'

'He talked *at* me for ten minutes. I saw you across the room looking at those hideous paintings and was about to make my excuses and come over to talk to you when he noticed I was watching you and without even excusing himself, he shot off to talk to you. I was weighing up whether to come and rescue you, when you disappeared with him into the conservatory. So naturally, I presumed you must like him.'

'He's a horrible man.'

Edmund gave a small nervous laugh. 'You *don't* like him?'

'I loathed him. At first sight and it went downhill from there.'

There was an audible sigh of relief from Edmund. 'Only if you'd thought him a good chap, I'd have had to cancel your apprenticeship.'

Alice shuddered. 'There's no danger of that. He was utterly obnoxious.' She looked up at him. 'In fact, he made a pass at me.

He implied I had loose morals. Then pushed himself on me when I made it clear I wasn't that kind of woman and had no interest in hanky-panky.'

Edmund spun round his eyes blazing. 'He did what?! He touched you? I'll kill him. Did he hurt you?' He placed his hands on her shoulders and Alice was immediately conscious of how different his hands felt from Fitzwarren's earlier. Edmund looked into her eyes, and she caught her breath.

'He pinned me against the wall and tried to kiss me. It was horrible.'

Edmund gasped.

'So I shoved my knee in a place I knew would hurt him.'

His eyes widened and his face broke into a smile.

'That did the trick. He had to let go. He called me a disgusting name.'

The hands on her shoulders moved down and she felt them wrap around her waist as he pulled her close to him. Her face was pressed into the rough fabric of Edmund's coat and she could hear his heart thumping. She almost stopped breathing. Then she felt him kiss the top of her head. Her stomach did a somersault.

'Oh, Alice. I'm so sorry that happened. I want to kill him. Punch his horrible smug face.' He drew back and looked down at her. His face was silvered by the light from the moon.

Alice trembled. What was happening? She looked up at him, her eyes meeting his. Then before she could say anything they were kissing. Their mouths soft against each other, then hard. Hungry. Longing. Holding onto each other as though if they let go, they'd be lost. On and on in the glorious, beautiful, unexpected discovery of each other.

Nearby, the church clock chimed the hour, breaking the spell. Edmund pulled away. 'I'm sorry. That was unforgiveable. I'd no right. I took advantage.' He held open the gate to the vicarage garden for her. She turned to say he hadn't. She was as much to blame as he was. But he was hurrying away back towards Bankstone.

Confused, and trembling, she opened the front door. Tears were threatening and she could feel her body shaking. She staggered upstairs and went straight to bed.

THIRTY

The following day was a Sunday so Alice wouldn't have to face
Edmund yet. She re-lived their kiss over and over in her head.
Until last night she'd never been kissed, only for it to happen
twice with two men in a manner that couldn't have been more
different.

Leonard Fitzwarren's kiss had been a violation, an assault:
ugly, repulsive, nauseating. Yet she was glad it had precipitated
the very different kiss she had shared with Edmund. A kiss that
had set her on fire and shaken her to her core. But Edmund had
seemed full of remorse and had left her bereft, bewildered,
abandoned.

She knew now, without any doubt, she was in love with
him. If she were honest, she'd known for a while but hadn't
allowed herself to admit it. It made her feel wretched because it
was a love without hope, without future. Edmund was married.
He was a father. His wife was beautiful. He'd rejected her once
before. Alice let the truth sink in. He must have been a little
drunk. Perhaps roused to jealousy by Fitzwarren.

Maybe, in the absence of his wife, Alice had been a willing
substitute. How could she tell, since she knew so little of men?

Her friend Harriet had once remarked that men thought only of one thing. Was that true of Edmund? Did he think of her in the same way Fitzwarren did – as a single woman grateful for any attention from a man?

She felt a rush of nausea.

Yet that kiss. Such passion. Such feeling. She struggled to believe it wasn't heartfelt.

Back at his cottage, Edmund was in a state of shock. How had it happened? How had he allowed himself to lose control? To give into the growing feelings for Alice he'd refused to acknowledge? Loss of control. A reckless irresponsible act – he'd humiliated her before when he'd married Dora and now he was adding insult to injury by taking advantage of her. His marriage was a sham, but it still meant he had nothing to offer Alice – other than potential shame.

After a sleepless night, he went into the studio early on Sunday morning hoping work might take his mind off what had happened, but as soon as he crossed the threshold he could feel Alice's presence even though she wasn't there. This place would always be associated with her. The hours they'd worked side-by-side. The conversations they'd shared. It had been the embodiment of every dream he'd ever had about a marriage of hearts and minds, a shared artistic endeavour. But now that he'd made that stupid impetuous mistake, she'd undoubtedly refuse to continue working with him. Who could blame her? His behaviour was indefensible.

Edmund couldn't bear to be in the workshop a moment longer. He had to get away from here. Had to get this out of his system. Walking usually helped him clear his mind, release his tension and work through difficult decisions. He grabbed his coat, slammed the door behind him and set off. Crisp frost-covered dead leaves crunched under his feet as he entered the woods. A fallen branch lay across his path so he picked it up and thrashed at the undergrowth with it as he walked, trying to release his anger at his own loss of control.

He was in love with Alice Dalton. No point trying to fool himself that he wasn't. He could never have her though, and now, thanks to his recklessness, he'd probably lose her friendship too.

The wood was on a hillside and he crashed through the bracken until he emerged into a clearing at the top of the ridge. The ground ahead fell away steeply, giving onto a wide view of the surrounding countryside.

But Edmund's eyes were not on the panorama. Sitting on a fallen tree trunk, Alice turned her head at his approach.

Their eyes met and for a moment time stopped. He was lost. Then they were moving towards each other.

Their words came out at the same time.

'Please forgive me,' he said.

'Did you mean it?' she said.

Then they each tried to answer.

'There's nothing to forgive.'

'Yes. I'm in love with you.'

No more words as they clung to each other, like a pair of drowning sailors. Kissing here at the top of this hill in the cold light of day, Edmund pushed aside his guilt. Here with Alice in his arms there was no room for recriminations. He loved her. Completely. Utterly. To the point where he could no longer acknowledge right from wrong.

Just a few minutes later, they stumbled back towards Bankstone. Towards his little cottage a few yards beyond the studio. They made no conscious decision. It was simply inevitable. Their progress was slow as every few paces they had to stop and kiss. Their hands were entwined. It was as if they feared if their mouths didn't meet again they would lose each other.

Edmund pushed open the door and they scrambled to undo

buttons, unbuckle his belt, unpin her hair. At some point he told her again that he loved her and she began to cry, saying through her tears that she loved him too.

'Are you sure you want to do this?' he whispered. 'There's no going back once we do.'

'There's no going back anyway and yes, I'm sure.'

Then they were on the bed, still kissing as though if they stopped they'd be unable to carry on breathing. As his hands explored her naked skin, Alice cried out. Edmund marvelled that just a few hours ago there had been only a shared but formal companionship in work. How were they the same people?

When at last he entered her, she locked her eyes on his and he knew he had found the love of his life.

They continued making love, until, sated, they fell asleep in each other's arms.

Edmund woke as the light was fading behind the flimsy curtains. Disorientated for a moment by the warmth of another body in the bed beside him, he watched Alice sleeping. Her unpinned hair was tousled on the pillow and her face peaceful. He felt a rush of tenderness and love for her.

He rolled onto his side and reached for her, drawing her close so that once again he knew the joy in the sensation of her naked skin against his. He began to kiss her tenderly but as she opened her eyes the realisation of what they'd done struck him forcibly.

'What's wrong?' she whispered.

'I've dishonoured you. I had no right.'

'Dishonoured me?' She laid the palm of her hand against his face. 'No! I was dead. You've breathed life into me. You've made me happy.'

He lifted his hand and began to stroke her hair, gently pushing away an errant strand from where it covered her eyes. 'And you me. I've never been happier than last night.' A sigh escaped from him. 'But I've made such a mess of things—'

'Don't say that.'

'It's true. When I married Dora I wronged you, Alice. And now I've made matters worse.'

She touched his lips with her fingers. 'That's not true.'

'If I hadn't been so impetuous and so determined to defy my father... If I hadn't pigheadedly assumed that whatever he wanted for me must be bad, you and I would have been together for the past five years. We'd be married.' He made an anguished sound.

'Stop it.' She saw the pain in his eyes.

'Instead we've both been alone and unhappy and now I've exposed you to scandal and disgrace.'

'Hush!' She pressed her fingers against his lips. 'What we did today was the most beautiful thing I've ever done.'

He breathed a long sigh, seeming to relax momentarily, only to frown again. 'But your aunt and uncle?'

A frown creased her forehead. 'I have to go soon. Dinner's after Evensong. I want to tell Eleanor on her own. Then she can tell Walter.'

'I'll come with you. I won't have you face them alone.'

'No. Please, Edmund, let me tell her myself.'

His face was full of concern. 'I want to be with you. They need to know how much I love you and you matter more to me than life itself.'

She smiled. 'Please, my love. I want to do this myself.'

He looked into her eyes. 'I'd be a coward if I don't stand beside you to face the consequences. The Hargreaveses are bound to think I've abused their trust and taken advantage of you.'

Alice leant over and kissed him slowly. 'They'll be concerned. Of course. They care about me. But I hope they'll understand.'

Edmund was less certain. Guilt and anguish at the position he'd put her in flooded him. 'Understand that their niece has committed adultery? With a married man? I don't think so. I wouldn't blame them if they told Mrs Bowyer and had me thrown out.'

'No!' she shook her head. 'They'd never do that. They'll see how happy you've made me. Happier than I've ever been.' She nestled against him.

'You are?' He bent his head and kissed her. 'Aren't you worried what people will say when they find out? And they will find out. I've opened you up to scandal.'

'Of course, I'm worried, but I can't regret what we've done. This isn't something you've done to me against my will. I wanted it. More than I've ever wanted anything. Please believe me, my darling.'

Alice raised herself up on one elbow and looked at him. 'When I was a baby Eleanor ran away with a man who turned out to be married and who abandoned her. Fortunately, she met Walter. My uncle doesn't judge – he leaves that to God and believes God is more compassionate than society is. Eleanor and Walter will be happy that I too have found love.'

He looked at her in anguish. 'I'll never stop loving you. Never. But I've done you wrong. First by rejecting you and now by compromising you.'

'Stop tormenting yourself, Edmund. I won't have it. All these recriminations. The past is the past, my darling. Only *now* and the future matter. I'll thank God each day for the rest of my life that it's happened.' She kissed him softly. 'No room for regrets. No time for might-have-beens. The only might-have-been is that we might not have met again. It's truly a miracle that we've found each other.'

Edmund looked into her eyes and drew her closer to him.

'And you don't really want to undo the past. You wouldn't want not to have had your daughter. If you'd married me Lottie wouldn't have existed. And if we'd been forced to marry, we might never have had the chance to fall in love as our marriage would have been a source of resentment between us. We can't undo what's happened. We can only move forward and embrace the future.'

'You're so wise, my beloved.'

She smiled. 'If we were never to see each other again after today it would break my heart, but I'd still be happier for our having had this – even for just a few stolen hours.' She bit her lip. 'You've given me something I didn't even know was lacking. Being without you would be torture but I'll never be completely alone again.' She turned onto her back and reached for his hand. 'Whatever happens, wherever I am and wherever you are, I'll treasure the precious time we have together. I'll store up memories and devour them for a time when you aren't here yourself.' She turned to face him again and kissed him on the lips. 'I'll know now that you'll always be thinking of me. I want you to imagine my hand at work on every piece of glass you cut. I want you to see my face looking back at you from the crackling depths of a fire on a winter's evening, in the patterns of frost on a windowpane. And even though it's not a pretty face it's a face that shines with love for you.' She brushed her lips against his. 'I love you, Edmund, and I'm so thankful I can say that.'

He gazed up at her. 'It's a beautiful face. The face I will never tire of looking at.' He paused, his hand cupping her breast under the sheet. 'I could never return to Dora.' His hands moved slowly over her breast, down her ribcage and onto her stomach, his touch setting her nerve endings alight. 'Until today I'd never seen a naked woman's body. Dora made me undress in the dark. Kept herself covered all the time. She thought sex was dirty. Something to be endured.' He caressed Alice's skin with slow strokes that made her gasp. 'I felt as though I was violating her.' He continued to touch her, his breath becoming ragged. 'Never like this, my darling.'

Alice moaned with pleasure as his fingers moved between her legs. She lifted her mouth to his and his lips found hers.

Later, they watched each other as they dressed. Alice felt no shyness, no shame. Sharing this intimacy and companionship was delicious and she wanted these moments to last forever.

'What will you tell them?' he asked.

'The truth. That I spent the night with you. And that I intend to continue to do so as long as you're here in Little Badgerton.'

'Even though I can't marry you?'

'When you married your wife I vowed I'd never marry and I meant it.'

His eyes widened. 'Why? You barely knew me then. Surely you didn't have feelings for me?'

Alice brushed her lips against his. 'No, I didn't. At least not those kinds of feelings. I can't lie – I despised you. I was angry.'

Ashamed, his mouth formed a hard line.

'But my anger at my parents was greater. They treated me as a commodity to be traded.'

Edmund wrapped her in his arms and stroked her hair.

'I thought a lot about marriage then and decided it wasn't what I wanted.' Alice shivered. 'My parents never showed each other any affection. They muddled along well enough but there's no love there. And my friend Harriet married entirely for money and a title. I had the sense that there was no love lost between your parents either.'

'That's true. Certainly not on my father's part. My mother married him for what she thought was love – a love that was never reciprocated.'

'That's sad. Until I met the Hargreaveses, I never saw a love marriage. It was only when I came here that I saw it was possible.'

'I remember the day I met your aunt and uncle. I had a sherry with them and as I walked back to Bankstone I was filled with envy. Their love was so evident. It was what I'd hoped for when I married Dora. Something I never experienced for even a fleeting moment.' He kissed the top of her head. 'Do you know, Alice, I harboured a dream where art and love came together. Dora's a talented illustrator but from the day I married her she refused to pick up a paintbrush. Working alongside you in the studio has been such a beautiful experience. Every moment I look up from my work I see you there working too. The sense of being united in a shared endeavour has made me so happy.'

'Really?'

'From the first day. I can't believe now that I was dreading you starting as my assistant. I never imagined you'd be as talented as you are. And I never dreamt that each day until now would have become an exquisite torture where I've longed to hold you in my arms, longed to show you how desperately I was falling in love with you.'

While Walter was conducting Evensong, Alice sought out her aunt and asked her to stay behind so they could talk. She explained the whole story including that Edmund was the man she had been meant to marry had their parents got their wishes.

Eleanor's eyes welled with tears. 'That's a real tragedy, Alice. I suppose it explains why he didn't want to take you on as his assistant. You cared for him then?'

'No! Not at all. I thought he was the most unpleasant man I'd ever met.'

'Why then?'

'I knew I wanted to learn a new skill. And I think the devil in me knew it would embarrass him. I wanted to rub his nose in it as I thought he'd humiliated me. I never expected to love the work so much and I certainly didn't expect to fall in love with him.'

'When did this start? Have you both known for long?'

'We had started to have feelings for each other but neither of us wanted to admit it to ourselves, let alone each other.' She told her aunt an edited version of Leonard Fitzwarren's assault.

'My poor darling. What a horrid man. To think that such an ugly event was the catalyst that brought you and Edmund together.'

Alice leant back in her chair, eyes shining. 'It would have had to happen eventually. Something would have prompted it. Our feelings are too strong to have been held back forever.'

'And you intend to continue the relationship even though it's outside marriage?'

Alice hugged herself. 'It's unthinkable us not being together now.

'But someone will find out eventually. Aren't you afraid of the scandal?' Eleanor's eyes were wide with concern.

'Only for you and Walter. I don't want people to think badly of you because of me.'

'We're big and ugly enough to look after ourselves, but it's you. Alice – you've no idea what you're likely to face when word gets out. People can be cruel. And merciless. Particularly where women are concerned.'

'I'm not ashamed. All that matters is that I love Edmund.'

'I can see that. And I'm happy for you. For both of you.' Eleanor sighed. 'It's apparent how much you care for each other. And I fear I may have seen it all too clearly before even you did. You two are made for each other. It breaks my heart now you've told me the whole story.'

Alice didn't want to dwell on the tragedy of how near she and Edmund had been to having a legitimate marriage, so she shifted the subject 'I was talking to Viola Fuller last week.'

Eleanor smiled. 'Ah! The Wanderer's Wife. You're fond of her.'

'I've never told you this before, but I know you'll keep the confidence – the Fullers aren't actually married.' Alice bit her lip. 'And if I'm honest, I love Edmund but I don't love marriage. Apart from you and Walter, I don't know any shining examples of married life.' She tilted her head on one side. 'Apart from Mrs Bowyer. Edmund says she and her husband were deeply in love. Who'd have ever thought that?'

'Why do you say that?'

'Because she's so old and crotchety.'

'So, you think that old people are incapable of feeling love?'

'No. Of course not.' She tilted her head, smiling. 'Only it's hard to imagine it in Mrs Bowyer's case. But Edmund told me she used to go to sea with the commodore on many of his voyages once he was a captain, as they couldn't bear to be parted. Before that it wasn't allowed. Anyway, marriage isn't possible for us. Edmund's wife will never divorce him. So we have no choice.' Alice smiled. 'I love Edmund. He loves me. I don't need a ring on my finger to prove it.'

Eleanor pursed her lips. 'What if you become with child? What then?'

She hadn't anticipated that possibility. 'Then I will become a mother. I don't need a ring for that either.'

'But the child?'

'The child would be loved more than any child on earth. And wanted.'

'But Edmund's already a father.'

'He is. And a good one. If I should bear him another child, then it would be blessed.' Alice clutched her hands together. 'Look I know what you're doing, dear Eleanor. I understand why. But nothing will stop me loving him and whatever the consequences I will find a way. *We* will find a way. Edmund and I.'

. . .

Despite Alice's conviction that she had nothing to be ashamed of in embarking on her relationship with Edmund, the couple decided discretion was needed. They were careful not to be seen about the village together – on Saturdays she would return to the vicarage to spend the night in order to set out for church on Sunday morning with Eleanor. The rest of the week they couldn't bear to be apart so moved between the studio and the cottage under cover of darkness. As the cottage was tucked away out of sight behind the studio this wasn't difficult but, as the days lengthened, it was becoming harder to conceal that she was living under the same roof as her lover. Alice also took care to set out for suffrage meetings from the vicarage and did everything possible to conceal what was going on.

The only person apart from the Hargreaveses whom she took into her confidence was Viola Fuller. Her friend was pleased about Alice's evident happiness but warned her of the obstacles ahead.

'Sometimes I wish Robert and I were married. Not only for the children's sake but because it feels we're living a lie. Robert thinks I should have been more brazen about it. Kept my own surname for a start. But why court trouble?'

'Does anyone else know?' Alice took a sip of tea.

'I don't think so. We keep ourselves to ourselves. But I live in dread of someone finding out and within no time the entire district knowing.'

'There's more cause for me to be fearful.' Alice's mouth turned down. 'Everyone in Little Badgerton knows me because of my uncle being the vicar and they all know I'm not married. Some people are anyway critical that I'm tied up in the Cause and work with a married man but if they knew the truth of our relationship, they'd doubtless burn me at the stake or at least revive the ducking stool.' She gave a sardonic laugh.

'You're brave, Alice. You must love him very much.'

'If you were in my shoes, would you do differently?'

Viola shook her head. 'I wish Robert were here with me and the children more often, but he has to earn a living. It must be hard knowing Edmund has a wife and child.'

'I feel for him being separated from his little girl. It breaks his heart. But that's not because of me. They'd be apart anyway.' She explained Edmund's feud with his father and Dora's decampment to Grosvenor Square. 'I hope that eventually the woman may relent and permit Charlotte to spend some time with him but there's no sign at the moment.'

One Saturday in April, when Edmund and Alice had been together for almost three months, the Hargreaveses were having guests to supper and Alice needed to be there. She left the cottage in the afternoon and hurried down the lane towards the village. It was a wrench leaving Edmund, who told her he intended to catch up on his reading.

As she walked, Alice tried to think of a way they could build a future together. If only they could do as Viola and Robert had done and move to a place where neither would be known. Once Mrs Bowyer's windows were complete there would be nothing to keep them in Little Badgerton. Yet Edmund needed to seek publicity for his work in order to gain new commissions. It was a dichotomy – the more the world knew of his skills as an artist and craftsman, the more he risked people probing his background and discovering his domestic arrangements. Preoccupied, Alice was oblivious to her surroundings and didn't notice the rider who had halted his horse at the brow of a hill, watching as she left Edmund's cottage.

Leonard Fitzwarren smiled, kicked his horse forward and cantered over the fields back to Padgett Hall.

THIRTY-ONE

All three panels of the Bankstone window had been fired and Edmund was showing Alice how to do the leading work. The glass had gone through several evolutions and she had relished the way the application of silver stain had transformed the pale yellow glass of the sun into shafts of deep rich orange and red, while tracts of the blue glass sea had assumed a greener tinge. Alice understood now that she couldn't have been more wrong when she had dismissed creating a stained-glass window as like assembling a coloured glass jigsaw puzzle. Watching Edmund painting, staining, stippling and creating a myriad of subtle effects in the glass, her respect for his artistry and craftsmanship had grown exponentially. Every day at his side she soaked up knowledge like a sponge and was grateful that she'd been given such a miraculous opportunity to learn from a master.

The strips of lead were malleable – long strips that they could form into any shape to bind the glass pieces together, but strong enough to support the weight. He showed her how to nail the leading in position before soldering it. They then made the panels strong and waterproof, by applying linseed oil putty to the spaces between glass and lead.

Mrs Bowyer had eventually agreed to the inclusion not of a mermaid but a cluster of sea nymphs. Edmund had won her over by telling her of the Greek mythological Nereids, protectors of sailors. While initially dubious, she warmed to the idea – the clincher being that pagan mythology was a direct contrast to the ecclesiastically-themed window that would adorn St Margaret's. The possibility that she was somehow cocking a snook at the vicar was the final spur. Edmund omitted to tell her that Walter had studied classics at Oxford and was a passionate Hellenophile.

Edmund's theory that his patron wanted the Bankstone window to remain a private commemoration of the commodore proved correct. While Mrs Bowyer was planning a public dedication service for the eventual church installation, the Bankside window was to be unveiled without guests.

'She told me she doesn't want half the county traipsing through her house and gawking at what she views as a personal shrine,' he said to Alice.

'Are you nervous about how she will react?'

'No. I know it's my best work. *Our* best work. And most importantly made with love.' He reached for Alice's hand. They stood side by side in the studio looking at the glass, marvelling at what they'd created from nothing.

'Of course, the true test will be seeing it in situ.' He leant against the edge of the studio table.

'I'll need you to assist with the installation and the placement of the reinforcing bars and support wires. A couple of the gardeners will help support the weight of the glass but you must be there. This is as much your work as mine.'

Alice glowed with pleasure. 'When are we doing it?'

'Tomorrow.'

'I've never been inside the house. Will Mrs Bowyer agree? She's never approved of my working with you.'

'She already has. I told her you were absolutely essential.'

Edmund pushed away from the table and took her in his arms. 'I could never have got through this without you, Alice. The work wouldn't have been as good.' He swung her round to face the glass again. 'It was you who insisted on the sea nymphs. That's where the magic has come from. It was your vision and your ideas.' He held her against him as they both looked at the window glass. 'When Mrs Bowyer told me it was to be a portrayal of her husband in uniform I was dispirited and saw no further than a fusty old portrait and some naval regalia. It was you who suggested all the magical ingredients. The glorious sunset, the dolphins, the seagulls and cormorants, the crested waves. It was you, my love.'

'We make a good team.' She rested her head against his shoulder. Her happiness was tinged by a growing desperation. It would all end soon. They had already made a start on the church window – the design was largely done and some of the glass cut. In a few months the work would be complete and then what? The idyllic days working together in the quiet of the studio, away from the rest of the world, the nights spent in the little cottage, lost in the pleasure of each other's company. All that must surely come to an end. How would she bear it?

That night, after they'd made love, they lay with his body curved around hers, and she knew she had to raise the subject.

'What will you do, Edmund, once the second window is finished? You'll have to go back to London?' She felt the tension immediately in his body.

'How can you think I'd ever go back to Dora now?'

'I didn't mean that. But back to Mr Whall's studio? Or didn't you talk about setting up on your own at Lowndes and Drury?'

Alice listened to his breathing and waited for his response, but he said nothing.

'We have to face the future, Edmund. You need to make a living. Our time here in this cottage and working together in the studio has been the most precious of my life and I believe that's true for you too. But we've always known it must end. Mrs Bowyer won't let you stay on here once the work is done. And you have to find the next commission.'

'I know. I know. I'd hoped she'd allow me to invite *Country House* magazine to come to look at the window. I need a photographic feature to get my work out into the world. But she's adamant that the Bankstone window is private and sacred to her husband's memory.'

'Yet she wants to celebrate his memory publicly in the church? I don't understand the difference.' She turned to face him, wrapping her arms around his neck. 'I'm going to try to speak to her tomorrow. I'm certain she's going to be so overjoyed by the window that she'll want it to be seen more widely. Even if she doesn't want to unveil it publicly, a private viewing for the most prestigious magazine in the country – read by all those county people she's so keen to be accepted by – that's a whole different matter.'

'You think so?'

'I'm sure.' She laid her hand on his cheek. 'And she adores you, Edmund. I also have that card to play. I think the idea of her being the woman who discovered the most exciting new stained-glass artist in Britain will appeal to her.'

'You, my love, are a genius.' Then he sighed deeply. 'It still doesn't solve the problem of *us*.'

The elderly widow was so thrilled at seeing the commemorative window in place that there was a suggestion of tears. Alice looked at Edmund in astonishment. Mrs Bowyer had never displayed such an extreme of emotion and it was touching.

'It's stunning, my dear,' She patted Edmund's arm while dabbing at her eyes with a lace handkerchief. 'You've done my beloved Algernon proud.' She stared up at the window open-mouthed. 'I never dreamt it would be possible to achieve such a likeness in a glass window. Remarkable. He looks just how he did when we married. It's more like him than the portrait in the dining room, when his final illness was already showing its signs.'

Edmund smiled. 'I must confess that I took a liberty. I made Mrs Harrison show me your wedding album.'

Mrs Bowyer moved closer to the window. 'My goodness. That's me!' she cried. 'It's my face on one of those sea nymphs.' She started to chuckle. 'Oh Mr Cutler, not only have you brought my husband close to me again, you've given me back my youth. What an achievement!'

'Alas, I can't take the credit. My assistant, Miss Dalton, is a fine artist and she painted the features. It was also her idea to add the nereids.'

'Thank you too, my dear.' Mrs Bowyer jangled a bell and Mrs Harrison appeared. 'Put that bottle of champagne on ice. The one my late husband bought for the anniversary we never got to enjoy.' She turned to Alice. 'It would have been our fortieth this year, you know. I never intended to open it once he wasn't here to share it with me, but now I have reason to. We will adjourn to the morning room and drink to Algernon's memory and your magnificent window.'

Before they left the house, Alice had won over a slightly tipsy Mrs Bowyer to the idea of the *Country House* feature. Alice stressed that not only would there be a chance to reveal the window, but it would be a tribute to the house itself.

Despite her earlier misgivings, Mrs Bowyer was enthusiastic. 'Algernon would have been so proud. Bankstone was his dream project, and your window has made it even more special.' She tapped her stick on the floor in a tattoo of excitement. 'I can't wait for the Hinkleys to see it. So much more spectacular than their window from Mr Whall.' Then she smiled. 'Of course, Mr Whall is pre-eminent in his field, but it takes a person of imagination to enable artists to produce their best work. I'm afraid the Hinkleys are rather too conventional and just don't have my vision.'

The *Country Life* feature did not disappoint. It was spread across ten pages, featuring both house and garden, crediting Mr Lutyens as the architect of Bankstone, and Miss Jekyll as garden designer. But pride of place went to Edmund Cutler and his memorial window. The report hailed him as a major new talent within the Arts and Crafts movement and predicted that his work at Bankstone must make him a strong contender to win a prize at the annual Arts and Crafts Exhibition, as well as leading to a swelling order book.

Alice had declined to be credited in the piece, telling Edmund that her mother was an avid reader of *Country Life*. Lady Dalton would be horrified at her daughter being mentioned by the magazine as an artist's assistant when she had once been the frontispiece portrait. Also, it was possible Dora might see the magazine and if Alice were mentioned it would surely antagonise her.

When the magazine arrived, Alice was overjoyed. She read aloud extracts from it. 'Listen to this! "The subtlety of texture, variety of shapes, and richness of colour make this window the vibrant heart of the house. The imaginative imagery and the intriguing detail elevate it to a work of significance. Mr Cutler is a former student of the Central School and a collaborator with the master stained-glass artist, Christopher Whall. This promising first solo commission indicates he has a stellar future." Oh, Edmund! It's everything we could have wished for. You're bound to get lots more work as a result.'

Edmund put his hands behind his head and grinned. 'Do you think so?'

'I know so, my darling.'

Mrs Bowyer was equally thrilled. The article had led to a number of invitations from people who had previously looked down their noses at the widow. A collection of calling cards piled up and Mrs Bowyer welcomed more visitors in a week than she'd received since her husband had died. She revelled in her new-found status as discoverer and patroness of a newly emerging artist.

Some of the visitors asked to meet Edmund and a steady succession of people crossed the meadow to the workshop to see the artist at work and enquire about the possibility of commissioning him.

'I can't believe it, Alice. We've got enough projects already to see us through next year. That last man wants me to quote for a window in a new tearoom he's opening in Portsmouth. There was a woman this morning who wants to commemorate her twenty-five-year-old airman son who was killed when his plane crashed into a hill.'

'How sad.'

'She wants to commemorate him and his love of flying. The joy of his life as well as the tragedy of his loss.'

'You must certainly do that one.'

'Then that architect who called in yesterday about a house in Hindhead – he was hinting there could be a whole stream of commissions from his clients. We need to get a move on with the St Margaret's window.'

'Now that you don't have to spend so long explaining things to me, we'll be able to get it finished much faster than the Bankstone window. And we've already done much of the preliminary work.' Alice stood behind Edmund, wrapped her arms around him and rested her head against the back of his shoulder.

THIRTY-TWO

Alice was at Sunday service when Mrs Harrison hammered on the door of Edmund's cottage.

'Sorry to disturb you, Mr Cutler,' she said, straining to look over his shoulder. 'Is Miss Dalton here?'

Taken aback, Edmund said, 'Of course not. Why would she be?'

Harrison was carrying a newspaper which she flourished at him. 'It's a bit late for that, Mr Cutler. I've kept my mouth shut about what's none of my business, so I don't want you thinking it was me or anyone at Bankstone who's talked to the papers.'

He stared at her, mystified.

'May I come in then?'

He stood back and let her pass, aware that Alice had left the latest monthly report from the national suffrage societies on the table and a shawl draped over the back of a chair.

If the housekeeper spotted them, she said nothing. She didn't need to. The bombshell she held in her hands was far more explosive. She opened out the newspaper, spread it on the table and stabbed at a column with her finger.

Edmund read the words with mounting horror. How had

THE ARTIST'S APPRENTICE 309

they found out? Who was responsible? It wasn't possible. They'd been so careful. Hadn't they?

His mouth was dry. Throat constricted. Alice – he'd done this to Alice.

He slumped into a chair, head in hands.

The News of the World reporter had done an excellent detective job. It was all there. Edmund's estrangement from his wife. Alice's identity as the Honourable Alice Dalton, daughter of Lord and Lady Dalton of Dalton Hall. A salacious description of the cottage as the secret love nest where he and the former debutante indulged in immoral and adulterous acts, while his poor abandoned wife and daughter had been given shelter by their generous father-in-law, a celebrated and successful stockbroker who had recently announced his intention to stand for Parliament as a Conservative.

The words swam before his eyes and nausea mounted. He had ruined himself – but worse he'd ruined the woman he loved.

'Not my place to judge, Mr Cutler,' Mrs Harrison said, in a tone that conveyed that actually it was very much her place to do so. 'I've known about the goings on with you and Miss Dalton, for some time. I suppose I ought to say her Ladyship now – that's another thing. You lied to me about her parents dying in India. Turns out she's nothing to do with India. Not sure why I didn't come straight out and tell Mrs Bowyer, but she was fond of you and I didn't want to upset her while you were doing that window. Her late husband meant everything to her.'

He looked up at the housekeeper. 'Mrs Bowyer doesn't know?' He felt a shiver of relief.

She shrugged. 'If she does, it's not from me. There was a fellow from the papers came asking lots of questions about you. No idea who talked to him. Mrs Bowyer certainly didn't. She wouldn't give the time of day to anyone from *The News of the World*.'

'May I keep this?' He pointed to the open newspaper.

'You're welcome to it. Filthy rag. I confiscated it from the housemaid who was reading it over breakfast. I don't want smut like that in the house. If you hadn't wanted it, it'd be going on the fire.'

'It will anyway, as soon as I've finished with it.'

Mrs Harrison left and Edmund spent the rest of the morning pacing up and down the cottage trying to decide what to do next. Should he show Alice the article? She'd be devastated. But keeping it from her would be worse as it could hardly be kept secret from the rest of the village.

He'd brought all this upon her. If he'd suppressed his feelings, Alice would never have been exposed to scandal. Despite the risk to her reputation, he'd gone ahead and kissed her after the colonel's party. He cared nothing for his own moral reputation but he had destroyed hers. He'd probably jeopardised his own future too. The kind of people who were his potential clients were unlikely to read *The News of the World* but it was likely that the more respectable press would pick up the story and cover it, albeit in a less salacious manner.

He couldn't think straight. Someone had betrayed them. But who? Why would anyone go to the trouble to do that? Who hated them? Dora? But no sooner had the thought entered his head than he dismissed it. She was selfish and shallow but she wasn't vindictive and she'd never do anything that could have repercussions for their daughter. His father? Likewise. He had nothing to gain – particularly if the article was right and he intended standing for Parliament.

And then he remembered the night it had all started.

Leonard Fitzwarren.

Hard as it was to believe that the man would go to so much trouble, Edmund reminded himself that the colonel's nephew had been humiliated and rejected by Alice – literally painfully so.

As soon as the thought entered his head Edmund was certain. He'd taken an instant dislike to Fitzwarren, to his supercilious manner, and casual snobbery. But most of all his assault on Alice.

Edmund stuffed the newspaper into the pocket of his coat and left the cottage.

Half an hour later, he hammered on the front door of Padgett Hall.

The housemaid who opened it looked startled and said, 'Colonel's at church. After that he's lunching with friends.'

'I'm actually here to see his nephew, Mr Fitzwarren.'

'He's not at home either, sir.'

'When do you expect his return?'

She shrugged. 'Mr Fitzwarren is out riding.'

He thanked her but she was already shutting the door.

Edmund walked round to the rear of the Georgian house. There was a paved courtyard with stables and a carriage house on one side, the latter with the doors open. There was no sign of life.

Two of the stalls were completely closed up and didn't look as though recently used. Two others had open doors: one presumably for the colonel's carriage horse and the other must house the nephew's mount. Edmund looked around. A gravel track ran down the side of the outbuildings towards a meadow with a grazing elderly donkey and, beyond it, open fields. Padgett Hall stood on a small hill with views over the surrounding countryside. He walked to the edge of the meadow and leant on the fence. Down in the valley below was Bankstone and there before it, clearly in view, was the cottage and beyond it the studio-workshop. Anyone standing here, let alone riding or walking closer, would be afforded an excellent view of the comings and goings to the cottage. Any shadow of

doubt he had held about Leonard Fitzwarren vanished immediately.

Edmund walked back to the stable yard and was about to
return to the road and head for Bankstone when a flock of birds
rose from some trees to his left. Immediately afterwards he
heard the pounding of a horse's hooves on the turf. Leonard
Fitzwarren emerged from behind the copse on a bay horse and
clattered into the yard. As soon as he saw Edmund he came to a
halt.

'What are you doing here, Cutler?'

'Came to call on you.'

'Where's your fancy woman? Pretending to be a virtuous
pillar of the parish at church with her uncle the vicar?'
Fitzwarren made a snorting snigger.

Edmund brandished the copy of the newspaper. 'This is
your work?'

'Oh, it's out, is it? Haven't read it yet. Must get hold of a
copy. Imagine it'll make for some interesting discussions in
Little Badgerton. A rather racy read, I'll bet.'

Edmund strode over to the horse and rider, anger swelling
inside him. He reached for the horse's reins.

Fitzwarren barked at him to let go. Edmund stood his
ground. The man began to beat him around the head and shoulders with his riding crop.

Incensed, stinging with pain, Edmund tasted blood and felt
it dripping down his cheek. He reached up and dragged
Fitzwarren from the saddle, knocking the crop out of his hands.

The man sprawled on the ground, shocked, gazing up at
Edmund with a bewildered expression. Evidently, he was used
to meting out punishment, without his victim retaliating.

Edmund pulled Leonard Fitzwarren upright then landed a
blow on the man's chin.

To his surprise Fitzwarren started wailing as he rolled
around on the ground. An angry cry of self-pity. The colonel's

nephew had obviously never been on the receiving end of a punch before. Edmund stared at the man who was clutching his chin, tears streaking his face.

'You hurt me,' he wailed. 'Just like that slut did.'

For a moment, Edmund contemplated hitting the chap again for insulting Alice. But what was the point? Fitzwarren was a cowardly wretch. Deserving only contempt. Edmund bent down, picked up the riding crop, tossed it into a nearby water butt and headed to the vicarage to find Alice.

As soon as he arrived, Alice knew something was wrong. His distress was written on his face. 'What's wrong? Is it news from London? Is it Lottie?'

They were alone in the drawing room. He held her against him. 'Everything I was afraid of has come to pass. It's my fault, my darling.' He showed her the paper.

Alice read it in silence, then screwed it into a ball and threw it on the fire. 'What possessed you to buy that rag?'

'I didn't. Mrs Harrison brought it to the cottage to show me. She caught one of the staff reading it.'

'Ah. That explains the whispering in church.' She sank into an armchair.

'What are we going to do?'

'Absolutely nothing. I refuse to be bullied by smutty tittle-tattlers.'

'But your reputation's ruined.'

'The only opinion I care for is what you, the Hargreaveses and my women friends think of me and you all know me well enough not to pay any attention to this.'

'What about your parents?'

'They're unlikely to read it.'

'They'll find out anyway. It's in a national newspaper. You can't put the cat back in the bag.'

Alice put her arms around his neck and looked up at him, then pulled away suddenly. 'You've cut your neck. There's dried blood.' She lifted a lock of hair to reveal another cut. 'My darling! What happened?'

'An encounter with a riding crop.'

She gasped.

'Wielded by our friend Fitzwarren.'

Alice stared at him, horrified.

'He's responsible for telling the press. There's a clear view of the cottage from the fields behind Padgett Hall. He must have seen us coming and going and after all the favourable publicity from *Country Life* decided we needed some negative coverage.'

'Oh, Edmund! You confronted him?'

'I was angry. But it turns out the fellow's a pathetic snivelling wretch. Probably wishing he'd never done it now.'

'You hurt him?' Her hand went to her mouth.

'Punched him in the jaw but he'll live. Not sure his pride will though.'

'Good. I wish I'd seen it.'

'Not pretty. The wretch actually cried.'

Alice's eyes widened and she grinned.

'But me socking him in the jaw will do nothing to restore your reputation.'

'I've told you, my love. I don't care who knows about us. As long as it doesn't harm *you*. That's what I'm worried about. For myself I don't care at all. I love you and that's enough.' She buried her head against his shoulder. 'Do you think this will cost you commissions?'

'I don't know. Most people happily assume that all artists lack morals.' He gave a wry laugh. 'It may cost me some ecclesiastical work, but I doubt other people will care. Scandals pass fast enough. Newsprint has a short life span.'

. . .

News of Edmund's and Alice's unconventional living arrangements spread rapidly around Little Badgerton. Edmund suggested Alice return to the vicarage for a while until the fuss died down.

Alice was defiant. 'I've nothing to hide.' Then hesitant, she added, 'Unless you want me to go.'

'No! Of course I don't. I hate being apart from you. Saturday nights are bad enough without you.'

But it was with mounting fear that Alice opened a letter delivered to the vicarage from Bankstone by Mrs Harrison. It was a request that she call on Mrs Bowyer.

The housekeeper did little to hide her disapproval as she showed Alice into the morning room, where Mrs Bowyer was waiting with a pot of tea.

'Come in Miss Dalton. Make yourself comfortable.' She offered tea which Alice, whose hands were shaking, politely refused.

'This morning, Colonel Fitzwarren paid me a visit.'

Alice squeezed her hands together tightly and readied herself for bad news.

'I'm sure you're aware of what he came to tell me?'

Alice nodded, mute.

'And precisely what is the relationship between you and Mr Cutler?'

Alice gulped. Her palms were sweating. 'We love each other.'

The elderly woman narrowed her eyes. 'And you are aware he is already married?'

'The marriage is not a happy one.'

'And you're prepared to risk your good name for this man?'

Alice nodded. 'Yes. I love him. Very much.'

Mrs Bowyer nodded, her expression solemn. 'I see. And Mr Cutler?'

'Loves me too.' She sat upright. She wouldn't cower.

'I'd prefer you to be married. I don't approve of adultery, but since marriage is out of the question and you genuinely love each other then you have my acceptance of the situation – if not my blessing.' She put down her teacup. 'I am a great believer in love.'

Alice's hands flew up to her mouth. A huge wave of relief rippled through her and her eyes filled with tears. 'Thank you, Mrs Bowyer. Thank you so much.'

'I can't abide the colonel. Sanctimonious old bully. When my dear Algernon was building Bankstone, Fitzwarren raised objections with the county council. Tried to stop us building.' Mrs Bowyer tilted her head towards Alice. 'Today he was ranting. Accusing you and Mr Cutler of debauchery. But truth told, he's a woman hater. So, he can jolly well mind his own business. Now that we've got that out of the way, will you have that cup of tea, Miss Dalton?'

When Alice's interview with Mrs Bowyer was over she ran across the lawn to Edmund's cottage, uncaring of who might see. He was sitting by the fireside, reading. He looked up when she burst in and rose to greet her.

'I've just had the most extraordinary conversation with Mrs Bowyer.'

Edmund raked a hand through his hair, his face full of concern.

'I won't be spending any more Saturday nights at the vicarage. I'm going to move my things over here. Mrs Bowyer knows about us.'

'What? How?'

'I was summoned for tea.' She relayed her conversation with Mrs Bowyer. 'So we have her blessing, Edmund.'

'I can't believe it!' His eyes lit up and he gave a joyful whoop.

'And you, my dearest darling, are the apple of her eye. She's convinced herself that she discovered you. Never mind the couple who recommended Mr Whall and never mind that Mr Whall recommended you. History has been rewritten!'

'Mrs Bowyer has a talent for that.'

'She wants to speak to you too. At six bells, whenever that is. You're to take tea with her.' Alice swept her arm around the workshop. 'She's going to suggest that you make Bankstone your permanent headquarters. Obviously, we'll need to pay rent once you start to earn other commissions but she's gifting you all the equipment and we can remain in the cottage.'

Edmund wrapped his arms around Alice. 'What did I do to deserve you?'

THIRTY-THREE

Late June 1914

The only flaw in their life was Edmund's lack of contact with his daughter. Since *The News of the World* article, Dora, apparently at the behest of her father-in-law, denied all further contact between Edmund and Lottie. His already infrequent meetings with his child were now non-existent and no matter how happy Alice made him, a dark cloud descended whenever he thought of his little girl. Mrs Bowyer's generosity and the growing order book meant he was able to pay for a solicitor to advise him about gaining access to Lottie, but the process was going to be protracted. The lawyer had warned Edmund that, pitted against Herbert Cutler's unlimited funds, their case would not be easy, and a successful outcome was far from guaranteed.

At least Lottie would be well provided for. Edmund had received a letter from his father's solicitor, informing him that Herbert Cutler had made a new will. Provision was made for Dora, including the lifetime use of the Grosvenor Square House and a generous allowance. Victor Dalton of New York

City was to inherit Cutler & Son, Stockbrokers, and Cutler's sole heir to the rest of his fortune was his granddaughter, Charlotte Cutler. As expected, there was nothing for Edmund.

When he read it, Edmund left the cottage, heading off alone to walk through the countryside. Alice continued their work in the studio, re-firing a section of the church window to better capture the subtleties of the face of Christ. As she worked, she thought of Victor getting his reward for his silence and long exile in America. Her parents would be happy as it would mean the future of Dalton Hall would be secure. How little she herself cared. Her family now was Edmund and the Hargreaveses.

Edmund didn't return until it was almost dark. He whispered an apology for his absence, took her in his arms and told her how much he loved her. Alice wished she had a means of washing away his sadness.

In late June, the church window was ready. The ceremony was fixed for Monday 29th June. During the Sunday service Reverend Hargreaves' announcement of the unveiling the following day provoked curiosity and interest across the parish – partly because the triple lancet was draped with a heavy cloth to prevent the congregation seeing it before the formal unveiling and partly because the tongue waggers were keen to see what the 'depraved couple' had produced.

Leaving church that Sunday morning, Alice had overheard someone say, 'It's not right. I wonder why the vicar's allowed it. A couple living in sin allowed to make the church windows.' The speaker was the chair of the Mothers' Union – someone who had hitherto been friendly towards Alice.

But nothing could mar her good humour. The balmy early summer weather, the plenitude of orders for stained glass and the sheer joy of living as man and wife with Edmund filled her with optimism.

On the day of the unveiling, they decided not to work in the studio but chose to spend the morning enjoying the sunshine outside the cottage until it was time to head to the church, Alice was absorbed in a book while Edmund read the paper.

She glanced up at him, but his face was concealed by the open newspaper. She saw the headline splashed across the front page: *Heir to Austrian Throne Murdered.* The sub-heading was *Archduke and His Wife Shot Dead in the Street.* 'Goodness me. Did you read that, Edmund? An assassination of royalty in Sarajevo. How terrible to think they were shot down in the street.'

'A bad business.' Edmund passed her the newspaper.

She started to read the front page. 'Where exactly is Sarajevo?'

'In Serbia. The Balkans. It's not going to go down well with the Austrians and Germans. There's talk of war over there.'

Alice shuddered. 'Let's hope it won't come to that. It won't affect us, will it?'

'Don't imagine so. Why would Britain allow itself to get dragged into a war on the continent? We've more than enough on our plate here with the troubles in Ireland and all the industrial unrest. Last thing we need is to get involved in armed conflict.'

'Gosh. I hope you're right.'

Despite the warmth of the sunshine, a little shiver ran through her.

The church of Saint Margaret was packed to capacity for Mrs Bowyer's unveiling of the memorial to her husband. As she pulled the cord to open the drapery there was a collective gasp. Edmund and Alice had surpassed themselves. This window was magnificent – larger than the one at Bankstone and comprising the three lancets surmounted by tracery. The images contained within were powerful, vivid, sparkling, intense. Sunlight projected the colours onto the white of the altar cloth in the side chapel. Applause burst forth as well as oohs and aahs as the congregation took in the scale and beauty of the achievement.

Alice looked at Edmund, then discreetly reached for his hand. He squeezed hers in return. Walter tilted his head in acknowledgement of the couple's achievement. Alice saw her aunt wipe a tear away with her handkerchief. Mrs Bowyer was glowing, puffed up with pride.

Around the church, people were murmuring. But instead of the unvoiced hostility that Alice had sensed ever since the villagers had discovered she and Edmund were lovers, the congregation had eyes only for the windows. Spontaneous applause broke out and someone slapped Edmund on the back. Alice looked about her and could see only admiration reflected back at her in the faces of the crowd. The sheer magnificence of the vibrantly coloured lancets appeared to have awakened a fierce pride among the residents of the parish, overshadowing any concerns about their creators' morality.

A weight lifted off her. Alice glanced at Edmund and reached for his hand. This was a perfect summer. She was in love with Edmund and knew she was loved in return. His fears about money had receded as they had a long list of interesting commissions swelling their order book. The future was as bright as the afternoon sunshine.

That night as they undressed, Alice took his hand and placed it on her belly. 'I have another reason for us to be happy.'

Edmund gasped. 'You're?'

'Yes. At least I think I am. I was going to wait until I've seen the doctor, but I *am* sure. I can sense it. I wanted to tell you today as it's such a special one – a day we'll never forget.

His eyes welled. 'My dearest love.'

· · ·

Next morning, Edmund woke from a dream. Not really a dream as it was too disturbing – but not quite a nightmare. A chill rippled through his body. Not fear. More like a premonition. A sense of unease and uncertainty. A kind of darkness enveloping him.

He rolled over. Early morning light came through the bedroom window, soft shadows dappling the sleeping face of Alice beside him. He remembered he was to become a father again. This time nothing would separate him from his child-to-be and from Alice. He would protect them with his life.

Pushing aside the odd feeling that accompanied his waking, Edmund picked up his pencil and the pocket-sized sketchbook he carried with him everywhere and began to draw his sleeping lover's face. As he drew, the darkness of his dream receded. A sunbeam touched her eyes. She opened them and smiled.

A LETTER FROM THE AUTHOR

Huge thanks for reading *The Artist's Apprentice*. I hope you were hooked on Alice and Edmund's journey and are eager to learn more about them. If you want to join other readers in hearing about my new Storm Publishing releases and bonus content, you can sign up for my mailing list here!

www.stormpublishing.co/clare-flynn

If you enjoyed this book and could spare a few moments to leave a review that would be hugely appreciated. Even a short review can make all the difference in encouraging a reader to discover my books for the first time. Thank you so much!

If you'd like to sign up to my mailing list for updates and extra content, you can sign up here!

www.subscribepage.com/r4w1u5

One of the things I most loved about writing this book was finding out about stained-glass window making. I'd never been a particular fan of stained glass before but it has become something of a passion. I've also loved looking at examples of Arts and Crafts stained-glass windows. My personal favourites – both near to me in Sussex – are the windows in Winchelsea church by Douglas Strachan and the spectacular lancets in the chapel at Ashdown Park by Irish artist Harry Clark. I also love the period in the run up to the First World War – the fight for votes for women and the innocent pleasures of the Edwardian age captured in that glorious summer before the war. It's always poignant looking at old photos from the period and wondering how many of those smiling young men survived the horrors they didn't realise lay ahead of them.

Thanks again for being part of this amazing journey with me and I hope you'll stay in touch – I have so many more stories and ideas to entertain you with!

Clare

clareflynn.co.uk

 facebook.com/authorclareflynn
x.com/clarefly

ACKNOWLEDGMENTS

Thanks to Lorna Fergusson who gave me a big kick when I was feeling devoid of inspiration. It's due to her that Mrs Bowyer and stained-glass windows presented themselves. Thanks, as always, to Margaret Kaine who has been a constant source of feedback and encouragement to stick at this and get it finished. Her wise counsel and support made a big contribution to getting me through this book.

Thanks to Carol Cooper who encouraged me to keep up the momentum when I was feeling discouraged during our writing retreat in Mousehole, Cornwall and subsequently.

To JJ Marsh, Alison Morton, Jane Davis, Debbie Young, Liza Perratt, Karen Inglis, Lorna Fergusson and Clare O'Brien, all of whom read a late draft and gave invaluable feedback.

To Gemma Court who is a terrific support to my writing and whose work on my website and newsletters and many other things frees up time for me to focus on my writing.

Several locations provided background inspiration for the book. A short stay at Ashdown Park in East Sussex to see Harry Clarke's amazing stained-glass windows, Douglas Strachan's spectacular windows discovered during an impromptu visit to Winchelsea church, and the beautiful Burne-Jones window in Rye parish church. None of Edmund's windows are based on these but collectively they were an inspiration for the kind of work he undertook.

Mrs Bowyer's Bankstone borrows heavily from Goddards in Surrey – a magnificent Lutyens Arts and Crafts house – where

I spent a writing retreat with some of my "Sanctuary" writer friends, Lorna Fergusson, Jane Davis, Debbie Young, Karen Inglis and Alison Morton.

Thanks also to my cousin, Joanna Ryan, who helped me drink a bottle of wine in the One Tun pub in Goodge Street while Salerno beat Lazio on the big plasma screen and we discovered there is unfortunately little to indicate how the interior of this pub would have looked in 1908. Jo has always been an amazing supporter of my ~~drinking~~ writing.

I used numerous books to help with the background – particularly for the craft of stained-glass windows. I took great inspiration from two stunningly beautiful books on stained glass, Peter Cormack's *Arts & Crafts Stained Glass*, and *Strangest Genius: The Stained Glass of Harry Clarke* by Lucy Costigan and Michael Cullen. But I want to single out the excellent little handbook to making stained glass by Christopher Whall, *Stained Glass Work: A Handbook for Students and Workers in Glass* from which I pillaged gleefully – as well as his speech to the Liverpool Art school. The book, *Making Their Mark* by Sylvia Backemayer was helpful in building a picture of student life at the Central School of Arts & Crafts.

Apart from Whall, most of the "speaking" characters in my book are fictional. Whall did have his studio at Ravenscourt Park in Hammersmith - an area I know well from my time living in Chiswick. Mrs Badley was also a real person and was the wife of the headmaster of Bedales, where Mrs Pankhurst spoke at her invitation in 1908. Karl Parsons is also a real person. He taught at the Central, worked for Whall and lived in Chiswick. Mary Lowndes is also mentioned and was a shining example of female stained-glass craftsmanship – as well as a strong and active supporter of the women's suffrage movement.

I'm also indebted to online access to the London County Council floor plans of the old (then brand new) Central School in Southampton Row, Holborn.

Printed in Great Britain
by Amazon